WITHDRAWN

I've travelled the world twice over,
Met the famous: saints and sinners,
Poets and artists, kings and queens,
Old stars and hopeful beginners,
I've been where no-one's been before,
Learned secrets from writers and cooks
All with one library ticket
To the wonderful world of books.

BLAYDE R.I.P.

The story begins with the funeral of Chief Superintendent Robert Blayde, one of the most remarkable police characters in John Wainwright's books. Blayde was a loner, an ambitious man, a man who hated crooks. The story—strewn with episodes of policing, many of them violent—describes the rise of a single police officer from Constable to Chief Super in one of the most demanding of all professions. Blayde was not a man to toe the line nor conform to the letter of established routines.

Books by John Wainwright in the Ulverscroft Large Print Series:

DUTY ELSEWHERE
LANDSCAPE WITH VIOLENCE
MAN OF LAW
BLAYDE R.I.P.

JOHN WAINWRIGHT

BLAYDE R.I.P.

Complete and Unabridged

ULVERSCROFT
Leicester

First published 1982

First Large Print Edition
published April 1984
by arrangement with
Macmillan London Ltd.
and
St. Martin's Press, Inc.,
New York

British Library CIP Data

Wainwright, John, *1921–*
Blayde R.I.P.—Large print ed.
(Ulverscroft large print series: mystery)
I. Title
823'.914[F] PR6073.A/

ISBN 0-7089-1121-8

Published by
F. A. Thorpe (Publishing) Ltd.
Anstey, Leicestershire
Printed and Bound in Great Britain by
T. J. Press (Padstow) Ltd., Padstow, Cornwall

Man is the shuttle, to whose winding quest
And passage through these looms
God order'd motion, but ordain'd no rest.

HENRY VAUGHAN
Silex Scintillans. Man

1

IT was a police funeral. More than that, it was a chief superintendent's funeral which meant wreaths galore, an escort of white-gloved officers wearing "best blue" and keeping perfect slow-march step as six of their colleagues carried the flag-draped coffin down the gentle slope of the path, towards the newly-dug grave near the farthest wall of the cemetery. There was no next-of-kin. The mourners were led by the chief constable, with Harris walking alongside him. The chief wore full uniform. Harris wore a dark blue suit, a white shirt and a black tie. Tallboy, wearing his chief superintendent's uniform, complete with soft leather gloves, walked behind the chief. Susan, Tallboy's wife, walked alongside her husband.

Behind, and in no particular order, walked friends and fellow-officers. Civilian dress and uniform mingled and, apart from an occasional murmured politeness as a mourner stood aside to allow a fellow-mourner to pass without having to tread on the sodden grass, there was very little talk. There was very little to talk about, because none of the mourners had really known the dead man.

"A damn good copper." That opinion had been expressed a score of times, and in a score of different ways, but it said nothing. It gave no hint of what else he'd been. There must have been a life before he'd become a policeman (and indeed his police records hinted at that life) but to those escorting and following the coffin, the facts and occasions of that life were unknown.

"No brothers? No sisters?" Susan Tallboy frowned in sadness as she murmured the words.

"Apparently not," repeated Tallboy.

"That's terrible," breathed his wife. "That's *terrible.*"

Tallboy knew what she meant. Their own presence at the funeral was perhaps part friendship, but the brutal fact was that it was mainly duty. With the chief constable and Harris it was wholly duty. As with every other officer there. Come to that, as with the civilians. Local dignitaries: magistrates and their wives; councillors and their wives. No friends. Nobody was there because a part of their own life had been removed. The cleric was there because he'd been paid to be there. The same with the undertaker and his men. The same with the two grave-diggers who stood apart, half-leaning on their shovels and ready to fill in the grave once the required rigmarole had ended.

No friends. No relatives. Plenty of floral tributes (to use the jargon) but the impression was that the wreaths and the bouquets were a form of silent apology. For not knowing him; for not going out of their way to get to know him.

"Should we stand at the grave?" whispered Susan.

"Why not?"

They shuffled to a position on the heavy canvas covering the boards which surrounded the hole in the ground. Not too deep a hole. Just the one coffin. He was going to be as solitary in death as he'd been in life.

The vicar had already started mumbling the Funeral Service. Such haste; such a hurry to get indoors and away from the wind as it swooped down from The Tops. Tallboy stared into the wind. His mind played with a near-forgotten memory; something to do with an old film—or was it a short story he'd once read?—something to do with Noel Coward—

had Noel Coward ever written short stories?—something to do with a man, drowned at sea and nobody wept for him, and he was damned but given one more chance to walk the earth again and change his ways and, when he "died" a second time, hope that somebody would weep for him. The film (the short story, whatever it was) had had an effect. People should weep. For this man, for every man and woman, they *should* weep, otherwise it was no different from planting a tree.

He felt the grip on his right hand tighten a little. He turned and saw the tears glinting in his wife's eyes. They spilled over and ran down her cheeks as he watched. He almost sighed with relief and held her hand a little tighter. It was silly—superstitious and silly—but somebody had wept and that fact, coupled with a half-remembered memory, seemed very important.

The undertaker tossed soil onto the coffin. Clay-heavy soil which splattered and covered the lower half of the silver rectangle, leaving only the words

Robert Blayde
Born Feb 25th 1922

as a last identity of the man in the coffin.

Harris fished a handkerchief from his mac

pocket, shook out its folds and blew his nose. It was noisy. Trumpeting. It could have been a parting opinion of the dead man. Indeed—knowing Harris and Blayde—it could have been an opinion.

2

"TWINS!" David Blayde glared at the doctor.

As he rolled down the sleeves of his shirt and buttoned the cuffs, the doctor added, "Your wife's fine. No problems at all."

"You said twins," said Blayde, angrily.

"Two fine boys."

"I don't give a damn whether they're boys or . . ."

"The midwife's cleaning everything up. She'll call you when you can see them."

"In hell's name, why couldn't you let them die?" The words were harsh, but deliberate. Spoken by a man almost out of his mind with worry.

"You don't know what you're saying." The doctor brushed the folds from his shirt sleeves. He was a patient man; he'd heard it all before, and knew what two extra mouths meant in a house where poverty was a daily fact of life. As he reached for his coat he said, "They're your sons, Blayde. They're fine babies and you were responsible for them."

"She should have had more gumption," groaned Blayde.

"Or you should have controlled yourself." The doctor settled his jacket onto his shoulders then, in a gentler tone, added, "Don't hate them, Blayde. It's not an easy world. Don't let them start life by being hated by their father. Give 'em some sort of a chance."

The doctor snapped his bag close, then let himself out of the house. The time was 4 a.m. The date was February 25th, 1922. The Saturday was four hours old.

Poverty. Hunger. Humiliation. David Blayde sat in the only armchair he owned; a second-hand, stained, worn and uncomfortable chair given as an act of charity he'd loathed but had lacked the manhood to refuse. He sat forward—bowed—resting his head in his hands and allowed his thoughts to contemplate those evils. Poverty, hunger and humiliation.

God, it wasn't all in the North-East. It wasn't all in Wales and in the Manchester-Preston-Liverpool area. It wasn't all in the big cities. Out here in the country .... it was here, too. That and more. Seven days a week, grafting your heart out for a pittance and not daring to say a word out of place, because you lived in a tied cottage. A hovel, that went with the job. A plot of land—oh aye, a plot of land you could use to grow your own produce—but when? You were out in the mistel, before dawn, milking the cows. Then for the rest of the day you were ploughing, or harrowing, or sowing, or reaping, or something else . . . anything, just to keep you at it till dusk. Seven days a week, because the beasts didn't stop giving milk once a week; their udders had to be emptied twice a day, year in, year out. So when the hell could you grow a few vegetables for your own use? When the hell had you the time, and when the hell had you the strength?

He wasn't a praying man. All this crap about being "nearer to God in the countryside" didn't include those who worked the countryside. Therefore, he wasn't a praying man. Nevertheless, he'd prayed. A miscarriage . . . something like that. Maybe the kid born dead. Anything! But *twins*.

He'd tell the foreman. Of course he'd tell the foreman, he couldn't not tell the foreman. Ask for a bob or two more a week. He wouldn't get it, but he'd ask. And he could already hear Dobson's reply. "Tha wants to keep thi fly buttoned up a bit more, lad." That or something along those lines. From Dobson, who already had five bairns and another on the way. But Dobson could afford. He handled brass. Everybody called him "the foreman" but his fancy title was "farm bailiff". Dobson was land-steward for Sir Some-Bugger-Or-Another who lived up in Scotland somewhere. And that wasn't right, either. Dammit, when a man worked for somebody—dammit, he had a right to know that "somebody". To see him sometimes. To talk to him sometimes. To know what a man who treated his beasts better than he treated his men looked like.

From upstairs he heard the tiny squeal of a new-born child.

He raised his head, stared at the ceiling, and muttered, "Tha's summat to cry about lad. 'Afore long, tha'll wish tha'd never been born."

It was warm in the mistel. The heat from the beasts countered, and more than countered, the last night frosts of February. Blayde liked the mistel on mornings like this; the farmyard tang which seemed to be concentrated within the white-washed, cobwebbed walls; the shuffling and snuffling of the beasts in their stalls; the light from the oil-lamps, each hanging on its own nail and, or so it seemed, creating shadows for the morning sun to find and eliminate.

He sat on the stool, his forehead resting against the warm flank of the cow, the pail held between his knees and the milk coming in rhythmical streams as his skilled fingers kneaded the teats.

He heard Dobson long before he saw him. The heavy, steel-studded boots fairly rang as he walked slowly the length of the cow-shed. That, and the sound of the ferrel at the end of his stick, as it tapped on the stained concrete. There was an arrogance in the walk; the life-and-death arrogance of a slave-master. Dobson would have had a good breakfast. Home-cured bacon, fresh eggs, home-baked bread, hot sweet tea. That belly of his took some filling. Good grub and good ale. Every evening he'd get his trap out and drive down to the village, to *The Bunch of Grapes,* and he'd swill it till closing time. Then his mates would lift him back into the trap, untie the horse and know he'd be taken home. No need for reins. No need for owt. That horse knew its way, there and back, as well as he did.

And the yard lad—first thing every morning, before he even started mucking out the cow-shed—would unharness the horse, stable it, rub it down and fodder it, then muscle the trap into its shed. Later, when he'd nowt else to do, the lad was expected to polish the harness, then the trap—clean any spew Dobson had brought up on the way home—make things ready for *that* night's boozing.

What a bloody life! What a bloody gaffer!

The slow walk stopped. Blayde knew that Dobson was at the entrance to the stall in which he was working. He pretended not to notice; continued emptying the cow's udder of milk.

"Well?"

Dobson's coarse voice asked the question, but Blayde continued to work the teats.

"Has she dropped it, then?" asked Dobson.

Blayde turned to look at Dobson, but without moving his head from the cow's side. He continued squirting milk into the bucket with expert ease.

"I'd like to see you, sometime," he said quietly.

"Oh aye?" Dobson raised his stick and poked the cow's rump. The cow tried to shift position, but Blayde's head held it firmly against the stall partition. Dobson asked, "What about exactly?"

"A bit more brass," said Blayde in an even voice.

"She has dropped it, then?"

"Twins. Two lads."

"Now, there's a bloody thing." Dobson grinned and slapped his stick against the leather gaiter on his right leg. "Two of 'em, at one go."

"I'll need more brass, Mr. Dobson." Blayde kept his voice level and reasonable.

"Oh, aye?" Dobson continued to grin.

"It's hard enough as it is," said Blayde. "With two more mouths to feed . . ."

"If tha can get more brass, tha's welcome to go," cut in Dobson.

"I mean here," said Blayde in a low voice.

"Not here, lad." Dobson shook his head. "We can get a man wi'out kids. If tha decides to go, that is."

"There's—there's the house."

"Aye, there's the house," Dobson nodded. He was no longer grinning. "Tha'll be flittin' then?"

"No." Blayde returned his attention to the pail and the milking. "I'll—I'll no'an be flittin'."

"If tha's looking for somewhere else."

"I'm asking for a few bob more. That's all."

"Oh, aye?"

"I'll work for it."

"No, lad." Dobson's voice was cold and mocking. "Tha'll work wi'out it." He pointed with his stick and growled, "An' them's teats tha's pullin', lad. Not bell-ropes."

"He's a bloody animal," snarled Hopkins. "A bloody animal an' an ale-pot."

"He's that," sighed Blayde.

"An' that's what we are . . . bloody animals."

"Happen."

If David Blayde could boast a friend, that friend was Seth Hopkins. Seth, who kept his job by the skin of his teeth and his uncanny skill with livestock, despite his openly expressed radical beliefs. And if David Blayde could boast—or even afford—a friend, that friend was undoubtedly Seth Hopkins.

"How's Meg?" asked Hopkins gently.

"She doesn't complain."

"No, she wouldn't." Hopkins glanced at the ceiling. "Twins. I doubt she's enough milk to feed 'em on. But she'll not complain."

"She's a good lass," said Blayde. "It's not her fault."

The two men sat facing each other in Blayde's cottage. They sat at a slight angle, facing what passed as a fire in the tiny grate; each seeking warmth, yet each not wishing to shield what warmth there was from the other. Blayde sucked at an empty pipe, an old briar, broken at the stem, then mended with a strip of cotton and tightly bound string. It was closing up to ten o'clock, and the oil-lamp was turned low enough to keep most of the tiny room in dark shadow. Seth Hopkins had called in to keep Blayde company; a short, less than a hundred yard walk from his own tied cottage, where he lived with his common law wife Elsie. Dobson had once called her "Hopkins's tame whore", and Hopkins had heard him. The pitchfork had actually punctured the skin of Dobson's belly as Hopkins snarled, "Call her that again, Dobson, and I'll see your tripes down there among the cow-shit."

Quite a lad, Seth Hopkins. Hard as nails, but an idealist. He was there with Blayde because he knew there was but the one double-bed, and a woman who'd just given birth to twins doesn't want somebody tossing and turning beside her all night. Blayde would be spending a few nights sitting alone, downstairs. He was there to share the vigil, or some of it.

When he'd arrived Blayde had offered the armchair, but Hopkins had waved aside the invitation and was now squatting, elbows on knees, on a broken-and-repaired milking stool.

Hopkins's eyes seemed to lose focus in the faint glow from the lamp and he said, "By God, the lads up north are showing 'em how."

"The miners?"

"The miners. The shipyard lads. They're getting organised. *Really* organised."

"Y'm unions?"

"Aye. They're showing the gaffers a thing or two."

"It doesn't seem right." Blayde scowled at the empty bowl of his pipe. "A bit too much like blackmail."

"Blackmail my arse. A fair day's pay, that's all they're asking. Not the moon. A fair day's pay, for a fair day's work. And they're getting it."

"They can't win," sighed Blayde. "Folk like us . . . we can't win."

"We can't win," agreed Hopkins bitterly.

"We're too scattered. All this tied-cottage business. That's why we can't win. But if we support 'em—let 'em know we're on their side—that's our way."

"I don't see . . ."

"We'll have our own party, see? Bugger the Liberals. Bugger that Welsh goat Lloyd-George. A Socialist Party. Down there in London. In Parliament. They'll do it, lad. One day we'll have a Socialist Government. Then we'll get rid of the tied cottages. Then we'll be able to win . . . all of us."

"Happen." Blayde sighed. He stood up from the chair, walked across the room and from a drawer of an ancient sideboard, took a child's notebook and the stub of a pencil. He returned to the chair, then said, "I don't like bothering Meg. Not now. But I think her mam and dad should know. You can write, Seth. Will you write and tell 'em, please?"

"Aye. Of course." Hopkins took the notebook and pencil, settled the open notebook on his knee, and said, "Now, what d'you want me to say?"

It was closing up to midnight. The fire was little more than a glowing coal, surrounded by a few charred logs, and the cool of the night was invading the room like a slowly rising tide. Hopkins had written the short, stilted letter, read it back to Blayde, then addressed an envelope and sealed the letter away. For almost thirty minutes neither of the two men had spoken; their friendship hadn't needed words; that they were together was enough.

Blayde said, "Elsie'll be wondering."

"Eh?"

"Elsie. She'll be wondering where you are."

"She knows." Hopkins smiled. "She's been left alone before. It doesn't bother her."

"Oh."

"The odd rabbit. Sometimes a hare. If I'm lucky a nice, fat cock pheasant."

"Y'mean poaching?" Blayde sounded mildly shocked.

"I mean making sure we eat."

"And—y'know—if you're caught?"

"Dave," Hopkins shook his head in bewilderment. "Dobson isn't God. He only thinks he is. Hares, rabbits, wood pigeons, the wild life . . . Dobson didn't create them. Why the hell shouldn't my stomach be as full as his?"

"It's your way, Seth." Blayde's tone was neither critical nor apposite. The dividing line between legality and illegality, as far as poaching was concerned, was blurred. A man lived in the country, he toiled hard in an attempt to tame the earth, it was arguable—maybe more than arguable—that he was entitled to what few perquisites that country-side had to offer. And (true enough) the wild life wasn't the property of Dobson. Wasn't the property of anybody or was the property of everybody. Blayde added, "When the hell do you sleep?"

"I sleep." Hopkins dismissed the question as being irrelevant. He glanced up at the ceiling again, and said, "That's what she needs."

"Meg?"

"Her belly's very empty, too."

"She's—she's had broth," muttered Blayde. "I'm no cook, but . . ."

"I know. Even you can boil potatoes, mash 'em then add water."

"She'll be up and about soon. She'll be able . . ."

"Elsie slipped over this afternoon."

"Oh." Blayde looked crestfallen.

"Potato water. What the hell good's potato water?" Hopkins seemed, suddenly, to become unreasonably angry. "She wants something with juice in it. Something to give her strength." He paused then, very pointedly, added, "I know where there's a few saddlebacks."

"Hey, Seth, for God's sake!" Blayde was genuinely shocked.

"He'll be home. Snoring like an old sow himself," argued Hopkins.

"That's not the point, Seth. Poaching's one thing, but . . ."

"D'you think he didn't steal 'em. Agh!" Hopkins waved a derisive hand. "Not in that way. He had 'em 'given'. But for what? For services rendered, lad, that's why. That low dry-stone wall, remember it? Five hundred yards. That if it was an inch. It's not our boundary. I've made it my business to check. I'm after Mister-bloody-Dobson. And one day . . ."

"What about the wall?"

"We mended it. And more than mended it. We damn near re-built the thing. For weeks, two of us down there, in all weather."

"And you think . . ."

"I know. I've made it my business to know. Five young saddlebacks. From Apple Tree Farm. I can even name the lad who brought 'em. Dobson, see? It's not our wall. But he made it our wall. Nowt out of his pocket, and a damn sight cheaper for the man who should have re-built it."

"Seth," pleaded Blayde, "it's still stealing. What Dobson does isn't our . . ."

"And you've got a lass upstairs."

"It's not the same."

"Don't you think owt about her?"

"Too much to have her wed to a thief."

"All right," mocked Hopkins. "Be honest. Happen you can afford to be honest. Happen you've more brass than I think you have. But happen you haven't. But remember this night, Dave. When you bury her—when you bury either her or one of them bairns—don't forget this night. The night she needed summat substantial in her belly to give her milk in her tits. And you were too bloody honest." Hopkins paused, his eyes hardened, and his voice was harsh with a passion almost beyond Blayde's understanding. "I'll tell you this, Dave Blayde. I'm no'an wedded to my woman, but *I'd* do it. And more. I'd kill for her. Willingly. Dobson? I'd kill that bloody animal and think nowt of it."

It was after 1.30 a.m. on Sunday, February 26th. It was a cloudless sky, and what moon there was gave sufficient light; not that they needed light; both men knew every turn, every door, every yard, every building in the farm complex. Seth Hopkins carried a hammer; a heavy-headed coal hammer, which he swung gently in his right hand.

"We'll regret this," whispered Blayde.

"We'll regret nowt. We'll have it cut up and hidden by daybreak."

They paused as they neared the bulk of the farmhouse where Dobson and his wife lived. They watched the horse, still in the shafts of the trap, and saw it raise its head as it scented their presence.

"Quiet my beauty," breathed Hopkins. "Quiet, lass. No need to fear. You know us well enough."

"That hammer . . ." began Blayde.

"One clout." Hopkins sounded very sure. "You hold the head steady. Just one clout in the right spot. Then we'll carry it somewhere to bleed it, and cut it up."

The sounds of the farm were all around them. The night sounds. The cattle soft-clomping in the mistel; the heavier clip-clop as the horses moved about their stalls; two screech owls hunting and calling to each other; the gentle rattle of a chain as the yard dog shifted position while it dozed.

Somewhere in the far distance a dog fox gave voice.

"You got that knife?" whispered Hopkins.

"Aye." Blayde touched the hilt of the razor-sharp kitchen knife stuck in his belt.

"Right, here we go."

Indian-file fashion they hurried, crouched and soft-footed, for the out-building in which the pigs were penned. They reached the door, paused for a last look at the darkened farmhouse, then Hopkins pulled the peg clear of the staple, eased the hasp and slowly opened the door. They were expecting the creak; they knew every door on the farm, but they also knew that, by lifting the door slightly, the creak could be softened. When the door was less than a yard open Blayde held it while Hopkins found the brick and jammed the door firmly. They knew the door. They knew it was hung badly; that without the brick it would swing closed, slowly and noisily.

They ducked into the darkness of the pig shed and stood there, gathering their senses and quietening their breathing. Gradually, their eyes became more accustomed to the gloom.

"We should open the door more," said Blayde softly.

"What?"

"To get the pig out," explained Blayde.

"Oh, aye." Excitement—something—gave Hopkins's voice a slight tremor. "Let's get the bloody thing, first. We'll get it out all right."

To their right, beyond the low wall, they could hear the soft gruntings and snufflings. The place stank to the high heaven of pig. Five saddlebacks, only five. Two in one pen, three in the next. The bloody stench! Muckiest things in creation, pigs. Muckier than cows, and they were bad enough. Funny thing, that. Folk counted pork a delicacy. And they liked beef. But horse-meat . . . who ate horse-meat? Who even wanted to eat horse-meat? But a horse was just about the cleanest beast of all. Almost finicky. Whereas a pig was the muckiest, smelliest . . .

"When you're ready, Dave."

Hopkins's words cut into Blayde's thoughts.

Blayde grunted, "Oh, aye," and at the same time vaulted the low wall.

It had to be done like that. Without thought. Without waiting. Without thinking about the possible consequences. In there and grab a porker but don't think about it. Don't even think about Meg. Or the twins. Think about nowt, otherwise it couldn't be done.

And then, it was all madness, and it seemed to go on for ever.

The squealing, the tossing, the grabbing of a struggling body, the straddling, the grasping of a tossing, twisting head, Seth cursing, the hammer missing its mark and landing, full-blooded, just above the snout, the second swing that landed as the head was turned and smashed the jaw, and then the pain in his leg. His right calf. Such pain as he'd never thought existed. The tearing of flesh and muscle. The cracking of bone.

There is a state of mental suspension; a never-never-land midway between consciousness and unconsciousness; a state in which everything can be heard, everything can be seen, everything can be felt . . . but nothing with meaning and nothing with comprehension. David Blayde hung there, suspended in the never-never land. He swung there, hanging by the thread of incandescent pain. He saw lights arrive and heard voices.

"Christ! The bloody sow has him by the leg."

"What are you two buggers up to at this . . ."

"Get a crowbar. Anything."

"By God, Hopkins, I've a mind to blow your head from your shoulders."

"A crowbar. *Something* . . ."

"She'll no'an let go. She'll need her jaws prized apart."

"For Christ's sake, get a crowbar."

"You've gone too bloody far this time. This time tha'll . . ."

"Shut your stupid gob, Dobson. There's a man here likely to lose his leg."

David Blayde didn't lose his leg; for the rest of his life he limped badly and could only walk slowly and with the aid of a stick. The terrible wound inflicted by the pain-mad saddleback was repaired, after a fashion, at the local cottage hospital, after which he stood in a Police Court and was sentenced to six months imprisonment. The Justices of the Peace who sat in judgement on him were fellow-farmers and an example had to be made, therefore both Seth Hopkins and David Blayde were denied any hope of a "second chance".

Meg Blayde was required to leave the tied cottage before her husband was out of hospital. She took her sorry sticks of furniture to the only place left; to her parent's home, on the outskirts of Lessford.

She also took her two newly-born twins.

When sentence was passed on him David Blayde limped from the dock and prior to transportation to prison, a kindly police officer allowed the man and wife a few moments of privacy.

"You'll come back, David." Meg Blayde fought back the tears.

"Nay." Blayde shook his head.

"But you must! You're my husband. I'll not let you . . ."

"Meg, lass." Blayde's voice was soft and filled with the sadness of despair. "I've brought you nowt but trouble. Your mam and dad won't be sorry. They'll . . ."

"They'll take you in, David. They're not . . ."

"They'll take me in." He touched her lips with a forefinger, to quieten her. "They'll take me in, because of you. They're good people. But they'll never forgive me, and I don't blame 'em. I'm a thief, luv. That's what it boils down to. I'm a thief. I'm a cripple an' I'm no good even to mi'sen. I've given your bairns a name. And that's all I'll ever be able to do. Be satisfied, Meg. An' don't tell 'em lies. When they grow up—when they can understand—credit 'em with being capable of accepting the truth."

And that was it. She never saw him again. Twice she visited H.M. Prison at Armley, Leeds, but on both occasions he refused to see her. Upon release he took to the road; work houses, common lodging houses, "spikes" . . . he grew to know them all. He begged for his food; a slice of dripping and bread and a mug of hot tea, usually at the homes of people not much more affluent than himself. When begging didn't fill his stomach, he stole; root crops which he chewed raw, left-overs which had been put out for some spoiled dog. In summer it wasn't too bad. In winter he shivered the nights away in some barn. Always moving; attempting to leave behind a past of which he became more and more ashamed.

Gradually—so gradually as not to be noticed—his mind went. First his memory, then his power of reasoning. He was never a nuisance; never a menace. Just a roadster, everlastingly muttering to himself as he dragged a crippled leg on a never-ending journey to nowhere.

On a March morning in 1932—Saturday, March 19th—a group of walkers found his body, huddled in the angle of two dry-stone walls on the high Pennines. There was no sign of foul play, and the pathologist estimated that the body had been there at least two days before it was found.

Who was he?

They never knew. Attempts at identification failed completely. Just some old tramp who'd been caught out on the slopes; one more life taken by some of the wildest country in the United Kingdom.

He was given a quick, Christian burial. A corner of a cemetery, reserved for paupers and people of no fixed abode; a cheap coffin, and no headstone. How could there be a headstone . . . they didn't know who he was.

3

LESSFORD, like every other city, was not what it made pretence it was. It was not a single unit. Much as fields are enclosed within a boundary and then called a farm, so districts are hedged within a single geographic area and are then given the name of a city. But each district had its own character, its own "feel", its own hidebound rules of acceptable behaviour. What was the norm in (say) North End would not have been tolerated in Hallsworth Hill. The factories and heavy industries of Mellow Road would never have fitted into the Park View scheme of things. A city, then, a conglomerate of houses, shops, factories, warehouses, offices, roads, streets, parks, squares and God knows what else—and in one corner of the Hallsworth Hill district, a sort of urban village called Hill Rise.

Sefton Wilkes was a man who enjoyed great respectability within this tiny community. Without being wealthy he was, nevertheless, "well off". Without being painfully sanctimonious he was an active elder at the local Methodist Church; his God was his friend, and Christ had long since pinned a reserved ticket on seats in the hereafter for Wilkes and his wife. He was the proprietor of a sprawling general store, and he sold just about everything, from apples to safety pins and, to those he trusted, there was almost unlimited credit; 1932 was a hard year, and good men were unable to find employment but, with the return of prosperity, those same good men would clear all their debts. Sefton Wilkes prided himself on his judge of character.

The idlers, of course, got short shrift. The world owed nobody a living, and those who thought it did were left in no doubt that they must seek that living in some place other than Wilkes's General Store.

It was nearing five o'clock in the afternoon of Thursday, February 25th and Wilkes, as was usual at that hour, was officiating behind the counter. The afternoon influx of customers had tailed off, and Wilkes was putting the world to rights with the help of his friend, George May.

"MacDonald." Wilkes unscrewed the top from a jar of boiled sweets. He held the opened jar for May to take a sweet, then he took one himself. As he returned the top to the jar, he sucked the sweet and continued, "I don't trust MacDonald. He blows with the wind."

"He's Labour."

May made the pronouncement as if it answered everything. May, like Wilkes, was self-employed; the local undertaker and (again like Wilkes) a staunch, Glory-to-God member of the Methodist Church.

"A Coalition Government." Wilkes paused to suck the sweet. "It's neither one thing nor the other. The ruling classes should rule. They're shirking their responsibility, that's the heart of the trouble."

"And," added May, as if this was a logical continuation of the proposition voiced by Wilkes, "the League of Nations should take Mussolini to task. He acts as if Italy was still Ancient Rome, and it's not."

There was a prolonged, sweet-sucking silence, then Wilkes consulted his pocket watch and said, "I'm closing at five sharp today."

"Oh. In that case . . ."

"No. Not you, George. I just mention it. It's their birthday, you see."

"Who?"

"The twins. A birthday tea. I promised Edna and Meg I'd be there."

"How old are they?" asked May.

"Ten years old, today."

"My, how time flies."

"It has wings," agreed Wilkes ponderously. "When we reach our age we become more aware of our mortality."

"Indeed."

May sucked and nodded his head, solemnly. As if Wilkes had voiced some previously-hidden truth; as if May's own profession did not constantly remind him that mortality was one of the few things common to all men.

The Wilkeses lived in a three-storey, detached house less than five hundred yards from the store. A tall, red-brick affair, with a high, steep-pitched roof—a "real hail-stone splitter" as one local builder was wont to remark—and, below ground level, a series of cellars. It housed Wilkes, his wife, his daughter and his two grandsons with room to spare, and that to its credit. On the debit side, it was ugly; it displayed some of the less charming features of Victorian architecture. Its chimneys pretended not to be chimneys; atop unnecessarily high stacks, they were frilled and fancy and looked remarkably like the cylindrical paper trimmings with which lamb chops are sometimes adorned. Its ridge-tiles were equally flippant; almost resembling frozen bunting stretched across the highest peak of the house. The cornices and window-ledges were great hunks of stone, ridiculously large and out of proportion to the windows and doors let into the brickwork. As if in neon lights, the whole house seemed to scream "Look what I can afford" at every passer-by.

The garden was a disaster. Surrounded by shoulder-high, iron railings it consisted of lawn—i.e. rarely mown areas of grass and clover leaf—ancient and untrimmed laurels, and black, soot-heavy soil where, each year, crocus and daffodil bulbs fought to continue life, despite almost impossible odds.

From the outside, then, it looked a cold and inhospitable dwelling. But the outside appearance was a visual lie. It was a home, in the true sense of that word. It was "comfy", "lived in" and, in its own tight-stay way, it contained humour. A quiet humour; a chuckling humour; a long-suffering humour . . . just as long as that humour did not stray too far from the strict confines of good taste and God-fearing decency.

There was certainly humour at the birthday table. Wilkes sat at the head, eyes twinkling and happy as he watched his family enjoying the thick-sliced ham he himself had carved from what was left of the whole leg on the carving-dish within easy reach on the table. The out-of-season lettuce and tomatoes. The great dollops of chutney. The home-baked bread—baked to perfection by his daughter, Meg—thick with rich, yellow butter.

"Eat up," he smiled. "More, if you want more. But don't forget the trifle to follow."

"Not too much trifle for the boys," warned his wife, Edna. "It has sherry in it."

And, if Sefton Wilkes was the head of his family, Edna Wilkes was its heart. She lived with pain; everlasting, never ceasing pain. Not agony—or, at least, not always agony—but the nagging, soul-destroying pain of rheumatoid arthritis. As she herself often put it, "It comes and goes," but this was an over-simplification, because it never completely left her. It was merely sometimes a little more tolerable than at others. Always—even in the better periods—she needed asistance when she walked; usually a walking-stick, sometimes two. But when the pain really drove itself into the joints, she also needed manual assistance.

And Meg. Meg, the treasure of Sefton Wilkes's heart. The hands and eyes of Edna Wilkes. Before she was born they'd wanted a boy; both of them . . . they'd both wanted a boy. But Meg had never been second best and she, in turn, had given them two boys. Robert and Richard Blayde. And never mind the name Blayde, they were as much children of their grandparents as they were of their own mother. As for their father . . . God bless him, wherever he was. He'd done a foolish thing—a shameful thing—but he'd been man enough to hold that shame close to his own breast, and not force his wife to share it.

They had trifle, and after the trifle came the cake. A square cake with pale-blue trimmings on pure white icing, and the trimmings divided the cake into two perfect halves and in each half stood ten tiny candles.

Having carefully lighted the candles, Wilkes sat back and said, "Right—both together—blow. Take a deep breath, and really *blow.*"

"And wish," added his wife.

The candles were all extinguished in a tiny hurricane of expelled breath, then the cake was cut, tasted and pronounced excellent. The birthday meal was ended and Meg Blayde made as if to move from the table.

"Not yet, Meg." Wilkes's voice was kind, but firm.

"Father, I don't think we should spoil this day by . . ."

"We decided, Meg." The tone was still kind, but as firm as ever. "We agreed—we *all* agreed—that when they reached this age, they must be told."

"Told what?" The boy, Robert, looked puzzled.

Edna Wilkes lowered her eyes and looked sad, but she made no attempt to dissuade her husband.

Sefton Wilkes smiled at the two boys and said, "Your father—you have a father, somewhere. He was—I've no doubt, still is—a good man. He and your mother were married. Happily married. But you don't know him. I doubt if you'll ever know him. And you're both old enough—sensible enough—to be told why you don't know him. Why you'll probably never meet him. But why, despite all things, you must always think kindly of him."

Sefton Wilkes told the story, second-hand. He told it honestly, without either making excuses or apportioning blame. He emphasised nothing, other than the fact that David Blayde, ten years previously, had done a wrong thing, but for right reasons.

"Hunger," he said. "Poverty. It can blind the best of men. All your life, you must remember that. The Bible puts it far better than I can. Faith, hope and charity . . . 'and the greatest of these is charity'. That's what it means. That's what it's talking about." He paused, smiled a smile which held nothing but genuine love for his grandchildren, then ended, "You're old enough to know. Old enough to understand. Old enough to feel nothing but charity for a good father who didn't want to visit a sinful act upon his wife or his sons."

That night, having given them time to bath, clean their teeth, put on freshly laundered pyjamas and climb into their beds, Meg Blayde paid her usual visit to her son's bedroom.

"Said your prayers?" she asked.

"Yes," said Robert.

"Yes," lied Richard.

She kissed them each in turn, tucked the flannelette sheets more firmly round their necks, wished them goodnight, warned them to behave themselves and go to sleep, turned out the light, then left.

There was a silence, until their mother was well out of earshot, then Robert said, "Why did you lie?"

"About saying my prayers?"

"Did you forget?"

"No." In the darkened bedroom, the voice had all the certainty and solemnity of a ten-year-old. "Why should I say my prayers? I don't believe in God."

"Richard!"

"I wonder where he is," mused Richard.

"God?"

"No. Our father."

"That's what I mean. You can't . . ."

"No. I mean *our* father."

"Oh!"

"I think he's a fool," said Richard calmly.

"If—if he was hungry. If they were poor. *Really* poor. If mother was . . ."

"I don't mean he was a fool for stealing," interrupted Richard. "He was a fool for trying to steal a pig. That was silly."

Robert Blayde made no comment.

Richard Blayde continued, "Why didn't he steal something worth stealing? Why did he need that man, Hopkins? Why didn't he just look after himself, and mother, of course? I think he was a fool and a coward."

Twins. Two where there should have been one; an embryo which, by some quirk of nature, has divided itself—doubled itself—and become a multiplicity of what it should have been. Sometimes almost opposites. Sometimes almost a mirror image. But always an affinity. A peculiar and unique affinity.

Robert and Richard Blayde were healthy, normal schoolboys . . . plus this affinity. They were not too much alike in looks, although they were obviously twins, but their respective thought processes were almost uncannily similar. At school—and quite deliberately—they were placed well away from each other in the classroom and yet when, for example, they were told to write an essay on any subject they chose, their choice always ran along the same lines. It was difficult to tell their handwriting apart. Even their spelling; they both seemed to have difficulty in spelling the same words. In no subject did one outstrip the other.

Their characters, too. Each had a strong, ruthless streak. What they started, either individually or together, they finished.

Thus, in 1934, when Hitler proclaimed himself Dictator of the Third Reich, their reactions—for twelve-year-olds—were parallel, but subtly different.

Richard said, "I suppose he took what he was after."

Robert said, "I think he's had that at the back of his mind, all the time."

They both left school at the age of fourteen. Neither was university fodder, neither was a dolt. A choice had to be made. Their grandfather looked towards one of them helping in the store, but knew there wasn't work enough for both.

"Should we spin a coin?" he asked.

"No." Robert shook his head. "I'd like to be a carpenter, grandfather."

"I can do that." The old man smiled his pleasure. "I can get you apprenticed to a real craftsman."

"I'd like that," said Robert.

"And you, Richard?" asked Wilkes.

"The shop," replied Richard. "You can teach me how to make money in the store."

"Always the edge," chuckled the old man. "Always Richard the careful one. You're both good boys. I'm proud of you both."

But the truth is, Robert Blayde soon learned

he wasn't cut out to be a carpenter. Well, a carpenter perhaps, but not a carpenter and undertaker. The one-man firm to whom Wilkes had arranged for him to be apprenticed was without doubt a firm which, despite its size, was held in high regard. His employer could make beautiful furniture; nothing slipshod; nothing "knocked together". The man was his own enemy, in that he took too much care. Nails were a form of minor blasphemy; fine wood could—indeed should—be cut and worked to an accuracy within which the whole piece stood firm and rigid by reason of various, skilfully positioned joints. Glue—glue boiled, in an old-fashioned glue-pot—was a mere means of fusing together what was already bonded by good workmanship.

The coffins, too. They took a day and a night—non'stop sawing, chiselling and shaping—before they were even ready for "finishing". And "finishing" meant sanding, then scraping and, finally, polishing with pure beeswax. The man wanted no varnish in his workshop. "Wood's a living thing, lad. Don't daub it with chemicals. Bring out its grain. Bring out its life. Then make that life shine with nature's wax."

No mere coffin was worth that much love.

Robert Blayde saw, and worked on, works of superb craftsmanship, which were destined to be buried for ever within a matter of days. Cabinets for corpses, and cabinets superior to the bulk of furniture to be found in everyday houses.

Blayde once said, "It's only a coffin, sir."

"Only a coffin." Near disbelief clouded the craftman's face. "It's a casket, son. It's being built to house something priceless. All that's left of a human being. That's how important it is. That's why it's got to be as near perfect as we can make it."

And Blayde accepted the reprimand as being deserved. He never again skimped any task he was set.

But the bodies!

The bodies worried young Robert Blayde. Sometimes they were stiff, sometimes they were boneless and as floppy as a rag-doll, and always they were cold. A strange, horrific coldness, as if beneath the skin there was iced putty; a coldness which, however many times he handled a corpse, young Robert Blayde could never get used to. And sometimes they were messy. Very messy. And on those occasions Blayde scrubbed his hands with carbolic soap and near-boiling water until they were almost raw, but he still felt unclean.

One evening in the spring of 1939—it was Saturday, May 27th—Meg, his mother, found Robert Blayde deep in thought in a corner of the evergreen-heavy garden.

"Worried about something?" she asked gently.

Blayde pushed his hands deeper into the pockets of his trousers and said, "You think there'll be a war, mam?"

"I hope not." Meg Blayde frowned. "I lived through the Great War."

"Didn't do much good, did it?"

"It didn't do what we all hoped it would do," admitted Meg.

"About this joining up . . ." began Blayde.

"You're in a safe job."

"Burying 'em, not making 'em," said Blayde bitterly.

"Robert!"

"Mam, I'm not going to be an undertaker." Blayde met his mother's eyes. "I like wood. I like working with wood. But the other thing . . . it sickens me."

"You're still apprenticed," she reminded him gently.

"I know. But if there *is* a war . . ." He didn't end the sentence.

"Yes?"

"Mam." Suddenly Robert Blayde was old for his years. "I think there will be a war. I think both Hitler and Mussolini intend to have a war. That's what the Spanish Civil War was all about. A try-out. A rehearsal. And I don't think Chamberlain can do much about it. It's coming, and when it comes, I want a say in where I go."

"Robert, you're in a . . ."

"Not for long, mam. Once it starts, being an apprentice undertaker won't count for much."

"You're . . . young," she said sadly.

"I'm seventeen," he said grimly. "I'm fit and strong. If there's a war and I volunteer, they'll take me."

4

THE lieutenant's lips moved into a dry smile, and he said, "A strange choice, Blayde."

"My choice, sir. If I have one."

"It won't keep you out of the fighting line, if that's what you think."

"That's not the reason behind my choice, sir."

"I'm glad to hear it." The lieutenant nodded a little pompously, then mused, "If my memory serves me well, originally one sergeant and ten men chosen in each regiment. Each man issued with a sword with a saw back, plus picks, shovels, axes and crowbars. Their duty to remove obstacles in the line of march. Rendering posts defensible. General repair work."

"That's going back a bit, sir."

"It is," agreed the lieutenant. He touched his tie; he was a very elegantly turned out young man, proud of his bearing and proud of his regiment, The Green Howards. For the life of him he couldn't see why any young man volunteering for the army wasn't prepared to move heaven and earth to serve in The Green Howards. He drawled, "It is, indeed, going back a bit."

"What's my chances, sir?" asked Robert Blayde.

"Good, I should think. We don't get many volunteers for the Pioneer Corps."

"I'm used to handling wood," said Blayde. "I'm not used to handling a rifle."

"We'll—er—we'll teach you how to handle a rifle."

"Yes, sir."

The conversation took place at 2 p.m. on Monday, September 4th, 1939, at an inner room of Lessford Army Recruiting Office. Blayde had told his employer of his intention, and the employer had looked sad, but resigned; in the outer office a ruddy-faced sergeant had beamed his approval and assisted Blayde in filling in various forms; in the inner office the lieutenant had noted Blayde's first choice, and remarked upon it accordingly.

Nor, in honesty, must it be implied that Blayde had much idea of what he was letting himself in for or, indeed, that he really knew why he was volunteering his services little more than twenty-four hours after the declaration of war.

Some of it had to do with Hitler and Mussolini, but much more of it had to do with his growing detestation of handling dead bodies. And to Blayde—as to the bulk of youthful volunteers at that time—the fact of war did not itself equate with more dead bodies than he'd ever seen or would ever see again. Some of it had to do with the Nazis and the Fascists, but again a great deal more had to do with Blayde's desire to have some control of his destiny in the event of a prolonged war.

Later in life, when asked, Blayde would be ruthlessly honest; so honest, in fact, as to be almost dishonest. "Christ knows. Because a lot of lads of my own age group were joining. Because I wanted to show 'em I'd as many hairs on my chest as the next idiot."

But that afternoon—the afternoon of Monday, September 4th, 1939—having taken the rest of the day off work, Robert Blayde was faced with explaining his action to his mother and his grandparents.

Edna Wilkes spent most of her waking life in a wheelchair these days, her joints were like ugly knots on a twisted cord. The continuous pain, too, had extracted its price; her eyes were sunken and dark-rimmed, and the corner of her mouth was creased where she'd held her lips hard together in order not to allow pain the freedom of expression. Nor had Sefton Wilkes weathered the recent years too well. The droop to his shoulders showed the weight of his years, and his walk was little more than a shuffle. He spent less and less time at the store; Blayde's twin, Richard, being by this time able to order, display and sell with as much skill as his grandfather.

As for Blayde's mother, Meg, iron grey had streaked her hair but she carried her age with the quiet pride of her kind. Had she been asked, had she understood, had she been able to view her own life objectively and had she been capable of putting it into words—she would have argued that she'd had her man, had her children and was now content to play housekeeper to parents who needed her in their ageing years. She was of a breed and of a generation capable of accepting "duty" without thought and without rancour.

Blayde told them what he'd done. As well as he was able, he explained why he'd done it. Meg gripped the apron which was part of her everyday attire and stared at her son as if seeing him for the first time. The grandmother's eyes shone with held-back tears.

In a quiet, sad voice Sefton said, "You could have waited."

"Probably," agreed Blayde. "But it would have come."

"And if Richard joins up?"

"I don't think he will."

Blayde sounded certain. Indeed, he was certain. Richard's job was here; working to bring money in; ensuring that this small family was able to ride out the period of this war without undue hardship. But there was something else . . . something inexplicable. Not cowardice. Richard was, if anything, more hot-headed—more ready for a fight—than Robert. And yet Robert was sure—absolutely sure—that while he could, his brother would keep out of uniform.

Three weeks later—on Tuesday, September 26th—a buff-coloured envelope dropped through the letter box. On Monday, October 2nd, Blayde boarded a train from Lessford for basic training.

It was a strange war. Those first few months became known as the Phoney War; a war which wasn't a war; a war of leaflets and propaganda. The field-marshals and generals pored over their maps and, with their trench-warfare minds, sought solutions beyond their comprehension. It was a "Cook's Tour War". It was a stupid war in which armies faced each other, snarled threats at each other and sang semi-comic songs about what they'd do . . . once the real war started.

But for the moment, the only real war was at sea. HMS Royal Oak was destroyed in (of all places) Scapa Flow. The Navy fumed at this shame, until they'd evened things out a little off the River Plate and watched the German warship Admiral Graf Spe slide beneath the surface.

Meanwhile, the continent of Europe shivered. Whatever else, it was a very cold war; the British Expeditionary Force shivered and struggled through snow and slush. The women at home knitted furiously, and every newsreel shot showed soliders bellied out to twice their size with pullovers, scarves, gloves and Balaclava helmets. And everywhere units of the Pioneer Corps built and re-built bridges which had broken under the weight of heavy vehicles and tanks; repaired or made shelters against the appalling weather.

Blayde had never been so cold, or as

miserable, in his life. The nature of his various tasks was such that it meant working either in icy water or in a raging blizzard. He'd been taught to be a perfectionist in wood; that things had to *fit*. Now "near-as-dammit" was the unit of measurement.

In the beginning he tried for some degree of accuracy.

"Sergeant, this timber's too short."

"How much too short?"

"Two inches, at least two inches."

"Drive a wedge in, then nail it into position."

"It won't last, sergeant. It'll go, the first time a tank . . ."

"Drive a wedge in, lad. If it goes—when it goes—we'll be back to guy it up again. That's what we're here for."

And gradually, reluctantly, Blayde accepted "near-as-dammit" as his basic unit of measurement; accepted that speed and immediacy was the army's only yardstick of practical efficiency. And that waste didn't matter because "there's a war on" and expense counted for nothing.

He lost count of the villages and districts he and his unit visited and re-visited. He seemed to spend half his life humping balks of unplaned timber and hammering them into position with six-inch nails, and the other half riding on trucks and half-tracks to somewhere else, where there'd be more balks of timber and more six-inch nails. At times he almost longed for the coffins and the corpses of the old days.

The army coarsened him, as it coarsens most men; the army, the weather, the frustration, the hard-living, the vulgarities of most of his comrades. Together they became coarsened, and Robert Blayde was no exception. He learned to eff and blind with the best of them. For the first time in his life he tasted hard liquor; he became drunk—paralytically drunk—and, when he sobered, he truly thought he was on the point of death. He had his first fist-fight—a raging, red-blooded set-to with a colleague, about some triviality hardly worth mentioning—and he was knocked cold.

The sergeant took him aside, when the scrap was over, and said, "You fight like a woman, lad."

"I'm sorry." Blayde touched his swelling jaw.

"Don't be sorry. Learn how to use yourself. And if you have to fight, fight to win."

"He's a better man than I am."

"The hell he is! You've age on your side, and muscle. Any other man in the team could have taken him apart."

"I'll learn," promised Blayde.

"The first clout," advised the sergeant. "If you're going to have a go, get that first clout in . . . and make it *matter*. After that, keep swinging. Don't just stand there waiting for punishment."

Blayde nodded. It was good advice, and Blayde recognised it as such.

By April, 1940, the snow had melted and much of the mud had dried out. The opposing armies were straining to get to real grips with each other. On Tuesday, the 2nd of that month, Blayde and four of his colleagues were granted leave and decided to spend the leave in Paris.

At eighteen years of age he was already old for his years. Even cynical. But still a virgin. That was rectified in a sleazy room of a back-street brothel, and Robert Blayde worried, for days, in case he'd "caught something". Then back to his unit, more bridge-building and the disheartening news that a British counter-invasion of Norway had been a failure. Chamberlain described the defeat in a long-remembered "missing-the-boat" excuse to the British Parliament and, as the German armies moved into Holland, Belgium and Luxemburg the British people roared their disapproval and demanded a fighting Prime Minister.

On Saturday, May 11th Churchill took over the reins of a National Government, and as from that moment, Great Britain refused to even contemplate final defeat.

On Friday, May 17th Private Robert Blayde became Lance Corporal Robert Blayde and, despite his lack of years, nobody begrudged him the small promotion. And by this time men of the B.E.F. realised that the Nazi war machine was rolling closer and might not be stopped. Monday, May 27th saw one of the war's darkest days: King Leopold ordered the Belgian army to capitulate to the Germans and the British army began a desperate rearguard action through Ostend, Ypres and Lille as it backed towards an unknown channel town called Dunkirk.

Dunkirk . . . where Lance Corporal Blayde was blooded and, at the same time, achieved complete manhood.

June 1st, 1940. It was a Saturday, and what was to add up to 299 British naval vessels and 420 "little boats" were rescuing 335,000 men from certain death or capture. The queues were already there; queues which stretched across the beaches and into the sea; queues which snaked into the puny shelter of the dunes. The British are great people for queuing—take your place, sir; no pushing or shoving; stand in line in an orderly fashion—even when you're being straffed from the air and shelled by enemy artillery.

The Messerschmitts came in line-astern, guns blazing and bullets kicking up the sand in a homicidal stitch-pattern. At the end of their run, they wheeled and came in from the opposite direction. It was a pure turkey shoot and the Bren-gunner hadn't a hope in hell. Nevertheless, and having lugged his weapon half-way across France, he swivelled it on its tripod and took each fighter as it came in low. Then, having slammed a fresh magazine into position and cocked the Bren, he died. Without a word. Without even having time to scream. For a split-second he crouched at the converging point of everything one of the Messerschmitts was throwing out. It was like a combined band-saw-cum-shredding-machine. He just didn't exist any more; torn flesh, shattered bone, a blood-soaked battle-dress . . . and that was all.

Blayde watched and went berserk. He dived for the toppled Bren gun, righted it and, shouting obscenities, took on the following fighter in a personal one-to-one battle. He survived, as did the fighter, but not the next fighter. Somebody—Blayde never knew who—fed a new magazine into the Bren, and Blayde kept the sights firmly on the spinner of the oncoming M.E. A man-to-man war between Blayde and some unknown fighter pilot; a war within a war; the spinner at the centre of the propeller and the lined-up sights of a stuttering Bren gun. Blayde felt the fighter's shells pluck at his tunic. His left leg was kicked from under him, but he clung to the Bren and kept the spinner glued to the sights. As he was spun sideways and lost consciousness he glimpsed smoke coming from the machine and, as from a lengthening distance, heard the cheers of men.

He caught passing glimpses of the world. Hazy, deformed glimpses; as if catching a sudden sight through the glass and moving waters of an aquarium. Men . . . men and waves . . . men passing him from hand to hand above the waves. A deck . . . a deck and a blanket . . . a gentle-handed man covering him with the warmth of a blanket . . . a slight pinprick in the arm . . . then darkness.

Sunday, September 8th, 1940.

The military hospital was in Gloucestershire, within easy reach of the Cotswolds and the Forest of Dean. Surrounded by good farmland and fruit-growing country; a million light years and a lifetime from the dunes of Dunkirk. And by this time the spin of the war had accelerated. It had taken to the skies. The Battle of Britain it was called, and the burning, pulsating heart of the battle was London; last night the capital had taken the hammering to end all hammerings and the boys in the Hurricanes and the Spitfires were bone weary but still fighting, and God only knew how, or when, it was going to end.

But the grounds of the hospital were peaceful, and the autumn sun sent afternoon shadows across the tree-lined lawns. Blayde walked between his mother and his brother. He was no longer in hospital blue but, instead, wore a fresh-out-of-stores battle-dress and boots which had yet to be broken in.

No, he wasn't going to have a limp; the bones of his left leg had knitted perfectly. Yes, the head wound was fine; little more than a graze, really; not much worse than being hit over the head with a pick shaft. No, he didn't know where he was going from here; and, if he had known, he wouldn't have told them. Yes, he was due for some sick leave, but he wasn't spending it all at home.

The army boots crunched slowly on the loose gravel of the path.

"Where . . ." Meg Blayde hesitated, then asked, "Where are you likely to spend it, Bob?"

"At home . . . some of it," answered Blayde awkwardly.

"And the rest?"

Richard Blayde chuckled and said, "He's found a girl, ma. Can't you guess?"

"No, it's not that." There was irritation in Blayde's denial.

"If it is . . ." began Meg.

"No."

"She'd be made welcome, if you want to . . ."

"It's not a girl, ma." Blayde's face clouded as he tried to explain. "It's just this—this sodding war."

"Bob!"

"I'm sorry. It's the way I feel. A lot of noise and no privacy. That's what's up with me. I need to be alone. Just by myself for a bit. No noise. Nobody else for miles." He smiled and ended. "You don't understand, ma, do you?"

"I—I think so," said Meg slowly.

"That's it, then. I'm sorry."

Of the fourteen days of the sick leave, he spent four at home. The first two, when he changed into civilian clothes, and the last two, when he collected his uniform. The rest he spent in The Dales.

He was looking for something, but it was something he couldn't put a name to. Peace, perhaps. But there couldn't be peace until this damn war ended. Therefore not that sort of peace. Maybe that snatched peace a ring-fighter finds between rounds. A breathing space. A chance to forget what had gone before, and not to remember what might be ahead. An identity, perhaps. His own identity; his own personality. In little more than a year he'd changed. That much, at least, he was sure of. His grandparents, his mother, his twin brother—he still loved them—but they were no longer *vital* to him. If he never saw them again he'd be sorry, but he wouldn't be heartbroken. Those first few months in the army had frayed the bond, and the Dunkirk episode had snapped it. Among other things, therefore, he carried a sense of guilt.

He walked lonely, leaf-strewn paths in Wensleydale, Nidderdale, Swaledale, and the loneliness went deeper—much deeper—than the surrounding solitude. It was a mental thing. An attitude of mind. In a strange way it paralleled the normal life-style of the folk of The Dales. Taciturn people. Undemonstrative. As silently immovable as the high peaks of The Pennines within whose folds they lived.

He spent his nights in farm and cottage bedrooms, sleeping on flock mattresses, kept warm by patchwork quilts and stone hot-water bottles. And the next morning he ate a breakfast big enough to last him until evening.

"How many eggs, lad? How many rashers?"

"I don't want to take your rations."

"Nay, lad." A quiet chuckle. "We keep our own hens. An' if tha likes home-cured bacon . . ."

And sometimes, in the evenings, after a day's walking and in front of a warm, spitting log fire, they'd talk. Blunt talk, with a paucity of words but a wealth of meaning.

"Sick leave?"

"Yes."

"Dunkirk?"

"Yes . . . Dunkirk."

"A bonny bloody mess, from what I read."

"A bit of a shambles."

"Some daft bugger needs a boot up 'is arse."

In a nutshell. The high command—the red-tabbed lunatics to whom a battle or, come to that, a whole war, boiled down to the movement of coloured flags on a wall-map . . . some daft bugger did, indeed, "need a boot up his arse".

Those days in The Dales. So many analogies. Like the purification of the soul; like a deep drink at a clear, cool spring; like an involved equation reduced to a simple two-plus-two problem.

Those last couple of days with his family were a form of anti-climax. Richard took him out to the local boozer one evening, but it was a monumental bore. Too many people, and all the wrong sort of people. Too much money to splash around, and too much back-slapping.

He was glad to put his uniform back on, pack his kitbag and board the train south.

5

THURSDAY, August 6th, 1942.

Cairo was a fly-infested dump, Egypt was the last place God made, and this bloody war was going to last for ever. The two sergeants sat at a table in one of the more popular bars, sipped iced beer, watched the huge blades of the ceiling-fans slowly stir the super-heated air and provide gentle relief from boredom for an assortment of insects, and talked "soldier talk". Rumours were rife, but in this hole rumours were always rife; rumours of this, rumours of that . . . as thick as fleas on the umpteen stray dogs roaming the narrow streets.

Sergeant "Taffy" Morgan said, "Some of the Long Range boys are back. Rommel's building up for a last push. That's what I hear."

"He's welcome." Blayde moved his shoulders to ease the sweat-soaked shirt away from the skin of his back.

"Mind you," mused Morgan, "we're doing a fair bit of building up ourselves."

Morgan was a sergeant in the Royal Engineers. Like Blayde, he was in charge of a unit of men who, when necessary, were detailed for a specific task. They'd struck up a friendship on the troopship and, whenever possible, they spent their free time together. Part of the reason for them liking each other was that neither of them fitted into the accepted pattern of the North African campaign. They were not professional soldiers, nor did they make pretence they were or ever would be. Not for them the shortened shorts, or the stripped-to-the-waist, he-man image. Nor, on the other hand, did they flout sun-bleached twill or eye-dazzling cravats. They were there to do a job, and they had each been issued with a uniform. They wore the uniform and, when ordered, they did the job. Rommel was Rommel and the Afrika Korps was the Afrika Korps, neither were "legendary"; they were a bloody nuisance, in that they stood in the way of a return to civilian life.

Morgan was a newly-married bank clerk and, because of this, the night life of Cairo interested him not at all.

"Go with one of 'em, man, and she's entitled to set up a brothel, with herself as top whore. That's what I say. It's one or the other. It's not a matter of degree, see?"

Which, although he was unmarried, was an argument that appealed to Blayde. He was no prude; maybe he'd once been something of a prude, but almost three years in the army had exposed him to a very earthy philosophy. And yet, at the centre (as with Morgan) he was a civilian in fancy dress. He held rank, and men, some of whom were old enough to be his father, obeyed him. But that was no sinecure. There was still England; specifically, there was still Lessford. And when he allowed himself to give thought to the future, he yearned to start a life of his own. To be his own man. To have some say in his own future.

Meanwhile . . .

On Friday, October 23rd, the guns opened up at a then unknown place called El Alamein, and by the end of May the following year the North African campaign was over and done with; Rommel was back in Germany and the Afrika Korps had had all hell kicked out of it. Blayde had helped to build more roads and, with the assistance of the Royal Engineers, had retrieved more smashed tanks, lorries, half-tracks and general battle-field debris than he'd even dreamed existed and, along with his pal, Morgan, was on a troopship bound for home.

Home.

Ah, yes, but where the hell *was* home?

He'd thought it was Lessford. Specifically, a somewhat ugly house in Hill Rise. He'd thought it was with his mother, his grandparents, his brother. And for the first few days of disembarkation leave it had seemed like home. But, within those days, the questioning—the "How", the "When", the "Where"—had got him down. Okay, they loved him—okay, they were proud of him—but he was no hero, not even a pretend-hero—and by the looks of things Richard hadn't done too badly out of this blasted war. Clothes, a mite too flashy, bundles of notes a shade too thick, friends a little too shifty-eyed.

He'd asked his mother.

"He's done well for himself." But it had been an excuse, not an explanation.

"How the hell can he 'do well for himself'? Things are in short supply."

"He seems to know where he can get things."

"Y'mean black market?"

"I—I don't think so." But she hadn't looked at him, and she'd added, "I don't ask."

"For Christ's sake!"

"Don't blaspheme in this house Robert." And there'd been a bite to the reprimand.

"Hey, ma." He smiled and put an arm across her shoulders. "Not at you. I'm sorry. But it is black market. It *has* to be."

"He's a good son," she muttered, but it had still been an excuse.

Blayde had sighed and, a little bitterly, had said, "I'll bet he is."

So after three days, he packed a knapsack and tried The Dales again, but this time it didn't work. The damn war had even reached that far. There was a moroseness — a gut-deep misery—which all the open fields and fresh air in the world couldn't banish. Everybody knew somebody—had somebody—the war had touched. The push after El Alamein. The Yanks, and the manpower and war material they represented. Uncle Joe Stalin and the Red Army killing Germans faster than they could count 'em. Great, Hitler *couldn't* win.

But so what?

The whole damn nation was punch-drunk. When *hadn't* there been a war in progress? When hadn't the people looked tired and drawn? When hadn't the army been Blayde's only way of life?

Some of it was self-pity. Some of it was a yearning for a life that was past, and the realisation that life would never return to that old plateau of pre-war normality. Some of it was the knowledge that a handful of fat cats had geared the war and the shortages to their own advantage. That all the bastards in the world didn't wear swastika arm-bands.

By comparison army life was simple. You received orders, you did what you were told, you passed those orders down the line and other men did what they were told. Uncomplicated. No sweat. You slept in a Nissen hut, maybe. Maybe under canvas. Some evenings you went on the town with a few mates. You bogged off on various courses. You learned how to use a Sten gun. Tank recognition. Aircraft recognition. New techniques for making makeshift runways. Always something new. Always busy. No time to think.

So, the war was going to last for ever, so what?

Then, suddenly, from nothing came everything. Blayde was posted south and, in the southern counties, his eyes popped at the monumental build-up of men and material. The end really *was* in sight . . . that or the biggest death toll in the history of the world. Blayde was dumped on the outskirts of a village in Sussex one day in May, 1944. A nice village; a very normal, very English village, except that it crawled with uniformed strangers, and you almost had to move sideways to pass the tanks, half-tracks, lorries and jeeps parked along every road and lane for miles around the village. Briefings were held, and the code-name "Operation Overlord" became something to make your heart skip a beat, then lodge at the back of your throat and threaten to choke you.

"Operation Overlord" . . . brother!

It left the start-line on June 6th, and needed more than 4,000 ships to land armies enough to smash a way into Hitler's Europe. And, on Friday, June 9th (D+3) Blayde saw the shambles of the landing beaches for the first time. He saw them—that's all—then he and his company were rushed inland to where all hell was popping on the outskirts of Caen. The Germans could still fight and, although Hitler might have looped a little, his generals played war as if it was a chess game and they were grand masters.

The major stormed, "The fornicating R.A.F! They were supposed to soften the place up, that's all. Soften it up. They've flattened the bloody place. They've made it into a citadel. We can't get the tanks through the rubble, and the blasted Germans are holed in there, fighting like hell."

The good old Sappers and the good old Pioneers—the non-fighting, non-blood-and-guts types—had a job to do. To clear a way for the tanks and the half-tracks; to move in, immediately behind the infantry, and undo the damage created by the bombers.

Just after dawn the next morning—Saturday, June 10th—the major led them forward, pointed, and said, "That street. The engineers are in already. We've cleared it of the enemy. Take your men in there, sergeant, and shift enough of that rubble to give the armour passage."

Blayde said, "Yes, sir," and led his team in at the double.

Mid-way down the street, somebody shouted,"Bob!"

Blayde skidded to a halt and because he

stopped, he lived. The sniper's bullet whined as it ricocheted from a stone.

Blayde shouted, "Take cover!" and dived for the doorway from where his name had been called.

Taffy Morgan hauled him into the shadows of the house and, as he did so, snarled, "That bloody major. He's a great one for wishful thinking."

"Taffy, of all the people." Blayde cocked his Sten gun. It was an automatic gesture; he was being shot at; training insisted that he prepare to shoot back. He said, "How long is it? When did you arrive at this . . . *behind you, Taffy.*"

And as he screamed the last three words, Blayde tilted the snout of the Sten and squeezed a milli-second before the German sergeant with the Luger pistol. Maybe he saved Morgan's life—maybe not—but that burst from the Sten was to pay dividends years later.[1] The Sten did its work as a close-range weapon; it embroidered a bloody pattern from the German's groin, up through his stomach, into the shoulder then into the head. The single, twitching-finger shot from the Luger

[1] An Urge for Justice, Macmillan, 1981.

was lost in the harsh clatter of the Sten in the confined space of the room.

Then silence and the lingering stench of cordite. Beyond the room, beyond the house, the symphony of battle could be heard, but strangely, that distant noise seemed not to disturb the silence of the room. Blayde stared at the shattered body of the first man he'd knowingly killed; stared at the torn holes, at the tiny rivers of blood; stared at the head which had been blasted wide open.

Morgan breathed, "That *bloody* major," then dashed for the stairs down which the German sergeant had come. His own Sten ready, he eased his way towards the upper part of the house. Blayde could hear him moving from room to room, but couldn't move. The sight of one dead enemy—one unknown man he'd blasted the life out of—epitomised the whole, damn, stupid, pointless, dirty business of war. He dragged his gaze from the dead German, lowered his head until the top of his steel helmet rested against the wall and spewed his heart up.

Morgan returned and said, "They're all dead. He was the last, now he's dead."

Blayde didn't answer. Didn't move. The spittle dripped from his lips.

"Bob . . ." Morgan sought the words. "It was him, or me. You've just saved my life, pal."

But if he heard, Blayde didn't heed. He didn't answer. He couldn't answer. His shoulders shook as he wept silently at the abomination the war had forced him to commit.

That, in effect, was Blayde's war. He didn't have nightmares; only movie heroes have nightmares resultant upon celluloid war. But without being consciously aware of it, he smiled a lot less and drank a little more. For the rest, he moved forward, behind the fighting troops; built and repaired roads and bridges; cleaned up after battles; performed the duties peculiar to the Pioneer Corps and throughout wondered how much more punishment Germany could take before somebody with a pea-sized piece of common sense would call a halt and let him and a few million other civilian soldiers go home and try to pick up the reality of normal life. Occasionally—rather like long-distance drivers bumping into each other at various cafes—he met up with Taffy Morgan . . . and always there was a drinking session.

He would remember certain high points. That on the day he trod German soil, some flaming idiot bit off more than he could chew and triggered off a massacre at Arnhem. That in the same month Roosevelt died, Mussolini was shot and Hitler killed himself and that, in some odd and illogical way, those three deaths seemed to bring the end of the war a little closer. That on Monday, May 7th, 1945, he deliberately stayed awake—chain-smoking in the silence of a barn in Germany—until one minute past midnight and the official ending of World War II.

He was still in Germany, helping to clear up the carnage of war when, on Thursday, August 9th, Nagasaki was obliterated by the second atomic bomb dropped in anger but that, of itself and because of the distance, cancelled out much of the horror and because, on that same day, he walked into Dachau Concentration Camp, and the atomic bomb, and the last six years, and the comparatively clean killing of armies locked in war suddenly became insignificant against the still-stained backdrop of man's supreme inhumanity to fellow-men. For some few hours of his life he could have happily committed murder: cheerfully and without hesitation had the victim in any way assisted Hitler's climb to power. The white heat of that initial anger died, but to the end of his life it remained smouldering and never forgotten.

In April, 1946—Friday, April 19th—he walked away from a Demobilisation Centre, wearing an ill-fitting, chalk-striped suit, and carrying his uniform in a badly-tied brown-paper parcel and, for Robert Blayde, the war was really over.

6

BLAYDE looked at his tool-box and felt saddened. It really was a beautiful piece of craftsmanship. His old gaffer had taught him the skills, and each fusion of wood with wood showed a row of tiny dove-tailed joints; his tools—the saws, the planes, the chisels, the scrapers, everything—had their own little purpose-built niches; the hinge of the box was a piano-hinge and, when you closed the lid, there was a sigh of escaping air . . . that was the measure of the absolute accuracy with which Blayde had lovingly built it.

And now?

A gratuity of a few hundred quid and the knowledge that he'd fought a war. But the skill had gone. Belting lengths of six-by-four into position had ruined the skill as surely and as finally as a sledge-hammer on the keys would ruin the finest Bechstein ever made. Anyway, the old gaffer had died while Blayde had been away in the Middle East, and the gratuity wasn't enough to set himself up in business on his own.

Blayde ran his hand across the silk-smooth surface of the tool-box and forced himself to face reality. He hadn't a skill any more, that was the top and bottom of it. Robert Blayde, Esq. Unskilled labourer. Good for digging ditches, shifting rubble and very little else. And to think he'd damn near prayed for this. For civvy street. For the day when, once more, he'd be his own man.

There was a timid knock on the bedroom door and Blayde called, "Okay. It's open."

Meg Blayde entered, stared at the tool-box, and said, "Oh! Are you . . ."

"Just looking at it," sighed Blayde. "Just admiring it."

"You'll be seeking a job."

"Not with these tools. I'd shame them."

Meg paused, moistened her lips, then said, "Ric's in some sort of trouble."

"Ric?"

"Richard. He's at . . ."

"Oh, aye." Blayde nodded sardonically. "He's 'Ric' these days. What's he want? A contract with Warner Brothers?"

"Your grandfather says you should go down and see."

"Go down where?"

"The—the police station."

"Ma." Blayde compressed his lips a little. "I'm not his keeper."

"He's your brother, Bob."

"And don't think that doesn't worry me, sometimes."

"Please, Bob. I think you should . . ."

"He keeps very strange company. He has some very weird tastes." Blayde waved a silencing hand, stood up from the bed, and said, "Okay. I'll go down, but if they've caught him with a hand in somebody's till, I'm damned if I'll make excuses."

It was a police station—a section station—although Blayde didn't know about such law-enforcement nuances at that time, and Blayde had passed and re-passed it hundreds of times throughout his life, but had never before been inside. Architecturally it was surprisingly like Sefton Wilkes's home; the only home Blayde had ever known. A gloomy place from the outside; red-brick, soot-darkened stone and a blue globe, with the word Police in white, fixed on a goose-neck bracket above the heavy door.

Blayde thumbed the bell-push and a uniformed constable, the choker neck of his tunic unfastened, answered the ring. The constable led Blayde across a tiny hall and into what should have been the lounge, had the building been a normal dwelling house, but which was now a large room in the centre of which was a massive polished, but scratched and stained, table. A couple of office chairs were pulled up to the table, and the surface of the table was littered with official-looking forms. Against one wall was a ceiling-high cabinet, one door of which was open; the interior of the cabinet was partitioned off, and each partition held its own pile of forms and documents. There was a wooden bench along one of the room's walls—opposite the chair in which the uniformed sergeant sat—and to the left of the form there was a door. A very heavy door, complete with large lock and a highly-polished brass lock-plate.

The sergeant was a man a few years older than Blayde. He had his tunic open, and braces showed against the collarless shirt. Above the left breast-pocket of the sergeant's tunic was a tiny row of medal-ribbons; the usual "fruit salad", and Blayde recognised the Air Crew Europe colours.

The sergeant struck a match and slowly

lighted a pipe before speaking. He watched Blayde through the flame of the match and the smoke from the bowl of the pipe. He waved out the match, dropped the match into an ash-tray, then spoke.

"You're the other Blayde lad." It was a statement, not a question.

Blayde nodded and waited. He wasn't afraid . . . what the hell had he to be frightened of? He wasn't even intimidated. For the first time in his life he was in the guts of a working police station, and he felt strangely at home. The coke fire in the open grate behind the sergeant's chair pushed out its warmth and made the whole room cosy; almost womb-like.

"Your brother's a receiver." Again it was a statement and not open to debate.

"I shouldn't wonder," said Blayde flatly.

"Butter. Sugar. Cigarettes. Even a couple of cases of whisky. Well over a hundred quid, all told."

Blayde said, "That's what I came down to find out."

"Oh, aye?"

"Was sent down to find out." Blayde corrected himself. It seemed important that the difference be understood.

"He won't have it," said the sergeant bluntly. "But that makes no difference . . . we have him by the balls."

Beyond the heavy door a whistling kettle climbed to a hissing scream.

As the constable moved towards the door, the sergeant asked Blayde, "Care for a cup?"

"Thanks." Blayde nodded.

"Make it three, Jim." Then to Blayde, "Sugar and milk?"

"Please."

The constable opened the door—strangely it wasn't locked—and beyond the door Blayde saw a passage, concrete floored and tiled to the ceiling with white tiles. The constable closed the door. Blayde and the sergeant remained silent until the constable re-appeared carrying three beakers. The tea had been mashed directly into the beakers and a slight scum of leaves floated on top of the hot liquid. There was only one spoon, and they passed it round. Blayde tasted the tea. It was good; hot, sweet and strong . . . what he'd once have called "sergeant major's".

The police sergeant removed the pipe from his mouth, drank some tea, then replaced the pipe before he spoke.

He said, "Tomorrow morning. There's an

Occasional Court fixed. Lessford Court House. We'll oppose bail."

"As bad as that?"

"More than a hundred quid." The sergeant raised an eyebrow.

"Will he need a solicitor?"

"He'll need more than that. He'll need a bloody miracle."

"That's it then." Blayde took a deeper drink of the tea.

The sergeant removed the pipe from his mouth long enough to enjoy another drink. The constable, Jim, seemed superfluous; only Blayde and the police sergeant need have been there. There was a rapport—a peculiar oneness—in which each recognised the other as a man capable of telling, and of being told, the unvarnished truth.

"You got out about ten days back?" The sergeant might have been talking about prison.

"Uhu." Blayde nodded.

"Pioneer Corps, wasn't it?"

"Pioneer Corps," agreed Blayde.

"I got out Class B." The sergeant talked as if to an equal. "This job. A few months earlier."

"The R.A.F.?" asked Blayde.

"Five Group. Lancs."

"Pilot?"

"No." The sergeant removed his pipe long enough to allow his lips freedom for a slightly shame-faced grin. "Pilots, navigators, bomb-aimers . . . they were the educated types. I was a wireless op."

"I wouldn't have liked to have been up there," said Blayde.

"Clean sheets?" The grin stayed on the sergeant's face. "We had it easy. Shit-scared occasionally. Other than that, a cushy number."

"I'm glad it's over," said Blayde sombrely.

"Who the hell isn't?" The sergeant replaced the pipe between his lips. It needed re-lighting. As he struck a match he said, "What now?"

Blayde moved his shoulders.

"You were a carpenter, right?"

"I've lost the knack."

"Bags of house-building." The sergeant stroked the surface of the burned tobacco with the flame of the match. "Should be easy to find a job."

"I don't fancy," said Blayde bluntly.

"You'll settle," promised the sergeant. As he waved out the match, he asked, "Want to see your brother?"

"Not particularly."

The sergeant looked mildly surprised.

"He's bent." Blayde didn't mince words.

"He's that," agreed the sergeant.

"Sod him. He deserves what he gets."

Thus, had it not been for the war—indeed had it not been for the politically motivated power-madness of a World War I corporal—Robert Blayde might have been a highly skilled carpenter; might have spent his working life fashioning wood and burying the dead. That war. It has much to answer for. At the time (1946) peace was a novel thing. A precious thing. A glittering, magnificent jewel whose brilliance tended to blind. But the "spivs" had waxed fat and shiny. The Kremlin had pulled its fighting men from East Germany and substituted uniformed louts from the backlands as a form of personal vengeance for what Hitler's armies had done to Russia. From the O.S.S. America had begun to create a monster called the Central Intelligence Agency; a monster which would, eventually, be capable of creating civil war and toppling governments. Small things, too. One of the finest, but gentlest, cricketers of all time, Hedley Verity, was buried in Italy of all places . . . where they don't even play the game. In the cinema, a new meaning was put into the word "chiaroscuro" and a young genius called Orson Welles became its accepted master.

Thousands of tiny and not so tiny changes . . . and one of them was Blayde's decision to leave home.

It was a very tear-filled parting. A very bitter parting on the part of Meg Blayde.

"We need you," she argued vehemently.

"You haven't needed me for the last six years."

"Now Ric's in trouble . . ."

"I don't give a damn about 'Ric'. He's a criminal."

"You've no right to say that about your brother. He's . . ."

"I know! He's kept you all in comparative luxury. And now, when all the chickens have come home to roost, you want me to take over. No thank you, ma. I want no part of it."

As they argued—as they fought each other with words—Blayde packed clothes into a suitcase. He felt a louse, but that was part of the price he had to pay for what he wanted. The mother, too, thought right was on her side; she said things she didn't mean; she said things she'd regret for the rest of her life.

Blayde took it—most of it—and made believe she *did* mean it . . . it made him feel just that less of a louse. Having pushed as many clothes as possible into the suitcase, he forced down the lid, snapped the catches and left the bedroom. Meg Blayde followed.

Downstairs Sefton Wilkes added his own small plea.

"We've loved you, Robert. We still love you."

"Good." Blayde didn't want to fight this old man.

"We've tried to give you a good home. Somewhere to come back to."

"I know."

Meg stormed, "He doesn't appreciate it. He's too selfish. He doesn't appreciate anything."

"I appreciate it," said Blayde heavily. "I just don't owe anything."

"Honour thy father and thy . . ." began the old man.

"Grandfather." Blayde lowered the suitcase. He faced the old man and Meg and, in as controlled a voice as possible, said, "Don't quote scripture to me. 'Thou shalt not steal.' Quote that to the man you seem to think so much about." He took a deep breath, then said, "I'm leaving. I'd like it to be on a friendly basis. But however you want it . . . I'm leaving.

"The store," said the old man weakly.

"You can pay somebody." The smile was ugly. "You may even find you're in pocket."

"Don't come back," spat Meg. *"Ever."*

Before Blayde could answer the old man said, "That's a right you don't have, Meg. Not while I'm alive." Then to Blayde, "When you've cooled. When everybody's cooled. This is still your home. At least visit us occasionally."

Blayde growled, "Maybe," then picked up the suitcase and left.

Had he given much thought to it, young Robert Blayde might have thought himself unique; a twenty-four-year-old, with a conscience big enough, clean enough, to force him to leave home rather than live under the same roof as a criminally-minded twin brother. That's what he would have thought. That's what he would have claimed. That, to that extent, he was unique . . . as unique as tens of thousands of other guys.

The truth was, he'd not merely lost a rudder, he'd lost an anchorage. For the first time in his life, he was on his own. He'd exchanged a family for the army, and now he no longer had the army and he was too old to allow the family back into his life as a prop. He had to think for himself; make his own decisions; go for broke and make a success or screw things up in his own individual way.

Way back—when he'd first worn uniform—some bloody fool had said, "It'll make a man of you, Bob." Some bloody fool who didn't know what he was talking about. Maybe if he'd married—if he'd had a wife and a home of his own to come back to, but he *hadn't* married, so what the hell? Maybe if his mother and grandparents had died during the war years—if he hadn't had a brother and if, while still in the army, he'd suddenly found himself on his own. But they hadn't died, and he had a brother. A twin brother. And (although he didn't realise it and, indeed, would have denied it) that twin brother was a very handy peg upon which he could hang all his excuses.

Richard Blayde was a thief; at best a receiver of stolen property. Big deal! Robert Blayde had, for the last six years or thereabouts, walked through a war; he hadn't stolen—not in army slang—he'd "won" things, he'd "found" things, the money he carried in his inside pocket was in a beautifully made leather wallet, which he'd "won" from a dead German officer in North Africa, and around his wrist was a watch he'd "found" on an equally dead German civilian on the continent of Europe. But they hadn't been stolen. The spoils of war. No more "stealing" than the German rations he'd helped to scoff after an advance; than the cigarettes he'd smoked after clearing the debris, looking for bodies in the remains of God knows how many destroyed shops; than the booze from a bomb-blasted cafe; than the eggs he'd lifted from the nests in a French farm.

Not stealing. Hell, not *stealing*.

Meanwhile, he had a room with breakfast at a so-called guest house in the Mellor Road district of Lessford, he had a gratuity that was dwindling fast, he hadn't a job and he'd better get a job.

Gradually, the idea of being a copper matured in his mind. It wasn't a sudden flash of inspiration; indeed, it began as a mere contemplation and a self-promise to "make enquiries". Not in the Lessford Constabulary. That would be too near his old home. Too near his brother and whatever future fun and games that brother might indulge in. The truth was, that bloody brother of his worried him a little bit. What (supposing he decided to be a copper) if he couldn't be a copper as an indirect result of Richard's sticky fingers? Just how unsullied had a man to be for acceptance in the force? Just how clean was clean? How white was white?

Well, that bridge could be crossed when it arrived.

Meanwhile, which force? London, perhaps? No, the hell with London; London was too big, too sprawling; London held out no temptation to Robert Blayde. Bordfield, maybe? Bordfield was the next city to Lessford; indeed, you had to know the district pretty well to know where Lessford ended and Bordfield began. But he didn't like Bordfield. Nobody in Lessford liked Bordfield, just as nobody in Bordfield liked Lessford. Bordfield tried to be too big for its size. Bordfield tried to do everything better than Lessford . . . and it always made a general balls-up. No. Wherever else, not Bordfield.

So, what about the county? The County Constabulary? Country lanes, open fields, hedges, farms, bags of fresh air . . . yes, the county might be worth a quick look-see.

He caught a bus to the administrative headquarters and quizzed the uniformed inspector in charge of recruiting.

"You're big enough. Fit enough. How's your education?"

"I left school at fourteen."

"That's no drawback. Can you do simple arithmetic?"

"Yes."

"Read? Write?"

"Yes."

"Write at slow dictation speed?"

"Yes. I held the rank of sergeant in the army."

"Good. You're what we're looking for."

"One thing." Blayde hesitated, then said, "I've a brother. He's been in trouble."

"With the police?"

"Yes."

The inspector frowned.

Blayde said, "There's a sergeant. I don't know his name. Rise Hill Police Station."

"Lessford?"

"He'll tell you all about my brother, Richard Blayde. He might vouch for me at the same time."

"But you don't know his name?"

"He was a wireless operator. Five Group, Bomber Command. He flew Lancs."

"We'll contact him," promised the inspector. "If he clears you, we'll make the usual enquiries. We'll let you know."

"What enquiries?"

"Debts. General character." The inspector stood up. The interview was over. As he opened the door of the office, he said, "We'll let you know, Mr. Blayde. Don't worry, it's *you* we want, not your brother."

On Monday, May 27th, 1946, Robert Blayde (having skated happily through the "medical" and "intelligence" examinations) was fitted out with uniform, then required to take the Constabulary Oath and finally, along with sixty-three other hopefuls, was bussed to a Police Training College. And as of that day he became Blayde, Robert, Police Constable Number 1718, and a very unimportant member of the County Constabulary.

7

"NOW we'll teach you how to be a bobby."

Blayde said, "Yes sergeant," and kept a straight face.

For three months, the instructors at the Police Training College had warned him of this day. "When you get out there in the wild and wicked world, the old hands will tell you. You've learned nothing here. Some of 'em—some of the real barmpots—might suggest you forget it all. Don't! At this moment you know more about Criminal Law than you'll ever know. More than most solicitors know. You'll forget a lot of it, but try to remember all you can. Try to keep up to date. And when you get outside . . . that's when you won't have an instructor to put you right. That's when you'll have to make it work. And *that's* what the old hands can teach you. You're not yet policemen, none of you. But here, at this college, we've done two things. We've made you capable of becoming policemen, and in the last three months we've given you the feel of the uniform."

The sergeant was saying, "Upper Neck Beat. That's your patch."

"Oh—er—yes, sergeant."

The sergeant moved to a wall map. He followed the marked-in boundaries with a banana-thick finger as he spoke.

"The red line. That's Sopworth Section, part of Beechwood Brook Division. That—that part inside the black line—that's your personal pigeon. Upper Neck. Got a bike yet?"

"I've one on order. I'm collecting it tomorrow."

"Good. You'll need it." The sergeant returned to the map. "There, next to Upper Neck Beat, is Rimstone Beat. Summat like a jigsaw puzzle. You'll get the hang."

Blayde nodded and allowed his mind to back-track to the three months of initial training.

The truth was, it hadn't been a bad three months. Enjoyable, in fact. As a new intake, they'd been chased around a bit by the drill pig—an ex-sergeant from one of the Guards regiments—but with the arrival of another new intake he'd eased off and blasted his broadsides at the fresh arrivals; one new intake every month, therefore for the last two months the mob of which Blayde was a part had been "old lags".

"That's your box." The sergeant rested a hand on one of a row of pigeon-holes, each with a number inserted in a holder above it. The box was numbered 1718. "Once a day, you visit here. Check the Telephone Book. Read it and initial it. Check your box. Warrants, summonses, accident enquiries. Owt needing your personal attention . . . it'll be in your box."

"I see."

And another thing—another plus—more than half (getting on for two-thirds) of the blokes had been ex-servicemen. Being shouted and bawled at by a drill sergeant had been a little like old times. And the drill pig had enjoyed himself on the quiet; nobody was going to run home to his mother heartbroken. The Army, the Navy, the R.A.F.—they'd all known the drill movements, basically. The Navy salute was something of a circus act, the R.A.F. hadn't a bloody clue about wheeling in line, but they'd soon pick it up. After that, it had been toffee.

"I live in the back, there." The sergeant jerked his thumb. "Me and the missus. Living quarters. I'm available twenty-four hours of the day, except on my day off."

"That's comforting." Blayde smiled.

"Just don't make a bloody pest of yourself, lad."

"I'll try not to."

"And at night—if you've any typing to do—shove some books under the machine. The bedroom's up there." The sergeant glanced at the ceiling. "Three o'clock of a morning . . . a typewriter sounds like a bloody pneumatic drill."

"I'll—er—I'll remember that."

The bullshit, too. They'd held a raffle; who could go on parade and put the drill pig to shame. Nobody had won. That crafty old bastard had known all the tricks. Boot-caps; spit and polish—never a brush—a soft cloth and tiny circular movements with the tip of a finger; plenty of spit to go with the polish and (a gag Blayde had learned for the first time) a drop—just one drop—of vinegar. Toe-caps like black mirrors. But never quite as perfect as those worn by the drill pig. The same with the crease of your trousers; iron them gently, and with brown paper and not a damp cloth; to make them razor sharp, run soap on the inside of each crease before ironing it. But—damn the man—none of them had ever reached his standard.

"Do I have to report here on duty?" asked Blayde.

"No." The sergeant shook his head. "The town lads report here on duty. But not the outside beat lads. They step out of the front door . . . they're on duty. But this is your nick, and I'm your sergeant. Get it?"

Blayde nodded.

"How's your digs?" asked the sergeant.

"Fine."

"Sure?"

"Oh, yes. Grand."

"Just one thing," warned the sergeant. "If owt goes wrong, let me know. Any complaints, don't go having a barney—don't sit on it and sulk—let me know. I'll iron the kinks out. Get you new digs, if necessary. That's what I'm here for." He glanced at the Charge Office Clock and ended the welcoming spiel. "Right, there's a bus due. Get back up there. Simon—Constable Sharpe—he'll be waiting for you. He's a bit of a job on, it's on your beat. You might as well go with him for experience."

"Er—where do I meet him?"

"He'll be waiting at the terminus."

That first day in uniform. Strictly speaking not the first day—he'd worn the uniform for three months, but always within the confines of a police college—but that first day in public. A sort of unveiling. The entrance onto the stage of a new character, and many of the audience—the inhabitants of the market town of Sopworth—recognised him as a new character.

Blayde felt it. All coppers feel it. The turning heads, the slightly surprised glances, the half-hidden smiles. There was a vague feeling of panic; a continuous prayer that nobody—*nobody* might rush up and demand the services of a policeman. On the bus, for example; the bus carrying him from Sopworth to Upper Neck. Blayde proffered the fare and the conductor pointedly ignored him.

On the platform, as he waited to leave the bus, the conductor touched his arm and said, *sotto voce,* "It's an understood thing, son. You're on our side. Any drunks, any silly buggers—you're here to help."

Police Constable 2111 Sharpe; Blayde's first mentor, therefore a man deserving some small examination. Portly, but spry. That was the immediate impression. Despite his slight tum, surprisingly agile on his feet. A man who wore his uniform with a certain swagger; whose helmet was ever so slightly on the tilt; whose cape, whether folded and slung over the left shoulder or draped to protect his tunic from the weather, seemed to be an adjunct of that hint of swashbuckling style peculiar to the man's own personality. A man of easy laughter, who seemed incapable of taking life too seriously. But (as Blayde was quick to appreciate) one hell of a copper.

They strolled through the village of Upper Neck. Leisurely; at the required four-miles-per-hour which, according to the book of words, was the normal constabulary pace. And as they talked, Sharpe imparted his own brand of wisdom to Blayde's eager ears.

"Your beat," observed Sharpe.

"Seems so." Blayde grinned a little self-consciously. "It'll take time to get used to the idea."

"From college to village copper."

"Is that unusual?"

"Not so unusual," said Sharpe. "A bit unfair, though."

"Why?" Blayde was genuinely interested.

"They'll try it on," promised Sharpe. "The young bloods . . . they'll try you out."

Blayde decided to bear this warning in mind.

Sharpe said, "Don't touch your helmet too much."

"Eh?"

"Y'know, touch your helmet. A sort of salute. You can always tell a good copper. They call him 'sir'. It's them who touch their hats."

"Ah." Blayde nodded.

"Don't try for popularity," advised Sharpe. "You'll have friends. Friends you don't want. Friends you can do without. It's not you they're friendly with, it's the uniform. They'll want favours. Little things. Tell 'em to take a running jump."

August was going out in a blaze of sunshine. June had been far from flaming. July had been very hit-and-miss and the first weeks of August had seen thunder-storms galore. But, having got it all out of its system, August now seemed bent on making up for lost time. The choker collar of his tunic chafed a little as it collected sweat from Blayde's neck.

After a brief period of silence, Sharpe said, "Keep your eye on Andy."

"Andy?"

"Andleton."

"Oh, y'mean Sergeant Andleton." Blayde waited for details.

"Okay when things are going rosy," explained Sharpe. "But when the fertiliser's ankle deep, don't look for him. He'll be on his bike, making for the hills."

"He—er—he seemed okay," ventured Blayde.

"He's a thwarted man." Sharpe chuckled. "Don't think I'm telling you what I haven't told *him* . . . scores of times. He wants to make inspector before he retires. That's all he lives for."

"Ambition," murmured Blayde.

"He won't get there," prophesied Sharpe. "He makes it too bloody obvious. He's a standing joke, but doesn't know it."

They'd reached a row of terraced cottages. They stopped their slow walk and, before hammering on the door with the side of his fist, Sharpe dropped a sly wink at Blayde. The door opened a fraction and Sharpe planted a size ten on the threshold to prevent it from being slammed shut again. He beamed into the face of a prematurely bald man who wore a collarless shirt, baggy trousers and a worried expression.

"Not at work, Tommy?" Sharpe's question carried mock-surprise.

"I've . . ." The man glanced at Blayde, then returned his stare to Sharpe. "I've 'urt me back."

"Carrying all that dripping?" suggested Sharpe cheerfully.

"Wot dripping?"

"That unopened box of dripping you lifted from the fish and chip shop, Friday morning."

"I dunno wot . . ."

"I know. You don't know what the hell I'm talking about." Sharpe loosened the middle button of his tunic and, speaking to Blayde, said, "Tommy Bellings, here. Always have a search warrant handy if ever you want to have a quick shufty round the hovel he calls a home . . ."

"You've no right to . . ."

". . .Because Tommy knows his rights, see? He knows the law. He should do. He's been in court often enough."

"Look. You've no right . . ."

"That's why I've brought a search warrant with me." Sharpe withdrew an official-looking document from an inside pocket, unfolded it and, turning his attention to Bellings, quoted, "To search the home and outbuildings of Thomas Bellings. And there to seize goods believed to have been stolen or received by the said Thomas Bellings." He re-folded the document and as he tucked it away again, inside his tunic, he smiled at Bellings and said, "So you've a very limited choice, Tommy. You either open the door, or we kick the bloody thing in."

Bellings stood away from the door and Blayde and Sharpe entered the cottage. It was what Sharpe had called it . . . a hovel.

Sharpe said, "Tell you what, Constable Blayde. You stay here and get acquainted with Tommy. You'll meet him often. He's a regular customer of ours. Chat him up a bit—make sure he doesn't get any daft ideas about making a run for it—I'll just have a quick look in all the likely places." Then to Bellings, "If I need to rip any floorboards up, I'll let you know."

There was, Blayde decided, a certain panache about the way in which Sharpe went about his duty. A certain happy certainty. He *enjoyed* bobbying, and saw no reason to hide his enjoyment.

Blayde stood with Bellings, and Bellings

eyed this newcomer to his life with a mix of distaste and curiosity.

"You the new copper, then?" he asked at last.

"That's me," said Blayde shortly.

"Straight from the new box?"

"Which box?"

"The box they've just opened." Bellings's grin was distinctly nasty.

"It is," warned Blayde, "a box of real ginger biscuits. It'll burn your tongue off, mate, if you're daft enough to take a bite."

"Oh, aye?"

"If what Contable Sharpe says is right, you'll soon find out."

Instinctively, Blayde knew he was saying the right thing; using the right tone of voice. Not threatening. Not bluster. But, instead, a cold warning in the only language men like Bellings understood. He'd met this sort in the army. The swingers who were always trying it on; bombastic little bastards you had to sit on, before they got on top.

Sharpe rejoined them and, in a voice moving towards boredom, said, "In the cupboard under the sink. Get your cap and coat on, Tommy, then you can fetch it."

"If you think . . ."

"I think," mused Sharpe, "that if you don't fetch it, I'll take this muck-hole apart, stone at a time, and see what else you have stashed away." Then to Blayde, "There's a phone box about a hundred yards farther along the lane. Give D.H.Q. a ring. Tell 'em we'd like a motor patrol car to transport a snivelling little tea-leaf and his loot back to Sopworth nick."

Back at Sopworth Police Station, Blayde marvelled at the way Sharpe handled the multiplicity of forms required to justify Bellings's arrest. Charge Form, Arrest Form, Crime Report Form, Prisoner's Property Form, Occurrence Report. These, and more, Sharpe collected from the stationery cupboard then, while Blayde searched the prisoner and locked him away in a cell. Sharpe fed them into a battered typewriter and with one-finger skill tapped out umpteen justifications in police jargon.

Sergeant Andleton poked his head round the door and asked, "Got what you wanted, Sharpe?"

"Why not?" Sharpe didn't even take his eyes from the typewriter.

"I'm away to meet Furnace. Keep Blayde under your wing till I get back."

"It's a pleasure." Sharpe still didn't look up from the typewriter.

When Andleton had gone, Sharpe said, "A brew-up . . . right?"

"Sounds fine to me."

"You'll find the makings in the cell corridor."

And less than half an hour later (by which time they were on Christian-name terms) Sharpe was leaning back in an office chair, tunic open, sipping tea, smoking a cigarette and, once more, imparting constabulary wisdom to the eager Blayde.

"Y'see, Bob." Sharpe waved a hand at the tiny pile of completed forms. "That's really what bobbying's all about. Lifting the horrible little sods is easy. The real knack is filling in the forms. All that garbage, and it all has to be filled in a certain way or else it'll come back with a squib tied to its tail. The way 'they' want it."

"Y'mean Headquarters?"

"No, bugger Headquarters . . . Headquarters couldn't care less. I mean Andy and the bloke above Andy. Inspector Perkins. Met Perkins yet?"

"No. Not yet."

"Right, a word to the wise. Use long words,

see? If you can come up with a word he's never seen before—summat he has to look up in his dictionary—you've a pal for life. That's the way his mind works. And get it past *him* . . . nobody else gives a damn."

"The super?" asked Blayde tentatively.

"Supers couldn't care less," said Sharpe with conviction. "Like Headquarters. It's got past Andy. It's got past Perkins. It *must* be right. Why bother to read the bloody thing?" Sharpe drew on the cigarette, then took a long drink of tea. He continued, "Lost property. Found property. A Lost and Found Report, easy. The prayer book says you've to make 'initial enquiries' before you send it in. A tip, for what it's worth. Six names. Get 'em from the voters' register. Get 'em from the headstones in a graveyard. Make 'em up, if necessary. Nobody's going to read 'em. Andy knows Perkins, and all Perkins does is count. Six. Seven names and it'll come back asking for a reason for delay. Five names and it'll come back for 'further enquiries'. But *six* names . . . it'll be filed somewhere, and you'll never see it again."

"As easy as that?" grinned Blayde.

"With Perkins . . . as easy as that." Sharpe returned the grin.

They smoked and drank tea in silence for a while. In such a short time there had already developed a trust. A rapport. Sharpe had medal ribbons on his tunic—ribbons which showed that he, too, had seen some of Hitler's war—and perhaps that had something to do with it. Blayde suddenly realised that Andleton's tunic was bare of ribbons. But if that was part of it, it wasn't all of it. It was far more than a past part-shared. Sharpe was the first 'working copper' Blayde had ever encountered; he was the matrix against which Blayde would measure every copper he was to meet throughout his service, but at the time he didn't realise this. Sharpe had style, and it was a style peculiar to himself. And because he instinctively liked that style—and because Sharpe recognised in Blayde a youngster much as he'd once been—the chemistry worked and the bond of friendship was already there.

"Would you?" asked Blayde curiously.

"What?"

"Have pulled his house apart? Floorboards? You could have. You've the warrant."

"Ah, the warrant." Sharpe placed his beaker on the desk and brought the document from the inside pocket of his tunic. "Y'see, Bob, know the bloke you're after. Know what you know. Know what he doesn't know. Bellings wouldn't recognise a search warrant if one got up and bit him."

Blayde reached across and unfolded the document. It carried a very fancy scrolled heading. The printed copperplate notified Simon Sharpe, Esq. that he'd won £20.2s.3d. It was more than a year old, and it had originated from the offices of one of the larger football pool firms.

"Keeps 'em happy." Sharpe retrieved his "search warrant". He folded it carefully and returned it to its pocket. "Keeps their bowels loose."

It was a new life and, as far as Blayde was concerned, it was a great life. Andleton, despite his shortcomings, was wise enough to see the ease with which Blayde and Sharpe worked in harness and, because recruits were required to work a two-week stint with an experienced copper, Blayde and Sharpe shared Upper Neck and Sopworth Town Beat side by side.

During those two weeks Blayde met "father"; Superintendent Kingston. A dapper man, nearing the end of his police service;

a man who rarely wore his uniform, but preferred natty suits in clerical grey.

"Welcome to the division, Blayde."

"Thank you, sir."

"It's a fine division. You won't find a better in the force."

"Whatever it is, it's not his fault," opined Sharpe later. "It could fall apart at the seams, for all he cares. He's free-wheeling to a nice juicy pension, and after that he intends to live as long as possible."

He met Inspector Perkins. A chisel-featured individual who, in some strange way, seemed to have more than his fair quota of arms and legs; an angular man whose corners seemed to be forever puncturing his own attempts at pomposity.

"Don't let the side down, Blayde."

"No, sir. I'll try not to."

"That's the main thing, constable. It's a team effort. Always bear that in mind."

"Yes, sir."

"Did he tell you not to let the side down?" asked Sharpe later.

"Yes. As a matter of fact he did."

"He always does. He must have read it somewhere." Sharpe sniffed his disgust, and added, "Christ only knows which side he's on."

Ted Furnace, the constable who shared Sopworth Town Beat with Sharpe. A huge man; not as rotund as Sharpe, but topping the six-foot mark by a good three inches, and with shoulders like an ox. But a very gentle, very patient man; soft-voiced and (as Blayde was later to learn) unconditionally devoted to a wife who'd been blind from birth.

And, of course, Tommy Mann. On sight, Mann seemed years too old to be a police constable; thin, haggard, stoop-shouldered and with a hollow-cheeked face whose eyes were forever watering and whose expression conveyed never-ending misery. Somewhere in the past Mann had offended someone in high authority—even Sharpe didn't know when or who—but, presumably as a punishment, Mann was "permanent office reserve". He crawled through Sopworth Police Station door at 5 p.m. each afternoon and, until 1 a.m. the next morning, he sat at a high desk, answered the telephone, made entries in the Telephone Book and brought all the other "books" up to date. This was his contribution to the policing of Sopworth Section. This and only this.

Nor was he popular with his colleagues.

His writing was almost indecipherable, his conversation was a perpetual whine and he had the filthy habit of hawking, then spitting at the tiny coal fire which kept the Charge Office warm. The early turn man—Sharpe or Furnace, usually—had the job of cleaning the grate and, with it, the added task of removing the snail-trails of dried-up spittle from the bars.

"He's a dirty, miserable old bugger," said Sharpe.

"I dare say." Blayde tried to be charitable. "But—hell's teeth—five till one every day. It's a bit much."

"He says it destroys his 'social life'."

"It must do."

"Can you," asked Sharpe, sarcastically, "see Tommy Mann jiving around some bloody dance-hall?"

"It's still a bit much."

"Don't trust him too far, that's all," warned Sharpe. "Anything you want Andy to know, tell Tommy in confidence. It's cheaper than a postcard."

Blayde was a good learner. With each day he absorbed a little more police wisdom; the law, not as taught at a college, but as applied on the streets. The sardonic view of life of the working copper. On Sharpe's day off he worked with Ted Furnace and appreciated in the gentle giant another way of "bobbying"; a quiet, soft-spoken efficiency based upon persuasion; the slow smile and the "Nay, lad. You know as well as I do" approach. It worked but, in Blayde's opinion, it worked only because it was backed by a veritable mountain of beef, and even then it didn't work with the flash lads.

Sharpe was his true mentor and when, after those first two weeks and when he was alone and cyling along the lanes of Upper Neck, it was Sharpe's way which gradually became Blayde's way and, as he grew in confidence, it never failed to pay dividends.

At first, he visited Hill Rise on his Weekly Rest Day, but the family—his family—gradually became more like strangers. To Blayde they seemed to be moving away from him, but the truth was he was moving away from them. Richard, his brother, did little to hide his distaste at having a policeman in the house.

"Fitted anybody out, recently, then?"

"It doesn't work that way."

"No? Now pull the other."

"Only the hooks."

"I was put away."

"In that case, you'll know what I'm talking about."

Meg tried to cushion the growing dislike building up between her two sons but, if she took sides—when she took sides—it was always to excuse Richard. In vain did Blayde try to argue sense into her.

"Ma, he's bent. He'll be caught and put inside again. Nothing surer."

"It's your job, Bob. You're paid to have a suspicious mind."

"You're wrong. He'll break your heart, but don't say I didn't warn you."

Sefton Wilkes was growing older at a terrifying rate. His faith in the Almighty was as strong as ever. Stronger, if anything. But despite this mild form of religious mania—despite the unsteadiness of his limbs—he had wisdom enough left to see what was going on.

"It should have been you, Bob," he said.

"What's that?"

"You should have stayed to look after the store. Ric's doing it all wrong."

"Wrong?" Blayde's tone neither condemned nor approved.

"I . . ." The old man hesitated, then said, "I don't want to see him go to prison again."

"That's up to him, isn't it?"

"It *should* have been you," said the old man sadly.

"You gave us a choice, grandpa. I chose not to."

"I shouldn't have let you."

"You couldn't have stopped me."

That was the tenor of the conversation each time he visited his grandparents' home at Lessford. He went less and less until, within the year, his visits were rare indeed. Nor was he an enthusiastic letter-writer. What few points of contact remained grew weaker, and he became what he was by nature: a true loner. He still liked working with Sharpe; still knew he had much to learn from both Sharpe and Furnace and, when Andleton was off duty—Weekly Rest Day, Annual Leave or Sick Leave—Sharpe it was who took over the authority of P.C. i/c, and Blayde was brought down from Upper Neck to help police Sopworth Town Beat. On such occasions, he found real pleasure in policing under the guidance of this devil-may-care, piratical copper. They worked well together but never once did he either see, or want to see, the inside of Sharpe's home. He was invited—indeed Furnace too invited him for an evening—but he always refused and in time both Sharpe and Furnace accepted the situation without rancour.

At Upper Neck he lived with Mr. and Mrs. Bowse. Good Yorkshire stock. Alfred Bowse worked on the administration side of the G.P.O. Angela Bowse was a good wife and an excellent cook. Their son—their only child—had been killed in the war and, at first, they tried to make Blayde fill the vacuum caused by his death. But without being ungrateful he refused to be pampered. He wasn't their second son and, without being hurtful, he refused to play the part. And yet they "fitted", perfectly. Liking and mutual respect filled the place where there'd once been love and, as their hurt at their loss gradually eased, they were appreciative. He wasn't their son . . . and their son could never be replaced.

Alfred and Angela Bowse (and, of course, Blayde) lived in a farmhouse. A farmhouse without a farm; one of the local farmers had bought the land for expansion purposes, then sold the farmhouse which went with the land as a means of making a little profit. Thus a farmhouse, but no farm. Nevertheless, there was a plot—little more than half an acre—which went with the house, at the rear of the house, and Alfred Bowse worked it for vegetables. Blayde helped him on off-duty periods; did some of the necessary spade work, patiently worked his way along the rows with the hoe. Sometimes he and Alfred Bowse worked together; for hours at a time without a word passing between them; content merely to be in each other's company. Blayde was no real talker—he spoke only when he had something worth saying—and Bowse sought to ease the pain of his son's death via silence and concentration. It grew to be a pattern and, when he stopped visiting Lessford, Blayde either worked in the garden or stayed in his room.

In his room, he read. That, too, became a pattern. Two hours every day, without fail. He remembered the advice given at the college. "Try to keep up to date". Moriarty's *Police Law;* Third Impression of the Eighth Edition. Stone's *Justices' Manual* and Harris and Wilshere's *Criminal Law;* each a couple of years out of date, but far too expensive for a young copper's pay; given to him by the local magistrates' clerk in the knowledge that they'd be both used and taken care of. There was a Stone's and a Wilshere's in the Charge Office, and the chances were they'd been obtained in a like manner—any solicitor's office worth its salt renewing the various editions as they came out in print—but they were even older than Blayde's copies and were consulted only when necessary. And finally, *Police Review;* the weekly magazine aimed at a police market. It was London orientated but, nevertheless, it was also up to the minute as far as new law and case decisions were concerned.

The law, to the enthusiast, is a set of involved but ever-shifting rules via which the game of life is played. The study of those rules—their patterns, their attempts to follow the changes in public attitudes, their occasional stupidities—can become mildy addictive . . . only let the patience and the enthusiasm be there.

Blayde disciplined himself to have the patience, and the enthusiasm followed.

In June, 1947 (Monday, June 9th) he returned to the Police Training College for the first of two Refresher Courses; a fortnight of cramming in which (because he'd schooled himself to a daily dose of Police Law) he shone and, much to his own surprise, took top honours when the examination results were made known.

Then back to Upper Neck, back to Alfred

and Angela Bowse, back to Sopworth, and Sergeant Andleton, Constable Sharpe and Constable Furnace. Back to what Blayde was already seeing as a comfortable rut from which, one day, he must hoist himself.

8

THE few lines in the Personal Announcements column read—

WILKES—September 14th. Edna, beloved wife of Sefton Wilkes. Friends please gather at Hill Rise Methodist Church, 2 p.m., September 17th.

That, then, was the size of the rift which had developed between Blayde and his family; had not Angela Bowse noticed the entry in the Monday edition of the local evening newspaper he would not have known of the death of his grandmother.

"Didn't you know?" Mrs. Bowse asked the question in an awkward, almost frightened, voice.

"No." Blayde's answer was low and harsh.

"That's—that's *awful.*"

"It's disgraceful," said Mr. Bowse.

"It's . . ." Blayde took a deep breath, then said, "It's unpleasant."

"Will you go?" asked Bowse.

"Of course he'll go. It's his grandmother."

"I might. I'll have a word with the sergeant. See if I can get my shift changed." A crooked, cynical smile touched his lips. "It says 'Friends please gather'. I think I was one of her friends."

The truth was, it hurt. Blayde wasn't a heart-on-the sleeve type, but, by God, it hurt. The old lady; she was free from pain at last. And she'd known pain. Those gnarled joints, those quick intakes of breath when she'd moved and, in moving, driven the knife deeper than she'd expected, those darkened eye-sockets . . . like caverns within which she'd tried to hide her agony. And she'd loved him. Dammit, he knew she'd loved him. He wasn't demonstrative—he never had been, and neither had she—but they'd both *known*. Of them all—mother, brother, grandfather, grandmother—she'd been the gem. The old man was good—always had been good—but his wife had been better. A damn sight better. When he'd left home—the day he'd made the big decision—he'd been able to face his mother and face his grandfather, but he hadn't dare to face his grandmother. She'd have understood—tried to understand and found excuses—but he hadn't had the guts. He'd left it to somebody else to tell her; to break her heart a little; to smash something he'd known she'd valued.

And now . . .

He came off duty at 1 a.m. the next morning. He garaged his bicycle in the garden shed, let himself into the house, walked to the kitchen where he knew there'd be a Thermos of hot soup waiting . . . and for the first time in his life he felt lonely. It was a reaction. He recognised it for what it was, but that didn't make it any easier to bear. He didn't weep. Grown men—coppers—don't cry. He blocked the tears by allowing his anger to rise; like capping a blazing oil well. Dangerous. As dangerous as that. But, nevertheless, he didn't weep, but nor did he sleep that night.

He was in the church at a little before 2 p.m. He chose his place with care; one of the rear pews, and half-hidden by a stone column. By 2 p.m. he was one of a number of friends and acquaintances gathered to pay last respects to the old lady. He watched the tiny cortege arrive; the coffin, followed by Meg and the bent and heartbroken old man; then his brother and a woman he didn't recognise; then close friends of the family, some of whom he knew from a distant past and others he'd never seen before. They sat on the front pews and listened (or didn't listen) as the cleric mouthed inadequacies; they sang a hymn, said a prayer, then followed the coffin to its burial place.

He joined the end of the procession, walked slowly down the path and stood well away from the grave. He watched the coffin lowered, but was too far away to hear the preacher's words. He continued to watch as Meg and her father, Ric and the strange woman moved aside to allow others to shuffle around the hole in the ground and gaze for a moment at the box in which the remains of a gentle old lady waited to be covered with earth.

He was sure they hadn't seen him, but he was wrong. Meg handed her father over to the care of Ric and hurried over to where Blayde was standing.

"So you decided to come, after all?" Her voice was low, but over-flowing with contempt.

"I came." Blayde spoke flatly. Softly. His voice was as expressionless as his face.

"You could 'fit it in', then?"

Blayde nodded.

"Telling Ric, that." She almost spat the words. "Excuses. We had to make excuses to father . . . to your grandfather. Hadn't he enough sorrow? Did you have to make it worse for him?"

"What did he say I said?" asked Blayde gently.

"Ric?"

"What did he say?"

"After he'd telephoned to tell you?"

"What did he say?" repeated Blayde.

"What *you* said. That you wouldn't be here. That you couldn't 'fit it in'."

"That was . . . very wicked," breathed Blayde.

"I'm glad you think so." Some of the fury left her voice. The occasion—the fact that he was her son—the look on her face softened and she touched his arm. "Anyway, it's done with. I'm glad you came. There's a bit of a meal . . ."

"No," he interrupted. He smiled and continued. "No, I can't make the meal. Just ask Ric."

"What?"

"I'd like a word with him."

"What about?"

"Just—things—to explain things." As she hesitated, he said, "Please, ma. Ask him to stay behind. Just for a couple of minutes. He'll tell you . . . if he wants you to know."

She was a mother. She looked puzzled—undecided—she had two sons and she didn't understand. Something was happening. Something she should know about, but something she didn't know about.

"Please," said Blayde gently.

She nodded and hurried away.

He stood and watched. He saw her speak to his brother, and saw his brother glance towards where he was standing. He saw the mourners begin to troop from the graveyard; saw Ric speak to the strange woman, then saw the woman hurry to a broad-shouldered man wearing a dark suit. A stranger. A big man who had "minder" written across his frame as blatantly as if he wore a placard. The big man nodded and returned to stand by Ric, alongside the open grave.

Blayde waited until the graveyard was empty; until only the three of them remained. Then he walked towards his brother and the minder. He didn't hurry. He walked casually, as if out for a quiet stroll.

He positioned himself between Ric and the minder; until they each formed the corners of a triangle. The minder might not have been there for what notice Blayde took of him.

He looked at his brother, smiled, then said, "Mother mentioned that you telephoned."

"I don't want trouble." Ric glanced at the minder.

"That you telephoned, to tell me," insisted Blayde softly.

"It was y'know—" Ric moved his hands.

"What?"

Ric's nostrils flared, and he said, "I didn't want a copper here. Does that answer it?"

"Yes." Blayde nodded, slowly. "As far as you're concerned, that answers everything."

The balled fist was as tight as a hammer-head. The sudden eruption caught both men off their guard. Every ounce of power he could muster—the muscles of his left leg, his back muscles, his shoulder muscles, the muscles of his right arm—all went into the punch, and the fist landed flush on his brother's mouth. The lips split wide open—he'd need six stitches to sew the torn flesh together again—and he catapulted backwards and sprawled across a neighbouring grave.

Blayde turned to meet the minder, weaved, caught the blow on his shoulder, then sank his second punch hard into the pit of the minder's stomach. As the minder doubled, Blayde spun round and back-heeled the minder in the head. That back-kick could easily have killed—Blayde didn't give a damn—but, instead of killing, it splashed the minder's nose across his face, lifted him off his feet and sent him crashing down onto the newly-lowered coffin.

Blayde's finger was as rigid as a gun-barrel as he pointed it at the bloody face of his sprawling brother.

"Don't," he snarled. "Don't ever come within reach of me again. Ever! If you do—so help me—I'll bury you."

He turned his back and walked from the graveyard. He heard his brother sobbing with pain—but he continued to walk and didn't look round. Sheer will-power kept his legs from trembling and kept the walk the same saunter it had been prior to allowing his fury to explode.

And if Blayde changed a little after the funeral of his grandmother, neither Alfred nor Angela Bowse saw fit to mention it. Saw fit to even notice it. He'd always been a quiet young man. A solemn young man. So different from so many of his age group. He'd never had friends. His colleagues—his fellow-policemen—they were nice enough people, and Blayde spoke of them with admiration, but no *friends*.

Meanwhile, Blayde went about his business of being a village copper. Of working relief duty whenever Sopworth Town was more understaffed than usual. Of handling petty crime and offences within the area of his own authority.

Gradually, he earned "the confidence of the court". A phrase he'd come to learn. A phrase which, in essence, meant that the magistrates knew him to be an honest and reasonable constable; a police witness not given to overstating his case; a policeman ready to say as much in favour of the defendant as possible.

And this, too, earned a down-to-earth observation from the worldly-wise Sharpe.

"Y'know, Bob, you're no mug. You say all the nice things . . . then they'll believe all the nasty things."

"We're bastards, didn't you know?" And the smile that went with the remark held a hint of bitterness. "We're animals, full of guile."

"Easy, Bob." Sharpe looked worried. "Don't let the job get at you. If you do . . ."

"I'm tired, Simon." And this time the grin was open and friendly. "I'm due some

Annual Leave. Get myself off into The Dales, somewhere. It's done the trick before."

But he didn't. It was too late in the year for holidaying in The Dales; not yet true winter, not yet frosty but, instead, a miserable wet period which matched his mood. The cycle tyres hissed on the wet road surfaces as he bent his head against the driving rain. Despite leggings and cape, he became soaked and felt the dampness on the skin of his shoulders. When he came off duty there was always a hot bath waiting, and he thawed out, dressed in dry clothes then, as a general rule, closed the door of his room and read his growing library of books. He was a loner. He was a recluse . . . and that's the way he wanted it to be.

Talking together, Angela Bowse said, "He hasn't been home since his grandmother died."

"I know." Bowse frowned.

"Not that I'm saying he ever—y'know . . ."

"I know. But at his age . . ."

"What do you say," said Angela Bowse, "what do you say to a party?"

"Eh?"

"A party?"

"I can't see . . ."

"A Christmas party?"

"He'll be on duty Christmas Day. Was last

year. Let the men with wives and kids be at home, if possible."

"Boxing Day," she suggested.

"If you think it'll help." Bowse smiled, and added, "Don't be disappointed if it doesn't work, luv, but if you think it'll help . . ."

Boxing Day, 1947. It was a Friday and, via one of those quirks of English weather, temperature apart it might have been a day in mid-summer. An eye-squinting sun shone from a cloudless sky and the hint of air frost added to the glad-to-be-alive feeling. Blayde had come off duty at 2 a.m. and by ten o'clock he was up, bathed, shaved and spruced out in white shirt, blue serge suit and polished black shoes.

A party. That's what Angela had said. "We've planned a party for Boxing Day. You'll stay, Bob, won't you? After all, you're almost one of the family." And why not? It might be what he needed; something to form a memory barrier between the funeral and the future. It was certainly what they needed; something to take their minds away—well away—from the loss of their son. They hadn't known—they hadn't even realised—but the silences had been filled with his memory. They wouldn't—

they *couldn't*—let the poor guy rest in the peace he deserved. His photograph there, on the sideboard; and every time they passed it they paused—only momentarily, but they always paused—and looked at it. Both of them. Both Alfred and Angela. They refused to allow themselves to forget. Refused to allow the wounds to heal.

And okay, maybe he was a little envious. Envious of a man he'd never met, and never would meet. Envious of a son who'd enjoyed such unqualified love from his parents. Both his parents. But if he deserved that love he wouldn't have wanted them to mourn the rest of their lives. Remember him, sure, but not mourn him. They still had a lot of their own lives to live.

As he walked into the living room, Alfred Bowse smiled, and said, "Thanks, Bob."

"What?" Blayde looked surprised.

"You look smart, lad. You've made a real effort. It'll please Angela."

"It's a party." Blayde returned the smile.

From the kitchen came the sounds and smells of good food being prepared and, when they strolled into the dining room Blayde saw that the table had been extended and places set for six.

"Punch." Bowse chuckled. He touched a silver-plated punch-bowl taking pride of place on a side-table. "A wedding present. First time we've ever used it. Angela insisted we should."

"Punch?" Blayde raised amused eyebrows. "Damned if I know how to make it."

"Or me."

"Right, we'll experiment." Bowse reached for a row of bottles standing alongside the punch-bowl. "We'll start with rum, and see what happens."

It set the tone of the party. Alfred and Angela Bowse; Alfred's brother Jim and his wife, Mary; their daughter, Ruth, and Blayde. It was a happy, let's-try-anything-within-reason get-together. The turkey, the stuffing, the roast and creamed potatoes, the vegetables, the Christmas pudding and the blazing brandy sauce. Everything and lots of everything. Dickens himself would have been pressed to do literary justice to the meal. And the laughter. *Real* laughter; laughter which (as far as Alfred and Angela Bowse were concerned) had a ring Blayde had never before heard.

After the meal Bowse and his brother took up sprawling positions at each side of the open fire; they lighted cigars, settled into the armchairs and made no pretence of doing other than dozing and smoking, pending their digestive juices working overtime. Angela and Mary began to clear the table, prior to washing the crockery, cutlery and glassware. Ruth made a movement to help.

"No." Angela waved her niece aside. "You two youngsters get from under our feet. Go for a walk. Work up an appetite for tea."

Ruth glanced at Blayde, and Blayde moved his shoulders, smiled and said, "Why not? It's a lovely day."

The chemistry of affection. The moon-June thing. With Blayde and Ruth Bowse it started with that afternoon walk on Boxing Day of 1947. Nothing was said—nothing was even hinted at—but they both knew. He helped her over a couple of stiles when, strictly speaking, she didn't need help; she was as fit as he was and a year younger; the clambering over stiles was no hardship. No hardship at all. Nevertheless, he held out a hand, and she grasped it and, when she was over, they held hands a fraction longer than was necessary. No more than that. That, plus spontaneous laughter. That, plus a relaxed happiness in each other's company. That, plus the fact that they walked a little farther and were out a little longer than they had at first intended.

When do people fall in love? At what precise moment? When does the pointer, firmly fixed at "good friends" flick over and arrow, equally firmly, at "sweethearts"?

Not on that Boxing Day walk, that for sure. Blayde was no ladies man, but Ruth Bowse was one of the very few women with whom he felt at ease. But as far as he was concerned, love was a thing you read about in books. In some books it was a sloppy, badly-described mish-mash of "dancing eyes", "ready lips", "firm embraces" and the like. In other, equally badly-written books, it amounted to animal passion and a wild rutting between sheets or on grassy banks. Occasionally—just occasionally—some word-wizard managed to convey that hint of honey-sweet emotion to which Blayde was a stranger. Not sloppy, not lustful, but . . . pleasant. A strange pleasure, a unique pleasure which started by being happy-to-be-with, then gradually grew until it became incomplete-without.

Over the months they saw each other often. Always on Blayde's Weekly Rest Day. Sometimes, in that following summer, when he had an early finish and could catch a bus to

Bordfield for an evening in her company. They never talked of love—never so much as hinted at it—but, occasionally, their fingers met and, for a while, they walked hand-in-hand. They laughed with each other, but never kissed.

Perhaps that was why: because Blayde took too much for granted, and Ruth was never quite sure.

He'd been on his second Refresher Course, and Christmas 1948 was coming up fast. It was the time for Police Dances, Children's Parties . . . the various excuses grasped by policemen for letting their hair down and making minor idiots of themselves.

Quite suddenly, she said, "Robert's asked us to the dance."

"Robert?" For a moment, Blayde was out of his depth.

"Robert Harris. He lives two doors away. He's a policeman, like you. He's asked us to the Police Dance." Then, rather hurriedly, she aded, "Both of us."

"Oh."

They were on the way home to Ruth's house, having been to the local cinema. The film had been David Lean's *Brief Encounter*. Perhaps that, too, was one reason why Blayde acted as he did; perhaps the superb acting of Celia Johnson and Trevor Howard had encapsulated something Blayde felt, but couldn't quite come to terms with; perhaps even the haunting background music of Rachmaninov's Second Piano Concerto had added to the mix-up of emotions. Perhaps so many things. But, for whatever reason, his voice carried barbs she'd never heard before.

He said, "At least you're consistent."

"What's that supposed to mean?" And she, too, spoke in a low voice which had danger signals attached.

"I don't dance," he muttered. "I can't dance."

Had she known it, that was the point when she could have made amends. It was as far as Blayde was prepared to go; to give her a loophole; to allow her movement enough to mend, at least in part, the hurt she'd inflicted . . . albeit unconsciously.

Instead, she said the one thing she shouldn't have said.

"This—my being 'consistent'—I don't know what you're getting at."

"Same job. Same Christian name," growled Blayde.

"Why shouldn't I be friendly with Robert?" she demanded.

"Because . . ." Blayde closed his lips, then said, "No reason. No reason at all."

"You don't own me."

"No."

"You've never said anything about . . ." She, too, closed her lips.

"No." Blayde was finding it difficult to be even moderately polite.

"I mean, if you're trying to tell me . . ."

"I can't dance, that's all."

"Look, if you want me to . . ."

"Nothing. As you say, I don't own you."

For the rest of the way, they walked in silence. Like strangers. Each trapped by a pride they could neither understand nor control.

At the door, Blayde muttered, "Goodnight, then."

"Aren't you coming inside?"

"No."

"That's up to you, of course. But . . ."

"I've—I've things to do. Some reports to finish."

"Oh."

"Goodnight."

"Goodnight."

"I'll—er I'll be in touch. I'll telephone."

But he didn't. Nor did she. It was the end, because Blayde lacked that touch of humility which might have bridged the rift and, in so doing, made it the beginning.

Three years later Ruth Bowse married Police Constable Robert Harris.

9

JUNE, 1949 saw Blayde's first headline case. He'd seen his name in print enough times: *Constable Blayde said in evidence,* but only in the local rag, and only as a result of petty theft, poaching, wilful damage, traffic offences and the like. And always at Beechwood Brook Magistrate's Court or at a coroner's inquest.

Then on Sunday, June 5th, 1949, he received a telephone call from Sharpe. Sharpe was Constable i/c Sopworth—Andleton was away on Annual Leave—and, although Blayde was off duty at the time, Sharpe telephoned the complaint through at just after 3 p.m.

"You've a flasher on your beat, old son."

"Oh, aye, where?"

"The Mills sisters. Know 'em?"

"Out on Rimstone Lane."

"That's 'em. Some randy bugger flashed his John Thomas at 'em, about an hour ago. Care to sort it out?"

Blayde said, "I'm on my way," and replaced the receiver.

It was a "crime enquiry" and, in those days, detectives were very thin on the ground; the nearest detective sergeant was at Beechwood Brook Divisonal Headquarters and, sure as hell, he wouldn't take too kindly to having his afternoon siesta interrupted because a brace of old biddies had been given a practical demonstration of the male anatomy. The nearest detective constable was at sub-divisional headquarters and, as Blayde knew, that poor guy was, in all probability, at Beechwood Brook Cottage Hospital worrying himself stupid about a young son who'd roller-skated into the path of a speeding motor car. And, anyway, outside beat men were expected to handle their own crime enquiries in anything short of armed robbery.

Nor was indecent exposure in the top league. Good for a quiet giggle. Good for a few bawdy remarks between coppers.

But . . .

Far too often there was a pattern. Indecent exposure, because the nerk was twisted, but lacked the guts to commit indecent assault. But given time he'd get brave. He'd commit indecent assault. Then braver . . . and commit rape. And rape wasn't a thousand miles short of murder. Like the rungs on a ladder; he climbed them slowly and tremblingly but, if he wasn't kiboshed, he'd get there.

Blayde slipped on a sports jacket and cycled out to Rimstone Lane.

The house stood in its own grounds; an uninspiring, shoe-box of a house with a fifty-yard long rear garden which ended at a railway embankment. And that's where the miscreant had stood; atop the railway embankment and facing the house. He'd seen them watching from the window—he *must* have seen them watching—and he'd dropped his trousers and under-pants, lifted the front of his shirt and given them the full treatment.

At first the Mills sisters—Ruby and Gemma—had been a little tongue-tied; a little embarrassed. They were maiden ladies, some way past their prime. Not yet old, you understand, but "of a certain age". They lived alone, they were pillars of the local church and they had been well brought up. And here was a young man—albeit a nice young man, a serious young man, and a policeman—nevertheless, a young man asking them questions about . . .

"We—er—we expected a police lady," Gemma had said.

"You understand," Ruby had smiled.

"There's only one policewoman in the sub-division," Blayde had explained patiently. "She'll probably be round to take a statement from you, maybe tomorrow. Meanwhile, I'd like a description. As good a description of him as you can give me."

And it had been some description. Whatever else, neither Ruby nor Gemma had averted their eyes.

"An elderly man," said Gemma.

"Not *old*," Ruby had chimed in. "Not really elderly. About our age, wouldn't you think, dear?"

"Yes. About our age. And very thin."

"We think we've seen him somewhere," said Ruby.

"Well—yes—we *think* we have." Gemma wasn't as certain.

"Where?" asked Blayde.

"Oh, that we can't remember."

"He's nobody we know," added Gemma.

"His clothes?" suggested Blayde.

They gave a very detailed description of his clothes. A very detailed description.

Ruby's final contribution was, "And he was wearing a tie. A dark tie. Dark grey, I think. With tiny little white dots."

"White dots?" Blayde frowned his doubts.

"It's a long way away. From the window, to where he was standing. I'm not suggesting his tie hadn't white dots, but . . ."

"Oh, we put the binoculars on him," smiled Gemma.

"You . . ." Blayde swallowed, and controlled his facial muscles.

"We wanted to be able to give as good a description as possible," explained Ruby. "We could certainly recognise him again. Both of us."

"You think?"

Blayde's voice was anxious. It matched the worried look on his face as he asked the question.

"I think it's possible." Sharpe, too, was unusually solemn. He stared at Blayde for a moment, then asked, "And if it is?"

"What else?" The anxiety was replaced by brusqueness.

"It's your case." Sharpe still stared at Blayde's face.

"I've already said. What else?"

"Okay." Sharpe took a deep breath, exhaled, then said, "Go for a walk, Bob. Meet me back here in about thirty minutes."

Blayde nodded and walked out of Sopworth Police Station.

Without deliberate direction, without even being conscious of the streets he strolled or the corners he turned, Blayde killed time. He smoked cigarettes, he forced himself to be objective and every five minutes or so he glanced at his watch. It was too late to back out now. He'd committed himself, and that's what he'd had to do.

Nevertheless . . .

Christ, it was only . . . Only what? Only the first step towards assault—then rape—then murder? No! Not that. A kink. Maybe only a sick joke. The Mills sisters. They were . . . Okay, they weren't quite all they pretended to be, binoculars and all that; in their own silly way, they'd enjoyed a bit of a thrill; as sure as hell they hadn't been insulted. Not even offended . . . not really. But they were people on his patch, and they'd made an official complaint. Not an empty complaint. That was their right and, along with that right was his duty.

And Simon?

Simon Sharpe was a damn good copper. A damn good copper. But, y'know, just for a few seconds he'd opened the door. He'd created a let-out. Which, in effect, meant he'd been prepared to carry his own can. P.C. i/c—acting sergeant—as sure as green apples Andleton wouldn't have said "It's your case". Andleton wouldn't have taken that risk.

Sure, it could have been hushed up. Reported, then forgotten. But if the can leaked, what then? Those Mills sisters talked a good deal. Gossip. Village tittle-tattle. And they just might remember . . .

He gave Sharpe five extra minutes to be on the safe side, and it was closing to 5.15 p.m. when he walked into Sopworth Police Station. Sharpe was already there; head bent at the sergeant's desk, filling in the Section Diary. Tommy Mann had settled himself within easy spitting-distance of the fire, and was scrawling in the Telephone Book. Sharpe glanced up, gave a tiny nod, then returned his attention to the Section Diary.

Blayde cleared his throat and said, "Tommy."

"Aye." Mann didn't even raise his head.

"This afternoon, about two o'clock." Blayde hesitated, then asked, "Mind telling me where you were."

"I can't see it's any of your bloody . . ."

"Please, Tommy." Blayde fought to keep his voice steady.

Mann lowered his pen, slowly raised his head, removed the steel-rimmed spectacles from his nose, and said, "Why?"

"I have reasons," said Blayde.

"Oh, aye?"

"Good reasons."

"Out in the park. Playing bowls, if you must know."

"The hell you were." Sharpe growled the remark, without looking up from the Section Diary.

"You *know*, d'you?" Mann turned his attention to Sharpe.

"Aye, I know." Sharpe closed the Section Diary and became part of the proceedings. "I know because I know that's where you usually go. And I've been round to the park. And where the hell else you were, you weren't playing bowls."

"You can prove that?" sneered Mann.

"If necessary."

"I can prove you were on my beat." Blayde risked the bluff, in an attempt to get it over with.

"Oh, aye?" Like a poker cooling, some of the red-hot certainty left Mann's tone.

"They recognised you," said Blayde softly.

"Who rec . . ."

"They even recognised this." Sharpe pulled a rolled-up tie from his pocket; a grey tie with tiny white spots. "I collected it from your missus when I'd left the park. It's the tie you wore this afternoon."

"You've no bloody right . . ."

"And you," exploded Blayde, "have no bloody right to come on my beat, flashing your chopper and thinking you can get away with it."

"Your bloody beat." Mann's lips curled. "I'd a beat before . . ."

"We know." Sharpe moved until he was alongside Blayde. "You'd a beat before Peel was out of the nappy stage. But we're talking about Upper Neck this afternoon. And a slight case of indecent exposure."

"They know you Tommy." Blayde had more control of himself. "They had binoculars on you. They even described the tie." He took a deep breath, then asked, "For Christ's sake, man, why?"

Mann didn't answer.

"It's not going to be tucked away under the carpet," said Sharpe, grimly.

"You could . . ." began Mann.

"Nothing!" Sharpe cut him short. "We clean the mess off our own doorstep, too. We do while I'm around."

Mann nodded slowly. Resignedly.

"Charge him, Bob." Sharpe's tone was coldly efficient. He picked up the phone, and said, "Caution him, then charge him. I'll get Perkins out."

It hit the headlines; even the nationals trotted out the "one bad apple" argument. In fairness, Tommy Mann pleaded guilty and threw himself on the mercy of the court; he was a completely broken man, but he tried neither to explain nor excuse. The magistrates were not merciful; the chairman—knowing the reporters were recording his every word—yapped on alarmingly about "good policemen" and "bad policemen" and a force "besmirched by the action of one of its officers". After which he hit Mann with the biggest stick the court had at its disposal; six months imprisonment.

As the Bridewell officer led Tommy Mann from the dock to the cells beneath the court Blayde felt sick. Physically sick. He turned and walked from the courtroom. In the corridor, he leaned his shoulder-blades against a wall and lighted a cigarette. His hand trembled slightly.

Sharpe, who'd given back-up evidence against Mann, joined him.

In a low voice he murmured, "Stand by for flak, Bob."

Blayde looked puzzled.

"You'll get bouquets, but you'll get the other thing."

Nor did Blayde have to wait for "the other thing". The elderly woman who'd been sitting at the back of the courtroom entered the corridor. She was grey-faced and her slow walk had a slight staggering quality about it. Her eyes searched the occupants of the corridor then, when they fastened on Blayde, she walked slowly until she was face to face with him.

"Proud, are you?" she said in a soft voice, and hatred and contempt filled the voice and shone from the eyes.

Blayde glanced at Sharpe.

Sharpe breathed, "Tommy's wife."

"Oh!"

"You needn't have, y'know." The fury quivered on the tone. "Don't think I don't know these things. You needn't have."

"Mrs. Mann." Blayde sighed. "He was . . ."

"He was old enough to be your father. He was a good man. A good husband. And now—thanks to you—he's nothing!"

She leaned forward slightly, spat directly into Blayde's face, then turned and walked away. Everybody in the corridor saw it. Everybody looked shocked.

"That's it!" breathed Sharpe. As he moved he muttered, "I'll book the silly old . . ."

"Leave it." Blayde caught Sharpe's arm. As he took a handkerchief from his pocket and wiped the spittle from his face, he rasped, "It's not important. It's out of her system."

Sharpe was right. The Chief Constable's Commendation came through; a congratulation, couched in stilted officialese. But fellow-coppers—in particular the older coppers—made snide remarks or pointedly ignored him. Blayde cared little for the former, and even less for the latter. He'd done his job; just that and no more. The hell with the All-Pals-Together Act; it wasn't on Blayde's statute book.

And when Andleton (making damn sure witnesses weren't around) said, "It wasn't a wise thing to do, Blayde," Blayde was in no mood for apologies.

"Why wasn't it a wise thing to do, sergeant?" he asked, in a dangerously modulated voice.

"It can be construed," said Andleton.

"In what way?" Blayde slipped his notebook and a ballpoint from the breast pocket of his tunic.

"People might think it's the whole bloody section."

"I don't follow."

"Me . . . that's what I mean. They might think I can't keep my own men in order." Andleton paused, watched Blayde for a moment, then asked, "What's that you're doing?"

"Recording this conversation." Blayde continued to write.

"What the hell for?" Mild panic hit Sergeant Andleton.

"Posterity," said Blayde sardonically.

"Blayde, I shouldn't . . ." Andleton stopped as Blayde looked up.

"Sergeant Andleton," said Blayde slowly, "in effect you've just told me it's 'unwise' to carry a crime to its conclusion. That your opinion and the opinion of the chief constable don't run on similar lines. I don't give a toss about the section—come to that, I don't give a toss about you—but I'm getting tired of all this good-boy-bad-boy bullshit. I did my job. I want neither praise nor blame. But, sure as hell, I'm not prepared to take a ticking off for putting a flasher where he belongs just because he's your pal."

"He's—he wasn't my pal," choked Andleton.

"Good." Blayde closed the notebook and returned it and the ballpoint to his pocket. "As long as that's understood. As long as nobody thinks they're going to ride on my back."

This minor run-in with Andleton saw the end of Police Constable Blayde, as far as Beechwood Brook Division was concerned. He was a dangerous animal to have around. Andleton had friends of his own ilk; friends who, while not in high places, nevertheless had access to files and indices at County Constabulary Headquarters. The policy of the force, at that time, was to move a man after an average of five years or so in any one place. It was a brainless policy. It was based upon the theory that, in five years, a copper might have made friends; it meant that any conscientious flatfoot was given time enough to sort the sheep from the goats . . . then he was shifted.

Blayde had been at Beechwood Brook for three years. All it needed was a slight re-shuffle of the index-cards; a gentle "jumping of the queue" while nobody was looking.

Blayde found the Proposed Transfer Form in his box at Sopworth Police Station. It wasn't too much of a surprise. Indeed, it wasn't too much of a disappointment; since the Ruth episode, and without it imposing itself between their friendship, he'd felt a little awkward, perhaps a little guilty, in the presence of Alfred and Angela Bowse. He therefore "noted and accepted" the transfer (knowing damn well that any attempt at non-acceptance wasn't even an option), enjoyed the forty-eight hours of Transfer Leave which went with the move and, on Monday, August, 22nd, 1949, reported for duty at Haggthorpe Divisional Headquarters.

10

HAGGTHORPE. Despite its name, it was a spa town; a municipal borough, perched atop an assortment of mineral wells and policed by the County Constabulary. The town gave its name to a division and was, of itself, a police section. As a section it was well staffed—compared with Sopworth over-staffed. The headquarters building held the superintendent's office and the office of his second-in-command, the divisional chief inspector. It even had an inspector clerk and a detective chief inspector; but these two worthies were expected to oversee the whole division . . . as was the superintendent and the chief inspector.

Nevertheless (and even as a section) people were available. A uniformed inspector, three uniformed sergeants, a detective sergeant, two detective constables and enough pavement-bashers to keep the citizens of Haggthorpe happy.

"Y'see, old son . . ." The sergeant's name was Lennox and, as always, he was giving the new arrival a general picture of the place he was to police. He continued, "It ain't like anywhere in the county. The hotels. Seventeen of 'em. Two four-star rated, the rest three-star rated. And that's not counting God only knows how many private hotels . . . digs, in other words. So we start off with two layers of the sandwich. Those who pay to live in the hotels and those paid by the hotels. There's a shifting population: the cleaners, the kitchen staff, the odd-job types. Some of 'em are as good as gold. Others . . . they're on the twist, they get what they can, then they move on.

"The shops. Woolworths, Marks and Sparks, that sort o' thing. But some shops—jewellers, furriers, that sort o' thing—they carry stock you won't find anywhere else outside London. Then there's the people who live here. There's a residential area, but there ain't a working class area. The reason for that's easy. We don't have industry . . . at least, nothing worth calling industry. So the bulk o' the population either comes from the top drawer or thinks it does, and those who think they do are a bigger bloody nuisance then those who do."

"Yes, sir—no, sir—three bags full, sir," murmured Blayde.

"No." Lennox chuckled. He was a fat man, with a bay-window gut. His belly wobbled in amusement. "Pass the time o' day with 'em, that's all. They'll talk. They'll tell you things." The belly wobbled again. "They pay over-the-top rates at this place, old son. They like value for their money."

"Bit different from Sopworth. Is that what you're telling me?"

They were alone in the Sergeant's Office, but the Sergeant's Office led directly to, and from, the Charge Office, and the door was ajar. One thing was different from Sopworth. The traffic into and out of the Charge Office was continual; constables, civilian clerks, typists, and Blayde had already noticed one uniformed inspector walking past the door. Lennox strolled to the door and, very casually, closed it. He returned to the desk before he spoke.

He said, "Blayde, old son, take it, or leave it, I don't give a damn. I'm out of here and to Bordfield next week."

"Changing forces?" Blayde looked surprised.

"An inspectorship. It was up for grabs in *The Police Review*. I applied. I was lucky."

"And," asked Blayde, "what should I take or leave?"

"You've a name," said Lennox calmly. "You haven't been in the bloody job five minutes . . . you already have a name. You're Jack the lad. You book your own kind, if necessary."

"And I'd do it again."

"Aye." The fat sergeant nodded. "And that's what makes 'em all nervous."

"Meaning I shouldn't?" Anger was in the question.

"Meaning you should." Lennox grinned. "Every time. I would."

"In that case . . ."

"Just don't think it makes you popular, old son. That's all."

"I don't give a damn about popularity. I don't . . ."

"And keep a weather eye over your shoulder." The grin had vanished. "You're new at the job, son. You are new, whatever you think. And Tommy Mann had—still has—acquaintances. I wouldn't call 'em friends, but—y'know—acquaintances. Some of 'em—not all of 'em, but some of 'em—it's a personal thing. Some snooty-nosed young brat hammers one of their own age group . . . that's the way *they* see things."

"Not quite like that."

"No. But the way they see things. Give 'em a chance . . . they'll chop you off at the stocking tops. It's as well to know."

Blayde took the advice. For almost a year he deliberately took things as they came. He obeyed instructions . . . to the letter. On night patrol he learned the beats; the back-alleys, the short-cuts, the yards and loading bays where thieves might work. It was town work. A totally different type of policing to Upper Neck. When traffic lights went on the blink a copper had to don white gloves and end a two-hour stint with aching arms. When cash, in large lumps, was handled—to or from banks, to or from stores—a copper had to be discreetly on hand, just in case.

With four years of service under his belt he could sit promotion examinations. Unlike the Met, in the provinces the passing of these examinations didn't necessarily mean you were going to be promoted. You sat the exam, and it was a full day's job. Above a certain mark you were home and dry for possible future inspectorship; below that mark, but above a pass mark you were in there ready for chevrons, but so what? It was pure lucky-dip games and, during the war years, some nerks had made pretty high ranks because possible opposition was wearing another cut of uniform.

Blayde didn't kid himself. Nor did he lose sleep. The Tommy Mann episode had earned him a name; in some places that name was in neon, in other places it stank to high heaven.

Then, for Christ's sake, he did it again. He booked the wrong guy. Okay, only a traffic offence—but not a hairline traffic offence. The mad bastard took the crossroads against red, and smack in the middle of town. Blayde flagged him down, and the usual cross-talk act got under way.

"Excuse me, sir, but those lights were at red."

"Were they?"

"Very much so. Can I see your driving licence, please?"

The driver produced the licence with quite a flourish. He was a thin man. His expression suggested that Blayde suffered from an advanced case of body odour.

As Blayde copied details of the driving

licence into his notebook, he said, "I didn't notice the lights. I was preoccupied."

Blayde grunted, but continued writing.

"You know who I am, of course?"

"Mr. Moyne. Mr. David Moyne. It says so here, on your licence."

Moyne gave a gentlemanly snort, then said, "I'm a very good friend of John."

"John?" Blayde handed back the driving licence.

"John Chapman."

"The only Chapman I know is . . ."

"Superintendent Chapman. John. We're very good friends."

"He and I aren't yet on Christian name terms," said Blayde flatly.

"Of course not. Nevertheless . . ."

"You're being booked, Mr. Moyne. You can mention that to all the friends you like . . . you're *still* being booked."

"Do you know who I am?" Moyne glared at this stroppy young copper.

Blayde said, "Yes, sir. You're David Moyne. You're the driver of this motor car, and you've just gone through traffic lights at red. I think you're lucky. Anything coming from your right or left and you might be the late David Moyne."

Blayde strolled away. The arrogant bastard had got up his nostrils, but things had been done strictly by the book. He was on safe soil. Sod the super. "John" could get stuffed . . . and take his friends with him.

He was on afternoons—2 p.m. until 10 p.m.— and, as he walked through the Charge Office on his way to the tiny canteen, he was given the news. Superintendent Chapman wanted to see Police Constable Blayde, in his office, pronto.

Chapman. A divisonal officer not given to keeping a whole kennel of dogs and barking himself. Not at all like Kingston, Blayde's superintendent in Beechwood Brook Division. Most of Chapman's career had been in C.I.D., *ergo* if the crime statistics of Haggthorpe Division looked healthy, Chapman was satisfied. Nevertheless, not a man to fool around with. He drove a modest enough Morris Minor and, when on night patrol, officers paled if that motor car pulled up at the kerb and a cheerful enough voice called, "Get in, constable. Let's have a spin round the town."

John Chapman knew Haggthorpe like the back of his own hand. Years ago he'd worked it as a detective sergeant, and he had something of a photographic memory; rumour had it he knew where every blasted fire hydrant was. And, once in the car, the sweating constable was expected to know the answer to every damn question thrown at him.

As they drove past the railway station; "Right. I want to get to London. Where do I change, and what time's the last train out?"

They approached a school; "The headmaster. What's his name? Where does he live?"

Or at the Central Post Office; "When's the last post to Leeds? What time do the sorters come on?"

The questions came, thick, fast and heavy. "Night porter at this hotel. What's his name?" "Early closing, Wednesday. Which stores don't close?" "Lloyds Bank. Who's the manager? In an emergency, is he the only keyholder?" Or, worst of all, "There's a bent sod lives in this street. Which house? What's his name? What're his previous convictions? Who does he pal around with?"

Questions, questions, questions. And let the suffering copper say, "I don't know, sir," and the immediate reaction was, "You should bloody well know. It's what you're paid for. Knowing things—knowing *everything*—that's what bobbying boils down to."

And the hell of it was, Chapman did know.

And this man—this walking encyclopaedia—wanted to see Police Constable 1718 Robert Blayde.

Blayde knocked on the door and, having received a sharp "Come in," entered the office, closed the door, stepped smartly to the desk and slammed a somewhat dazzling salute at the man with the crowns on his shoulders.

He said, "Constable Blayde, sir."

"Ah, yes." Chapman consulted a scribbling pad. "You had your notebook out this afternoon, Blayde?"

"Yes, sir."

"David Moyne?"

"Yes, sir."

"Jumped the lights a fraction, so he tells me."

"No, sir." Blayde gazed straight ahead; staring at a point on the wall above Chapman's head.

"Right, let's hear your side."

"He went through at red, sir. Smack in the middle of red. I don't think he even noticed the lights."

"Uhu." Chapman nodded slowly. "I believe you. Know who he is?"

"A friend of yours, sir. That's what he said. He asked . . ."

"Blayde." Chapman's voice hardened a little. "I have no friends when they break the law. I don't give a damn if it's only spitting on the pavement. That clear?"

"Yes, sir." Blayde relaxed a little.

"D'you know who he is?" insisted Chapman.

"He's David Moyne, sir. He lives at . . ."'

"He's the bloody mayor!"

"Oh."

"Didn't you know that?"

"No, sir."

"You've been here long enough."

"Yes, sir," agreed Blayde.

"So . . ." Chapman paused. "What happens now?"

"He gets booked."

"He'd *better* get booked." Chapman matched tone for tone. "Any fish-flesh-and-fowl antics in this division, and I'll have somebody's guts on a plate."

"The report'll be in before I go off duty, sir."

"Good." Chapman's tone became less cold. He said, "Take that flowerpot-man helmet off your head and sit down. I was intending to have a chat. This afternoon's episode gave me an excuse."

Blayde removed his helmet and lowered himself on to a strategically placed chair.

"Smoke?" Chapman held an open cigarette-case out.

"Thank you."

Blayde reached across, Chapman thumbed a lighter and pushed a heavy glass ash-tray to a position, mid-way between them, on the desk surface. When they were both smoking, Chapman opened the conversation.

"Happy in your work?" Chapman grinned as he mouthed the age-old opening gambit.

"Yes, sir." Blayde returned the grin.

Suddenly Chapman was something very special. It really was as simple as that; that spark, from which grows respect almost amounting to affection, flashed between them. Despite their years, despite their difference in rank, they were of a kind, and each recognised the fact at the same moment. Loners. Don't-give-a-damn types. Chapman lowered his head, opened a folder and glanced at the cards and papers it held. Blayde watched, noted (not for the first time) the D.F.C. ribbon and the Air Crew Europe ribbon which took pride of place on the superintendent's double row and, as a fleeting thought, wondered whether it was fighters or bombers. He was a fighter type and yet, if Blayde's knowledge of gongs meant anything, fighters didn't earn A.C.E. So . . . bombers. Christ, this one must have been hell on roller-skates behind the controls of a Lanc or a Halifax. His crew must have . . .

"You've passed your exams?" Chapman looked up, and cut into Blayde's thoughts.

"Yes, sir."

"A chief's commendation?"

"Yes, sir."

"You're on take-off?"

"Sir?"

"You're going places?" The smile robbed the question of any sarcasm.

Blayde hesitated a split second, then risked it.

He said, "If I get as far as you, I'll be happy, sir."

"You want this chair?" Chapman cocked a quizzical eyebrow.

"If ever it comes empty . . . and if I'm available."

"Now that . . ." Chapman leaned back in the chair in question. "That I like to hear." The eyes twinkled mischievously, as he added,

"Mind you, booking local government officials might not help."

"In that case, I don't want it."

The chuckle grew into a quick laugh, and Chapman said, "My God! You have it all worked out."

Blayde didn't answer.

In a more serious tone, Chapman said, "C.I.D.?"

"I hadn't thought about it, sir."

"No?"

"If it makes for experience."

"It will," said Chapman solemnly, "make for experience." He consulted the contents of the folder. "Digs. Mrs. Buckmaster. The usual arrangement?"

"A sort of bed-sit, sir. I come and go as I please. Not—ye'know—one of the family, like my last place."

"And it suits you?"

"I like it that way."

"Uhu." Chapman linked his fingers on the surface of the desk. "So if we say 'next stop C.I.D.' there'll be no complaints?"

"No complaints at all, sir."

"Fine." Chapman smiled. "Keep cracking, Blayde. Don't get a headache wondering and worrying. It'll come."

"Yes, sir."

Blayde stood up, replaced his helmet, saluted and left the office. He'd met a man he liked. First Sharpe, now Chapman; a constable and a superintendent. Blayde didn't realise it, but those two officers would, with others, mould the type of copper he was to become. In that, he was no different to any other police officer.

Saturday, September 16th, 1950. Despite the calendar—despite the weatherman's optimistic predictions—it was cold working nights. Great-coat cold. Haggthorpe wasn't as exposed as Upper Neck had been, but the force 5-6 tended to whistle along the canyons of streets and roads and nipped at the ears. The sergeant had just left him and Blayde was skirting The Common, making his way to the private-nursing-home district of the town; to where a cinema and a municipal car park needed checking on the first round of the night.

The Common. The citizenry of Haggthorpe loathed the name. It sounded "common". Had they been able, they would have re-christened it and called it The Stray; to them it was on a par with The Stray of their near-identical North Yorkshire town of Harrogate but, like The Stray they envied, it was protected by Act of Parliament. Nevertheless, and despite its name, it was jealously guarded. No football was ever played on The Common; no game at all, in fact. Its grass was kept trimmed and tidy by the Parks Department. Its fringe of almond trees, rowans and horse-chestnuts were nursed and guarded as if their like had never before pushed their branches to the sky. The grass was criss-crossed by tarmac paths upon whose surface no bicycles were allowed. As for motor cars—the whole of The Common was surrounded by no parking zones—motor vehicles were prohibited from parking alongside The Common, much less on its sacred turf.

But there was one there. Smack in the middle of the grass. As Blayde watched it zig-zagged slightly, then stopped.

Blayde muttered, "Bloody marvellous!" checked the time as a few minutes to midnight, then swerved off the pavement and towards the offending vehicle.

It was a Morris Minor. It was *the* Morris Minor. Blayde remembered remarks as he'd come on duty; a party—a booze-up—at a local R.A.F. establishment, and "father" had accepted an invitation. And there he was, slumped forward over the wheel—Superintendent John Chapman, in rumpled civilian clothes—pissed to the wide!

Strangely, Blayde didn't hesitate. There was no decision to make. Nor did he do what he had to do with any eye on the future. A nice guy—a guy after his own heart—but if some of the other narrow-minded bastards ever saw this . . .

Blayde opened the door by the driver's seat and, as Chapman swayed sideways, caught him.

"Hup, mate. Into the other seat."

Blayde struggled a little, Chapman muttered unintelligent noises, but eventually the big white chief of Haggthorpe Division was jammed, unceremoniously, into the front passenger seat.

Blayde switched off the lights, started the engine and crawled the car carefully to the edge of The Common. In its own way, it was a little like knitting gossamer; nobody—copper or passing pedestrian—*nobody* must witness this little episode, otherwise . . . two for the high jump.

He stopped in the shadow of a horse-chestnut. Still with the lights switched off. He waited until the road was clear of traffic, checked for possible walkers, then bumped the car across the pavement and onto the road, switched on the lights and drove along back streets to D.H.Q.

At Chapman's house, at the rear of D.H.Q., Blayde parked the car by the front door. Leaving Chapman snoring, he pressed the bell-push alongside the door. He kept his finger on the button until a light showed in an upstairs window. He waited until he heard movement inside the house, then he walked away and turned the nearest corner.

From here on it was Chapman's wife's pigeon.

The next night—Sunday, September 17th—the Morris Minor drew to a halt alongside the patrolling Blayde. Chapman wound down the window and called, "Get inside, constable."

Blayde settled himself in the front passenger seat and for all of five minutes, Chapman drove the car along the streets of Haggthorpe. Nothing was said. The usual—the normal—question-and-answer session didn't take place.

Then in a gruff voice Chapman asked, "Why didn't you book me?"

"Sir?" Blayde pretended puzzlement.

"Don't arse around, Blayde." Chapman's tone was heavy. "We both know what I'm talking about. Why didn't you book me? I could name a dozen who'd have jumped at the chance."

"They didn't get the chance."

"You haven't answered the question. Why didn't you book me?"

Blayde took a chance. With as much respect as the words would allow, he said, "For the same reason you're not slapping me on a Misconduct Form for not booking you."

"A very devious answer," complained Chapman.

"It's as near as I can get to the truth."

Chapman stared at the road ahead and said, "It's earned you no favours, Blayde."

"If it does—if it even looks as if it is doing—you can lay book on being arrested next time . . . sir."

"If there is a 'next time'."

"Yes, sir."

They drove in silence for about half a mile. A strange silence; an awkward, yet companionable, silence. Had it not been for the impossibility, due to the difference in rank, they could have been friends.

Chapman said, "What I'm going to say. It's no favour. I had you in the office the other day to get the feel of you."

Blayde didn't say anything.

"D.E." said Chapman quietly. "Know what it means?"

"Duty Elsewhere."

"Know what that means?"

"Canteen gossip," said Blayde. "Basically it means nobody knows."

"Nobody does know." Chapman stopped at a crossing to allow a group of pedestrians right of way. "Nobody has to know . . . and that includes me. They asked for an officer. I suggested you. And that was before I had you in the office."

"They?"

"County Headquarters. Specifically, Detective Superintendent Kegan. If you're willing, he'll see you at County Headquarters at two o'clock tomorrow afternoon." Chapman paused, then said, "It's voluntary. It's your decision."

Blayde said, "And that's it? Nothing else?"

"I don't know anything else."

"What would you do? In my shoes."

"I'd make up my own bloody mind," said Chapman brusquely.

"No favours," grinned Blayde.

"As I remember, that was the arrangement. Your arrangement."

"I'll take it, sir," said Blayde. "What do I do as far as Haggthorpe is concerned?"

"Keep your mouth shut and disappear." Chapman concentrated on the road ahead as he continued, "Force Headquarters at two o'clock tomorrow afternoon. After that, you'll know more than I know. Forget Haggthorpe until you come off D.E. You live here, that's all. Don't come near D.H.Q. Your pay will be re-routed to Headquarters. On the duty rota you'll be marked up D.E. until further notice. And when you *do* come back . . . keep your mouth shut."

Blayde said, "Yes, sir," and wondered what the hell he'd let himself in for.

At 2.30 p.m. (thereabouts) the next day—Monday, September 18th—Blayde began to learn. County Constabulary Headquarters was just as big, just as awe-inspiring, as when he'd last seen it; more than four years previously when he'd first joined and spoken to the chief constable for the first and only time to date. the inhabitants had that same cocky walk; as if they knew things far and above anything known by common-or-garden beat-bashers. Even the cadets had that stupid, arrogant attitude.

Blayde had walked to the Reception Desk and given his name and number.

The cadet had raised supercilious eyebrows and asked, "And what do you want?"

"Detective Superintendent Kegan."

"I don't know whether he's in the building."

Blayde had glared, then snapped, "Use your crystal ball, sonny. That . . . or ask."

"He doesn't see people without an appointment."

"He wants to see me. Now, contact him, and tell him your troubles."

A deflated cadet had gone to an inner sanctum and, when he'd returned, he'd said, "In about half an hour. In the Billiard Room."

"Where's the Billiard Room?"

The cadet had told him the way.

On the way to the Billiard Room Blayde had spotted a door marked Canteen; he'd entered the canteen and purchased a beaker of hot, instant coffee, then he'd continued on his way; around corners, along corridors and up stairs.

It was some billiard room. It boasted one table, with a stained and slightly torn cloth, an incomplete set of snooker balls, a triangle that had come adrift at one corner and a set of cues, any of which could have done stand-in duty as a crummock. A man of about Blayde's age, also dressed in civilian clothes, was the only occupant of the room. As Blayde had entered he'd stopped rolling one of the reds against the tired cushions of the table.

He'd said, "Superintendent Kegan?"

"Who? Me?" Blayde had stared.

"Sorry." The other man had smiled his embarrassment.

"Kegan's who I'm waiting for," said Blayde.

"Yeah, me, too." The stranger had resumed the nervous play with the red ball. Then, as Blayde settled on to one of the benches which ran the length of one wall, had said, "My name's Copeland."

"Blayde," Blayde had said shortly.

"Duty Elsewhere?"

"I wouldn't know," said Blayde carefully. "Maybe Kegan knows."

"That's—that's why I'm here." Copeland managed a sickly smile.

"That a fact?"

End of conversation. Two coppers stepping into the unknown. One anxious for moral support, the other not knowing who the hell to trust.

Then Kegan had arrived.

He was unmistakable. A stocky man;

heavily built; close-cropped salt-and-pepper hair; dark suit, dark tie, white shirt. He paced into the room, and his first words left neither of the waiting officers in doubt.

"Right. Bolt the door. We don't want interruptions."

Copeland bolted the door. Blayde stood up from the bench, and screwed out a half-smoked cigarette into a tobacco-tin ash-tray. Copeland came to stand alongside Blayde, and they waited.

Kegan glanced at each in turn, then said, "You both know why you're here."

"No, sir," Blayde answered, before Copeland could speak.

"You were told to report to me. You're both . . ."

"We don't know who you are, sir," interrupted Blayde.

"Kegan. Detective Superintendent Kegan."

"Yes, sir. But that's only who you say you are. I don't know you. This chap might, but . . ."

"No, sir." Copeland swallowed. "I've—er—I've never met Detective Superintendent Kegan in my life."

"Neat." Kegan cocked his head to one side,

like an inquisitive sparrow. "Unusual, but I approve. Identification, then."

He fished a folded pasteboard from his wallet and allowed Blayde and Copeland to inspect it.

Blayde said, "I'm Police Constable Blayde."

"And I'm Police Constable Copeland, sir."

"Right . . ."

Kegan shoved his hands into the pockets of his jacket, with his thumbs hooked over the openings. He strolled slowly and stiff-legged to and from in front of the two constables as he talked. He kept his eyes fixed, in an unseeing glare, at a point about a yard ahead of his strolling feet.

He said, "Keeton. Neither of you know the place. You haven't policed there, you haven't lived or worked there. Something we've already checked. The Whiff 'em Whaff 'em Club. A bloody stupid name, but that's where you're going. A glorified working men's club, that's all it is. Boozing. Club acts. The usual thing, but something extra. It's that 'extra' we're interested in.

"Boozing till all hours. That's the least of it. There's also a nice market in nicked merchandise going on. A sweet little bastard called

Fellows . . . we think he's holed up there. He's on the run from the Midlands. A big store job and, when he made a run for it, he crippled a copper.

"All this we think, all this we're pretty sure of. But—I don't have to tell you—a club isn't like a pub. More like a private dwelling house. Which means we need a warrant. Which means we need evidence enough to get a warrant. It might also be nice if somebody opened the front door when we arrived." He stopped his slow pacing, looked at the two constables, and said, "That's the size of it. That's the meal we're asking you to swallow."

Blayde glanced at Copeland, then asked, "How do we get in, sir?"

"That's your first problem, son." Kegan smiled. "If it was that easy we'd have been there weeks ago."

"This—er—this man Fellows," murmured Copeland.

"You'll have a photograph before you leave. To look at, not to take away. We don't want *that* to slip out of your pocket at the wrong time."

There were a few moments of silence. Deliberate. Kegan may have outlined the problem in easy-to-understand language, but the two constables had to be given time enough to understand fully what was required of them.

Kegan rested his rump against the edge of the billiard table and said, "Inspector Black. He's your go-between. Out beyond Keeton there's a socking great stretch of moorland. There's a lay-by, out at the back of beyond. Black will meet you there. Three o'clock, tomorrow afternoon. After that, you fix your own meetings."

"Er—how do we get there?" asked Copeland. "The lay-by, I mean."

"Bus from Keeton," said Kegan. "I'll give you the location of the lay-by. There's a stop, less than a mile away."

And that was it. A few more details—not much to mean anything—then Kegan wished them luck, unbolted the door and left. The two innocents lighted cigarettes and walked slowly from County Headquarters building.

Copeland said, "This your first spell on this lark?"

"Aye."

"Mine, too. By the way, my name's Jim."

"Bob."

"Christ!" James Copeland sighed. "A bit different to trying doorknobs."

They walked slowly towards the lay-by. Blayde wore a zip-up wind-cheater, stained flannels and a cap. Copeland wore an ancient tweed jacket, worn army-twill trousers and a weatherbeaten trilby. They both felt slightly ridiculous.

A yellow VW Beetle was parked in the lay-by. At the wheel was a woman, with the collar of her driving coat turned up to hide her face. Alongside her in the front passenger seat, a thick-built, grey-haired man was slouched back in apparent sleep. As Copeland slowed to a halt, Blayde fished a packet of cigarettes from the pocket of his wind-cheater, walked to the nearside of the car and tapped on the window. The grey-haired man opened his eyes, sat up and wound down the window.

"Could you fix me with a light, please, sir." As he held the cigarette ready Blayde put slight emphasis on the sir and met the man's eyes.

The man produced matches, and murmured, "Which one?"

"Sir?"

"Blayde or Copeland?"

"Blayde, sir." Blayde took the matches, smiled and, as he lighted the cigarette, nodded towards Copeland and stood aside to allow Black to open the door of the VW.

Black said, "Into the back, the pair of you."

When they were settled, Black said, "My daughter, Liz. She's in on this thing. She'll take you into Keeton, bring you out of Keeton. Either this car or a Morris. She'll give you a number to ring, not a police number. Today she'll drop you in a street behind Woolworths. Other pick-up and dropping points . . . arrange it between you."

As he unfolded a street map of Keeton, Black continued, "This is the fourth try. Getting into this bloody club after hours is like getting into Fort Knox. So far, we haven't been able to get beyond the doors in drinking time. In short, it's not an easy number. Now, here . . ."

He stabbed the street map with a forefinger. Pointed out where the Whiff 'em Whaff 'em Club was situated. Gave a quick run-down of the main roads and streets of the town. The more important buildings and stores. Blayde and Copeland leaned forward in the rear seat and peered over the shoulders of Black and his daughter.

As he re-folded the map, Black said, "What's your capacity for drink?"

Blayde said, "I don't drink much."

"I'm no ale-can," added Copeland.

"Right." Black tucked the map away in his pocket. "An old copper's trick. Not too much to eat and a teaspoonful of olive oil before you start drinking. It floats on top of the booze, and keeps the fumes from your brain. It'll keep you sober until it's been absorbed into the system. But don't push things. It can't handle a whole bloody brewery." His lips bent into a quick, crusty smile as he added, "It'll also keep your bowels loose."

"The Fellows character?" murmured Blayde.

"We think he's in there. We think he's holed up in the flat above the club. Just get us in, that's all. Get us enough to swear out a warrant, we'll winkle the bastard out."

Copeland said, "Other than that, after-hours drinking and stolen property."

"Just the one, if that's all you can get." Black's tone was low and harsh. "They've thumbed their nose at us too bloody long.

There's even talk of back-handers. Just get us *something.* I'll get the warrant."

The object—always the object to be first surmounted on this sort of D.E. assignment—to get where coppers shouldn't be. To out-fox the opposition. To con, to connive, to prove they weren't coppers. That for starters.

Liz Black had dropped them in the street behind Woolworths and, on this the first evening, they'd arranged that she pick them up at five minutes past midnight—"Not dead on midnight. That's too neat a time"—at their dropping off place. They'd mooched around the town, familiarising themselves with the location of the target club, and the streets and alleys surrounding it. As advised, they'd called at a chemist's and bought a bottle of olive oil, but it was still unopened in Copeland's pocket.

And now they were in a cheap, not-too-clean cafe, sipping tea and risking their teeth on appropriately named rock buns.

"Ideally," mused Blayde. "Ideally we should be invited into the club. Then—once we're accepted—apply to join."

"Some hopes!" remarked Copeland.

"No." Blayde broke a piece from one of the

rock buns and popped it into his mouth. He talked as he chewed. "They don't like coppers. Okay, let's behave as if we don't like coppers. Let's start with the nearby pubs."

"As good a way as any," agreed Copeland without over-enthusiasm.

Blayde said, "Background. We'll stick to our real names, that'll eliminate one possible slip-up. I'm a joiner, you're my mate. We've just been sacked for nicking timber. We're looking round for work."

"And if they ask questions?"

"Tell 'em to mind their own bloody business. Be touchy. Aggressive. Give the impression we've missed jail by the skin of our teeth."

"Can you—y'know—joiner a bit?" asked Copeland. "In case we meet somebody who can."

"Enough," said Blayde.

"Seems as good a way as any," sighed Copeland.

"Can you think of a better way?"

"No." Copeland smiled. "You're the boss. One of us has to make the decisions . . . I'll just tag along and say the right things. I hope."

That was the way they worked it. The slow

way, the probing way, the careful way. Pubs, within easy walking distance of the target club, and they played darts and dominoes, and drank pints, and talked. Their talk was rough and Blayde was surprised to learn that the inoffensive-looking Copeland had a fund of filthy jokes, plus the ability to tell them well. Copeland became the more popular of the two, and Blayde was content to stay in the background and keep a scowl on his face.

The plan paid dividends. By the evening of Thursday the 21st they'd found a taproom visited by members of the Whiff 'em and Whaff 'em. Amid the general gabble of talk, they'd caught the exchange. "I'll see you in the club, later." "Aye. I'll be along when I've finished this pint." Blayde earmarked the two men. One or the other—possibly both—represented a possible way through the doors of the club.

They staggered the place and time of their pick-up and drop-off. A bus to Keeton then, when the night's work was ended, Liz Black drove them back to their respective homes. It was necessary. It was far too late for public transport.

Sometimes the yellow VW. Sometimes the

Morris. She never asked questions. Indeed, she hardly ever spoke.

Once Copeland said, "This job must be very inconvenient for you."

"Not really. Mother died about two years ago. I act as housekeeper to father."

"Oh."

"Anything you want him to know, tell me. It'll stay with the four of us."

On the Thursday night Blayde said, "Inspector Black might be interested. We've spotted two club members, we think it's the target club. We'll cultivate them and let you know."

"Fine. I'll tell him."

And the next night, Friday, they waited until the two club members were at the bar, then went into a pre-arranged routine.

It needed less than an hour to closing time. The taproom was crowded and Blayde pushed his way forward for re-fills. As Blayde lifted the glasses, having received the change from the landlord, Copeland jostled him, and called, "Twenty Players, while you're at it, mate."

The beer slopped from the glasses, and some of it splashed down the trousers of one of the club members.

Blayde snarled, "You clumsy, ham-fisted sod!"

Copeland glared and snapped, "Hang about a bit, mate. You don't think I did it on purpose."

"I don't give a damn why you did it. All I know is . . ."

"If you want to make a big thing out of this . . ."

"And what if I do?"

"I'll bloody soon oblige, mate."

"All right." Blayde returned the glasses to the bar counter. "If that's the way you want . . ."

"Hey! Hey! Hey!" The landlord moved hurriedly along the bar. "If you two want to . . ."

"It's all right, Tom." The club member straightened from brushing spilled beer from his trousers. "It was an accident. Nobody's fault, really."

Thus the key was gently inserted into the lock. The quarrel was patched and rounds of drinks were bought. The two club members were gradually, skilfully, brought within the orbit of friendship and, each evening, that friendship was coaxed into a fuller bloom. Blayde and Copeland concocted deliberate phrases which, at the right moment, could be inserted into an otherwise normal public-house chin-wag. "God! We'll have to find another boozer. This beer gets worse every day." "What! Time already? It *can't* be . . . there's summat wrong with that bloody clock."

On Friday, September 29th, Charlie Close, the club member upon whose trousers Blayde had spilled beer more than a week before, said, "Where are you working, then?"

"Oh—y'know—anywhere," said Blayde vaguely.

"You're not out of work?"

Blayde timed the hesitation carefully, then said, "Officially."

Close's club-friend, Walter Whitaker, said, "What you mean is you're drawing Unemployment, eh?"

"A bit here, a bit there," said Copeland guiltily.

"Moonlighting," insisted Whitaker.

"What are you two?" Blayde scowled. "Bloody coppers?"

It was, of course, the perfect double-bluff . . . and it worked. The club, it seemed, had bought a baby grand piano. "Some of the vocalists, see? They like a piano. They're not too happy with an electric organ." But the stage was beginning to feel the strain. An electric organ *and* a large piano. "That damn stage. It's like a springboard when you walk across it."

"We'd like it strengthened," said Whitaker.

"And," added Close, "we've put out some estimates and, frankly, we don't seem to be getting far."

"Shoring up," said Blayde.

"Aye. Summat like that," said Close.

"We'll have to see it, first. See what it needs."

"Naturally."

"All right." Blayde nodded and frowned. "We'll do it. Make a good job. You provide the timber, we'll provide the labour. There's just . . ." He didn't end the sentence.

"Just what?" asked Whitaker.

"We'll have to fit it in, that's all."

"We're a bit ploughed under at the moment. A job here. A job there. We've work to last us . . ."

"What about at night, when the club's closed?" Close asked the question he'd been led by the nose to ask.

"Happen." Blayde seemed to give the proposition careful thought.

"No double-time. Owt daft like that," warned Close.

"No, but I like my pint. So does Jim."

"It's a *club*, mate. Not the Y.W.C.A."

"Eh? Oh!" Understanding dawned on Blayde's face. "In that case we can have a look, get measured up and get cracking."

On paper—when it was reduced to official verbiage—it looked easy. "Superintendent Kegan, sir, I respectfully report . . ." The cold, police jargon destroyed all the nuances, the gentle manoeuvres, the moments when Blayde and Copeland had held their breath, crossed their fingers and prayed.

But, as Black glanced through copies of the reports, he knew what they represented, and murmured, "You're to be congratulated, gentlemen. You've done quite a job."

Blayde took on duty as spokesman.

He said, "We can spin it out until Saturday, sir. As it is, the stage is strong enough to hold an elephant act."

"Saturday, then. What's the best time?"

"One o'clock." Blayde didn't hesitate. "One o'clock, Sunday morning. They have a pattern. They shut shop at turning-out time. On the button. Those in the know stay on. They lock the doors . . . one lock, two bolts. There's a peep-hole in the door. About eye-level. The sort of thing banks use. There's also a button under a small shelf, on the right of the door. It's linked to a red light above the bar. A warning."

"You suggest one o'clock." Black brought Blayde back to fundamentals.

"Yes, sir. It's usually going on for three when the heavy drinkers leave. One o'clock . . . there's usually between twenty and thirty still there at that time."

"And how do we get in?"

"The gents toilet . . . to get to it you have to pass the main entrance. The one I'm talking about. I'll have the door unlocked and unbolted at one o'clock. Come in through the main door, down the passage and into the main room. That's where they'll be."

"Passing of stolen goods?"

"It goes on. Most of it after hours. Close—that's one of the men who got us in there—most evenings he has a case. Watches, bracelets, pendants, that sort of thing. That's a hit-and-miss thing. But, being Saturday night, there's a good chance he'll have it with him."

"And Fellows?"

"He's there," said Blayde. "He acts the part of the steward's brother. Lives upstairs above the club. The door to the living quarters is backstage. Near the dressing-rooms. It's marked 'Private' and leads to a flight of stairs."

"Right." Black smiled his satisfaction. The impression was that it was a smile he kept tucked away for special occasions. "Now—for your information and reassurance—I'll arrive at one o'clock . . . exactly. Time your watches by the Speaking Clock before you go into the club. I'll time mine the same way. Twenty men . . . including myself and a sergeant. All in uniform. All hand-picked. They'll be pulled off duty from various parts of the division. As they arrive at divisional headquarters they'll be kept strictly incommunicado. They'll be briefed—by me—at twelve-thirty. There'll be no leak. No possibility of a leak. You have my word on that."

Saturday, October 7th, 1950—strictly speaking, 12.45 a.m., Sunday, October 8th—and the butterflies were fighting each other in the pit of Blayde's stomach. Copeland had a worried look on his face, and kept licking his lips. They were squatting under the club stage. Their only light was from an electric light bulb, running on a lead from a socket of the footlights. At odd intervals Blayde hammered on one of the uprights supporting the stage.

Copeland crawled forward and squinted through a tiny gap in the stage front.

"About two dozen," he whispered. "They're still at it."

Blayde grunted.

"Close is still with us."

"Good," breathed Blayde.

"And Fellows."

"All we need now, is Black and his merry men."

Copeland crawled back to where they were crouched. Blayde hammered the upright again. He glanced at his watch.

"Four minutes to go," he muttered.

"Unless there's a cock-up."

"There won't *be* a cock-up." Blayde's taut nerves made his voice harsh.

At three minutes to one o'clock Blayde crawled from under the stage. Copeland followed. In the narrow passage which led to the dressing rooms and the door marked "Private", Blayde paused and took a few deep breaths.

"Jim." Blayde forced a smile. "Take that look off your face. Otherwise they'll send for the midwife."

"Sorry." Copeland rubbed the back of his hand across his mouth. "I'll—er—I'll not let you down."

"Who made the suggestion?" Blayde touched Copeland's arm. "Those jokes—the filthiest you can come up with—keep 'em listening at the bar."

They walked through the door leading to the main room of the club and strolled the length of that room. As they neared the bar, Blayde turned and headed towards the toilets.

Somebody called, "I'll set one up for you, Bob," and Blayde raised a hand in acknowledgement.

Out of sight of the main room, Blayde worked fast. He glanced into the toilets to make sure they were empty, then he returned to the corridor, unlocked the door then, carefully and not allowing them to squeak, he withdrew the bolts, top and bottom, from their sockets. To be doubly certain, he turned the knob and eased the door an inch or so open. Then he turned his back and walked towards the main room.

Even as he entered the main room he heard

the cars arrive. Heard the doors slam and the thump of boots racing along the corridor.

Then all hell broke.

The man Fellows hared for the door alongside the stage, and Blayde gave chase. Fellows reached the door first, and tried to slam it in Blayde's face. Blayde twisted, charged the door with his shoulder, touched Fellow's shoulder, but couldn't grip. Fellows belted for the door marked "Private", jerked it open and tried to take the stairs two at a time. Half way up the stairs he spun round and aimed a kick at Blayde's head. Blayde swayed, caught the foot, pulled and twisted.

They both ended in a heap at the foot of the stairs, with Blayde underneath. There was the glint of a switch-knife blade, then a rolling and a wrestling and Blayde felt the steel go in, hilt-deep.

He gasped, "I'm a copper. You're nicked," and, with the blade still in his side, heaved himself sideways and upwards and clamped an arm-lock across Fellows's throat.

The rest was a little hazy. How long . . . he didn't know. Just that this bastard was well and truly nailed.

He heard a voice—a strangely gentle voice—and saw a uniform.

The voice said, "Easy, old son. You'll break his neck."

The gathering darkness and a pain in his side like nothing on earth.

"Always the hard way." Chapman smiled down at Blayde. "You're a glutton for punishment."

Blayde returned the smile. The tiny side-ward was light and airy. The central heating was warm without being stuffy. The sheets were cool and comfortable. The nurses—even the medics—tended to make a fuss of him. His side was a little stiff, the bandaging tended to restrict his breathing a little, but the pain had left him. If this was the hard way he wasn't complaining.

"How did it go?" he asked.

"Grand slam." Chapman was in civilian clothes. He pulled a chair nearer to the bed and sat down. "Black thinks you're Superman and Robin rolled into one."

Blayde didn't say anything.

"The club's folded." Chapman's eyes twinkled. "The old gag. Wound up. Closed. Finished. They can say that at the trial . . . then they'll open again under new management."

"Fellows?" asked Blayde.

"I doubt if the pigeons will crap on him for a few years."

"Close?"

"Receiving. He'll be lucky if he only gets three."

"He wasn't a bad chap," mused Blayde.

"He was a bent bugger. Don't start feeling sorry for 'em."

"When are they up?" asked Blayde.

"They're pleading Guilty. With Copeland and the others there'll be enough coppers. You won't be called." Then almost as an after-thought. "How are you feeling?'

"Fine."

"It could have been worse. Much worse. It missed all the important bits."

"So I'm told."

"The doc tells me you could be out of here within the week."

"I hope so."

"Then Sick Leave?"

"Yes, sir."

"The West Riding crowd . . ." Chapman moved his head to stare out of the window. "They run bloody good Detective Training Courses. On a par with the Home Office shindigs. November the twentieth. There's a vacancy for a non-West Riding type."

"Is that an offer?" asked Blayde gently.

"November twentieth," murmured Chapman.

Blayde grinned, and said, "I'll be jumping over five-barred gates."

11

THE syllabus read, *West Riding Constabulary Detective Training Course for Junior Officers: 20th November 1950—10th February 1951. To be held at the Detective Training School, Wakefield.*

In the class of forty officers not more than half were West Riding men. The others came from neighbouring forces; Salford, York, North Riding: it was a get-together of differing methods to form a great conglomerate of enthusiasms. In many ways, it was like a university. The men lived out (Blayde, a Salford man and a West Riding man were billeted out at a small public house, less than ten minutes' walk from the training school) and when they were in class they were encouraged to argue points of law, discuss personal cases, criticise and generally enjoy themselves. The men who taught them were all coppers; working coppers who'd made the law fit the streets, but at the same time men who'd kept abreast of the law.

Nor was it all law. The tricks of surveillance,

the cons of the race track, the modes of interviewing various types, the use of forensic science, the manner in which the police services of America went about their business, sketching and plan drawing, the methods of confidence tricksters, sharepushers and long-firm fraudsmen. It was all included. It meant work—much of it evening work—but Blayde knew he'd been given the chance of a lifetime, and he took it.

Soon the pub where he and his two colleagues were billeted became the meeting-house for many of the other trainees, after the early evening graft at the books and notes was completed. They felt apart—yes, even superior—as far as the non-police customers were concerned. It was a club. Not just the members of the course, but the whole police service. A large, but at the same time, very exclusive club. Blayde felt it for the first time on that course. Until then he'd been a noviciate; of but strictly speaking not *in*. Now he was a fully-paid-up member . . . for life. The knowledge—the realisation—gave a warm and contented feeling. And, in turn, this feeling drove him to listen and understand; to appreciate that his tutors were men of vast and varied experience and that, as far as they were able, they were passing that experience on to a younger generation of their own kind, that it might be treasured and built upon.

As his fellow-lodger from Salford put it, "It's a damn good job they're on our side. They know every gag in the joke book."

There was a break in the course. From Saturday, December 23rd until Wednesday, December 27th. On the day before the break Blayde telephoned Hill Rise. Twice his brother answered, and Blayde replaced the receiver without speaking. On the third time Meg, his mother answered.

"Bob here, mother."

"Oh."

"It's a long time since we talked."

"Yes, it's a long time." Her voice had changed. Much of the pride had been squeezed out of it. She said, "Your grandfather died. Did you know?"

"No."

"More than a year ago."

"I'm sorry." And he meant it.

"It was . . . We expected it. He was an old man."

"Uhu."

"Heartbroken."

"I'm sorry, ma." He choked a little and

almost wished he hadn't telephoned. He asked, "Who's living there now?"

"Just the three of us. Ric and his wife . . . his woman really."

"Does he . . ." He forced himself to ask the hurtful question. "Does he change the model very often?"

There was a hesitation, then she said, "Sometimes."

On an impulse he said, "Spend Christmas with me, ma."

Again there was a hesitation before she said, "No . . . I can't."

Blayde felt a louse because, before she'd answered, he was regretting his suggestion. That damn twin brother of his. He'd have been there between them; not in person, but in spirit. There'd have been rows. Arguments. Things said. Maybe things left unsaid but, nevertheless, *known*.

In an awkward voice he said, "Well, that's it, ma . . . nice to hear your voice again."

"And yours, son."

"Have a good Christmas."

"You, too."

"I'll try."

"Ring again, son." It was a plea, and it hurt like the devil.

"Aye." He cleared his throat. "I'll do that ma."

So Christmas 1950 was Christmas 1950 . . . and that's all it was. For Blayde it was a novelty, because he went off the rails a little. Maybe it was because of the telephone conversation. Maybe it was because all the other guys on the course were going to their homes and their families and the gaiety that was Christmas, and that . . .

Maybe it was everything, all rolled into one. Maybe it was nothing more than a delayed backlash of over-work and very little relaxation.

Take your pick. Who knows? Blayde didn't.

All he knew was that he was closing up to his twenty-ninth birthday, and that he was both alone and lonely. This loner business. It demanded its price occasionally, and it wasn't a very low price. One Christmas three years ago . . . But what the hell did that mean? What the hell did that matter? One good Christmas in a lifetime. Maybe that was his quota. And if it *could* have meant something, *could* have led up to something . . . okay, he'd blown it.

So, let's flip the coin and see what pictures

we can draw in the muck of the "tails" side.

Christmas at Blackpool. Like a tart with tinsel round her neck. The two-star hotel, "Special Christmas Festivities", a whole building creaking under the weight of make-believe bonhomie. Revelry with stained and tattered edges. The one thing Christmas was not about. Slap and tickle, nudge-nudge, wink-wink and make sure your knicker elastic can stand the strain, darling. He didn't even know her full name. Pam, that was all, and maybe that wasn't her real name.

They each seemed to recognise their own kind; to see, in the other, a mirror-image of a tight-jawed and very personal desperation. It was Christmas, and people had to do things. She wasn't a whore. Whatever else, she wasn't that; she lacked the teasing quality, the pseudo-seductive gestures, the elephantine subtleties of double-talk. She was, perhaps, a little afraid. Afraid in the way Blayde was afraid. As if she—like him—had momentarily escaped the confines of a private and invisible strait-jacket. That plus the fact that, at around midnight, the damn hotel had more giggles and whispers and opening and closing doors than a French farce.

They lusted silently and without joy. It

was "part of Christmas"; as meaningless as pulling crackers; as unimportant as the wearing of a paper crown.

And when it was all over—when they each returned to their own world of reality—they didn't even say goodbye.

Saturday, January 20th, 1951. Thirty minutes past noon, and the class had had more than two hours of the "Official Secrets Acts". Not the easiest of subjects. Not the most stimulating. Blayde and his colleages left the training school and made their way to their respective billets. The next session began at 9 a.m. on Monday morning, and most of them were anxious to dump their books and make for a bus or a train home. Blayde didn't hurry. It was his custom to stay in Wakefield, at the pub, through the weekend. Wakefield was no swinging town, but it had cinemas and the pub sold good beer, and—what the hell—where else?"

The letter was waiting for him. The buff coloured envelope and the coat of arms told him it was from County Constabulary Headquarters. The document was terse and to the point. As from Monday, February 12th—the Monday after the Detective Training Course ended—he was to report to Bigton Sub-Divisional Headquarters, Haggthorpe Division, as Detective Sergeant Robert Blayde. Just for a moment he thought it might be some form of off-beat joke. In effect two rungs up; missing the usual stint as detective constable. It had been known, but not often. Then as the truth dawned—that it wasn't a joke—he felt humbled and for a few seconds unsure of himself. Detective Sergeant. Responsible for the day-to-day enquiries into crime throughout a whole sub-division. Christ, that was a mouthful for a first bite. Four years in the force—just over four years—by the old-time yardstick he still carried nappy-marks. That's what they'd say. The oldsters. They'd curl their lips and whisper about "pissing in the same pot", and nothing he could do, nothing he could say, would budge that opinion.

So, the hell with them!

He scrawled his name under the word "Noted", added the date, then tucked the document back in its envelope and slipped it into his inside pocket.

That afternoon he caught a train to Haggthorpe. By early evening he was in the

Divisional Headquarters building. He asked to see Chapman.

"I think he's knocked off for a few hours," said the duty sergeant.

"Check," suggested Blayde.

The duty sergeant contacted the switchboard and, from there, the superintendent's office.

As he replaced the receiver he said, "Just in time. He'll give you five minutes."

Blayde hurried along corridors, knocked on the door of Chapman's office and, having been invited, entered. Chapman faced him with a look of quizzical innocence on his face.

"Sit down, Blayde." Then when Blayde was seated. "Now, what's your trouble?"

"This, sir." Blayde took the envelope from his pocket and passed it over the desk.

Chapman read the form, raised his eyebrows and, still with the innocent look on his face, said, "And this is trouble?"

"No, sir, not trouble. Unexpected. A pleasant surprise. And I think the least I can do is thank you."

"Me?" Chapman flicked the form with his finger. "These things come from headquarters. See the signature? The A.C.C."

"I still think I owe you more than a few thanks."

"Blayde." Chapman dropped the form onto the desk top. The mock-innocence left his expression. He said, "I give nothing. Please believe that. Nothing! The vacancy came at Bigton. You were eligible . . . just. I'd far sooner have somebody I know than some dumb cluck another superintendent wants to see the back of. Okay, I pulled a few strings. But you may well live to wish I hadn't. I am a very demanding man. Be warned. I expect my detective sergeants to work their balls off . . . and I give them hell if they don't."

"I'll expect hell if I don't," said Blayde quietly.

"So . . ." Chapman's lips moved into a slow and lop-sided smile. "We both know where we stand. That's the way I like things."

And by God he worked. He bought himself a banger—a slightly battered Lancia which had seen better days—and as from Monday, February 12th, 1951, Bigton Sub-Division knew it had a detective sergeant who was going places. Sure, he made enemies. He had enemies before he even reported on that Monday morning; uniformed sergeants—some almost old enough to be his father—soured and bitter that some unknown young pip-squeak had dropped for a job they themselves had had their eyes on; detective constables, at the various sections, who'd worked The Old Pals Act for years and didn't take too kindly to the possibility that their "nawpings" might be brought to a sudden end. And, within the month, everybody knew the score. Sub-divisional crime was no longer merely re-corded. It was bloody-well detected, or if not it wasn't for the want of trying. He pulled no punches. "Jacks don't work office hours. If that's what you're after, find yourself a place behind a pen." He was realistic enough to acknowledge that twenty-five percent of crime was (to use a phrase he loathed) "undetect-able"; crime committed by strangers passing through the district. "We can keep 'em out. Make it too damn hot for 'em. Get around. Talk to people, and warn 'em. If we do enough work before the crime, the crime won't be committed."

It didn't make for friendship, but who the hell needed friendship? Respect—respect from the men with the same idea as himself—and from the others trepidation which almost amounted to fear. Nobody knew better than

Blayde that, if he crawled out on a branch, certain bastards would form a queue to use the saw, but at the same time enough real coppers were there to make damn sure the saw lacked teeth. In the whole division, no sergeant fought harder in the cause of a detective constable who'd justifiably chanced his arm in the name of law-enforcement and come unstuck. In those first two years he had toe-to-toe slanging matches with Chapman himself in the privacy of the latter's office.

"Damn it, sir, in those hovels, the law doesn't run."

"He over-stepped the mark, sergeant."

"He did what I'd have done."

"What the hell is that supposed to mean?"

"He took a gamble. If it had come off, you'd have been the first to pat him on the back. Don't break his bloody arm for trying."

Then in 1953 he pulled a blinder which in time became part of the weft and weave of the history of the force.

Introducing Harry Rath. Detective Constable Harry Rath. Nobody could figure out the relationship between Rath and Blayde; just that one was a D.C. and the other was a D.S., and they both worked out of Bigton Sub-

Divisional Headquarters. By all the rules of the game—by all the rules of Blayde's game—they should have been mortal enemies. Rath was a detective for one simple reason; he'd been an embarrassment in uniform. The force didn't want to know. In effect they disowned him. His initial mistake was joining the police force . . . *any* police force. A circus, sure, he'd have earned a fortune as a clown, merely by being his normal self. As a stand-up-comic—by all means, he'd have had the audience in tears of laughter, merely by explaining his own back-to-front logic. But a policeman? Never in a thousand years.

Rath did not take a crime and, from then, find the criminal. Rath did it his way; the only way he knew. He had a criminal—*one* criminal—and he bust a gut to fit every crime ever reported to that criminal. Had the crown jewels been nicked while Rath was actually watching Don Shelton . . . no matter. The reaction would have been the same.

"Shelton. It has his hallmark all over it."

"How in hell's name . . ."

"I'm telling you. I've studied that bugger. It's him."

From rape to pinching milk bottles, from fraudulent conversion to unlawful wounding:

Shelton . . . it was a one-man race. And, indeed, Shelton had form. Not much—helping himself from supermarket shelves a couple of times, three "drunk-and-dizzies"—but he had form.

Then on Monday, October 5th, a crate of whisky went missing from a van outside an off-licence; the driver had nipped into the back of the shop for a quick tea and biscuit with the proprietor and, when he'd returned to his van, a crate of Red Label wasn't where it should have been.

Harry Rath took the complaint, went through the required motions, sent the van driver on his way, then said, "Shelton."

"Not again," murmured Blayde.

"Bob, I keep telling you," pleaded Rath. "He's laughing at us. He's a one-man crime wave."

"Harry," sighed Blayde, "he's a snot-nosed little tea-leaf and when he goes on the twist we'll grab him. Then you can sleep at nights."

"Him and that cousin of his," pronounced Rath.

"Hanson, the bookie?"

"He sups whisky like it came out of a tap."

"And because Hanson likes his tipple, Shelton nicked the whisky?"

"They're thick. They're close. Hanson'll have had his share."

"Harry." Blayde shook his head, slowly. "Leave it. I'll have a word. We'll twist Hanson's tail a little. See which key he sings in. Then, if you're right, we'll have some idea."

Rath was content. To him this young detective sergeant—a man almost young enough to be his son—was something special. Something unique, in that there was never that hint of mockery in the eyes or in the tone.

Later that morning Blayde spoke to the uniformed sergeant in the Charge Office.

"Started on the bookies, yet?"

"Some of 'em."

"Hanson?"

The uniformed sergeant took a typed list from a desk drawer, consulted it, then said, "No. Hanson's still to come."

"Leave him, eh?" said Blayde.

"Why?" The uniformed sergeant looked puzzled.

"Something Harry Rath's come up with. Leave Hanson to stew. I want him worried.

"Okay."

The uniformed sergeant made a careful note alongside a name on the list, and returned the list to the drawer.

The year was 1953. Off-course, ready-money betting was illegal. It was a stupid law; every copper in the U.K. knew it was a stupid law. But it was the law, and it was broken every race day of the year, therefore coppers, bookies and magistrates went through mutually accepted tricks.

Each betting shop was raided once a year. The day and time of the raid was agreed upon by the bookie and the uniformed sergeant who was to stroll into "unlawful premises" with a couple of flatfeet. The evidence, in the shape of betting-slips, sporting pages, etc., was ready and waiting on the counter. Four or five pensioners had been given a quid to be available as "resorters" and (in order not to interfere with the betting in progress) the coppers took along half-completed bail forms, to be filled in on the spot. The bookie and the "resorters" were arrested and bailed in seconds. The "evidence" was collected. Everybody said the right things and when, a fortnight or so later, the bookie and his "resorters" appeared in court, everybody pleaded Guilty, the bookie paid all the fines . . . and that was him clear for another twelve months. It was a game. The fines were standard. Nobody asked for, or expected, a rake-off. The letter of a particularly silly law had been applied and the bookie had coughed up what was, in effect, an annual licence fee.

On Tuesday, November 17th, Hanson visited Bigton Police Station. The uniformed sergeant listened sympathetically to his tale of woe, made appropriate noises of commiseration, then directed him to the C.I.D. Office where both Blayde and Rath were "at home." It was just after three in the afternoon. Rath's eyes widened, then a slow smile of contentment gathered itself at his lips. Blayde looked up from the Crime Report he was checking, nodded silent greeting, waved to a vacant chair, then returned to the checking of the Crime Report.

Hanson sat down and began, "They told me, downstairs . . ."

"I'll be with you," interrupted Blayde without looking up. "Just cross your legs and hold your water."

Hanson began to look worried. Really worried . . . which was how he was meant to look.

Blayde signed the Crime Report, placed it carefully into the Out basket, lighted a cigarette, then leaned back and gazed at Hanson for a moment.

He said, "Okay. Let's listen to your funnies first."

"What—what 'funnies'?"

"Unless this is a social call."

"No, it's . . ." Hanson seemed at a loss for words.

"Well?" encouraged Blayde.

"They—they haven't raided me," stumbled Hanson.

" 'They'?"

"The cops. They haven't done my place yet."

"I see." Blayde showed mild, but bored, interest.

"I'm losing money," complained Hanson.

"How?"

"The bloody customers. The punters. Even some of the regulars. They're going to the other places."

"The other betting-shops?"

"Aye."

"Why should they do that?" asked Blayde innocently.

"Because my place hasn't been raided. All the others have."

"And?"

"Look, for Christ's sake." Hanson sounded desperate. "We all know the score."

"You break the law," said Blayde flatly.

"The hell I . . ." Hanson checked himself, then said, "We *all* break the law. But that's not the point."

"Not the point?" mocked Blayde. "In a police station?"

"I'm losing custom," groaned Hanson. "I'm losing money, hand over fist."

Blayde clicked his tongue and murmured, "My heart bleeds for you, Hanson."

"I'm serious, Mr. Blayde."

"And I'm not?"

"Look . . ." Hanson leaned forward a little and used his hands to emphasise his words. "The other bookies. They're making money. *My* money, from *my* customers. Everybody thinks there's summat on. That you people have a down on me. Me personally. So they're keeping away, just in case."

"Just in case what?"

"All right. All right." Hanson ran the fingers of one hand through his hair. He licked his lips, then breathed, "How much?"

"I don't follow." Blayde smiled.

"How much is it going to cost me?"

"For what?"

"To raid my place. To get me off the hook for another year. How much?"

"Harry." Blayde glanced at the beaming Rath. "Harry, I think Mr. Hanson's offering us a bribe, don't you?"

"Sounds like it," agreed Rath.

"No. It's not that," gabbled Hanson hurriedly. "It's just that . . ."

"Bribing a copper to do his duty," mused Blayde. "It's a new twist, even if it's an old gag."

"Please! I'm not . . ."

"But bribing a copper—*attempting* to bribe a copper, attempting to bribe two coppers—you're up queer street, Hanson. You're really in trouble."

"All right." Hanson's sigh was one of utter defeat; of unconditional surrender. "You tell me. What is it you do want?"

"Ah." Blayde smiled. And such a smile. The smile of a hungry tiger within easy reach of a good breakfast. He purred, "What have you to offer, Hanson?"

"The—the bloke downstairs. He said . . ."

"He sent you to me. I left word."

Hanson waited.

Blayde said, "We don't raid you, you go bust eventually? Am I reading the instructions correctly?"

"Eventually," admitted Hanson heavily.

"Whereas, if we do raid you?"

"That's all I'm asking."

"And," said Blayde softly, "if we do our job properly? If we raid you every day for—let's say—six months?"

"You—you wouldn't!"

"Don't make the odds too high," warned Blayde, and his voice was suddenly very business-like. Very cold. "We'd be doing our job. Doing it as it should be done."

"Harassment," breathed Hanson.

"Don't make me laugh," snapped Blayde. "It's what we're paid for. I doubt if you'd last six months."

"I—I wouldn't last three," whispered Hanson.

"Fine." Blayde's tone thawed just a little. "So, now we come to the price. Not a bribe. Information. Information about Don Shelton."

"D—Don Shelton?" For a moment Hanson looked like a badly trained horse, terrified at an approaching motor car.

"He's your cousin," Blayde reminded him.

"I—I know. He's my . . ."

"You're great friends. Real buddy-buddies."

Hanson nodded.

"Tell us about him," encouraged Blayde.

"What—what d'you want to know?"

"Anything. Everything."

"Look, I don't wanna . . ."

"You don't want to go bankrupt," Blayde reminded him.

"He's—he's my *cousin*," breathed Hanson.

Blayde nodded and waited.

"We're pals. More like brothers."

"You know how much you owe him," said Blayde softly. "You know how much you're prepared to pay. All I've done is name the price."

"How—how much do you know?" It was a plea, barely audible.

"Enough," lied Blayde. "Maybe enough to stand you alongside him in the dock."

"No . . . I didn't. We were drunk one night. He—he told me. How the hell you got wind of it . . ." Hanson closed, then opened, his eyes then, in a strangely steady voice, said, "You're right. He murdered his wife. Poisoned her. We both thought—y'know—it wouldn't come out."

"It's come out." Blayde, in turn, managed

to keep his voice calm and steady. He glanced at the open-mouthed Rath, then continued, "Everything you know, Hanson. Every last thing he told you. Detective Constable Rath will take the statement. He'll—er—take time off from fishing, I'm sure."

"Fishing?" Hanson stared.

"He fishes," explained Blayde. "Sometimes he's very lucky. If the water's deep enough, he occasionally lands a shark."

Over the years that short, but immaculately paced, interview became a yardstick of "possibility" within the county constabulary. How to shake the machine gently and, without even putting a coin in the slot, collect the jackpot. What to say, how and when to say it . . . and when to say damn-all.

To Rath, it raised Blayde until he sat alongside the gods. He (Rath) was no longer a joke. True, Blayde had pulled the blinder, and never once did Rath seek to deny or hide that fact, but Rath took the statement—four foolscape pages of it—and on the strength of that statement H.M. Coroner authorised the opening of the grave, and from that moment Shelton was on his way to the hanging shed.

It was Blayde's first murder. The detective

inspector, from Haggthorpe D.H.Q., arrived and fannied around, but that was merely for the sake of appearances and to make it look like a murder enquiry. It was Blayde's case, and Chapman sat quietly in the background and made sure it stayed Blayde's case and, if Blayde wanted to hand more than a fair shair of the kudos to Rath that, too, was Blayde's prerogative, but no high-ranker was going to slip in and do a soft-shoe-take-over job.

It was Blayde's first murder. It was Rath's first murder. It was also their first exhumation . . . and that, too, was something to live with them for the rest of their days.

The coffin was the first one down, therefore the grave-opening could be authorised by H.M. Coroner; had it been lower than the top coffin it would have needed Home Office approval. But the ghouls and general rubber-neckers who make up a percentage of the population being what they are, the usual pattern had to be followed. The gates of the cemetery were closed at the normal time. Gradually, in order not to arouse undue curiousity, uniformed officers were delivered to the outside of the cemetery and took up patrol positions, in order to isolate the whole cemetery from the outside world. A high tarpaulin screen was rigged up around the grave, and a police van, with layers of tarpaulin spread on the inside floor, was parked within easy carrying distance. Light came from a single bulb, with a hand-holder and a length of wire which snaked under the tarpaulin screens to a socket in a brickbuilt tool-shed about twenty yards away. Two muscular grave-diggers, the Home Office pathologist, his secretary, Blayde, Rath and a volunteer uniformed constable were the only people allowed within the tarpaulin surround.

At just after 11 p.m. the pathologist glanced at his watch and spoke to the grave-diggers.

"Right, I think we'll start. As gentle as possible, please. She's been buried almost three years. The coffin will have started to rot, and I'd like it as intact as possible. I suggest you keep your feet as near the side of the grave as possible and when you touch wood, stop."

The pathologist lighted a cigarette. His secretary jotted an entry into her notebook. Blayde, too, took out cigarettes, offered the packet to Rath and the uniformed constable, and they stood to one side and watched the grave-diggers go about their task.

There was complete silence until the pathologist spoke.

He craned his neck and gazed at the sky, then remarked, "A nice night for it, anyway. No sign of clouds."

"There might be a frost before morning." Blayde tried to meet ease of conversation with equal ease of conversation. "We're pretty exposed up here."

"Yes . . . I suppose we are."

It was something to marvel at; the quiet, everyday manner in which this highly educated man accepted a scene which might have been lifted from a horror movie. Presumably he knew what to expect when they reached the coffin. Blayde certainly didn't. He'd seen corpses; scores of corpses; bodies bloody and mangled after fatal road accidents. He'd been present at post mortem examinations; the P.M. Room held no horrors for him. But this! After three years what the hell did a corpse look like? After three years underground and encased in a coffin?

The diggers worked on, silently and skilfully. Carefully, too. The top soil had been removed, and that had been steady muscle-work. But because they'd opened other graves with coffins already long-buried—because in the past they'd been obliged to take the requisite care—they gradually began to scoop rather than dig. They worked facing each other, feet straddling the deepening hole, boots thrust into the sides and seeking foot holds other than on the loosened surface of the bottom.

The others—the pathologist and his secretary, the two detectives and the uniformed constable—all wore gumboots. The pathologist chain-smoked but, as far as his outward demeanour was concerned, this was habit rather than nerves. The impression was that he had infinite patience. Blayde tried to match the pathologist's impassiveness. Rath's expression was set—as if he'd forced his facial muscles to remain motionless—but he was unable to hide that final hint of trepidation from his eyes. The uniformed constable stood apart, stamped his feet to assist his circulation and had his hands thrust deep into his overcoat pockets.

The single light bulb had been fastened to a suitable upright—one of the uprights holding the tarpaulin in place—and its harsh glare seemed to give an excess of light and an excess of shadow. Black shadows and a light which robbed whatever it touched of any depth of colour. The shadows of the diggers moved and spilled over onto the growing mound of earth.

Bobbying. This, too, was bobbying. This fearful place of the dead. This grave-robbing in search of evidence. This tightening of nerves already at piano-wire tension. It wasn't all beer and skittles . . . not by a few light-years. It was also *this.* A situation on which any normal man might turn his back and from which he might hurry away. But coppers weren't expected to be "normal men". The stuff of which nightmares are made was also part of their duty.

One of the diggers said, "It's here."

He tossed his shovel onto the heap of earth alongside the grave and, steadied by his mate, bent forward and scooped the soil clear with his hand.

The pathologist laid a sheet of plastic alongside the lips of the grave and lowered himself onto his stomach.

"The light," said Blayde, and the constable fumbled the knots loose and held the bulb above the head of the partly exposed coffin.

The woodwork of the lid was rotting. The grain had curled upwards, opening itself as the combination of damp and time had worked their destruction.

The pathologist said, "One of the bags, please," and the secretary stopped note-taking long enough to hand him a self-sealing plastic bag. He handed the bag to the digger and said, "Soil samples from above the coffin, please. Then, more samples from the sides of the coffin and, when we've lifted it, from the soil under the coffin."

The digger, still steadied by his colleague, worked silently and carefully as the pathologist handed him the bags, one at a time. The secretary tagged each bag, and continued taking notes.

It took almost fifteen minutes to clear the coffin lid of soil, then as long again to clear the soil, handful at a time, from around the sides. The wood was oak—Blayde knew enough about wood to recognise good oak when he saw it and despite its condition—and that was a small mercy. Anything less, and the coffin would have been split and rotten.

The digger said, "If you can steady us, I think we can lift it high enough for you to take over."

"Not without gloves."

The pathologist motioned to his secretary, and she handed heavy duty rubber gloves to the grave-diggers. Then similar gloves to Blayde and Rath, then to the constable and the pathologist.

"If you'll just steady us, for the first few feet," said the digger.

They spread polythene sacks along the two sides of the grave, then—Blayde and the constable at one side and the pathologist and Rath at the other—they sprawled and reached down to grasp the diggers by the shoulders. The diggers worked their boots into secure footholds, then leaned forward and forced their fingers under the coffin.

"Take your time," murmured Blayde.

One of the diggers grunted acknowledgement. The single bulb—replaced to its previous position by the constable—swung gently and, by its sway, seemed to add a final dimension of horror to the scene.

One of the diggers muttered, "When you're ready."

"Ready," echoed his colleague.

"Very gently," warned the pathologist.

The diggers tensed their muscles, began to straighten their backs and their legs, and the men on the lips of the grave tightened their grip on the shoulders of the diggers. The coffin came away from the floor of the grave with a soft and disgusting sucking sound. Sweat was shining on the faces of the diggers by the time they were upright, with the coffin held between them.

One of them gasped, "Okay . . . take it off us."

The four men at the lips shifted their positions, knelt on the polythene sacks and took the weight of the coffin. They raised it high enough for the diggers to duck and scramble out of the grave and, from then on, it was a matter of patience to ease the coffin onto the plastic sheeting used by the pathologist, wrap the sheeting around it and carry it to the waiting van.

Then they peeled off their gloves, Blayde passed round the cigarettes and they steadied their nerves and their breathing in complete silence.

Later—at around three o'clock in the morning—Blayde and Rath played out the final scene under the strip lighting of a tile-walled mortuary. The law required them to be present in the dual capacity of coppers and coroner's officers, when the coffin was finally opened.

The pathologist, now wearing a heavy rubber apron, surgical gloves and a clean pair of gumboots, wrestled the screws from their sockets and eased the warped lid clear of the coffin. Rath clapped his hand to his mouth and hurried towards the toilet. A fleeting look of disgust touched the secretary's face, then she went on with her note-taking. Blayde gritted his teeth and forced himself to watch as the off-white slime striated with bilious green, slopped down the sides of the casket and clung in thinning, mucoid strands to the lid.

The pathologist leaned the soiled lid against the post mortem table, walked to the sink, swilled the surgical gloves clean, then returned to the coffin and plunged his hands deep into the foul goo that had once been living flesh.

When he removed his closed hand the gloves were alive with tiny, writhing maggots. Life from the entrails of death. The stage well beyond that of mere putrefaction.

He looked up and smiled at the grey-faced Blayde.

He said, "We're lucky, sergeant. Any poison, we'll find it in these little chaps."

The boffins did their work. The poison was identified as a barbiturate, and the dosage was estimated as being well beyond the fatal threshold. Enquiries and statements left no doubt in anybody's mind; the late Mrs.

Shelton had "enjoyed ill health"; she'd been God's gift to the drug manufacturers and a pain in the neck to the local G.P. As a mate to a healthy, red-blooded male she was a non-starter. As far as Shelton was concerned, poisoning was both more final and cheaper than divorce, and Shelton had always been a man to count the pennies. The doctor issuing the Death Certificate took a grilling at Lessford Assize Court but, as he almost tearfully explained, his patient had insisted she was a sick (even a dying) woman, and when she had died the issuing of the certificate had almost amounted to the final move in a personal wish-fulfilment. A certain amount of tear-jerking histrionics on the part of the Defence failed to convince a hard-headed jury that the poison had been self-administered and, in due course, the judge allowed the square of black velvet to be positioned atop his wig.

Both Blayde and Rath received commendations from the court "for pressing home a particularly difficult enquiry" and, within the stipulated time-scale, Shelton dropped into eternity.

"And all," remarked Blayde, "because some light-fingered germ nicked a crate of whisky from a parked van."

The theft of the whisky remained undetected.

12

YET, and despite this undoubted flair for policing, Blayde remained aloof from his colleagues. Even Rath handled their friendship with a care usually reserved for dangerously thin ice. Nor was it consciously Blayde's fault. He wasn't snooty, he wasn't officious, he wasn't in any way untrustworthy. He just didn't mix. The various social and sporting functions, which to other officers were part and parcel of the job, held no interest for Blayde. He could interview, he could interrogate, but when it came to ordinary, everyday conversation he was awkward and gauche. Pretence was not part of his nature. If he was asked a question, he answered it honestly . . . who the hell it hurt or who the hell it offended. If the subject of a conversation was beyond his knowledge, he was blunt enough to admit his ignorance and refused to express an opinion.

In September, 1954, Lessford University began a series of extra-mural evening classes on Criminology at Haggthorpe Y.M.C.A.

Blayde enrolled. In a class of fifteen, he was the only police officer, and this fact both surprised and saddened him. Bobbying, while not an art form, was nevertheless a skill; it had to be learned and, other than on the streets, there seemed little enough opportunity seriously to study its multifarious subtleties and side-issues. The book of words insisted that a police officer should present the evidence for a conviction and after that divorce himself utterly from the court's decision, but that (in Blayde's opinion) was a crackpot attitude. Bobbies dealt with crime, therefore they dealt with criminals . . . and criminals were people. A man went inside for a stretch, but outside prison he might have a wife and family. They suffered, too. Often they suffered more than the convicted man. And, anyway, after his spell of imprisonment he'd be one of the community again. What was he going to be like? Which of his attitudes would have changed and why? What the hell was the point of banging a thief up for a few years with the knowledge that, when he returned to circulation he was not going to be only a thief, he was also going to be a cop-hater? And so often putting a first-timer into a prison stuffed to the ceiling with old lags was tantamount to sending him to a university; he'd come out knowing a damn sight more about general villainy than when the court sentenced him.

Hell's teeth! That classroom should have been stiff with coppers.

The classes were held every Thursday, from 7.30 p.m. until 9.30 p.m., and Blayde's fellow-wisdom-seekers, both male and female, were a mixed bunch. Trainee probation officers, Do-It-Yourself students eager to acquire snippets of knowledge with which to baffle their way into some tin-pot do-goodery position, pensioners who refused to allow their brains to stagnate merely because their bodies had become a little creaky, a couple of run-of-the-mill housewives seeking some outlet for pent-up mental energy . . . as mixed a bunch as you could wish for.

The tutor was a middle-aged man, soft-spoken and round-shouldered, as if weary of carrying the great weight of learning with which he was burdened. But a pleasant, smiling man, with a tendency to start most points open for discussion with the words, "Let us assume . . ."

For the first two evenings Blayde was content to sit quietly and be reminded of already-half-forgotten aspects of the theory of Criminal Law. "Let us assume we are dealing with a statutary crime and the Act makes no mention, express or implied, of mens rea . . ." "Let us assume that a man or a woman vanishes from his or her home leaving a note which suggests that he or she intends to commit suicide and, as a result thereof, a great deal of expense is involved in police searches and the like when, in fact, the note was a hoax . . ." "Let us assume that an extreme political party secretly organises a march or a demonstration without notifying the chief officer of police of that district of their intention . . ."

It was all great stuff; the fruit and fibre of forensic wrangling. And Blayde (although, occasionally, he could have given a dogmatic answer backed by some Court of Criminal Appeal decision) sat back and listened to the sway of lay argument. These people—or at least most of them—respected the law; wanted it to work, but in the main were unaware of the difficulty of framing a legal system capable of checking lawlessness, while at the same time retaining the full freedoms of law-abiding members of the public. The tutor smiled benignly and quietly turned one argument against another. His task was to make people think; to encourage them to feel their way towards an acceptable solution . . . sometimes a solution which had yet to be pronounced by an appeal court.

Then on the third Thursday (it was October 7th) Blayde found himself involved in a great treadmill of discussion concerning criminals and some of the more obvious reasons why they were criminals.

The tutor had said, "Let us assume you are a criminal. A convicted criminal, with previous convictions for serious offences against the law. For some reason—any reason—you genuinely wish to make a new start as a decent, responsible member of the community. How would you go about it?"

The obvious answers had been aired—moving house, moving jobs, all the pretty-pretty, pat solutions—and each solution had been gently stone-walled by the smiling tutor.

The tutor murmured, "And assuming you were the daughter of such a man?"

"She hasn't much hope," said Blayde bluntly.

"She could leave home," suggested one of the housewives.

"Let us assume she couldn't leave home,"

said the tutor. "Let us assume she has a sick mother and, because she loves her mother, she feels a strong moral obligation to stay at home."

"In that case, she has even less hope," said Blayde.

"You mean you're condemning . . ."

"Let us assume it is harsh reality," interrupted the tutor gently. "Mr. Blayde, why do you think it harsh reality?"

Blayde felt the eyes of the others on his face. Angry eyes. Outraged eyes. The eyes of ordinary people, in the main decent people, to whom crime was little more than a column in a newspaper. To them the criminal—even the most hardened criminal—could be coaxed out of crime. Nobody was beyond redemption. More than that even. Everybody, deep down, was anxious to be redeemed.

The tutor murmured, "Mr. Blayde."

"All right." Blayde felt irrational rage rise within him. If these nincompoops wanted the truth, they could have it. From the horse's mouth, and no holds barred. "You get a lass, there. Her father's as bent as they come. That's her family, remember. The only thing she's known. All through her childhood, all through her teens, every minute of her life.

Her father's nicking things. In and out of prison. Maybe a tearaway for good measure. What's she supposed to think? What yardstick has she?

"Because of her father, she knows others of his breed. They're her father's friends. They're her friends. Their children are her friends. Everything—everybody she comes in contact with—bent. She lives in this world. It's her only world. And if she can't free herself, she's done for. And when she reaches marrying age, who the hell's going to marry her, other than her own class? It's a self-perpetuating cycle. And, what's more, she knows it. If we grant her compassion enough to stay with a sick mother, in spite of a criminal father, logic insists that we credit her with knowing what goes on around her. Of being able to see the tight limits of her own life." He paused then, in a gruff voice, ended, "As I've said . . . she hasn't much hope."

"Crime," sneered one of the student types, "being hereditary?"

"Crime," said Blayde, "having a lot to do with a person's immediate environment. How he's brought up. What examples are set for him."

"And assuming," murmured the tutor, "she

meets and marries a man from a similar background to herself? And with her own ideas?"

Blayde said, "She can count herself lucky."

"What if she meets a convicted thief and sets out to reform him?" asked one of the women students. "Isn't that a way out?"

"A convicted thief?" Blayde raised a quizzical eyebrow.

"Yes." The woman nodded.

"A recidivist?" pressed Blayde.

"Yes, if you like."

"And she marries him in the hope of reforming him?"

"Yes."

"He'll break her heart," said Blayde bluntly.

"That," said one of the housewives angrily, "is one of the most narrow-minded remarks I've ever heard. What you're saying, in effect, is that some people are beyond hope. Beyond help. Beyond understanding."

"What I'm saying," replied Blayde, "is that here we are discussing crime, discussing criminals, and this is the first time we've touched the bottom of the barrel. Some of 'em don't want help. Some of 'em don't want understanding. They're rotten, because they like being rotten. A percentage—not quite the small percentage some of you people might think—and certainly a percentage large enough to need taking into consideration . . . otherwise a lot of time is going to be wasted getting nowhere. Outside prison, they live in their own tight communities and they like it there. It's their chosen way of life. You measure them by their yardstick . . . otherwise you get a headache and that's all you do get. They inter-marry. Produce offspring of their own kind. They may be rich, they may be poor. They may be outwardly charming. But they're still criminals, because they've been taught that criminality is both a normal and a very desirable way of life."

"Let us assume," said the tutor quickly, and acting as referee. "Let us assume that Mr. Blayde has argued a good case. Let us accept the proposition he makes. In that case, what course of action might be appropriate?"

The expression "opening a can of worms" flitted across Blayde's mind. The arguments were many and tortuous; they ranged from a blind belief that nobody was beyond redemption to the "special unit for persistent offenders" theory, from the use of corporal punishment in order to fight terror with terror to an out-of-the-world proposition that the drug manufacturers should be encouraged to come up with some wonder potion capable of turning all men from wickedness.

It was quite a session, and the tutor's eyes twinkled mischievously as he deliberately flicked the ball of controversy from one student to another.

At half-past nine he chuckled and said, "Quite a stimulating evening, ladies and gentlemen. One of the most interesting evenings I've had for a long time."

The class-members wandered out into the darkened street, and Blayde felt a touch on his arm. He turned and saw the quiet woman smiling shyly, apologetically, at him.

He said, "Yes?"

"I'm sorry." The smile wavered a little.

"What for?" Blayde returned the smile.

"For being rude. For saying you were defeatist . . . and starting it all."

"That's okay." The smile expanded into a friendly grin. "It's what we're here for."

"Still, I really shouldn't have . . ."

"It's a little like training tigers," said Blayde gently. "You can read books on the subject. You can even listen to experts. But once you're in the cage with 'em . . . that's a different matter."

"Are they?" Without conscious thought, they fell into step as they walked slowly towards the car park. "Are they really as bad as that?"

"Some." He paused, then added, "Others are ordinary folk with a kink in their personalities."

"It must be interesting," she mused.

"What?"

"Being a policeman. Being a detective."

"It's hard work. Time-consuming." They continued a few steps, then he asked. "What about you?"

"Me?"

"What brings you to these classes?"

"I'm looking for work, eventually. Sociology, I hope."

"Oh, my God!"

"You don't approve?" There was a touch of angry impatience in the question.

"Oh yes, I approve." The slow smile was a complete apology. "But they don't approve. That's the trouble."

" 'They'?"

"The thieves, the muggers, the crooks. They don't want to know what makes 'em tick. And unless they want to help . . ." He left the sentence unfinished.

"My husband wouldn't have agreed," she said quietly.

"In that case he's a very optimistic chap."

"He's dead," she said flatly.

"Oh. I'm sorry. I didn't mean to . . ."

"A car accident. Almost two years ago." She gave the information in a staccato voice—a "name-rank-and-number" voice—as if that was all she was allowed to say, and all she was prepared to say.

As they neared the car park, she slowed and said, "I'll leave you here, Mr. Blayde. I mustn't miss my bus."

"I thought . . ." Blayde stopped.

"What?"

"The car park. I thought you had a car."

"No." She allowed a quick smile to touch her lips. "I—er—I can't run a car since Bill died."

"Where's your home?" asked Blayde.

"Just outside Sayworth, but . . ."

"It's on my way."

"To Bigton?" she mocked teasingly.

"It's not far out of my way." Blayde corrected himself.

"No, I suppose not."

"So. Why can't I run you home?"

"You can," she said. "On one understanding."

"What's that?"

"It isn't a pick-up."

"You," grinned Blayde, "picked *me* up . . . remember?"

"It isn't that either."

"Just a friendly gesture," promised Blayde. "No more, no less."

Her name was Margaret Ogden. Her age, in the late twenties . . . possibly the *very* early thirties. She personified "moderation"; she was moderately good looking, moderately well educated, moderately appealing in every way. Perhaps that was one reason why Blayde felt at ease in her company. She showed genuine interest in his work, but even then only in moderation . . . she wasn't nosey. He called for her on the way to the class, dropped her off on his way home after the class, and those comparatively short rides began to assume something of importance. The warm silences. The few times she opened up a little about her late husband. Not seeking sympathy, but merely remembering and voicing those memories to somebody who seemed to understand.

She lived in a maisonette—a purpose-built

block of small apartments—on the outskirts of Sayworth and to afford it and at the same time live (again) moderately, she helped out in a pre-school kindergarten for children of working mothers. "Which is strange, because I don't have any real feeling for children."

"What's so strange? Who does like the horrible little brats?"

She'd laughed, and thought he was joking.

On November 18th, he picked her up as usual and, as she settled into the front passenger's seat, he said, "We cut off as soon as the class closes tonight."

"Oh . . . why?"

"We're eating out. I've booked a place. I know Haggthorpe well. It's a nice little restaurant. You'll like it."

"We go Dutch," she said quietly.

Blayde engaged first, moved from the kerb, then said, "In that case we go hungry."

"Bob, I can't let you . . ."

"It's not expensive. It's not The Savoy. Nice, but with realistic prices."

"All the more reason . . ."

"I'm treating myself." His tone carried little expression, and he stared at the road ahead. "I don't often treat myself, but tonight I'm going to make an exception. And you're part of the treat."

"You're a nice man, Bob," she said gently.

"That's why I'm doing it. I'd like at least one person not to think too badly of me."

It was one of those restaurants rarely found mentioned in standard *Good Food Guide* publications. This, not because it was less than excellent, but rather because it was treasured, like a secret garden, by both the proprietor and the clientele. It was a private place, serving fine food to customers who returned and returned again. The waitresses were pleasant and efficient. The linen was starched and spotless. The tableware sparkled in the light of tiny individual stand-lamps. And—that extra touch which made so much difference—the vase on each table held a tiny spray of freshly-cut but inexpensive flowers.

Margaret Ogden inhaled cigarette smoke and said, "I didn't know such places still existed."

"Not many." Blayde smiled his pleasure. "Being a bobby has its hidden perks. We know where these spots are."

"Thanks," she said simply, but it was far more than a polite word.

They were at the coffee-and-cigarettes stage. The meal had been mouth-wateringly good. The rainbow trout had been fresh—indeed it had been swimming around in the water of a trout-farm that same afternoon—and the trimmings had been just right and just enough. The half-bottle of wine they'd shared had relaxed them without making them garrulous, which was what a good wine should. And now the meal was over and they were talking and smoking and sipping good black coffee.

Quite suddenly she said, "What's it like being a policeman?"

"Fine." That was his immediate answer to the question, then he drew on his cigarette, and added qualifications. "Sometimes you curse the job. The hours. The inconvenience. The fact that you handle so much crass stupidity." He paused again, then ended, "It can also be very lonely."

"No friends?" she asked with a smile.

"You have to make them very carefully."

"But you must have friends."

"Not many," he confessed. "I don't rush things . . . not *those* sort of things. It's not my way."

"But you get there?"

"Eventually, if they wait."

"Bob." She leaned fractionally forward across the table. "We might be getting too friendly."

"Wouldn't you want that?" he asked gently.

"I don't know." A tiny frown etched itself across her forehead. "No . . . that's wrong. That's unfair. I do know. What I don't know is how far."

"You're a nice lady." It seemed a strange thing to say, and yet the way he said it made it the only thing to say; the only combination of words to make sense. He stretched out an arm and touched the back of her hand with his fingers. He repeated, "You're a nice lady, Margaret. That counts for a great deal."

"Enough?" There was a hint of sadness in the question.

"I'll settle for that," he said quietly.

She raised her head, stared into his eyes for a moment, then shook her head as if in mild amazement.

"Have I said something wrong?" he asked.

"So much like Bill," she breathed. "So very much like Bill. I wouldn't have believed."

"No." He drummed gently on the back of her hand with his fingertips. "Bill was unique . . . like the rest of us. Nobody quite like him. There never is. That's what makes life so interesting. You never meet the same person twice. No comparisons. There can't be. There mustn't be. Otherwise, you . . ."

"Excuse me, sergeant."

Blayde looked up. The proprietor was standing at his shoulder, looking a mix of worry and embarrassment.

He said, "There's a telephone call for you, sergeant. It's urgent. It's from a Mr. Rath."

"Okay," sighed Blayde. He patted the woman's hand, smiled and said, "That's another of the joys of being a policeman. Within reason, you have to be on call . . . just in case."

He was away from the table less than five minutes and when he returned he was a changed man.

He said, "Sorry, pet. I can't drop you off, you'll have to come too."

"What is it? Why should . . ."

"Please!" he urged. "I've settled the bill. I'll tell you on the way."

Rath had notified Blayde before he'd notified anybody else. Because (as far as Rath was concerned) Blayde was *Blayde* . . . and Blayde could work miracles. Nevertheless, the street was sealed off and some fairly heavy brass—

including Chapman—made up the police presence when Blayde braked to a halt. Blayde said, "Stay there, pet. I'll be back," then opened the car door and sprinted to where the action was.

"Where is he?" he demanded.

"Up there. Second floor. Third window from the left." Chapman pointed.

"And he still has the twelve-bore?"

"We wouldn't be standing here like spare pricks if he hadn't."

"What's he done so far?"

"He thinks he's killed his brother-in-law. Some sort of a family set-to. Now he's threatening to shoot anybody who tries to arrest him."

"Who's tried?" asked Blayde.

"For Christ's sake, sergeant. There's a lunatic up there with a . . ."

"I don't give a damn if he has the Brigade of Guards up there with him. Either we run Bigton, or he does."

Chapman breathed heavily through his nose. This bloody sergeant, Blayde, was mad. Stark, staring bloody mad! Nobody with an ounce of gumption argued the finer points of etiquette from the wrong end of a twelve-bore.

In a brittle, controlled voice, Chapman said,

"We've sent to Headquarters for firearms. When *they* arrive . . ."

"I know, we'll play Cowboys and bloody Indians."

"Sergeant! You may not agree with what . . ."

"Has he killed anybody yet?"

"No. I've already told you. His brother-in-law's been shot. He might have to have a leg off, but . . ."

"In that case, we'd better take that shotgun off him before he kills somebody."

"Sergeant, I forbid you to . . ."

"I'm off duty." Blayde turned to leave the group. "I'll come on duty when I arrest him."

It was lunacy, but magnificent lunacy. Blayde walked towards the house at a very normal, very everyday pace. Chapman, and about twenty other policemen, held their breath and watched. Rath sprinted from a group of uniformed coppers and fell in step alongside Blayde.

"There's no need," said Blayde.

"His name's Eric." Rath ignored the invitation to return to safety. "Eric Gold. It's a twin-barrel. I think he's terrified of what he's done. That's just a guess, of course."

"A good guess." Blayde neither slowed nor hastened his pace.

"Second landing, last room on the right," said Rath.

"You'll do as you're told," grunted Blayde.

"Aye."

"*Exactly* what you're told."

"You're the boss, Bob."

As they neared the house, Blayde asked, "Any coppers in the house?"

"A uniformed sergeant. Three—maybe four—uniformed coppers."

"Let's get them out first."

They reached the house and walked into the hall. A worried uniformed sergeant nodded silent greeting. The hall was well lit, as were the stairs and the landings. Blayde peered up the stairwell.

Blayde said, ""Everybody out, except Rath and me."

The uniformed sergeant said, "I've a man on each landing and . . ."

"Get 'em all out," snapped Blayde. "Walk away. Walk where the street-lighting can let him see."

"Er—what if he shoots?"

"He hasn't shot *us* and we were coming. He won't shoot anybody leaving."

"You seem bloody sure. He's had a go at his brother-in-law."

"We aren't his brother-in-law."

The uniformed sergeant shrugged, called his men from the stairs and the landings, then left.

"Keep behind me," said Blayde as he started up the stairs. "Not a move—not a word—unless I tell you."

Rath grunted understanding.

It was a good house; "upper-middle-class"; some of its neighbours had been turned into flats, but this one was as it had been built. Well carpeted, good lighting, solid, old-fashioned furniture. As Blayde climbed the stairs the thought struck him that they didn't make banisters and handrails like this any more. They wouldn't know how.

On the second landing Blayde paused. He nodded towards a closed door.

"That the room?" he asked.

"Aye."

"Right. Stay near the wall. Keep out of range. And *nothing* till I tell you."

"Understood."

Blayde walked quietly along the passage, stopped in front of the door and checked what he was up against. A four-panel door. It looked solid, maybe it wasn't quite as solid as it looked. The knob was on his right as he faced the door. It opened away from him . . . and before anything else it had to be opened.

He positioned himself by the wall alongside the doorknob, then reached out a hand and knocked, moderately loudly, on the upper panel.

"Who is it?" The voice was high-pitched. A man's voice, but on the verge of sounding like a woman's scream.

"Police." Blayde kept his voice low and steady. Loud enough to be heard beyond the closed door, and lacking the flutter which was making his stomach muscles quiver a little. He added, "Detective Sergeant Blayde."

"Go away," screamed the voice. "Go away or I'll shoot."

"I'm not armed," said Blayde.

"Keep away from that door."

"There's only me," lied Blayde. "All the others have left."

"Two of you came in."

"The other detective's downstairs," lied Blayde.

"I don't believe you."

"Eric. Eric Gold . . . isn't it?"

"What's it to you?"

"You're being foolish, Eric."

"You don't know. You don't know what . . ."

"You could have killed your brother-in-law."

There was a pause, then the voice said, "You're bluffing. Of course you are. You're bluffing. You're trying to . . .'

"I don't know what you mean," interrupted Blayde.

"He's dead. I meant to kill him. It's what he deserves. So don't try . . ."

"He might lose a leg. He won't lose his life."

"You're—you're just saying that." The high voice had a sobbing quality.

Blayde pulled a handkerchief from his pocket and wiped the gathering sweat from his forehead. Rath made a move, and Blayde waved him back against the wall.

He called, "Eric, don't be a damn fool. Don't make things worse."

"Keep away from that door."

"You're a lousy shot, Eric. Your brother-in-law's alive."

"I don't believe you."

"I can't prove it." Blayde fought to make his voice reasonable. "I can't bring him along for you to see. He's in hospital. Possibly on an operating table having his leg amputated. But he's alive . . . and he'll live."

"You're telling lies."

It was an impasse. Verbal communication had been established; the first step had been made. But if something more wasn't done, the guns would arrive from County Headquarters, and after that . . .

Blayde called, "I'm coming in, Eric."

"Keep away from that door."

"I'm coming in."

"I'll shoot. I swear, I'll shoot."

Blayde took a deep breath, glared at Rath to stay where he was and keep quiet then, with his back to the wall alongside the door, he stretched out a hand and turned the knob as quickly and as noisily as possible.

He jerked his hand clear as the double roar filled the passage and the landing with noise. The woodwork of the door was blasted to hell generally, and especially around the lock. The shot patterned the plaster of the opposite wall . . . but two shots had been fired. He *thought* two shots. He *hoped* two shots. He hoped to hell two shots.

He left the wall, faced the smashed door and slammed the heel of his right shoe against the lock. The door flew open and, steadying his action, Blayde stepped into the room and faced the man with the shotgun.

Gold had broken the gun and was fumbling fresh cartridges into the breech. He closed the gun with a snap, thumbed back the hammers and levelled the barrels at Blayde's chest.

"Do *that*, boy, and you really *will* hang."

Blayde knew he was talking for his life. He watched the fingers thread themselves through the trigger-guard.

"Do it, and look me in the face," he challenged.

The man was panting. Sweating. Wild-eyed and capable of just about anything. Blayde prayed he wasn't quite capable of *everything*.

"We talk," he said and this time he put authority into his voice.

"I've—I've nothing to say."

"You've still something to say," snapped Blayde. He deliberately kept his eyes from the barrels of the shotgun; looked the man, Gold, full in the face. "You've excuses to make. Kill me . . . *then* you'll have nothing to say. After that, excuses won't mean a damn thing."

"He—he called me . . ."

"That's not important."

"He accused me of . . ."

"That's not important," repeated Blayde.

"I—I lost my temper." Gold lowered his eyes from Blayde's gaze. The barrels of the gun tilted a little lower, but the fingers remained inside the trigger-guard. Slowly, tears spilled from his eyes and rolled down each side of his nose.

"Not now," Blayde reminded him in a less harsh tone. "You're not in a temper now."

"No," whispered the man. "Not now."

"And," said Blayde deliberately, "I'm going to take that gun away from you before you do any more damage."

The man raised tear-filled eyes, but the barrels remained lowered.

"Nobody's going to lay a glove on you," said Blayde soothingly. He moved forward gently. "Just let me have that gun. Just that . . . then we can all stop worrying."

"No." But it was a half-hearted objection.

"Come on, Eric." And now Blayde's voice was coaxing and reasonable. "You've been foolish, but so far no real harm done. Leave it at that."

Blayde's outstretched hand grasped the gun barrels. For a moment Gold tightened his grip, then he released the hold and allowed Blayde to gently take the twelve-bore, slide it away from the fingers and ease down the hammers. Finally, Blayde swung the gun and sent it spinning through the window, shattering glass and, in so doing, breaking the tension.

The reaction set in in the street. The trembling, as if with great cold. The near-inability to hold a cigarette steady enough for Rath to touch the end with a match flame.

Chapman said, "My office at ten o'clock tomorrow morning, sergeant."

Blayde nodded and walked a little unsteadily towards the car and Margaret Ogden. She needed no telling. She moved to behind the steering wheel and Blayde flopped into the front passenger seat.

Blayde opened his eyes and, for a moment, didn't understand. It was a strange bed, a strange bedroom and the pyjamas he was wearing weren't his own.

Then he remembered . . .

He really hadn't been fit to drive the car back to Bigton. He'd wanted to. He'd tried to wave aside her worry, her objections. He hadn't wanted this. Truly, he hadn't wanted it . . . not in the circumstances of last night.

He'd wanted to drop her off—let her drive the car as far as Sayworth—then return to his own place.

"Bob, you mustn't."

"I'll be okay. I'll drive slowly. Carefully."

"At least come inside for a drink. Something to steady your nerves."

And he'd accepted the invitation and even *then* . . . Jesus Christ, even *then!* Hot sweet tea, laced with brandy. And cigarettes. And the warmth and comfort of her maisonette. And then, the talk. Perhaps most of all the talk. The things said. But, more important, the things left unsaid.

"You could have been killed." There'd been real concern in her voice.

"Not face-to-face." He grinned—tried to grin—and it had come out a twisted grimace.

"He'd already shot somebody."

"Not killed him."

"He must have meant to kill him."

He'd shrugged.

"It was a silly thing to do, Bob. Thoughtless."

"Thoughtless?"

"What about . . ." She'd closed her mouth, blushed slightly, then whispered, "You could have been killed."

"It's what I'm paid for." He tried to steer the conversation along safer lines. Away from things that might have been said and might have been regretted. "We take an oath . . . we're supposed to understand it. To mean it. If there *has* to be a killing—and if there's a choice—let it be a copper. When the boom drops, that's what he's there for. To protect life. With his own, if necessary."

So po-faced. But he'd meant it. He still meant it. Last night he'd said it for a reason, but it had meant damn all.

Damn what the medics called delayed shock. In that upstairs room, facing Gold, facing the shotgun. He'd been scared—who the hell wouldn't have been scared?—but his job was not to be scared, and he'd done his job. A calculated risk, but if it hadn't come off . . . At the time he'd been very objective—he'd forced himself to be objective, because absolute objectivity had been the only hope—but then, like being hit across the back of the neck with a cricket bat, subjectivity had taken over. Delayed shock. The shakes. The trembles. And then her presence, and the brandy-laced tea, and Crosby . . .

Crosby, "The Old Groaner." These days the kids went wild about Sinatra and, indeed,

Sinatra could belt out a ballad like few people on earth. But Bing . . . nobody was quite like Bing. That easy, one-to-one voice; soft, with a gentle chuckle on each line. The voice of a happy and contented man singing happy and contented melodies. *Out of Nowhere, Just One More Chance, Sweet and Lovely.* The never-to-be-forgotten songs, sung by a never-to-be-forgotten singer.

Crosby, too, had had something to do with it. Blayde couldn't remember when she'd put the disc on the record-player. Couldn't remember how, or why, she'd coaxed him from the armchair. He couldn't dance—he'd never been able to dance—and yet he'd danced. Well, maybe not actually *danced.* A few square feet around the furniture . . . you couldn't call that a dance floor. And as for dancing? A sort of "in time" movement of the feet; a one-two-three-four movement which had been a fancy excuse for them to hold each other. That had been the beginning. Then that first tentative touching of lips. Then the real kiss. Then more kisses, and Crosby had still been singing, but they'd stopped dancing. Suddenly, they'd had more important things to do than dance.

And how had it happened? Dammit, how had it *really* happened? Whatever else, he was no Lothario. He wouldn't have . . . And she'd once said she disliked kids, so it couldn't have been a "mother-substitute" job. So how in hell . . .

In a low voice, she said, "Are you awake?"

"Yes."

She had her back to him. She was gazing out of the window, at the first cold light of early morning. She wore an ankle-length dressing-gown, and she continued to look out of the window as she spoke.

"We . . ." She paused, then said, "We made fools of ourselves last night, didn't we?"

"It's possible," he admitted softly.

"I swore . . ." She stopped.

"What?" he asked, softly.

"When Bill died, I swore I'd never let another man . . ." Again she stopped.

"We make promises." He tried to catch her mood; tried to be kind to her. "We're human. Sometimes we can't keep the promises."

"That sort of promise," she murmured.

"I'm sorry, pet."

"It wasn't your fault." Without seeing her face, he knew the remark was accompanied by a bitter smile. "You wanted to go home. I wouldn't let you."

"But for a different reason."

"Do you—do you want breakfast?" Her voice was low, but harsh. "I don't know much about these things, but I understand the professionals provide breakfast for the client before he leaves."

"For Christ's sake!"

"Do you want breakfast?" she repeated in a dull voice.

"It hasn't been that sort of a night." His voice had the ugly edge of suppressed anger.

"Not for you, perhaps. For you—what is it?—a one night stand."

"Do *you* call it that?"

"I don't know what to call it. I don't know what to call myself."

"A woman?" suggested Blayde.

Her shoulders drooped a little, then they straightened and, when she spoke it was in a voice which left no doubt.

"I'm going to the kitchen. If you need breakfast . . ."

"No breakfast, thank you."

". . . that's where I'll be. If not, let yourself out, please.'

She turned and walked from the bedroom. Not once did she look at him.

He'd been home, bathed, shaved and changed clothes from the skin out by the time he knocked on Chapman's office door. He entered and Chapman waved him to a convenient chair.

Blayde murmured, "Thank you, sir."

"That makes a pleasant change," said Chapman drily.

"Sir?"

"Last night at Bigton I just wondered who the hell *was* in charge of this division. Not a 'sir' spoken, as I recall."

Blayde remained silent. The hell . . . he could do nothing right. First Margaret. Now Chapman. And the signs were that Chapman was in a very dangerous mood.

"Last night," said Chapman in a hard, cold voice, "saw medal-chasing at its worst. Gold was isolated. All we had to do was wait."

"For guns." Blayde had had enough stick. He began to hit back. "For the curtain to rise on a good, old-fashioned, Wild West shoot-out."

"The guns were back-up. They wouldn't have been used."

"In that case, why send for 'em?"

"Blayde, I'm not going to argue with you. I'm not . . ."

"But I'm going to argue with *you* . . . sir. What about Gold? The poor devil who thought he'd shot somebody to death. Didn't he count? Coppers waving revolvers. Snipers hiding behind chimney stacks. That's what Gold would have seen. All he'd have seen. And you think he'd have recognised it as a bluff?"

"Who the hell d'you think you're . . ."

"He might have put up a fight." Blayde blasted on, and refused Chapman the time, or the right, to pull rank. "And if he had, don't tell me the guns wouldn't have been used. My guess is he'd have shot himself . . . but doesn't that count?"

"Blayde!" Chapman exploded the name across the few feet which separated them. Then as Blayde listened, stone-faced, he snapped, "All right, you're a bloody hero. You deserve a medal . . . you might even get one. But, better or worse, I don't allow a detective sergeant to take the reins from my hands in my own division." He quietened fractionally, and continued, "It doesn't make for discipline. Dammit, you did the right

thing—of course you did—but you didn't ask, you didn't volunteer . . . you just went ahead, and the hell with what anybody else said."

"To that extent, I'm sorry," muttered Blayde.

"I don't want you to be sorry." Chapman blew out his cheeks, and the fury evaporated. "Hell's teeth, sergeant, can't you see things from my point of view? My job goes a bit farther than polishing the seat of this chair with my arse. I'm supposed to run this division. My way. Last night you put your life on the line and prevented a tragedy and, for that, there's a recommendation on its way to the chief, suggesting that you be in line for a Queen's Police Medal . . ."

"I don't want a damn medal."

"You . . ." Chapman glared. "You will accept a Queen's Police Medal and *like* it . . . if it comes off. And that's an order."

"Yes, sir," muttered Blayde.

"But, having said that, we come to the real reason why you're here." Chapman paused, then continued, "This division. It can't carry *two* mad sods. Last night—okay, you did the right thing, and you were a brave little policeman—but what if Gold had blown your stupid head off?"

"Somebody would have organised a whip-round for a wreath."

"Somebody would have had his neck stretched across the chopping-block. And that somebody would have been *me*. Not because I ordered. Not because I asked for volunteers. But because a hair-brained detective sergeant arrived on the scene and, off his own bat, went barmy. That's why you're moving."

"Moving?"

"Pinthead Pike Division," said Chapman gently.

"If a Proposed Transfer Form comes through for . . ."

"It's already on its way," interrupted Chapman. "As a uniformed inspector. A peg up . . . and you're an ambitious man, aren't you?"

"Police politics," sneered Blayde.

"Don't knock them, sergeant. They've been with us a long time. They're here to stay."

"Who's the super up there?" asked Blayde.

"Hale." Chapman's mouth looped into a sardonic smile. "You'll love him."

"The Gauleiter of Outer Siberia," mocked Blayde.

"You're a hot-head, sergeant." Chapman shook his head slowly and sadly. "You're a damn good copper, but not quite as good as you think you are. 'Outer Siberia', as you put it, might do you the world of good."

13

IN acreage it was near enough the hundred-thousand mark as to make no real difference. It included what was known as The Tops, and The Tops was a frightening place. The Tops had peaks and overhangs capable of making the finest rock-climbers in the world pause and swallow. The Tops included an ocean of ling and heather; of bracken and stilted, wind-bent trees; a petrified ocean whose waves marched as far as the eye could see in all directions. If The Tops had a call, it was the lost and lonely call of the curlew; if it had a sound, it was the never-ending sound of the wind, sometimes raging in a tempest against which a man must lean in order not to be plucked from his feet and hurled like the toy of a spoiled child, sometimes moaning gently as if mourning the scores—hundreds—of lives it had claimed over the years. Foolish men. Foolish women. Mere human beings who'd thought they could tame nature there on The Tops. In winter the snow had taken them; blinding, whirling snow which more than once had frozen their tired and lost bodies within a hundred yards of some squat dwelling where they could have found shelter. In spring and autumn—yes and in summer also—the sudden mists had claimed victims as easily as the snows of winter; mists which made a mockery of even the best of maps; mists which enticed climbers and fell-walkers away from the well-worn tracks, then forced them to walk in circles until they were exhausted . . . then left them to die.

The Tops were part of Pinthead Pike Police Division. In effect, The Tops were Pinthead Pike Division. The only other parts were tiny hamlets and villages, sheltering in the folded skirts of The Tops. The only town (so-called) was Pinthead itself; a huddle of shops, houses, pubs, a Methodist chapel and a cattle market at which the hill farmers gathered once a week to sell livestock and to exchange news. And, towering above Pinthead, the Pike—a great, raw, limestone grit outcrop, like the broken tooth of a giant—which, along with the township, gave the division its name.

It had the reputation of being the "punishment division" of the force and this, too, requires some small explanation. Every force has its "punishment beats", its "punishment sections" and, sometimes, its "punishment division". Areas of various size which it is almost impossible to police with any degree of efficiency. A beat may be a veritable ghetto of villains, tearaways and madmen to whom the sight of a copper's uniform is like the sight of a cape to a fighting bull. A whole section may be that also, but a "punishment section" is more often on a par with a "punishment division" and a "punishment division" is where damn-all happens from one year's end to the next. To understand the sheer, blind boredom of such a division—a division like Pinthead Pike—it is necessary to appreciate the fact that every square inch of the United Kingdom is part of some police division, some police section, some police beat. The fells and wilderness of the High Pennines. The vast solitude of the North Yorkshire Moors. Every outcrop, every sprig of heather, every blade of grass is on some poor copper's beat, and the beat is part of a section, and the section is part of a division.

"Punishment divisions". "Punishment sections". The punishment is the knowledge that, short of a miracle, you are never going to have a case or an enquiry worth a damn; the conviction that, to all intents and purposes, you've been buried and forgotten, and that any ambition you might once have entertained is now a particularly sick joke.

The New Year of 1955 saw Blayde—Inspector Blayde—settling in at Pinthead Pike. He worked from Divisional Headquarters and, to cover the distances, he bought himself a good, second-hand VW Beetle. Built like a miniature tank, and without the problems of a water-cooled system, it was the ideal, moderately-priced car for the job. It had no flash turn of speed; it was a workhorse rather than a Derby winner, but a Derby winner wouldn't have lasted a single winter up there on The Tops.

And on Thursday, January 6th, Blayde met his new boss, Superintendent Hale, and the only good thing that could be said about Hale was that he was unique. There was only Hale . . . no force on God's earth could have carried two!

Blayde visited his office and as he opened the door he almost stepped back as the blast of hot air hit him in the face. Hale had had a "bit of a break" for Christmas, and that "bit of a break" had stretched itself out for almost three weeks. The office had an open fire, piled high with blazing coal. Hale was in civilian clothes, with his coat off and the sleeves of his shirt rolled high to reveal hairy, muscular forearms. Hale's face carried a two-day stubble of beard, and the motif was continued up and over the dome of his head where the impression was that he'd dispensed with the services of a hairdresser and instead allowed a sheep-shearer loose on his scalp.

"Siddown." Hale waved sausage-thick fingers towards an empty chair.

Blayde sat down.

Hale was holding a used match. As he talked he tore tiny splinters from the stalk, then used the thin end to pick his teeth.

"A bit of a hot 'un," he remarked in a rumbling tone.

"Sir?"

"You. So I hear. A bit of a hot 'un."

"I do my job."

"Oh, aye?" Hale dislodged a crumb of food with the makeshift toothpick, turned his head and spat the morsel into the flaming coals. As he resumed his poking, he growled, "Courts . . . and such."

"I've attended court enough times," admitted Blayde.

"They don't like courts in these parts."

"I don't see what . . ."

"On a par with cheques and banks and suchlike. Very down to earth. They like the real thing. A thump across the lughole . . . that's what they understand."

"And major crime?" asked Blayde gently.

"A boot up the arse, six laceholes deep."

"Unusual," observed Blayde carefully.

"It works." Hale spat another crumb into the fire, then dropped the matchstick into an ash-tray on his desk. He continued, "Another thing, I don't carry anybody."

"I'm not expecting to be carried," countered Blayde.

"Good." Hale nodded ponderously. "You'll deal with all the garbage that comes your way."

"Garbage?"

"Forms. Paperwork. Where it says 'Divisional Office', *you* sign it . . . put the word 'for' in front of 'Divisional Officer'.

"*You're* the divisional officer, sir," Blayde reminded Hale softly.

"Aye." Hale nodded.

"You're supposed to check things."

"*You're* supposed to check 'em first."

"Agreed."

"I've already mentioned. I don't carry

anybody. I've better things to do than see that every comma and every dot is in its right place."

Blayde remained silent.

"The same with any two-five-two lark," rumbled Hale. "We don't use 'em in this division."

"No Misconduct forms?" Blayde raised one eyebrow a fraction.

"Y'see, young feller," Hale squared his shoulders, stretched his arms and yawned. "We don't need 'em, in these parts. Anybody gets stroppy, he does a few nights. Sheep stealing. We get a bit of sheep stealing now and again. Some young tup gets too big for his britches, you slap him on night patrol. Pick him up about eleven and tell him he's on 'observations'. Looking for sheep stealers. Drive him ten miles up onto The Tops, and tell him to keep his eyes open . . . while he makes his way back." Hale's shoulders shook as he added, "That cools their bloody ardour faster than any two-five-two."

"An understood thing?" queried Blayde gently.

"Oh, aye. This division . . . its *my* division. I run it as *I* see fit."

"Can I ask a question?" asked Blayde.

"Aye."
"What about the periodic H.M.I. inspection? What does he say?"
"Nowt."
"Really?"
"The chief constable." Hale grinned. "He decides which divisions. He's more gumption than to drag a blood H.M.I. out here."
"I see."
Hale stood up and lumbered to the office door. As he opened it in a gesture of dismissal, he said, "Owt else you want to know, just ask."
"Thanks."

By the rules of the game—indeed by the rules of his own game—Blayde should have loathed Pinthead Pike Division and that he didn't was solely due to The Tops. As the seasons passed he grew to know them in their varying splendour. He didn't realise it, because he wasn't given to self-analysis, but they epitomised his own life-style. They couldn't be tamed. They were aloof and their rugged independence could terrify lesser men.
And, in its own way, Pinthead Pike *was* a well-run division. It was a back-to-front way; a way which might have given any divisional

officer other than Hale ulcers within a year. But it worked, and that itself was something to marvel at. Its "authorised strength" included a chief inspector and four inspectors. Its actual strength was two inspectors: Blayde and a middle-aged, perpetually frightened man called Clare. As for Hale? Forget him. Blayde or Clare signed everything "for the Divisional Officer". It was three sergeants and God only knew how many coppers light as far as manpower was concerned, but that was okay because everybody "covered" for everybody else and, huge though the division was in area, there was a distinctly family attitude within its personnel . . . with, of course, Hale commanding the unqualified status of *pater familias.*

Clare was terrified of Hale and made no attempt to hide the fact from Blayde.

"He's an oaf," he whined.

"He's an oaf," agreed Blayde. "He's soldiering on to his pension, and who can blame him?"

"He'll accept no responsibility."

"Should he?" asked Blayde mischievously.

"He makes us sign everything. Then, if there's trouble, he's the perfect let-out."

"The copper signs it. The sergeant signs it.

Then you or I sign it. Jesus Christ, man, how many signatures do you want?"

"But if it's wrong. If it's not quite right."

"Send it back to the sergeant. He'll send it back to the copper. It's a glorified form of General Post . . . treat it as such."

"It's all right for you. I've a wife and two kids to think about."

"Fine, let *them* sign it."

"That's not a nice thing to say."

"Clare, for Christ's sake stop worrying. Hale doesn't give a monkey's toss. Why should we?"

And yet, he did. Deep down in his bones Blayde knew that this couldn't last. It *mustn't* last. A man could be a copper for only so long—for only so many years—then a pension reared up and bit him. And Blayde had too much self-respect, was perhaps too self-opinionated, to be satisfied with a mere inspectorship. This cushy little number at Pinthead Pike was only a respite. Chapman might have thought he was squeezing the vinegar out of Blayde by fixing a transfer to a division where damn-all happened, but if so Chapman had added his sums up wrong.

After a year of feeling his way into things (on Friday, January 6th, 1956, to be precise)

Blayde walked into Hale's office and voiced a proposition.

"I think we should have a purge," he announced.

"Oh, aye?" Hale, as was usual during the winter months, was coatless, with a roaring fire threatening to set the office chimney alight.

"Rear lights," said Blayde solemnly.

"What about rear lights?"

"Up there on The Tops. I estimate that one vehicle out of every six has a dicky rear light."

"By God, you'll earn another Queen's Police Medal chasing duff rear lights."

"It's dangerous," insisted Blayde. "And if we do it right it'll give some of the lads court experience."

"The locals won't like it."

"The locals can bloody-well lump it," said Blayde flatly. "I want a purge on rear lights and, while they're stopped, we can look for other things."

"Such as?"

"From the North Riding to Durham—and from Durham to the North Riding—if anybody wants to travel the quiet way they cross this division."

"Villains, you mean?"

"On the way from some job," amplified Blayde.

Hale sucked at his upper lip for a moment, then growled, "I'm not going up there, freezing my balls off on the odd chance."

"I'm not asking."

"Rear lights!" And the utter disgust with which Hale spoke the words brought a grin to Blayde's face.

Nevertheless, it paid dividends. The local magistrates court seemed quietly pleased at the idea of imposing fines on a handful of drivers each week; it made them feel wanted; it also demonstrated that their district was policed more tightly than might have been imagined. One of the shooting-brakes stopped carried a stolen ewe in the rear, and that was one for his nob and delighted the hill farmers who, in turn, figured that the local rozzers might, after all, be earning their corn. The "big 'un", however, was a Ford, carrying three hard-eyed men haring north, having just lifted a small fortune in rings, watches and general knick-knacks from a jeweller's shop at Bordfield.

The Bordfield man in charge of the enquiry was a certain Detective Inspector Harris and, at first, the name meant nothing. Indeed, had not Harris opened the memory—opened the wound—Blayde might have been none the wiser.

The Bordfield Court of Quarter Sessions had slammed the villains and, having given evidence, Harris suggested a quiet celebratory pint at a local pub.

"Blayde?" Having tasted the beer. Harris wiped the moustache of froth from his upper lip with the back of his hand, and mouthed the name in a questioning tone.

"Uhu," grunted Blayde.

"The man who used to work Upper Neck?" asked Harris.

"Some few years back." Blayde frowned.

"My wife was once a bit keen on you."

"Eh?"

"Ruth Bowse, that was her unmarried name. You lodged with her aunt and uncle."

"Ruth!"

"Even today, she keeps mentioning you." Harris's eyes narrowed ever so slightly. "She was really taken."

"I think she's exaggerating a little."

"No . . . I think I caught her on the rebound. I've wanted to meet you for a long time."

"What do you suggest?" Blayde suddenly found himself matching Harris, tone for tone. "Pistols at twenty paces?"

"Just to let you know," said Harris coldly.

"What? That if I'd accepted an invitation to a police dance Ruth would have been *my* wife by this time?"

Maybe it hurt a little. Maybe more than just a little. Blayde was no womaniser. He was sufficient unto himself and, moreover, he had the sense to realise that only a very special breed of woman can make a success of being a copper's wife, especially if that copper happens to be ambitious. Maybe Ruth *was* of that breed, and if so . . .

Hale called off the rear light caper.

"Bugger rear lights. That wasn't what you were really after. You've netted your catch for one year. The others won't use this route till they're sure. Let 'em think it was a one-off job. They'll be back. Try again next year."

"You think I'll still be here next year?" asked Blayde grimly.

"And the year after *and* the year after that." Hale chuckled. "It'll break your bloody heart to leave us, lad."

Blayde didn't argue. Nothing less than a

nickel-coated .303 could penetrate Hale's hide and, anyway, there was enough truth in the remark to block any real argument.

So . . . back to supervising sheep-dipping, back to strolling around the Pinthead Cattle Market and the weekly chat with the local R.S.P.C.A. inspector ("Watch a horse when it's coming towards you, inspector. It nods its head. If it nods it to its left, there's pain at that side. The same if it nods it to the right. It's a good rule of thumb, it's rarely out"), back to the issuing of Swine Movement Orders. And anthrax.

In May a farm on the lower slopes was hit by anthrax. A farm which was little more than a smallholding. Joe Benton's place. And anthrax meant slaughter, burning, a cordoning-off, a sluicing down of sheds with caustic soda and, all in all, a full week of muck and graft. Joe Benton worked for himself; just Joe, his wife and his son, Little Willie, and thank God for Little Willie.

Not yet twenty, he was a giant with the brain of an obedient child. Joe and Sarah kept him at home as much as possible. Pixilated they called it—the pixies had touched him at birth. He couldn't read, he couldn't write, he couldn't add up, he couldn't hold a conversation, but with his parents and the livestock he was supremely happy. But he had strength—phenomenal strength—strength enough to carry a hundredweight sack of barley under each arm and without conscious effort, and the Bentons were terrified that should he be allowed to roam abroad he might be subjected to the taunts of stupid people, and that the taunts might cancel out his normal happy disposition, and if Little Willie ever lost his temper and lashed out, he'd be hard pushed not to kill somebody.

Nevertheless, when anthrax struck, thank God for Little Willie.

Five cows had to be slaughtered and burned. They had to be burned away completely, and the burning had to take place in a huge grave where the ashes had to be covered with quick-lime prior to the grave being filled in. It was one hell of a task, and poor Joe Benton was almost in tears.

"I'm insured, but it doesn't cover. I can't afford men to help dig a pit *that* size."

"I've some holiday due," said Blayde. "The three of us—us two and Willie—we'll do it."

"I can't afford to pay you much, Mr. Blayde."

"Don't worry, Joe. The exercise is what I need."

They did it, too. Benton and Blayde swung picks and wielded shovels until their hands were blistered, but Little Willie shifted more earth than the combined effort of both of them. The pit was dug, Blayde telephoned around, Hale pulled strings and old railway sleepers, huge drums of old sump oil, two tons of coal and a lorry piled high with used car tyres arrived to form the basis of the pyre.

The burning took three days and three nights. Joe Benton and Blayde took it in turn to stand guard over the fire; to fuel things up whenever the moisture from the burning beasts threatened to dampen the roaring furnace. Then came the scrubbing down of the sheds, and that took another two days.

When it was all over the Bentons and Blayde drank each other's health in the stone-flagged kitchen of the tiny farmhouse. Willie drank home-made lemonade. Benton and Blayde swallowed draughts of nettle beer and, for Blayde, it was one more new experience; it went down like liquid silk, but it had a delayed action capable of making run-of-the-mill booze seem like tap-water. Sarah Benton contented herself with sipping elder-flower wine.

Joe Benton smacked his lips and said, "Back to Square One."

"I'm sorry," said Blayde.

"Nay, lad. Thanks to you we can go back to Square One."

"We can't thank you enough, Mr. Blayde," said Sarah.

"You can thank me." Blayde spoke gently, but with meaning.

"How?" asked Benton. "Just say the word."

"There's a plough shed," said Blayde carefully. "At the far end, where your land dog-legs to the Beechwood Brook boundary." He added, hurriedly, "To buy it from you . . . that's what I mean."

"That broken-down bloody thing. There's no roof left. I've been going to flatten the thing for ages. It's nowt but an eye-sore."

Blayde said, "I'd like to buy it."

"Tha can have it. It's no damn good to . . ."

"To *buy* it," emphasised Blayde. "The shed. About half an acre of land around the shed . . . building-land price."

"Be damned for a tale! It's agricultural land. I'll not . . ."

"Joe, there's a building on it."

"Aye . . . of a sort."

"I want my own place. It's as simple as that. I'm tired of living in digs."

"It's an old plough-shed." Benton stared. "A broken-down old plough-shed. It's no bloody good to anybody."

"Look . . ." Blayde tasted nettle beer before continuing. "Between the four of us. There's mains electricity, there's water, all within easy distance. A good septic tank system. Oil-fired central heating. This isn't a sudden thing, Joe. I've given it some thought. There's already a building—a building of a sorts—on the site. That gives me a thin end towards planning permission. Hale can do the rest. Hale . . ." Blayde chuckled. "With the people he knows, I could build a Hilton Hotel on the site."

"Which builder?" asked Benton.

"Myself."

"Tha'll kill thi'sen."

"No." Blayde shook his head. "I have most of the know-how from the past. Bit at a time. It'll get done."

Sarah Benton said, "Willie can help."

"Aye." Benton nodded slowly. "Whatever it is, just tell him. He'll do it."

Little Willie grinned with delight at the prospect of working with his new-found friend.

"It's settled, then?" said Blayde. "I'll make enquiries about the current price of building-land. About half an acre, plus the plough shed. I'll meet the costs of solicitor's fees."

"It—it doesn't seem right. Damn it all . . ."

"Do myself a favour. Give myself roots of a sort." Blayde smiled, and added, "And at the same time give you a nudge from Square One."

The summer of '56 saw Blayde a contented man. At first Hale had treated the notion of building a cottage on the land occupied by the plough shed with some derision but, having been made to realise that this slightly barmy inspector of his was deadly serious, words had been whispered in quiet corners and the planning permission had gone through without a hitch. Blayde's own popularity had helped, plus the fact that he'd spent hours drawing the plans and itemising the specifications and, whatever else, it was going to be one of the best built cottages for miles.

Blayde bought himself a caravan—a second-hand, two-berther which he converted into home-cum-office. He parked the caravan on the site he'd purchased from Benton, arranged for electricity, water and a telephone to be installed and thus was able to spend every spare moment "on the job".

Little Willie was a godsend when it came down to the sheer graft of digging the foundations and Blayde was happy to pay him standard labourer's rate per hour, knowing that no two labourers could have kept pace with this young giant. And those foundations were meant to last.

"Solid, Willie. Deep, broad and solid. Something to really build on."

And Willie grinned cheerfully and humped great boulders to give the concrete something with which to hold the cottage firm and solid.

Blayde chose his materials with great care. Sharp sand—not the usual stuff made of pulverised sand stone—sand which, when mixed four-to-one with good cement, gave a bonding material which over the years would weld itself granite-hard between the stones. The stones, too; good Yorkshire stone, trimmed lovingly and with a texture firm enough to shrug off all weather and, in doing so, mellow in colour until it was one with the surrounding landscape.

The damp-course . . . it was a *real* damp-course. Not the slap-bang-wallop damp-course of the jerry-builders. Sheet-lead bedded firmly on a bed of tar, with more tar spread atop to take the first layer of stone. And, when it came to the woodwork, every inch of timber was personally chosen; the beams fitted exactly, each window, each door, was tailor-made on the spot. It took time, it took patience, but pride and a peculiar sort of love went into the building and it showed.

In retrospect—and with hindsight—what was left of 1956 and most of 1957 was a respite for Blayde. A sort of unofficial sabbatical. He policed, and nobody could fault the manner of his policing but, for the first time since he'd joined the force, bobbying took a second place.

He'd touched the truth when he'd told Benton he was seeking roots. Somewhere he could truly call home; not just a room—maybe two rooms—in somebody else's house. One spot on God's earth which was uniquely his. It took priority over everything.

Clare complained, "You've eased off a lot, since you arrived."

"Eased off?"

"Policing, I mean."

"I do my share . . . a little more than my share, at a guess."

"I'm—y'know—I'm not saying you don't."

"So what the hell's the gripe?"

"No. I'm not griping."

"Just stating the obvious?"

"Yes, I suppose so."

"If it's obvious it doesn't *need* stating."

He was still the same Blayde. Still as touchy, still as stroppy, still ready to give as much, and more, than he received. On top of which, he was tired. Physically tired as well as mentally tired. He drove himself to the point of exhaustion; set himself a seemingly impossible pace and, literally, fought his own body in order to maintain that pace.

The only people he was prepared to call friends were the Bentons, and perhaps once a month, never more than twice, he dragged his weary body to their tiny farmhouse, flopped into a chair and accepted good country fare. A pint of hot, sweet tea, home-made bread, home-churned cheese, home-made butter. A feast fit for a monarch compared with the snatch meals he usually allowed himself.

Sarah Benton looked worried and said, "You're killing yourself, lad."

"I'm beating it." He grinned a tired grin.

"Is it worth it?" asked Joe Benton.

"To me."

"Folks think you're daft," said Joe bluntly.

"Maybe they're right."

"Ease up a bit, Bob," pleaded Sarah. "You're losing weight. One man to build a whole house. It's nigh impossible."

"Willie helps a lot."

"Willie," said Joe Benton, "isn't you. You're trying to match him, that's what I reckon, and *that's* what's killing you."

"It's my house, not Willie's."

Sarah hesitated, then asked, "Haven't you any family, Bob?"

"A mother. A brother. I think."

"You only *think?*"

"Lessford," sighed Blayde. "I haven't seen either for years."

"Don't you keep in touch?"

"No. Nor do they. They could be dead and buried for all I know."

"For all you care?" she pressed.

"Maybe," growled Blayde.

Then he worked and drove himself even harder—as if it was a form of penance. He was up before the sun topped the horizon and he was policing or building until the light had faded. To Clare's surprised relief he took over much of the night duty; supervising the division until the small hours, snatching a short sleep, then out of the caravan and working on the house.

On Sunday, September 1st, his body called a halt. The rafters for the upstairs floor were in position and he was sawing and fitting the floor-boards, otherwise he might have fallen and killed himself. At the very least he'd have broken a limb. For a few seconds he felt it approaching, like a great wave curling to envelope him; the rushing, the roaring, the spinning, the darkness.

He managed to call, "Willie!" before his limbs turned to jelly and he crumpled onto the newly-positioned boards.

His next conscious thought was that the sheets of Beechwood Brook Cottage Hospital were clean and cool and very comfortable.

A gruff, no-nonsense voice said, "So? You've decided to join the human race again?"

"What . . ." Blayde squinted up at the grizzled medic.

"You've too big an opinion of yourself." He was a G.P.—one of the rota who took turns at officiating at the tiny hospital—and, if he'd ever had a bedside manner, he'd misplaced it years ago. He said, "You're only a police inspector. You're not yet God."

"What? I mean what . . ."

"You flaked out." Hale spoke from the foot of the bed. He spoke through a grin which threatened to split his face. "Willie Benton lugged you all the way to their place. They telephone D.H.Q. Now, you're here."

"And you're staying here," added the medic.

"What's—what's wrong with me?" asked Blayde.

The medic grunted, "You're well and truly knackered. A dog or a horse . . . you'd have been shot by this time. As it is . . ."

He left the sentence unfinished, but the tone conveyed the impression that medical practitioners were treated unfairly because they couldn't resort to humane-killer treatment.

"And," added Hale, "for at least a month—at least a month—'The Little Grey Home In The West' is strictly off-limits."

Blayde smiled a tired smile. He was, as the medic had put it, knackered. Completely, utterly and absolutely knackered. Both physically and mentally. His body was drained of strength and his mind seemed incapable of coherent thought. Had somebody told him he was on the verge of death, he wouldn't have argued, he wouldn't have been surprised, he wouldn't even have minded. Once more he tried to smile, but couldn't quite make it.

As he closed his eyes and drifted off into blessed sleep, he heard the medic say, "I've never seen anything like it before. The man's a bloody fool. I'll wager he takes more care of his car's engine than he does of his own body."

Ten days later, on Wednesday, September 11th, Blayde left the hospital for a spell of convalescence. He went to the Police Convalescent Home at Harrogate, mixed once more with his own kind and, thanks to good food, good air and the quiet pace of the spa town, once more began to feel comparatively fit. Agreed, there was still a hint of wobbliness about the legs, and the old noggin wasn't always as clear as it should be, but with each day the strength returned and, with it, the clear-headedness.

On Sunday the 15th he took a train to Lessford, then a taxi to Hill Rise. It was almost a spur-of-the-moment decision, probably prompted by Sarah Benton's shock at hearing he hadn't kept in touch with his family. That, plus a certain feeling of guilt which invariably accompanies the recovery from a serious, but vague, illness in a man used to good health. Something not far removed from self-pity; the need for reassurance that he really *has* been ill, and hasn't been swinging the lead.

He rang the bell and a strange woman answered the door. A plump, middle-aged, kindly-faced woman.

Blayde said, "Mrs.—er—Blayde. She . . . Doesn't she live here any more?"

"You mean old Mrs. Blayde?"

The word "old" came as something of a shock, but Blayde nodded, and said, "Yes. Mrs. Meg Blayde."

"She's . . ." The woman looked uncomfortable, then said, "She's in Greenfields."

"Oh."

"Didn't you know?"

"No, I . . ." Blayde shook his head, and muttered, "I'm sorry. I didn't know."

"We bought the house more than two years ago."

"I'm sorry," repeated Blayde. "I—y'know—didn't know."

She watched him as he walked to the gate. It

saddened her that a man could look so dejected. So defeated.

Blayde caught one of the infrequent buses to the city centre, then a second bus to the outskirts. To beyond Hallsworth Hill and to the very edge of the city boundary. The place was known by the name it had always been known by. Greenfields. Its full name was Greenfield Mental Hospital and, despite the humane advance of modern medicine, it still carried echoes of its Victorian past. "Tha needs sending to Greenfields." "Tha's that daft, tha musta come from Greenfields."

A terrible and terrifying place. Huge grounds, surrounded by a high wall. Like a prison, but in some ways more frightening than any prison.

"Meg Blayde," said Blayde.

The matron looked uncertain.

"I'm her son," explained Blayde.

"The one who had her . . ."

"No! The *other* son. I didn't even know she was in here."

"She won't recognise you," said the matron gently. "She doesn't recognise anybody. She doesn't even know where she is."

"Is she . . . bad?" Blayde substituted bad for

mad. He couldn't bring himself to voice the other word.

"She's where she should be," said the matron quietly. "She'll never get better. She'll die here. In her own way, she's happy . . . in her own way."

But she wasn't. She was neither happy nor unhappy. She was *nothing*. She sat in a room—a large, airy room, with tiled walls and geometrically positioned chairs—and she, along with about a dozen other pitiful creatures, sat and stared at out-of-focus nothingness. Her fingers played everlastingly with a tiny handkerchief, twisting it, turning it, picking at it. As if the madness had reached her finger-tips, giving them a spasmodic life of their own. The room was clean—spotlessly clean—but it stank of disinfectant and stale urine.

The matron murmured, "Some of them are incontinent, I'm afraid."

"Mother?"

The matron nodded sadly and said, "I'm sorry."

He stood in front of her. He spoke her name. He touched her and pleaded with her to recognise him, but it was no good. Only the fingers moved as they plucked at the handkerchief. The eyes still stared. The rest of her remained motionless.

"You're wasting your time, Mr. Blayde," sighed the matron.

"Why?" Blayde's voice was low and hoarse as they walked from the room.

"I beg your pardon?"

"What caused it?"

"Her mind went."

"I realise . . . but what caused *that?*"

"Who knows?" The matron smiled sympathetically. "Pressures . . . that plus age. That's the usual story."

"What sort of pressures?"

"It's difficult to say."

"Family pressures?"

"Part of it, I suppose. It often is." Blayde had the impression she was being deliberately vague.

"I have a brother. Is he . . ."

"Mr. Blayde, we don't know. Some people lead tranquil lives. Some people have the strength to withstand any amount of emotional upheaval. Other people . . ." She moved her shoulders. "Everybody's different, Mr. Blayde. Your mother's one of the unfortunate ones but, in her own way, she's happy."

"Look after her," mumbled Blayde. "She—

y'know—she deserved better than this."

He took the bus back to the city centre, then walked into Lessford City Police Headquarters, identified himself and asked to see somebody from C.I.D. A detective sergeant was the only plain clothes man available and the two of them sought privacy in one of the Interview Rooms.

"Well?" smiled the D.S.

Blayde said, "Richard Blayde. Same name as mine, we're brothers. He has form—at least one previous—do you know where I can find him?"

"Uhu." The D.S. nodded. He was no longer smiling.

"We're brothers, sergeant," said Blayde heavily. "But don't let that make you coy. As far as we're concerned 'brotherly love' is listed alongside perpetual motion and the dodo. I'm in the county, Pinthead Pike. We're out of touch with civilisation. So . . . brother Richard. I'd be grateful for small mercies."

"Ric Blayde," murmured the D.S. ruminatively.

"A bloody stupid name. But he's a stupid man."

"What we know? Or what we can prove?"

"Anything you care to come up with."

"Well now," the D.S. pushed his hands into the pockets of his trousers, tilted his chair onto its back legs, and gazed up at the ceiling. "Lessford's a big place, inspector. Say about fifty hotels, and about seventy pubs worthy of consideration. Say about half of each. That's on the low side. Plus a few betting shops. Plus a handful of clubs. Plus this, plus that, plus the other. It makes a steady income. Fifty quid a week, that's Ric's going rate. A form of insurance. That much we *know*. Unfortunately, that much we can't yet *prove*. People tend to be scared."

"The protection game?" growled Blayde.

"Strictly cash. No credit."

"And he's getting away with it?"

"He's a careful man," sighed the D.S. as he allowed the front legs of the chair to lower themselves. Then very solemnly, very deliberately, he said, "He's an evil sod. The last three years. Fires. Arson. We can prove arson. Four people were burned to death."

"You can *prove* arson?"

"Just so far. After that a brick wall."

"He was never *that* smart."

"In that case, he's learned," said the D.S. grimly.

"Right." Blayde's face was expressionless,

but he nodded. "I believe you, sergeant. Now . . . where can I find him?"

It was what an estate agent might have described as "a superbly maintained, private, double-fronted residence of handsome proportions". The impression was that the guy who ran the place must have come to a private agreement with the Royal Mint, that or must have control shares in Fort Knox. And "the guy who ran the place" looked the part.

Richard Blayde had a role to play, and he played it well. His study, where he received his visitor, had floor-space upon which to stand the whole of his brother's half-completed cottage. And it was furnished with wall-to-wall wealth. Wealth which went with the sharp, made-to-measure clothes; the open-necked silk shirt; the hand-made sneakers; the manicured fingers.

From the depths of the leather wing-chair, he smiled at his brother and murmured, "Long time."

"Not long enough."

Blayde walked slowly, cat-footed across the carpet. He ignored the three men and the flash-looking tart who shared the room with his brother.

Richard Blayde smiled and said, "But there's a reason?"

"I saw mother earlier today," ground Blayde.

"Was she well?"

"Who drove her to that place?" breathed Blayde.

"People lose their marbles. All sorts of people. She lost hers."

"I think you."

"Not a nice conclusion to come to." The brother grinned mockingly.

"The big boss." Blayde's contempt twisted his lips into an ugly sneer. "The smart-arse who couldn't even run a general store without getting his fingers sticky."

"Not a friendly visit." The eyes hardened. "Like last time . . . but not *quite* like last time."

Richard Blayde moved a hand, and two of the men stepped silently across the carpet. Each grabbed one of Blayde's arms and twisted, viciously. They knew their job. The wrists were within a fraction of being broken. The shoulder-blades were on the point of dislocation.

Richard Blayde lighted a cigarette. He allowed the smoke to drift from his nostrils as he contemplated the mix of fury and contempt on his brother's face.

"Mouthy coppers," he murmured. "They give me a pain."

"Call your keepers off." Blayde's voice was low and hate-filled. He winced as one of the men gave an arm an extra twist, then gasped, "I'll bury you, little brother. Call them off and I'll bury you now. Either way I'll live to bury you and spit on your grave."

"If *I* let you." Richard Blayde glanced at the third man, then inhaled cigarette smoke before he continued, "I owe you, remember? A little interest, too. I pay my debts. Certain debts." He smiled a knowledgeable smile. "Assault on police? No, I think not. That wouldn't be in the league you're talking about. You want more than that. You want the top cherry or nothing. But just in case . . ." He moved a shoulder in an off-handed gesture. "One phone call and we aren't here. None of us. Not you, not me, none of us. And the people prepared to take an oath on that carry more weight than you'll ever carry. You do understand?"

"I'll nail you for more than assault," whispered Blayde.

"Of course . . . you'll try. Meanwhile the

payment of that little debt." He turned his head and spoke to the third man. "Not on the face, Harry. A few bruises around the body . . . and one in the balls for luck."

The two heavies held him; he was still weak and didn't take much holding and, with each turn to lessen a blow he threatened to tear his shoulder-blades from their sockets. Richard Blayde settled in the wing-chair and watched with the bored interest of a connoisseur who'd seen it all scores of times before. The woman watched, too, her eyes shone with excitement and a thin dribble of spittle left one corner of her mouth. The third man—the man called Harry—wielded the hard rubber truncheon like the expert he was. The ribs and the guts. Each blow delivered with careful accuracy; each blow bringing a gasp of pain from behind Blayde's clenched teeth. Nobody was in a hurry. The swings were wide and full-blooded; they landed and hurt, then landed again and again, until the hurt was almost unbearable. Blayde's legs began to buckle. The two heavies held him upright and Harry brought the truncheon up in a wide arc to land a last crippling blow to the crotch . . . and Blayde fastened his teeth onto his lower lip to stop himself from screaming.

Consciousness remained with Blayde until the two men dragged him from the room, across the hall and heaved him onto the gravel drive. Then he fought the pain, steadied himself on his knees and stiffened arms, and was violently sick. It seemed to take him a small infinity to haul himself upright; to walk like a drunken man to the street; to find a kiosk and to telephone for a taxi.

As he flopped into the rear seat, he gasped, "The station."

"Police station?" asked the driver.

"No. The railway station."

The next day he discharged himself from the convalescent home and returned to Pinthead Pike. He still ached like the very devil and it pained him to walk upright, but although he wore a magnificent assortment of bruises, he was sure no bones were broken. For two days he stayed at the best hotel Pinthead could offer; resting and soaking the pain from his bruises in hot baths then, on the afternoon of Wednesday, September 18th, he visited Hale's office.

"You're home early." Hale scowled. "I thought I gave you strict orders to . . ."

"Don't!" Blayde lowered himself onto a

handy chair, and the way he spat the single word stopped Hale's objections before they were completed. In a voice not far from a snarl, Blayde said, "Don't order me to do anything else but bobby. And I *mean* bobby. Fair warning . . . sir. I'm going to tear this back-of-beyond division limb from limb. All this you-scratch-my-back-I'll-scratch-yours bullshit. I have every intention of flaying the skin off those backs."

"Oh, aye?" Hale's jaw-muscles hardened.

"Yours, too, sir."

"Think you have it in you, lad?"

"Don't try to con me, Superintendent Hale." Blayde's lips moved into a slow, sardonic smile. "You're up to the armpits in it, and you enjoy it too much to sit back and let me even try."

Hale said, "That's very heavy talk from an inspector to a superintendent, wouldn't you say?"

"It's blackmail," said Blayde bluntly.

"Blackmail?"

"I want a transfer . . . for personal reasons."

"Any particular place?" asked Hale sarcastically.

"Out of this division. That for starters. I'll make my own way from there."

"Just like that?" Hale sniffed disdainfully.

"Just like that, and don't tell me you can't do it."

"Happen I can." Hale gave an inch or so of ground, then added, "But what about this happy homestead you're busy building."

"It'll get finished. And I'll live there."

There was a silence. It lasted all of thirty seconds. The two men stared at each other; rank versus obstinacy; a comfortable ride to a good pension opposed by a fury prepared to destroy that ride.

"It's not you I'm after, superintendent," said Blayde quietly.

"Comforting," grunted Hale.

"You can keep your friends—all that booze you get given at Christmas, all the perks you enjoy from the local officials—just as long as I'm not here."

"Now you're threatening." Hale suddenly seemed to relax. A grin dawned, widened, then burst into a great guffaw of enjoyment, and he boomed, "Of all the stroppy young buggers! Chapman warned me. But *this.* Christ, I think you would, too."

Blayde nodded solemnly.

"By God, yes. You would."

Blayde seemed to hesitate, as if giving

careful thought to the words, then said, "Superintendent, I owe you nothing. You owe me nothing. Just . . . Let's say something's cropped up. Something I have to do if it takes the rest of my service. I don't stand a cat in hell's chance of doing it from Pinthead Pike."

"From where then?" Hale seemed to be giving Blayde an option.

"I don't know," admitted Blayde. "It's not even in the county area, but it might spread."

"But not to here?"

"No." For the first time since entering the office, Blayde smiled. "The fertiliser isn't thick enough in this division."

"Pick a division," suggested Hale.

For a moment Blayde thought he was being mocked, then he said, "Haggthorpe."

"Back to Haggthorpe?" Hale sounded surprised.

"I know the place. The conditions—the conditions I'm looking for—it's possible. And I'd soon know."

"What about Chapman. He wanted rid. That's why you're here."

"No, he wanted me tamed. *That's* why I'm here."

"And *are* you tamed?" asked Hale mischievously.

"I've been a well-behaved inspector."

"True." Hale nodded ponderously. Somehow the exchange had developed into a game of words, and Hale was beginning to enjoy himself. "You've done your job. More than your job."

"Which means I'm tamed."

"What," mused Hale, "if you storm into Chapman's office one day and start twisting his arm?"

"Would I?"

"You might."

"Ah, but could I?"

"Let's say you'd catch a draught up your kilt."

Blayde nodded his agreement.

Hale took a deep breath, blew out his cheeks, and said, "Y'know, lad, anybody but me. Any other divisional officer in this whole bloody force. You wouldn't have got away with it. Not even with me . . ." He waved Blayde silent. "Those—er—'friends' I have. Between us, we could have fitted you out. It's been done. It'll be done again. Fitted you out so tight you wouldn't have been able to breath comfortably. But . . ." Hale moved a shoulder in a gesture of mock-philosophy. "I'm only a hick superintendent. I don't have burning ambitions. I don't want to trample anybody to death. Not even you."

As he spoke the last few words Hale reached out, scuffled through the untidy paperwork in his In-tray, found what he was looking for and tossed it across the desk towards Blayde.

Blayde had seen enough of them to be able to recognise the heading and the general layout before he picked it up to read the contents.

A Proposed Transfer Form.

"It arrived while you were taking the waters at Harrogate," grunted Hale.

The document proposed that Inspector Robert Blayde take up duties at Haggthorpe Divisional Headquarters, as detective inspector.

"I—er—I didn't know," muttered Blayde.

"You don't say!"

"I'm sorry."

"The hell you're sorry," rumbled Hale bluntly. "You've never been sorry for anything in your young life. You never will be."

"Nevertheless . . ."

"Sign the bloody thing," interrupted Hale. "And come Christmas—if you've time, that is—come round and help get rid of some of that booze you were talking about."

14

THE rank and authority of detective inspector. It sounds big. It sounds important. And indeed, to a degree, it is both big and important, but only to a degree. In practical terms a D.I. is a general dogsbody, albeit a rather important dogsbody. He lacks the God-like authority of a detective superintendent, or even a detective chief inspector; much of the time he is merely the conduit via which such exalted beings communicate with mere sergeants and constables. On the other hand, he is not expected to waste too much time on the street; what talent he possesses is counted as being wasted if he fannies around with run-of-the-mill crime. Not yet big enough to really throw weight, but nice and handy for catching more than a few cans before they land on wider laps.

And yet to a man like Blayde . . .

Ah, but what sort of man had Blayde become?

Something special, that for sure. Something different. To reach D.I. at the age of thirty-five, and with little more than ten years service tucked under his belt . . . special and different. He certainly wasn't the innocent whom Police Constable Sharpe had escorted around Upper Neck Beat a small lifetime since. Not even the man who'd done Duty Elsewhere and, as a reward, had been sent on a Detective Training Course. He was certainly a suspicious man; a man distrustful of anything and everything required to be taken at its face value. He granted no favours, and he asked none. He was a copper—waking and sleeping he was a copper—and the force, in particular the County Constabulary, was the very mainspring of his life. He wasn't popular, but on the other hand he wasn't unpopular; he wasn't a bastard other than on the rare occasions when it was necessary to be a bastard, but when it was necessary, he pulled out all the stops. He neither hated nor loved. Emotional entanglement was something he shied away from like a startled horse. Some tagged him as a misogynist, and perhaps they were partly right; certain it is that on the two occasions when he might have shared his life with a woman things had gone very wrong, and that because he was a proud man.

And that (his infernal pride) was his only

weakness, although he, himself, never counted it as a weakness. Nevertheless, it prevented him from unbending. It prohibited him from even contemplating the periodic pub crawls which for so many other coppers was a form of safety-valve. Blayde's relaxation was to drive out to Pinthead Pike Division, and there graft away at his cottage until he was almost too tired to drive back to Haggthorpe.

But as a detective inspector he'd earned himself a reputation within a year. His trade, and the trade of those under his supervision, was catching criminals, and he worked at it until it was a craft and almost an art. Name a man in the whole division with previous and the chances were that Blayde knew every crime he'd ever committed, every crime he'd been suspected of, his accomplices, his marital status, his fancy women, his weaknesses, his attitude under interrogation and, very often, his Criminal Records Office Number. As Blayde saw things, that was what he was paid to know, much as a good medical practitioner was expected to know the various vilenesses which afflict the human body.

Nor was he ever "off-duty".

At 9.30 p.m. (thereabouts) he was having a

quiet pint in the bar parlour of one of Haggthorpe's pubs when, by sheer chance, he overheard a conversation between two other customers. It was a Saturday (July 19th, 1958) and, amid the general chatter, one phrase caught his immediate attention.

"I mean, dammit, she's only fifteen and she's in the club."

"Aye, I know. Lynda! I'd give her bloody 'Lynda' if she were my lass."

"Nay, you can't blame the father."

"I can."

"Oh, be damned for a tale. He's up all night, waiting for passengers getting off the trains. He has to sleep sometime."

"If he'd brought her up right."

"Happen. But her mother's as much to blame. If she looked after her kids a bit better, instead o' arsing around reckoning to be a club singer. Ever heard her?"

"No, can't say I have."

"Bloody awful. 'Mary O'Connor. The Rose of Tralee'."

"Tha what?"

"That's what she calls herself. Lizzie Finchley. 'Mary O'Connor. The Rose of Tralee'."

"Bloody hell!"

Blayde tipped what was left of his beer down his throat, then left the pub. Without actually hurrying he strode purposefully along the pavements and round the corners until he reached Haggthorpe D.H.Q. There he strode through doors and along corridors until he reached the large, buckshee room at the rear where uniformed officers paraded and were briefed prior to moving out onto the street. The night-shift men were listening to the last of the information being read out by a uniformed inspector, while a uniformed sergeant stood at one side, idly cleaning his finger-nails with a straightened paper-clip.

Blayde murmured, "When you've finished, Jerry."

"Eh?" The uniformed inspector looked up from his clipboard, then said, "That's the lot. Something you'd like to say to 'em?"

"Uhu." Blayde turned to the half-dozen uniformed constables. "A taxi-driver. Finchley. Usually works nights, picking up passengers at the railway station. Anybody know him?"

A middle-aged man hesitated, then said, "Tom Finchley. Yes, sir. I know him."

"Know him well?" asked Blayde.

"Fairly well, sir."

"He has a daughter, right?"

"Two daughters. One son."

"Lynda?"

"That's his younger daughter, sir. The elder daughter's married."

"His wife's a club-singer?"

"Of a sort." The middle-aged constable smiled. "No Dame Melba, from what I hear."

Blayde turned to the uniformed inspector and said, "Can you pull this man off the street for a few days?"

"I—er . . ." The uniformed inspector consulted the papers on the clipboard. "Yes. I don't see why not. A little doubling-up. It shouldn't be too difficult."

"Starting tonight?"

"Sure." The uniformed inspector spoke to the parading men. "Right. Dobey, you stay here. The rest of you, on the street and keep your eyes skinned for those car numbers."

When the patrol constables had left, Blayde said, "Do we have a policewoman handy?"

"Woman Police Sergeant Flinch, maybe." The uniformed inspector glanced at his clipboard as if to double-check. "She went off duty at eight. She's had a long day. She's been . . ."

"Is she on the telephone?"

"Yes."

"Give her a ring. Ask her to be ready."

"She's had a long day," repeated the uniformed inspector pointedly.

"So? With luck, she'll have a long night."

The uniformed inspector sighed. He was a kind-hearted man. He said, "I'll see she's on stand-by."

"Dobey." Blayde turned his attention to the uniformed constable.

"Yes, sir."

"Finchley. Should he be at the station now?"

"Should be," said Dobey. "Should just about have started."

"Fine. Let's visit him."

The uniformed inspector said, "Am I allowed to know what this is all about?"

"You're too young." Blayde grinned. "You still believe in birds, bees and little black bags."

Thomas Jefferson Finchley. British born of Jamaican parents. Skin the colour of top-quality mahogany. And that, for Blayde, was the first surprise. He'd expected white. From the conversation he'd overheard in the public house, he'd also expected the man to be something of a couldn't-care-less slob. On both counts he was wrong. The man spoke well; politely without even so much as a hint of subservience.

He nodded a friendly greeting to Dobey then, after introductions had been made, moved the car from its position in the rank to a quiet corner of an adjoining car park.

Blayde settled himself in the front passenger-seat. Dobey spread himself in the rear seat. Before either of them could speak, Finchley beat them to the punch.

"It's about Lynda, isn't it?"

"It's about Lynda," agreed Blayde.

"Her mamma and I don't seem to be able to control her too well."

"Fifteen years old," said Blayde.

"Fifteen . . . closing sixteen."

"And pregnant."

"Yeah." Finchley sighed. His hands gripped the top of the steering-wheel rim. "We're gonna have a lot of trouble with that gal."

"Kids run wild sometimes," murmured Blayde.

"Running wild and fornication. They ain't the same thing, mister."

"Know who the father is?" asked Blayde.

"No."

"Has she hinted?"

"No. She don't know." Finchley hesitated,

then whispered, "She's a whore, mister." He lowered his head until it rested on the hands gripping the steering-wheel then, in an even softer voice, repeated, "She's a whore, but she's young and she's my daughter."

"Your wife?" probed Blayde gently.

"Liz." Finchley raised his head. In a heartbroken voice, he said, "She's ashamed. We've worked . . . both of us. The 'nigger' tag. We've worked to get rid of it. Mister, we've *worked.* Now Liz is ashamed to show her face outside the house." The hands loosened, then re-gripped the rim of the steering-wheel. In a voice suddenly angry, he said, "I'm English, mister. I was born here. So was Liz. We're as English as you are—as English as any of the trash who use that damn word. Our skin ain't white, that's all."

"I hadn't noticed," said Blayde solemnly.

"What?"

"The pigmentation. It's not important."

"It's important, mister." And now bitterness had joined the anger. "And you noticed."

The house was one of the better class, terrace-type on the outskirts of the town. Finchley owned it, and Finchley had looked after it. The paintwork, the pointing, the sharp edges of the well-kept lawn, the trimmed hedges, the weed-free flower beds. All the outward signs of a well-cared-for house. Inside was the same. Fitted carpets, a handful of popular prints on the walls, multi-store furniture, but good multi-store furniture, and looked after by a woman proud of keeping her home spotlessly clean.

Elizabeth Finchley wore pyjamas and a dressing-gown. In her mid—or late—forties, she'd also looked after herself. A little heavy perhaps, but in her youth she must have been a real beauty. Like her daughter, Lynda. That subtle beauty, the pride of bearing, which comes naturally to most black women. And she loved her man, and he loved her . . . and that, too, was very obvious.

The two of them, with Blayde and Dobey, sipped good percolated coffee at the kitchen table while in the front room the W.P.S. teased a statement from the pregnant fifteen-year-old.

Blayde had given firm instructions.

"The lot. How, when and where. Plus a description. We have to build the case on that statement, sergeant."

"You'll know everything," the W.P.S. had promised.

"Even the four-letter words."

"Her own language, sir. Whatever she knows, you'll know."

And now they were waiting. The four of them. Waiting, wondering and, as far as the Finchleys were concerned, worrying.

Dobey asked, "Who's the complainant, sir?"

"Mr. Finchley." Blayde didn't hesitate.

"Hey, mister," said Finchley, "I didn't make any . . ."

"I think you would have done."

"Send my own kin to prison?"

"She won't go to prison," promised Blayde with a smile. "The man responsible . . . *he'll* go to prison. I'll see to that, personally."

"If you find him."

"We'll find him."

"And what about my Lynda?" asked the coloured woman. "You gonna take her from her mammy and daddy?"

"Why should we do that?"

"They'll say we can't bring her up good."

" 'They'?"

"You know who we mean, man." Finchley chipped in alongside his wife. "Those Social Services people. They get their hands on things, they're gonna take Lynda and put her in a home or something."

Dobey said, "No, Tommy, that's not going to happen."

"And you?" Finchley looked accusingly at Blayde.

"You're not going to believe me," said Blayde bluntly. "Why the hell should I express an opinion?"

"You're gonna . . ."

"I'll tell you what I'm going to do, Mr. Finchley. The crime has a name. It's called Unlawful Carnal Knowledge. And I'm going to feel the collar of the criminal. The Social Services? You're more bothered about them than you are about your own daughter, that's the impression I get. Let any filthy pig handle your daughter—let him do what he likes with her—just as long as the Social Services don't hear about it."

"That ain't fair, mister," muttered Finchley.

"That's what it's beginning to sound like," snapped Blayde.

Elizabeth Finchley said, "Mister, I don't wanna lose my child."

"You won't, ma. Believe me, you won't." Dobey tried to be the peacemaker.

"He ain't said so."

"I'm not going to say so." Blayde's voice softened a little as he faced the distressed woman. "I don't know, and that's the truth. Constable Dobey doesn't know either, and that, also, is the truth."

"In that case, I don't wanna . . ."

"What you want doesn't count any more, madam. I'm not laying blame. But she's fifteen, she's pregnant and I don't believe in storks. That, basically, is all I'm interested in. I don't make promises I can't deliver. But I'll promise this: if the court asks I'll say she comes from a good home, with law-abiding parents. That much I'll say. If it helps—if it carries weight—I'll say it."

It was past 2.30 a.m. Blayde, Dobey and the W.P.S. were in Blayde's office, and Blayde was re-reading the statement the W.P.S. had taken from the fifteen-year-old Lynda Finchley.

> ...it was about two months ago. I think it was May 3rd. It was on a Saturday. I was on The Common, just walking. I was alone, this man was walking his dog. It was a terrier dog and he was throwing a stick. The stick just missed me and I threw it back, so we got to talking and he asked me whether I liked Blackpool and I said I'd never been to

Blackpool . . . it seemed okay and a good idea . . . daddy was in bed after working all night and mammy wasn't at home and was going out singing later. We went in his car and he drove fast . . . I don't know the make of the car, just that it was open. A black sports car. I didn't notice the number, a fast car. A two-seater. The dog sat between us . . . parked on the front . . . we just walked on the prom and on the sands. I paddled and wiped my feet on his handkerchief . . . so he took me to the Pleasure Beach and we had a ride on the Big Dipper . . . a meal at a cafe on the Pleasure Beach, then came back . . . he drove fast, to his place, up a sort of back street . . . cobbles. It was a dirty house and the sort I think they call back-to-back and as he opened the door a cat came out and the dog flew at it . . . bit it very badly on its back, near the top of its back legs . . . made some tea . . . I didn't really want it because it wasn't a very clean house . . . gave me a pound note . . . started to mess about with me. I was a bit frightened but it seemed okay . . . on the rug in front of the fire . . . there wasn't a fire in the grate . . . it hurt bad, I was really scared . . . ran out of the house but he didn't run after me . . . a bus stop or it might have been a trolley stop. I was frightened and can't be sure . . . either sixpence or a shilling to Huddersfield . . . the pound note, but there was no copper in the change . . . was still very frightened . . . a bus from Huddersfield back to Haggthorpe . . . didn't tell anybody until . . . then mammy made me tell her and she took me to see the doctor . . . having a baby. It has to be his, never been with anybody else. I think he was about forty . . . an old man. Almost as old as daddy I think. Perhaps older. Thin and with dark hair. No moustache . . . called him Malcolm. That's the only name he used . . . dark coloured clothes . . . I didn't hear him call the dog a name . . . I didn't notice the name of the street . . .

"Three foolscap pages." Blayde dropped the statement onto his desk. He looked at the W.P.S. and said, "What impression, sergeant?"

"She's a tease," said the W.P.S. bluntly. "Good looking and knows it. She enjoyed it up to the point of no-return. Then she was scared. She even enjoyed talking about it. But," added the W.P.S. solemnly, "she's scared of having the baby. That really scares her."

"Poor kid," murmured Dobey.

"Don't kid yourself," snapped the W.P.S. "She'll brag about it to her friends. A blow-by-blow description and inter-round summaries."

"First time?" asked Blayde.

"So she claims. First time with a man, I'm prepared to believe that. But chances are she's played feelie-for-feelie with her own age group, more than a few times."

"Look! She's only . . ." began Dobey.

Blayde cut in on Dobey's indignation and said, "She's a fifteen-year-old tart, constable. She lets herself be picked up by a man old enough to be her own father, she lets him take her to Blackpool for the day, she lets him take her back to his own place, then she lets him screw her . . . for a quid! What the hell else but a tart! She's scared because she's in the club. Without that minor coincidence we wouldn't know a damn thing. Nor would her parents."

"Do I make the Crime Complaint out, sir?" said Dobey in a flat, expressionless tone.

"You do. From her father . . . it might make the court think that little better of him. Time it for when we met him at the railway station. Get it down on paper, then go home. We start at nine o'clock, and you're C.I.D. Aide until further notice. I'll fix things with the inspector."

"Yes, sir. I'll do it now."

Dobey left the office and, when he'd closed the door, the W.P.S. smiled and said, "Another disillusioned man, inspector."

"He should have learned by this time."

"Pity, though," murmured the W.P.S.

"A pity?" Blayde sniffed his contempt. "Why the hell's name did he join if he wanted to keep his innocence?"

The trick was to find the elusive "Malcolm" . . . working on the problematic assumption that that was his real name. The starting point had to be Huddersfield. Huddersfield, because that was the place she first reached and recognised. So, Huddersfield. Blayde telephoned Huddersfield Public Transport and asked the first question. For sixpence how far could he travel on a bus or on a trolley? The routes? The various stopping places? Okay, now up it to a shilling: how far for a shilling?

On a large scale map he linked the minimum

and maximum points together. It looked like an out-of-shape doughnut, but he tapped it with the marker and said, "That's where he is, Dobey. Somewhere inside those two lines. He owns a sports car—open—black. It's not very new, it's not very shiny. Not if he lives in the sort of place she describes. Some creep called Malcolm who runs a black sports car. All we have to do is find him."

It wasn't very exciting. Criminal investigation rarely is. But it called for patience and the ability to move one step at a time. The garages first. For three days they moved from garage to garage; from filling station to filling station. And always the same questions.

"Somebody called Malcolm who runs a black sports car . . ."

"Okay, somebody not called Malcolm who runs a black sports car . . ."

"Somebody—anybody—who ran a black sports car on May 3rd . . ."

"Somebody who might have borrowed a black sports car on that day . . ."

And sports cars? Black sports cars? The outskirts of Huddersfield crawled with men running black sports cars. Huddersfield was the black-sports-car centre of the universe. And more than that, most of the guys who ran black sports cars were called Malcolm. And they all had to be checked out. The Malcolms and the non-Malcolms.

At the end of the third day, as they drove back to Haggthorpe, Dobey asked, "How long will it go on, sir?"

"Till we find him," said Blayde flatly.

Dobey tried to kill a sigh.

"Not romantic enough?" suggested Blayde drily. "No tyres screeching? No punch-ups?"

"It's a bit harrowing," admitted Dobey.

"Harrowing?"

"I wouldn't like it." Dobey warmed to his theme. "Some of 'em. Like me . . . happily married with kids. And coppers come knocking on the door asking whether I've tailed a fifteen-year-old. It's a bit rough."

"It puts 'em off their grub," admitted Blayde.

"There must be an easier way."

"Sure."

"What way's that, sir?"

"Let everybody get away with everything, then we can all sit back and draw the dole."

And so it continued. Four days. Five days. Quizzing mechanics and pump-assistants. Writing names and addresses in pocket books. Knocking on doors. Asking questions; embarrassing questions. Watching the man's face — watching his eyes—trying to guess whether he was telling the truth or working a flanker. Listening to answers, but never quite believing those answers.

"May 3rd? How do I know where I was on May 3rd?"

"Look! I'm not given to messing about with fifteen-year-old kids . . ."

"Go to hell. That's an insulting suggestion to even make . . ."

"Sure, I'd like to help. But I don't keep a diary, so . . ."

"So, I haven't an alibi. I don't need an alibi. It wasn't . . ."

Then, on Sunday, July 27th and a miserable, drizzling, cloud-heavy afternoon . . .

It was the right sort of house. The man's name was, indeed, Malcolm . . . Malcolm Piper. And Blayde had trotted out the same old questions.

"May 3rd?"

"May 3rd," agreed Blayde.

"What day of the week was that?"

"Saturday."

"Uhu." Piper seemed to ponder. "I don't work Saturdays. But I've no set routine."

"But you'd know?"

"Know? Oh, sure I'd know." Piper smiled. "It wasn't me. That much I do know. But I'm trying to think . . . trying to come up with somebody I might have been with."

"Were you at Haggthorpe?" suggested Blayde.

"No . . . no, no." Piper shook his head with certainty. "I wasn't there. Can't remember when I last visited Haggthorpe. Must be years ago."

"Blackpool?"

"No. Last year I went to see The Lights. Before that? When I was a kid. I don't often . . ."

"Ever been approached by a teenager?"

"Who? Me?" Piper looked amused and amazed. "I'm past the forty mark, inspector. If I need a woman—well, y'know — they're readily available. You pay your money, you take your choice. Bang away for the night and no harm done. I don't want some young amateur."

Dobey was making his way towards the door. One more interview, one more dud. How many more prize nerks were going to explain their sexual likes and dislikes? How many more "Malcolms" was this mad detective inspector going to probe and prod? The bloody crime was dead . . . dead as a ten-year-old corpse. Maybe Blayde got some sort of vicarious kick from listening to other men spouting buckets about the women they'd . . .

"Just that you're not married," murmured Blayde.

"Oh, aye, I'm married, inspector." Piper screwed his face into what was a mix of mild sorrow and cynical humour. "We're separated. Not divorced, separated. About six years ago. She found some bloke—y'know — he must have something I haven't."

Something you haven't? Something you have, boyo. Blayde could sense it and, if that sounds a little far-fetched, it was no less than the truth. The great detectives have—always have had, always will have—this sixth sense. Like a tribal witch doctor smelling out guilt, but with a good jack it's real. He was being taken for a ta-ta. He was being conned. Ask the right question. Phrase it in the right way . . .

Dobey turned the knob of the door very pointedly.

Blayde said, "It's a pity. About May 3rd, I mean."

"Aye, I know. I wish I could help."

"I mean, you would know . . . wouldn't you?"

"Eh?"

"A black teenager. Something you wouldn't forget?"

"I keep telling you, inspector."

Dobey opened the door a fraction and the cat nipped in out of the rain . . . and it was there! The healed scar, not yet furred over. Near the hip joint. It must have been one hell of a bite.

Blayde saw it, Dobey saw it and Dobey closed the door and held back a sigh of relief.

"Where's the dog?" asked Blayde softly. Coldly.

"The—the dog?" The change in Blayde's tone scared Piper.

"The dog that bit the cat, that killed the mouse . . ." Blayde stared unblinkingly at the paling face of Malcolm Piper. "This is the house that Jack built, Piper. This is the place. You're the man, and if you start squirming you'll end up on an identification parade just for laughs."

"I—I it wasn't altogether my fault."

"May 3rd," said Blayde relentlessly.

"You're—you're not going to believe this . . ."

"Probably not. After all the bullshit you've thrown at me I'm unlikely to believe anything. But try me."

"She—she asked for it."

"She got it, whether she asked for it or not. She's in the family way."

"Oh, God!" Piper bent slowly into a chair and covered his face with his hands.

"Get it off your chest, Piper. The constable, here, will write it down, then we'd like your autograph."

"Will they—will they . . ."

"Send you to prison?"

Still with his hands covering his face, Piper nodded.

"For a very long time." Blayde pulled no punches. "The next time you see a teenager, you'll be well past feeling randy."

It was used at police colleges as a text-book example of how a crime should be pressed to its absolute limit; of how statements should include everything—relevancies and irrelevancies—in order to give the enquiring team the maximum information to be used if necessary; of why it was essential to believe nothing without proof of its accuracy.

For Blayde it was one more chief constable's

commendation. For Chapman it was an opportunity to deflate any ego Blayde might be building up. "On paper, it looks good. But you know—and I know—that bloody cat solved the crime. If it hadn't walked in at that particular moment . . ." For Dobey it represented his first and only visit to an assize court, and the relief of returning to a more mundane life pounding the streets. For Piper it ended up with a five year stretch, and the knowledge that, once inside, the other cons would work to cripple him as a man who committed abominations upon children. For the Finchleys it meant . . . nothing. Public stupidity being what it is, their shame was considered to be on a par with Piper's and one more black family lost a little more faith in the British police system.

1958 became part of history, as did 1959. Blayde flogged on, always learning and always willing to learn. He reached the point where it was difficult to remember when he wasn't a copper. He finished and furnished his cottage, had a toe-to-toe slanging match with Chapman, but in the end got his own way; he could commute between the cottage and Haggthorpe. "But," warned Chapman, "you'd better be around when you're needed. Any policing by proxy and you won't know what the hell's hit you."

In retrospect those years were Blayde's proving time. He was a copper and he loved being a copper, but he insisted upon bobbying in his own way. He gave ballockings when they were needed. He took ballockings, but only when he considered them justified. He favoured no man, nor did he allow any man to trample on him simply for the hell of it. It was a very narrow plank he walked, and more than one wished him ill; hoped that his foot might slip and that, figuratively speaking, he'd break his neck. But he learned the art of balance and in time that plank became as safe to walk along as a six-lane carriageway.

In his private life, if it can be said he had a private life, he was content. Not happy; it would be incorrect and misleading to say he was happy, but at the same time it would be equally wrong and misleading to suggest that he was consciously unhappy. What he had was what he mistook for happiness; he wasn't miserable but spontaneous laughter never touched his lips. He was, therefore, content.

His cottage was his retreat. His womb-substitute. And he was everlastingly making minor improvements, both inside and out.

Loft insulation and double-glazing was coming into fashion, therefore he insulated the loft and fitted his own double-glazing units on every window and external door. He estimated how much of a garden he could keep clean and tidy, decided on a small lawn at the rear and a limited number of flower beds in which he could grow roses; the rest of the area he flagged, and the result added to the charm of the place. He had a telephone extension installed at his bedside, invested in a good second-hand Jag and learned all the short cuts, cutting out possible traffic bottlenecks, between the cottage and various parts of Haggthorpe Division and could, therefore, arrive at the scene of any crime within minutes (and sometimes even before) of the arrival of an official squad car. And Chapman was conscious of these efforts on the part of his divisional detective inspector to improve his efficiency and get-at-ability.

As for women . . .

He was reaching the forty mark, and sex had never been a prominent, or even important, part of his life. Sex, as he saw it, was a mere habit, a pleasant habit but a habit which, if uncontrolled, could grow into an addiction. For a few weeks (no more than three months, if that) he was the deliberate target for a young and attractive widow from Pinthead; a petite woman, perhaps a couple of years younger than himself, whose husband had been killed in a car crash and whose only child—a teenage son—was seeking a career in the merchant navy. She was lonely and she tipped her bonnet in Blayde's direction, and for those few weeks she regularly shared his bed. She was an excellent cook and, in his own slightly sardonic fasion, Blayde took what was on offer, but neither made nor implied any promises. Eventually she grew hungry at the obvious lack of progress.

"I'm not a doormat, you know."

"Have I given that impression?"

"There are other men who'd happily exchange a wedding ring for what you seem to take for granted."

"I don't doubt it." Blayde had smiled a tired, couldn't-care-less smile. "Don't let me stand in your way."

And that had been that. She'd left in a huff. It may well be that she'd expected Blayde to seek her out and make amends. If so, she was a disappointed woman.

Joe Benton—an occasional visitor who liked to share the warmth of the cottage kitchen while he and Blayde enjoyed a quiet smoke away from nagging women—said, "Tha's a real one-man-band, Bob."

"I'm happy. I don't need an army of friends."

"She damn near had thee."

Blayde chuckled knowingly.

"Well, she thowth she had," Benton corrected himself.

Thus the cottage became a home in the real sense of the word, while policing remained the mainspring of his life. House- shop- and store-breaking was the bread-and-butter level of bobbying, and within the area of Haggthorpe Division he could make an educated guess at who might be responsible merely by noting the method of entry. The professionals, the semi-professionals and the rank amateurs could be spotted, merely by glancing at the manner in which, say, a bedroom had been searched for loot. A quick catalogue of what had been stolen gave an indication of which known fence might have accepted the property from the thief. A man on the cadge one day then, the day after a break-in, lashing drinks all round to his cronies . . . nobody had to look far for the thief. These, and a score of other equally simple guidelines, coupled with a never-ending accumulation of local knowledge and a handful of reliable snouts. Thief-taking was a game; as skilled as bridge and as cunning as chess, but nevertheless a game. And Blayde worked at learning every rule and every move in that game.

Crimes of violence proliferated, but only slightly. The great upsurge of assaults and muggings of the 'seventies was just beginning to show itself. And, of all crimes, Blayde loathed those involving smashed bodies. The men working under him knew exactly where they stood.

"The hell with any pussyfooting around. Those bastards aren't going to be allowed a monopoly as far as the infliction of pain is concerned. Every last one of 'em . . . they all resist arrest. They all arrive at the nick with blood on their clothes. Nor do we play at Queensbury Rules. It's not a matter of who's the best man. The copper's the best man—he'd *better* be—if he has to hit the other bugger over the head with the side of a house."

More than once Chapman had him in his office.

"Is it necessary?"

"As necessary as what he did."

"You're getting this division something of a name, inspector."

"That's what I'm after, sir."

"I'm getting some flak from headquarters, that's what I'm saying."

"Good. Give 'em my compliments, and suggest they remove their respective arses from all those comfortable chairs. Come out and show us how to do it. I'll give you my contribution to the wreath now."

And always Chapman grinned and said, "Consider yourself ballocked, inspector."

"Yes, sir."

"Just don't break anybody's neck, that's all."

"Unless it's strictly necessary, sir."

There was a rapport between the two; that plus a mutual respect which was near-unique. Chapman fielded the bouncers and, where possible, returned them to the sender. Blayde tore into the criminal fraternity and earned respect via fear. He weeded the Haggthorpe C.I.D. of all deadwood. He demanded men—if possible ex-servicemen who'd been part of the shooting war—willing to work by the case-load and not by the hour. Men who didn't give a damn about the odds. Dedicated men to whom crime detection was a form of religion.

They still talk about that Chapman/Blayde period in the history of Haggthorpe Police Division. Legends have been formed around the cases, around the chances which were taken, around the almost unbelievable blinders pulled to slap some crook, some tearaway, in a dock.

There is a "Golden Age" in every force, in every division; a period—long or short—when the chemistry of practical law-enforcement works with a smooth efficiency bordering upon magic. Men bring about such periods. Men—sometimes singly, sometimes in pairs, sometimes in groups—but men who stamp a personal trademark on the area over which they hold sway. And when they leave, when the team is broken up, when retirement or some other reason takes away all, or even a part, of that magic the crooks know. They smile, rub their hands with glee and know that they can now get away with villainies they would previously never have contemplated, because one more "Golden Age" has run its course.

And always—in every inquiry touching upon Lessford or the people of Lessford—

Blayde asked questions. Additional questions. Subtle questions which had little or nothing to do with the investigation in hand. Private questions, the answers to which he stored away in his memory and never forgot.

On the first day of March, 1960, Blayde answered a call to Chapman's office. It was a Tuesday; a dreary, miserable Tuesday; a Tuesday which seemed to be hellbent on staving off even the first hint of the end of a dreary winter.

Chapman waved Blayde to a chair and said, "Sit down, Bob."

Blayde sat down and waited.

Chapman seemed to have unaccustomed difficulty in saying what he had to say. He chose a devious route and asked questions—made remarks—which puzzled Blayde and made him wonder about the reason for this summons.

Chapman said, "You still have that uniform? The one you wore at Pinthead Pike?"

"Yes."

"Moths been at it?"

"No. It's still in the wardrobe. Both of'em . . . I have two, of course."

"Of course. Of course." Chapman paused, then asked, "How's the fit?"

"They fit I suppose. I haven't tried 'em on for years. But I haven't put on weight."

"Fine." Chapman nodded, as if relieved. He fiddled with a pencil, didn't look at Blayde, as he continued, "I've—er—I've never asked you to take acting rank."

"You've always known what my answer would be."

"Yes."

"If a man deserves a rank he *deserves* that rank. Acting means not-quite-up-to-the-mark, but let's wait and see."

"No. Not quite that."

Blayde growled, "Superintendent, don't flannel. We know each other too well."

"We know each other," sighed Chapman.

"If you're offering me an acting rank—with respect—stuff it."

"They all have acting ranks," said Chapman sadly.

"You're talking in riddles, sir."

"It comes through substantive before they return to active duty."

"I still don't know what the hell . . ."

Chapman looked up, and almost blurted, "You've been recommended as an inspector at the training college. Acting chief inspector."

Blayde stared, then breathed, "Christ!"

"A two-year stint. Subject to renewal, if you want it renewed. You'll *be* a chief inspector by the time you get back."

"Who the hell . . ." began Blayde.

"I did." Chapman, having broken the news, was his old assertive self. "I recommended you. I want coppers, not book men. Not just in this division, either. Throughout the force. There's a new breed coming through the pipeline, Bob. They're being brainwashed by idiots, and when we get 'em they're no bloody good."

"We teach 'em," argued Blayde.

"But first we have to unteach them. And that's a waste of time."

"I'm no bloody school-teacher," grumbled Blayde.

"Damn it all, you'll be third in command!" exploded Chapman. "Don't make things worse for me. I don't want to lose you, but what I do want is you back here, with three pips and a whole sub-division under your control."

"Third in command?"

"The commandant—a chief superintendent—acting. The assistant commandant—superintendent—acting. Then *you*. Official designation . . . senior instructor. Three, maybe four, inspectors—acting. All the others, sergeants—acting." Chapman glared and opened the throttles wide. "Blayde, you're going because I want you to go. I've pulled strings as thick as bell-ropes to get . . ."

"Police politics," sneered Blayde. "Always police politics."

"I don't give a damn if it's international brinksmanship. One day you'll thank me. Damn it, man! Two years . . . it's not a lifetime. You can do good. Give the infernal recruits something more substantial than book knowledge. Then come back here, and take up the position of Number Two."

"It's an order, then?" growled Blayde.

"No. I can't make it an order, you know that as well as I do. I wish to hell I could."

"Tell me I have to," said Blayde gruffly, "and, whether you can make it an order or not, I'll accept it as one."

"I'll make it a personal request."

"In that case . . ." Blayde shrugged. "I'd better invest in some chalk and a sponge."

Round pegs in square holes. The force—every force—displays a positive genius for putting the wrong guy in the right place. For the best reason in the world, of course. No police authority wants its officers to be miserable . . .

it just doesn't give a damn if they are.

And yet . . .

Blayde expected to hate the job. He arrived at the training college prepared to make as big a bloody nuisance of himself as possible. Damn the eyes of the man who wrote the book, Blayde was determined to open secret doors and let these grass-green recruits see the filth, and the twisting, and the sheer, soul-destroying slog which went to make up successful bobbying.

He was surprised to find he had a friend; a man with similar ideas, but a man unable to put those ideas into practice. The assistant commandant. A roly-poly Yorkshireman from Doncaster. A droll man whose stone-faced sense of humour left some of the recruits unable to decide what was serious and what was leg-pulling. "A broken collar bone. First Aid. You ram a billiard ball into the armpit and strap the arm firmly to the side of the body. Always use a billiard ball—never a snooker ball—and if you happen to be miles from anywhere, way and gone to hell on the Yorkshire Moors, you're in luck . . . you can't move for billiard balls."

Or when he was announcing an end-of-course dance. "You may each bring a guest.

Preferably female, otherwise people might get the wrong idea. Your wife. Your girlfriend. Even some girl you may have met in the town. Not, however, the sort of girl one young hopeful escorted here a few months back. She wasn't the biggest whore in the district . . . that reputation was held by her sister."

His name was Alf Morrison and he literally ran the college. He carried the crown of a superintendent on his shoulders and, when necessary, his tongue could sand-blast any dim-witted recruit out of existence. He didn't hate the commandant, he merely despised him and did nothing to hide the fact.

"A rare breed, Bob. A career policeman. All his life he's been locked away in one college or another. Four years to a pension, and I've worked it out, he's spent slightly less than two years out on the streets. And that pin-brained creep is responsible for training working rozzers."

Not that it mattered. The commandant spent his life in the high atmosphere of his own making. Passing Out Day saw him in all his splendour, chatting to various chief constables and Home Office officials, but for the rest he sat in a comfortable armchair, in a plush office, dictating memos to underlings who, having read them, burned them or screwed them up and tossed them into the nearest waste-paper basket.

Alf Morrison—now assisted by Blayde—made the college work. Morrison gave pep-talks and the like. Blayde stood in and either took over a lecture and, in so doing, brought out the usual lecturer in a muck-sweat, or slammed questions at a gasping class of recruits.

Blayde it was who devised the "observation question" with which every lecture opened.

"Okay, you've just walked down the corridor to this classroom: how many light bulbs?"

"You've all looked at the wall-clock in the dining-hall: roman numerals or arabic numerals?

"Superintendent Morrison's motor car, it's parked in the Staff Car Park enough times, what's its make, what's its registration number?

"By this time, you've all been down to the town, how many traffic roundabouts between the college gates and the council offices?"

Every day, for three months, a different question. A never-ending search for such questions by the instructors. In time, an eager awaiting for that first "non-police" question which opened every lecture. The recruits didn't realise it, but they were being taught observation, and observation was the rock upon which local knowledge would, eventually, be built. And local knowledge detected crimes.

His stand-in lecture on the Judges Rules:

". . . thought up by bewigged hermits who do not live in this world. The Official Caution. You all know it, and rest assured that ninety per cent of all crooks you'll ever interview will know it better than you do. You administer it to an accused person when in your opinion, he might be charged with the crime under investigation. In your opinion. Very important words. Only you know when you reach that opinion. The defending barrister doesn't know. The judge doesn't know. Only you. So, don't have a suspicious mind. Keep asking questions. Be dumb. Be trusting. Give His Nibs the benefit of every doubt under the sun. Then, when he's tied himself into small knots—when he's admitted everything you *want* him to admit—reach your opinion. Decide that he might be charged with the crime, and administer the Official Caution.

"Do it in a clear voice. Pronounce every

word distinctly. That's what the Judges Rules instruct you to do. But unless you want His Nibs to shut up like a clam, walk from the Interview Room, close the door, and then administer the caution. The judges say you have to rattle off that ridiculous rigmarole, they don't add that the accused has to hear it. If he can't hear what's said behind a closed door that's his tough luck . . ."

Or ". . . at which point the prisoner is allowed a telephone call. *One* telephone call. The law doesn't say so, but the judges leave no doubt . . . the prisoner must be allowed *one* telephone call. Let me remind you what the judges don't say. They don't say when. They don't say you have to give every snivelling little tea-leaf—every smart-talking con merchant—complete freedom of a police station switch-board. He makes that telephone call at your convenience, not his, and you decide when it's 'convenient' . . ."

Morrison fairly gurgled with delight when whispers of the type of lecture delivered by Blayde reached his ears.

"You're priceless, Bob," he chuckled. "All those po-faced, would-be-schoolmasters are peeing their frilly little panties in case word reaches the commandant."

Blayde said, "I didn't want to come. But now I'm here, I'm damned if I'll perpetuate the 'friendly family policeman' gag."

"I'm behind you, old son." Morrison dropped an eyelid. "This particular commandant . . . he'll never know. Officially. He won't even ask. He won't even question. It might put his own job at risk."

Nor was Morrison a slouch when it came to lecturing in front of a gawping audience of embryo-flatfeet. His favourite lesson had the grand title of "Ranks, Insignias and the Chain of Command."

". . . crossed tipstaves, surrounded by a laurel wreath. I tell you that, purely as a point of academic interest. There isn't a snowball's chance in hell of any of you lot ever reaching the rank of chief constable.

". . . there are many ways to the top in the Police Service. You can, of course, work your balls off and hope. You'll thus become eunuchs, but the chances are that's all you'll become. You can mow the superintendent's lawn during off-duty periods. With luck, and supposing he's feeling less liverish than usual, that might bring on the chevrons.

". . . the most certain way to advancement is to find a chief constable's daughter. It doesn't matter if she's a face like a horse and a figure like a sack of spanners. You're looking for advancement, not love. Put her in the family way, offer to marry her, and you'll end up a superintendent before your next-shift comes round. It's a hard, harsh world my little innocents. The Police Service invented nepotism. I know of one piffling little force—no names, no pack-drill—authorised strength, one chief constable, two superintendents. The chief constable, the assistant chief constable and one of the superintendents are brothers. The odd man out—the other superintendent—is their cousin. In short, a family business. The reverse side of the coin to the Mafia . . ."

Strangely, and thanks in no small measure to Morrison, Blayde quite enjoyed his stint as a police college instructor. Each weekend was free, and each weekend he drove back to his cottage and was able to relax without the possibility of interruption by an urgent telephone call. At the college he lived in a compact little flat on the second floor; bedroom, bathroom and tiny lounge. He was awakened by one of the civilian staff who brought him an early-morning cup of tea, he took all his meals in the massive dining room and, each evening, before he retired, he liked to change into a sports jacket, stroll into the communal lounge and exchange small-talk with the recruits. They were what Morrison regularly called them . . . innocents. That great influx of ex-servicemen had trickled, then dried up. These poor young devils were being thrown in at the deep end. Often the sign of homesickness was there at the back of their eyes; decent kids who had to be taught law but (and of equal practical importance) also when to push the law aside and deal with tearaways in the only language tearaways understand.

"You've a truncheon. Carry it, *always*. You'll need it when you least think you need it. And never bluff with it. If you have to draw it, *use* it."

They chatted as near-equals. The youngsters, eager to learn, and Blayde equally eager to pass on tips and wrinkles.

"Don't try for popularity. Sod popularity. Try for respect, a respect based upon impartiality. And don't soften. Let some smart-talking bastard get away with a minor motoring offence—let him butter you up to your face—that night, in the pub, he'll be bragging about how he conned a stupid young copper."

A thousand and one ways. The difference

between policing and merely wearing a blue uniform. And, because he talked quietly but with authority, they listened and remembered.

"When you get out there, find yourself a model. A good policeman. A practical policeman. A policeman happy in his job. They aren't hard to recognise. Start off by doing things his way. The way he walks, the way he interviews, the way he goes about his business. Then very gradually, as you gain experience, add your own variations to his way. Don't forget everything you've been taught here, but don't think any of it's holy writ. Me? I'm not proud. I moulded myself on another copper. A damn good copper. A Police Constable Sharpe. I owe him a damn sight more than I'll ever owe a police training college."

On Monday, March 5th, 1962, Blayde's acting rank became his real rank. Chief Inspector Robert Blayde. He was offered a second two-year stint as assistant commandant (acting superintendent) at another police training college, and the truth is he was tempted. Only Morrison had the wisdom to point out the obvious flaw.

"He's not the same as this commandant, Bob. I've worked under him. Leave the rails once and he'll nail you. He goes strictly by the adverts, the poor buggers only learn the truth when they've left the college."

That was enough. On Saturday, March 31st, Blayde shook hands with Morrison, drove back to his cottage and, on Monday, April 2nd, he reported to Chapman's office as a working, uniformed, chief inspector, and second-in-command at Haggthorpe Division.

It was good to be back. Chapman and he were almost level-pegging; they could use first names without a vague feeling of awkwardness and during those first few weeks Blayde set about sorting out the weaknesses and evaluating the strengths throughout the whole division.

Then on Sunday, May 6th, 1962, Chapman suffered a heart attack while reaching high to re-paint the ceiling of his lounge. Despite the care lavished at the hospital, despite Chapman's own fierce will to stay alive, it was too much. Too massive an attack. He died four weeks later to the day, and Blayde mourned the passing of a friend . . . perhaps also the passing of a protector.

Chapman's place was filled by a man Blayde already knew. Perkins. Inspector Perkins—now, of course, Superintendent Perkins. The man who liked long words. The one-time pipsqueak who'd counted names on Lost and Found Reports.

From the sublime to the ridiculous . . . and Blayde wondered *how* ridiculous.

15

SUPERINTENDENTS. Don't let the rank fool you. Don't let the lady novelists, whose superintendents are always hawk-featured, bronze-skinned, dark-eyed and unmarried, lead you up their own particularly romantic garden path. Man, not God, makes superintendents, and man can drop some awful googlies. *Ergo,* superintendents can come in all shapes, all sizes and all degrees of idiocy. Short and fat, long and thin; taciturn and garrulous; long-sighted and as blind as a bat. Some are anatomically on the skew; they think the crown on their shoulder is, in fact, on their head. Some rarely wear their uniform, other than on official occasions, others damn near go to bed in it. Some, quite a few, are aware of their own shortcomings and, in order to shroud their own dimness of wit, surround themselves with hand-picked officers in order to play at paper tigers, in the happy knowledge that, if something comes unstuck, there's always the guy down the line to whom the messy baby can be passed.

Perkins was of a kind. Put briefly, a pompous prat, but unfortunately carrying the rank which entitled him to enjoy his pomposity to his heart's content and to be as pratish as he wished, without anybody around to slam on the brakes.

His first clash with Blayde occurred within the first week of his superintendentship.

"Direct from training school?" Perkins lounged in the chair, behind the desk which Blayde would always know as 'Chapman's desk', and eyed Blayde with open contempt. "It doesn't help much, does it?"

"I wasn't a pupil," said Blayde gently.

"Nevertheless, you lose touch . . . with reality, I mean."

"That has yet to be seen."

"Now—er—as I remember . . . correct me if I'm wrong. You were a constable—a recruit—at Sopworth. I was an inspector at the time."

Blayde nodded.

"You've done well for yourself."

"I've—er—'not let the side down'," mocked Blayde quietly.

"I beg your pardon?"

"Your own advice. The first—the only—advice you ever gave me."

"Ah, quite." Perkins shifted his angular

frame into a more nonchalant position in the desk chair. "We must work together, of course."

"Superintendent Chapman had that in mind."

"Ah, yes. But Superintendent Chapman's methods . . . they're not my methods."

Blayde waited.

"I intend," explained Perkins, "to make this division the show division of the force. Smartness of turn-out. Uniforms clean and creased. Nothing slovenly. Slovenliness, in any form, will be dealt with severely."

Blayde continued to wait.

"As with reports, statements, general paper-work. There is a way—the *correct* way—and I want nothing less. The same with the section stations, the outside beat stations, they will be kept clean, they will be kept tidy and, above all else, only officers entitled to be there will be there. The rest—inspectors, sergeants, constables—they'll be doing what *they* should be doing. Out on the various beats, enforcing the law and supervising the enforcement of the law."

"And crime?" asked Blayde in a deliberately off-hand tone.

"I expect the crime rate to plummet," said Perkins with absolute confidence.

"May I ask why?" asked Blayde politely.

"I've already told you, Blayde." Irritability in Perkins's tone almost triggered Blayde's temper. "A good turn-out. That makes for a tidy mind, and tidy minds detect crimes."

"I see."

"On duty on time. Work . . . don't waste time in public houses, drinking with scum, in the hope that they'll do your work for you. And leave no aspect of an enquiry open to chance. Detecting crime isn't difficult, Blayde. All it needs is proper application."

"And, of course, a smart turn-out."

"Eh? Quite . . . therefore, crime statistics will plummet."

It didn't work. There wasn't a hope in hell of it ever working; successful policing being based upon far more than well-polished boots and clean fingernails. But (and here the uninitiated may be pushed to understand) Perkins was allowed to live in his own fairy-tale world, and think it worked. Blayde was the brick wall from which everything Perkins shouldn't know bounced. Word went down the chain of command like wildfire; if a working copper dropped a clanger he did his best to cover it up, if he couldn't cover it up, the sub-divisional inspector tried to cover it up, and if he couldn't cover it up it arrived in Blayde's In-tray.

Thereafter it was held in limbo pending Perkins's Weekly Rest Day—or perhaps Annual Leave—at which point Blayde handled things, tore mens' balls out by the roots if necessary, but whatever shunted the offending incident through D.H.Q. with a covering minute.

Perkins thought he was running the best police division since Robert Peel thought up the idea. He was encouraged to hold that belief. The whole of the division, led by Blayde, worked like the clappers to build the windowless ivory tower in which Perkins took his ease in comfortable ignorance.

Over those first few months every inspector and every sergeant received the same instructions . . . off the record, of course.

"Bugger Perkins. Anything that smells a little crappy, let *me* know. At my office, if I'm there. If not, at the cottage. But—wherever—let *me* know first."

It meant work. It meant inconvenience. It meant un-logged overtime by the ton. But there was a reason and the reason, as far as Blayde was concerned, was a sufficient reason. Haggthorpe Division was still Chapman's division. Perkins and his cock-eyed ideas was a sick joke. An insult to the memory of a man whose shoe-laces he wasn't fit to tie.

That, then, was Blayde's reason. But the real reason—the deep-down, unacknowledged reason—went farther than that. It had to do with the Police Service itself. It had to do with an abstract feeling of belonging; of the force, and the fact that the force had become part of him no less than he was part of the force. He knew every man in the division; knew his name, knew his number, knew the beat he was responsible for. In many cases he knew the name of the man's wife. Knew the names of his kids. He might have denied it, but the truth was that Blayde gradually began to look upon Haggthorpe Division as *his* division. His personal responsibility, with Perkins a mere annoyance in the background. And, whenever possible, he took a perverse delight in making Perkins look foolish.

Christmas, 1964 . . .

The incident occurred at Dingsby Section; a single sergeant, six-man section well away from Haggthorpe itself. Blayde received the message at his office as he was contemplating ending the day and returning to the cottage for a quiet Christmas Eve, alone. Some damn-fool motorist had parked his car, then opened his offside door directly into the path of a pedal cyclist. The cyclist had tried to swerve, caught the front wheel of his machine against the door and purled over the handlebars. He'd landed on the tarmac, head first, fractured his skull and was now in the morgue of Handley General Hospital.

Blayde drove over and at Dingsby Police Station met the Police Constable i/c the section.

"The sergeant's off duty with a 'flu bug." Blayde verified what he already knew.

"Yes, sir." The P.C. i/c was a man in his middle years and a good, conscientious copper. He looked worried. "The motorist's in a hell of a state, it's spoiled *his* Christmas. He's given a full statement, accepting complete responsibility."

"And the cyclist?"

"Dead on Arrival. We just don't know who he is."

"What's happened so far?"

"Well—like I say—the motorist. He's made a statement, and he's on his way home. I've had the Photography Section out, they've photographed the scene. The cyclist, he's a gonner. They took a morgue shot of him—head and shoulders—for circulation. We've searched his clothes . . . nothing. He could be an office worker on his way home. Or a not-too-well-off chap starting his Christmas holiday. There's nothing to tell. No identification of any sort. Fingerprints came out with the Photography Section. They've taken dabs in case he's any previous."

Blayde grunted his satisfaction.

"I've notified the coroner," continued the constable. "It's being treated as a Sudden Death. I haven't yet circulated his description, but that's the next step . . . through the division, I thought."

"Throughout the force," suggested Blayde.

"Yes, sir," The constable hesitated, then added, "And the newspapers, sir. The locals. I've notified them."

"Why not?" smiled Blayde.

"They'll be out again on Monday. If he isn't traced by then . . ."

"Good thinking." Blayde nodded. "Meanwhile, we'd better keep on hand in case he's reported Missing From Home."

"Yes, sir. The body's on ice, waiting for identification."

"You've just about done everything," congratulated Blayde. "Fatal Accident. Sudden Death. Missing From Home. No fault there. Get on the blower and circulate things."

The constable said, "Yes, sir," and felt duly self-satisfied at his ability to handle what could have been a tricky situation.

That was Christmas Eve. The following morning Blayde nipped back to Dingsby to check possible progress. Nothing further had happened, and the P.C. i/c said, "Looks as if we'll have to wait over the holiday period, sir. My guess is a Missing From Home, but he won't be missed until after Christmas."

"You're probably right," agreed Blayde. He glanced at his watch, and added, "Christmas dinner?"

"Next job, sir," grinned the constable. "Strict orders from the missus, it'll be on the table at one o'clock sharp."

"Wish her the compliments of the season from me."

"Thank you, sir, I will."

At which point Perkins walked into Dingsby Police Station. With a bare grunt of acknowledgement, he checked the section books and found no fault. After initialling them, he turned to the constable.

"That fatal accident yesterday. What have you done, so far?"

The constable rattled off the various steps he'd taken to identify the dead man, then waited for some form of congratulation. Instead of which he received criticism.

"Forensic science?" snapped Perkins.

"Sir?" The constable looked puzzled.

"Nail scrapings. Hair clippings. For forensic examination. Initial action, surely?"

"I—er . . ." The constable swallowed. "No, sir. I haven't taken nail parings or hair clippings from the corpse. I—er—I arranged to have his fingerprints . . ."

"You're not a *recruit*, constable."

"No, sir."

"That being the case, surely . . ."

"The fault's mine, superintendent," interrupted Blayde flatly.

"What?"

"I was here when the officer was handling the case. He told me what he'd done. I thought it sufficient, and said so."

"It is most certainly not sufficient." Perkins coloured as the anger touched his tone. He turned to the constable and snapped, "Now—

immediately—you'll go to Handley General Hospital. You'll take nail parings and hair clippings from the dead man and deliver them to whoever's on duty at the forensic science laboratory and request an examination."

The constable moistened his lips, and croaked, "Yes, sir."

"And in future, you'll handle these incidents with a little more efficiency. A little more imagination."

"Yes, sir."

Perkins left and for a few moments neither Blayde nor the constable spoke.

The Blayde said, "Your wife should be just putting the finishing touches to the meal."

"Yes." The constable sighed heavily. "I'd better ring her and tell her . . ."

"Go home. Enjoy your Christmas dinner," interrupted Blayde.

"Y'mean go to the morgue after . . ."

"I'll call at Handley General on my way back to Haggthorpe. I'll see to the nail parings and the hair cuttings."

The constable frowned indecision.

"I'll make it an order, if that'll clear your conscience," said Blayde.

"No sir." The frown disappeared. "Thank you, sir. Thank you very much."

On Wednesday, December 30th, the dead cyclist was reported as a Missing Person by the Preston police. Later that day the body was identified and on Friday, the first day of 1965, an inquest was held and that was (or should have been) the end of it. But Perkins (being Perkins) couldn't leave well alone.

The assistant chief constable arrived at Haggthorpe D.H.Q. It was one of those things; an Olympic god descending on a periodic visit, in order to assure mere mortals that he hadn't bogged off and left them in the lurch to fend for themselves. The luck of the draw . . . both Blayde and Perkins were in Perkins's office when the great man arrived.

There was much puff and panic and, the new year being but three days old, Perkins dived in at the deep end in an attempt to impress. Among other things, he rattled on about the pedal cyclist who'd been killed on Christmas Eve.

". . . something of a puzzler, sir. Something of a problem. I visited Dingsby the next day. Christmas Day. Fortunately, as it happened. All avenues of enquiry had not been explored. I ordered that nail scrapings and hair clippings from the body be forwarded to the laboratory for examination."

"Really?" The A.C.C. cocked a quizzical eyebrow.

"The body was identified . . . when was it, chief inspector?"

"Wednesday," said Blayde in a flat voice. "Reported Missing from Home at Preston."

"Ah, yes." Perkins smiled happily. "Fortunately there was no need to call the forensic people as witnesses at the inquest. But I had a confidential report from the lab. They'd pinpointed him. Lancashire. *Industrial* Lancashire."

"From the parings and clippings?" The A.C.C. sounded very impressed.

"Oh, yes." Perkins nodded. "A narrowing down of the field, you see, sir. Had he not been reported missing, we should, at least, have known where to make enquiries . . ."

About thirty minutes later, the A.C.C. left and Perkins and Blayde lighted cigarettes. Perkins had a thin film of sweat on his face. Blayde's expression was as impassive as a stone wall.

Blayde lowered himself into a chair and in a quiet, but unusually hard, voice said, "A heart-to-heart talk, Perkins. Do you mind?"

"What?" Perkins looked surprised. He sounded a little breathless; as if the visit of the

A.C.C. had been as physically exhausting as a well-run race.

"All that crap about pinpointing the cylist to industrial Lancashire."

"I—er—what exactly are you getting at, Blayde?"

"You asked a man," said Blayde slowly, "to scrape the fingernails and take hair clippings from a corpse immediately before he went home for his Christmas dinner."

"Naturally. It was . . ."

"What it wasn't going to do was help him enjoy his meal."

"That's of no great importance, Blayde. As divisional officer, I demand . . ."

"I told him not to," cut in Blayde.

"What?"

"I told him *I'd* take the parings and clippings on my way back to Haggthorpe."

"As long as they were taken," snapped Perkins.

"And they pinpointed the cylist to industrial Lancashire?" murmured Blayde.

"I had a confidential report. I was informed . . ."

"Balls."

"What?" Perkins's eyes widened.

"You're a liar," said Blayde calmly.

"Chief Inspector Blayde, I don't wish to pull rank . . ."

"You'd still be a liar."

". . . but when I make a statement it can be accepted as nothing short of absolute truth . . ."

"Not this time."

". . . and, moreover, it is blatantly obvious that you have no conception as to the skill of forensic scientists . . ."

"Skill! They must be bloody magicians. It was *my* nail parings and *my* hair clippings they were buggering about with."

"They can . . ." Perkins suddenly closed his mouth. Then, in little more than a whisper, he said, "What was that?"

"My nail parings. My hair clippings," repeated Blayde calmly. "I had a meal waiting, too."

"You—you mean . . ."

"I mean," said Blayde dangerously, "you've just fed an assistant chief constable up to the eyeballs with sheer crap . . . and I can prove it."

There was a silence; a silence in which trepidation, fury and contempt formed an invisible but explosive mixture. Perkins drew hard and long on his cigarette, and the cigarette trembled slightly as he came to reluctant terms with the exposure of his stupidity. Blayde remained cool; in complete control of the situation; knowing what he was going to say next, but giving the other man time enough to appreciate his own impossible position.

Then in a flat statement of fact Blayde said, "We don't like each other."

"Can you—can you wonder, when . . ."

"Don't bluster," snapped Blayde. "Agree or disagree. We don't like each other."

"We don't like each other," breathed Perkins.

"Lyndon Johnson," said Blayde calmly. "He didn't like Hoover, the boss of the F.B.I. But he didn't sack him, and Hoover asked why. Johnson put it in a nutshell. 'I'd sooner have you inside the tent pissing out, than outside the tent pissing in.' That's now your option, Perkins. Inside or outside. My way or your way."

"Your way?" Perkins looked genuinely amazed.

"It's been my way," said Blayde, "since the minute you took over this office. Chapman's way, if you like. The whole damn division. Pulling blinders to keep it running the way he ran it. We've let you kid yourself, and I've been putting up the biggest smoke screen. But no more, eh?"

Perkins moistened his lips.

"Police politics," said Blayde gently. "I've been taught by experts. Hale at Pinthead Pike. Chapman here, at Haggthorpe. I don't like it—I don't enjoy it—but it's sometimes necessary."

"What . . ." Again, Perkins moistened his lips. "What had you in mind?"

"You're still divisional officer." Blayde's tone was cool and certain. "You sign everything through this office, but *I* check it first. And no snowstorm of Misconduct Forms. That's a sure sign of a lousily run division. Just act out the role. 'Superintendent Perkins'. Draw the salary and be happy. Let *real* coppers run the show."

Perkins took a deep, shuddering breath.

"Otherwise," warned Blayde, "the nail parings and hair clippings fiasco might get leaked to County Headquarters."

Perkins nodded his head, once.

"Good." Blayde stood up and made for the door. He smiled as he added, "Look upon it as a clanger you've dropped. But it's been picked up, and it's done good all round."

As Blayde reached the door, Perkins breathed, "I'll get you for this, Blayde."

"You'll try," agreed Blayde. "But you'll have to concentrate on other things than highly-polished boots."

It happens, and it happens at all levels. At section level a sergeant can be a mere figurehead while a senior constable holds the section together. It happens at divisional level. It even happens way up top; the chief constable is little more than a rubber stamp, while the whole force is run by an A.C.C. Sometimes it is done quietly, and nobody is any the wiser. At other times, the whole damn force knows who the real boss is and the paper chief is allowed to go about his socialising unhindered and unheeded, because while he's knocking it back with the big-wigs he isn't getting under people's feet. In this respect, coppers are a queer tribe. They choose and recognise their own leaders, and all the tin-ware on the epaulets, and all the scrambled egg on the peaked caps, means damn-all. Within the orbit of his own authority a village bobby can carry far more weight than the Head of C.I.D. Within the tight area of a city beat a pavement-basher can raise a finger, and the citizenry will happily do what they would refuse to do at the behest of a police commissioner.

These men—these natural-born law-enforcers—have an air. A panache. A unique charisma. They can stroll into the very heart of a near-riot and, merely by their presence, cool things to the point of reasonableness. They can walk up to a half-mad tearaway—a rogue of the species capable of terrifying a whole neighbourhood—and grip his arm above the elbow and, like a new-born lamb, he'll allow himself to be guided to the nearest nick.

They have "the touch", and beyond that there is no known explanation.

Blayde had it. He had it by the ton. He had the knack of being at the right place at the right time. He had that luck without which no man—no woman—can demonstrate absolute and easy superiority.

But at a price. There is always a price and, more often than not, it is a high price.

More than ever, he became a very solitary man. He'd never been one for belly-laughs, but gradually what sense of humour he'd once had became whittled away until he rarely smiled. In a perverse way he both loved and loathed the job he did so well. He saw stupidity labelled criminality and his profession was such that he sent men to prison when, in fact, they needed skilled psychiatric treatment. On the other hand he saw money buy innocence and respectability; in the area of local—even national—government he saw the small fry netted, while the sharks continued to swim free.

And yet occasionally—just occasionally—he saw goodness almost beyond comprehension, blazing through some of the darkest of crimes . . . even murder.

By 1967 Blayde had become something of an institution. Perkins had slowly faded into the background; even he had realised that a superintendentship was the ultimate of any hopes he might have entertained within the Police Service, and that he'd been damn lucky to get as far as that. He never grew to like Blayde, but gradually and reluctantly he was forced into a personal admission that the division under Blayde worked. That, given freedom of action, Blayde could keep the pulse steady, keep the crime rate within manageable limits, keep the rate-payers happy, keep the men on their toes and, generally, run an uncommonly tight and happy division.

And in a strangely back-to-front way, Blayde enjoyed himself. He didn't realise it, but he was creating something. Handling seemingly impossible situations without panic, and infusing confidence in every Haggthorpe officer so that, whatever the situation, there wouldn't be panic. A couple of killings; they could hardly be called murders in the true meaning of that word. Man-and-wife squabbles, a history of extramarital screwing around, a surfeit of booze and (in both cases) a kitchen knife handy and ready to be used. The squalid pattern of nine out of every ten murders. No detection needed; the killer and the killed were both there when the police arrived in answer to some neighbour's nine-nine-nine call; just a matter of photographing, taking a few statements, compiling a file for the D.P.P. and another plus on the crime stat figures.

Then in May 1967—Saturday, May 13th—a *real* murder, and yet a murder which rocked every officer involved back on his heels. It couldn't happen. Even within the pages of wildly exaggerated novels, it wouldn't have been accepted. And yet it did happen and, in its own small way, it impinged itself on the life and personality of Chief Inspector Robert Blayde.

The Waynes and the Bonds. Alfred and Liz Wayne and William and Doris Bond. They knew each other; they'd known each other since their schooldays. They were friends, always had been friends and the friendship had grown to be a vital part of their life-style. Of an age—all four of them mid-thirties—Alf Wayne was a schoolmaster and Bill Bond was a conveyancing clerk at a local solicitor's office; Liz and Doris were closer than most sisters. Middle-class, decent, pay-your-way sort of people to whom crime—any sort of crime—was as alien as booking a passage on the next flight to Mars.

And yet at 2 p.m.—give or take a couple of minutes—a patrolling constable had picked up Alfred Wayne and guided him to Haggthorpe Police Station amid turning heads and staring eyes of every passer-by. Because Alfred Wayne was, literally, lathered in blood.

Blood dripped from the sleeves of his jacket, it formed a great map of scarlet across the front of his shirt, it was soaked into the material of his trousers and stained the leather of his shoes. It bespattered his face and even clogged his hair. It was everywhere! Had he just walked from a particularly badly managed slaughter-house, he could not have been more blood-covered.

The constable locked Wayne in a cell then—in effect—yelled for Blayde.

Blayde was taken aback. Had he been asked, he would have sworn that nothing—*nothing*—could shock him any more; that he'd seen it all and heard it all; that he was, in the vernacular, bomb-proof. Nevertheless, he stopped dead at the cell door and stared as the gore still dripped from the man sitting silently on the edge of the cell bed.

"Just like that?" he said, and his voice was a little hoarse.

"That's how he was, sir," verified the constable.

"Contact Sergeant Preston, then come back."

"Yes, sir."

Blayde walked slowly towards the sitting man, stopped, then spoke in a gentle, coaxing voice.

"Mr. Wayne, isn't it? Mr. Alfred Wayne?"

The man didn't answer. His out-of-focus eyes flickered slightly, as if he'd been reminded of something he should have remembered.

"You know me, Mr. Wayne." Blayde's voice was still coaxing. "I've lectured on road safety to your class. Chief Inspector Blayde."

Wayne raised his head and stared, without seeing, at Blayde's face.

"What happened, Mr. Wayne?" asked Blayde, gently.

There was still no reply.

"You're in a bit of a mess, old son. What caused it?"

Wayne lowered his head, gazed at his scarlet hands—at the blood which still dripped from his cuffs and onto the floor of the cell—and his eyes widened in horror.

"Take it easy," soothed Blayde. "There's a reason. We'll find it. Just take it easy . . . we've all the time in the world."

Wayne raised staring eyes, and whispered, "Black and Decker."

"Okay." Blayde lowered himself onto the edge of the cell bed alongside Wayne. He took one of the blood-soaked hands, squeezed it gently, and said, "Take your time, old son. Just take your time. You've had a bit of an accident . . . that right?"

Wayne began to shake his head. Slowly. Continuously. As if unable to stop. Then came quiet meeowing noises from behind his closed lips; noises which made Blayde's nape-hairs tingle, but which meant nothing other than some inner, inexplicable hurt.

"Bloody steaming Christ!"

Preston had arrived. Detective Sergeant Preston. Preston of the raucous voice. Preston of the size elevens which trampled in where lesser mortals might tread with fear and wonder. And Preston compressed all his immediate reaction in that single blast of astonishment.

"Bloody steaming Christ!"

"Cool down, sergeant," warned Blayde coldly.

"What the hell's happened?"

"We don't know, yet." Blayde switched his eyes to the constable. "Know where he lives?"

"Yes, sir."

"Okay, get there. Find out what you can. And bring him a complete change of clothes.

"Yes, sir." The constable hesitated, then added, "What about his wife?"

"She can come. But get the Charge Office sergeant to fix her up with tea and biscuits in an Interview Room. And tell her as little as possible."

Wayne continued his slow head-shaking and tiny whimpering. He was also beginning to tremble a little, as if cold to the point of freezing. The cell stank of blood and added to that smell was the stench of urine as Wayne lost control of his bladder.

"What . . ." began Preston.

"Doc Jones," said Blayde. "This is more than a straight police job."

"I'll get him."

Preston hurried away and Blayde was left with the wretched creature moaning and trembling on the edge of the cell bed. Instinct, rather than experience, prompted Blayde's attitude. Although awake, the man was obviously deep in the thralls of a personal nightmare. For some unknown reason, his senses had left him. The impression was that he was alive—just—but wished he *wasn't* alive. Certainly he couldn't be left. He needed care, he needed hospital treatment, he needed drugs . . . but where, in hell's name, had all the blood come from?

Within the hour they knew the truth of it. Alfred Wayne had been about to fix some shelves in the kitchen of his home. To help him he'd needed an electric drill: the Black and Decker, the only two words he'd uttered in the cell. He'd gone to his pal's house to borrow the drill, but William Bond had been out buying border plants for the garden. There was no doubt that Doris Bond had invited Wayne into the house . . . and then he'd gone berserk.

He'd hit the poor woman about the head and face with just about everything he could lay his hands on. Including a kitchen chair, including a coal hammer, including a poker. He hadn't killed her, quite. But that same evening the surgeon from Lessford Infirmary, to where she'd been rushed, telephoned Blayde to break the news that Doris Bond had died on the operating table.

"And," added the surgeon sadly, "it's a good job out of a bad one. Had she lived, she'd have been a vegetable."

But why?

As they choked on their sobs, as they drowned in their misery, Liz Wayne and William Bond asked that question over and over again . . . *why?*

"Bloody sex, what else?" bawled Preston. "Cross-tupping. Wife swapping. It's bloody obvious."

But it wasn't obvious and Wayne, when he was able to talk and think with some degree of clarity, was shocked that sex—in any of its forms—might be the motive for what he'd done. Nor did Liz Wayne or William Bond subscribe to even the possibility that Preston's belief was anything other than ridiculous.

But the police have very basic minds. They dug deeply enough to strike any oil that might be hidden under the surface. They questioned Bond and Mrs. Wayne; questioned and questioned and questioned. They sought the answer—*any* answer—from neighbours, from workmates, from relatives. They questioned Wayne until he broke completely and almost screamed, *"I don't know. I don't KNOW!"*

Blayde took Doc Jones aside, and said, "It's something new, doc. Something I've never met before. Why the hell *did* he kill her?"

"You're the copper," Jones reminded him with a sad smile.

"Okay, I'm the copper. And we don't have to prove motive. I'm curious. He didn't just *kill* her. He went crazy."

"Just that," said Jones flatly.

"What?"

"That very old-fashioned expression, a 'brain storm'. It's out of vogue at the moment. But that's my guess."

"Y'mean . . ."

"I mean," said Jones solemnly, "we don't

know a tenth—not a hundredth—of what happens up there above the eye-line. Something snaps. Some tiny cog misses an equally tiny pawl. In an engine there's a misfire. But in the brain . . . you end up with a Doris Bond."

"Christ!"

"It's only a guess."

"But an educated guess," said Blayde sombrely.

"Education? Civilisation? It's only skin-deep, chief inspector. I don't have to tell you that."

And that was as far as they ever got—as near to the truth as anybody ever *could* get—other, that is, than the heartbreak.

It was spooky. It was as near unbelievable as no matter. But it was true, and it happened every fourteen days and Blayde had never seen the like before and knew he'd never see the like again.

Pending the compilation of the Murder File, Wayne was brought before the magistrates each fortnight, to be remanded in custody pending the trial itself and, because of the circumstances of the case, the police made no objection to him being visited in the police cell, prior to and after his brief appearance in the dock. And *always* Liz Wayne and William Bond were there to comfort him. Twice the dead woman's parents were there, too. And *always* the heartbreak and the compassion could be felt, almost like an electric spark; the love they had for this man; the blind misery they felt at the thought of his being punished. Had it been possible—had there been any *way*—each and all of them would have joyfully forgiven him for what he had done . . . and, as Blayde began to know Wayne, he could comprehend their reason. The man had killed, but he wasn't a killer. He'd caused suffering, but the suffering he'd caused paled before the suffering he himself was being subjected to. The trial? The sentence? They were superfluous; they didn't mean a damn thing. Wayne had already tried himself, found himself guilty and with no mitigating circumstances, and whatever sentence the court imposed would be as nothing compared to what Wayne's own conscience was dragging him through. Whatever the sentence, Wayne wouldn't live it out . . . and his wife and the husband and parents of the dead woman realised this.

The feeling even penetrated Preston's elephantine hide.

He rubbed the back of his neck, frowned and grunted, "It gets you, doesn't it?"

"Cross-tupping?" snarled Blayde sarcastically.

"No," growled Preston. "Dammit . . . I'd have staked my life on it. But, no. Not this time."

"We've a lot to learn," said Blayde savagely. "We think we know it all. All the answers. All the blacks, all the whites, all the greys. And we haven't even started. We're scum, sergeant. To people like that we're scum, and compared with them we *are* scum. We've no bloody option. It's what we're paid to be. Not to forgive. Not to understand. To put the boot in, that's all, who the hell it hurts."

Coppers sometimes do have these misgivings. They know—they know far better than the man-in-the-street—how big a sledgehammer the criminal law can be, and how small the nut it sometimes has to crack. The thinking coppers. The humane coppers. Not the red-necked bully-boys to whom small authority is a personal lollipop they must always be licking.

Blayde? He was no red-neck, but on the other hand he was no halo-carrier. Even after the Wayne affair he fought off the doubt and taught himself to be as ruthless as before, but pictures of those unhappy people, helplessly trying to comfort a man who would never again know comfort, remained in the back of his mind.

Meanwhile he handled criminal law. It was his profession; to handle it, not to modify it and not to interpret it. Good or bad, he had to accept it in its entirety.

Mind you . . .

They were re-decorating the court-room and for a couple of weeks the regular Haggthorpe Magistrates' Court sat in a disused chapel about two hundred yards from the police station. And Nick Houseman, breaker and general thief, had to be escorted from the police cells to the court, and Nick Houseman didn't like it one little bit. He argued and pleaded with the detective constable, but the D.C. was adamant.

"Cuffs, Nick. You could run for it, and I'd feel very lonely."

"Please!"

"No way, friend. That's something you should have thought of when you were breaking in."

Blayde strolled into the Charge Office,

and Houseman pleaded with the detective constable's boss.

"Please, Mr. Blayde!"

"What's that?"

"He wants to walk without the cuffs, sir," said the D.C.

Houseman said, "We pass the school, Mr. Blayde. See? They'll be out in the playground. My two kids'll be there. They'll see me."

"So?" asked Blayde.

"The missus can tell 'em things," pleaded Houseman. "She has before. 'Daddy's away on a business trip.' That sorta thing. They believe her, and I keep their respect. The other kids don't rib 'em. Kids can be awful cruel, Mr. Blayde."

"So?" repeated Blayde.

"If I'm wearing *handcuffs* . . ." The impression was that Houseman was prepared to go down on his knees.

Blayde motioned to the D.C. and said, "Unlock the cuffs."

"But sir . . ."

"Just unlock the cuffs," repeated Blayde. "You go first, Houseman follows a few yards behind, I follow a few yards behind Houseman." Then to Houseman. "One promise . . . and I keep my promises. Make a break, and we'll catch you. Believe me, we'll catch you. And I'll personally escort you *into* the school and let every pupil there sit and watch you make excuses to your own kids."

"It's a deal, Mr. Blayde." Houseman grinned his delight. "I won't let you down, I swear."

And Houseman acted his part like a dream. He even waved to one of his sons beyond the playground railings.

The magistrates were feeling lenient. They dealt with him, and sent him down the line for a mere six months; a sentence he could endure on his head. And (perhaps because of the Wayne affair) Blayde ensured that the detective constable put his priorities in their correct order. "He's a thief, and that's all he is. He isn't violent. He's a good husband, and he worships those two kids of his. He has this kink. He's a thief . . . other than that, he's a good man."

The D.C. didn't quite understand. Blayde—Blayde, the man who, when the need arose, could be a ring-tailed, gold-plated bastard—he was obviously losing his grip.

But that same evening, Houseman's wife telephoned Blayde, said her husband had told her before they trucked him off to Armley, thanked him, then named real villains who were busy setting up a bank raid.

"Nick said I'd to tell you," she said.

"I'm obliged, ma'am. If there's anything I can do to help . . ."

"I'll help, Mr. Blayde. Whenever I can. So will Nick, when he comes home."

And he did. For the rest of Blayde's time at Haggthorpe Nick Houseman was a veritable gold mine of information; he mixed with the hookers and the wide boys—they'd been, and would always be, his normal companions—but to Blayde, and *only* to Blayde, the shady corners of Haggthorpe Division were constantly illuminated.

In 1969 Houseman came up with a nugget of information Blayde had been digging for for years. Tatholme Section; one of those hide-in-a-corner sections which go to make up every police division. A flash roadhouse; a drink-and-dance joint catering for the would-be jet-set of the surrounding area; a shining little plastic anything-goes, far enough out not to be a nuisance, but within easy motoring distance of either Lessford or Bordfield.

The proprietor of The Silver Stocking looked the part. He reminded Blayde of one of those pig's bladders, filled solid with lard which in the old days were sold by grocers who catered for middle- and upper-class customers. Fat to the point of obesity. Fawning. With a perpetual sheen on his skin which suggested that his sweat glands all needed new washers.

"I have it on good authority," said Blayde.

"No, chief inspector, you have my word."

Blayde had dressed the part; full uniform, up to and including soft leather gloves and a black, silver-knobbed cane. He looked very impressive. He was out to impress and Morley, the proprietor of The Silver Stocking, was, indeed, impressed . . . and terrified.

"I have good customers, chief inspector," he said.

"Who's talking about customers?"

"They wouldn't . . ."

"I'm talking about protection, Morley. Pay up or get knocked down . . . *that's* what I'm talking about."

The Tatholme sergeant stood, silent. He was a quiet, peace-at-any-price guy. He ran an easy section, and he wanted things to stay that way. Blayde worried him; threatened to smash his comfortable way of life . . . as, indeed, did Morley and his damn glorified whorehouse.

"You might like to kid yourself," said Blayde calmly. "You might call it 'insurance'."

"Sure, I pay insurance. With a place like this . . ."

"*Weekly* insurance?"

The sweat oozed out of Morley's pores.

"Every Thursday? Three o'clock, thereabouts?"

"Chief inspector, I've a living to make. I don't want . . ."

"Trouble?" Blayde ended the sentence for him.

"The one thing I can live without," moaned Morley.

"A straight choice." Blayde was merciless. "Trouble from *us*. Trouble from *them*."

"Look, why can't we . . ."

"We'll close you down in a week, Morley," said Blayde. "I, personally, will 'visit' this place every night. Names and addresses. Car numbers. The clientele you handle . . . in a week you'll be empty."

Morley ran a forefinger around the top of his shirt collar. He loosened the knot of his tie and unfastened a button. His neck seemed to be swelling and threatening to choke him.

"What—what the hell can *you* . . ."

"We can," said Blayde calmly, "shift *them.* On the other hand, they can't shift *us.*"

"You'd be wise, Mr. Morley." The Tatholme sergeant figured it was time he said something, if only to remind everybody that he was still around.

"Or," added Blayde, "you can be a complete mug."

"If—if you nick'em, they'll only . . ."

"Don't tell us what to do. Don't tell us how to do it," said Blayde coldly. "Just don't tell *them* anything. Go through the motions next Thursday . . . then forget they ever existed."

Morley gave a miserable nod of defeat, and Blayde knew he'd taken the first hurdle without any real problems.

Outside the roadhouse he turned to the Tatholme sergeant and said, "Leave it clear, sergeant."

"Yes, sir." The sergeant sounded relieved.

"No coppers within two miles of the place till further notice."

"I—er . . ." The sergeant swallowed. "I understand, sir."

"You don't," contradicted Blayde. "Just obey orders, and don't try puzzling things out."

"Yes, sir."

The sergeant left, and Blayde returned to Haggthorpe D.H.Q.

It was dangerous. Indeed, from a career point of view, it was suicidal. The men had to be picked with all the care needed to pluck a daisy from a bed of stinging nettles. Not merely tough, not merely trustworthy, but also mad enough to venture well outside the law, knowing that if they were caught, or if anybody dropped an inadvertent hint within distance of the wrong ear, they'd all finish up behind granite walls. Nothing surer, because 'our policemen are wonderful' and an innocent public would never stomach an argument which insisted that the only *real* answer to terror was counter-terror.

He chose four men. Detective Sergeant Preston, Detective Constable Rath, Police Sergeant Sykes and Police Constable Philby.

Preston, because Preston had the necessary muscle and the necessary madness; to Preston, policing was a form of open warfare and, if the law impinged itself on Preston's mode of policing, the hell with the law. Preston had no finesse. His was the crash-bang-wallop school of bobbying. He'd been on five Misconduct Reports for doing things his way. Despite this, he'd made detective sergeant, and he still did it his way. Moreover, his absolute loyalty could be taken for granted.

Rath, because he was Rath. He'd be the oldest and, to that extent, he'd be the most vulnerable should things get over-heated. But Rath's respect for Blayde amounted to nothing short of hero-worship. Hot irons and thumbscrews wouldn't drag the truth from Rath, should things go amiss.

Sykes, from Beechwood Brook Division, because Sykes personified all that a section sergeant should be. Teak-hard, knowing every gag in the joke book, not giving a damn about anything under the sun and a sworn enemy of criminal capers imported from America. Sykes, much like Blayde, had become a legend in his own lifetime. He'd never be other than a section sergeant, because he was too good a section sergeant and, whereas inspectors came by the carton, sergeants of Sykes's calibre came once every Preston Guild.

Philby because Constable Philby sported the D.F.M. and Bar, was the area light-heavyweight champion and was renowned for 'sorting 'em out' rather than carting people off to court. Philby was a born toughie and, had he not chosen to wear police uniform, might have been the sort of tearaway every copper fears . . . a man who truly doesn't know when he's defeated. To Philby it would be a lark. He'd enjoy himself, but keep mum about it later.

Blayde saw them all, at first separately, then together. He didn't tell them the where or the when, but he left them in no doubt.

"It's the only way we'll squash it. Once and for all. If it comes off, we have the satisfaction. . . but that's *all* we have. If it doesn't come off, I'll accept full responsibility, but that won't mean much. It isn't even Duty Elsewhere, in that it's *really* unofficial. I'm asking you—all four of you—to put your head on the chopping-block, in the hope you can duck when the axe swings."

And, such was Blayde's reputation throughout the force, not one of the four even argued.

Thursday, July 24th, 1969. Blayde's watch showed five minutes past three. He sat at the wheel of the Ford van and behind him, in the body of the van, his team of four squatted, waiting with the rear door of the van already ajar. They were within yards of the car park at the rear of The Silver Stocking and the car Blayde was watching was a dark Cortina.

All five were officially on Annual Leave; a basic precaution, in order not to embarrass the force more than was necessary, in the event of things getting screwed up. They all wore navy-blue boiler suits and dark plimsols. Across their foreheads the folds of stocking-masks were ready to be pulled into position.

Suddenly, but in a calm voice, Blayde said, "Here they come."

He opened the door of the van and stepped out. Philby joined him. Preston dropped from the rear of the van and took over the driving seat. In the body of the van Sykes and Rath pulled down their stocking masks.

The two "collectors" were heavily built men—men well able to give an account of themselves in a rough-house—but they weren't expecting trouble and Blayde and Philby timed things perfectly. As the "collectors" opened the front doors of the Cortina, they were shoulder charged and, almost simultaneously, their heads hit the rim of the car roof. Still dazed, they were shouldered into the car, then Blayde slipped into the rear seat behind the driver, and whipped a length of cheese-wire across the driver's throat and brought the two handled ends together behind his neck.

The driver's hands flew up to his throat, and Blayde said, "Don't! You'll only die with broken finger-nails."

The man in the front passenger-seat made as if to open the glove compartment and Philby administered a hard rabbit-chop across the nape of his neck.

Philby growled, "Just sit there. Don't even talk. They may be the last words you ever say."

Once in the car—once out of public view—both Blayde and Philby pulled down their stocking masks. Blayde did it one-handed, while he held the handles of the cheese-wire with his free hand.

The "collectors" knew the name of the game. They knew all the do's and don'ts. Had the positions been reversed, there might have been a killing. At the very least there'd have been a maiming. Thus the strict rules of the game and the "collectors" knew when to behave.

The Ford van entered the car park. Its number plates were caked with dry mud. It made a wide circle, and Blayde said, "Just follow the van."

Philby hooked an arm across the front of the passenger's throat, just to be on the safe side. The driver handled the car with his head well back, trying to ease the pressure of the cheese-wire. Other than this it was just four guys in a Cortina driving behind a Ford van.

Blayde had planned the route carefully. The van skirted villages and hamlets, left Haggthorpe, cut across Beechwood Brook, entered the Pinthead Pike area and climbed slowly to the wild desertion of The Tops. The Cortina followed. They left the few roads and lumbered along unmade tracks and, at a few minutes before four o'clock the van pulled off the track and braked to a halt. The Cortina stopped behind it.

Rath and Sykes opened the rear door of the van and dropped onto the springy turf. They each wore stocking masks. They each carried a twelve-bore shotgun. They opened the front doors of the Cortina, and motioned with the guns. Blayde released the cheese-wire and Philby removed his arm from the neck of the second collector. The collectors climbed from the Cortina, each massaging his neck. They looked scared. They were tough men—hard men—but they each thought they could count the rest of their lives in minutes, therefore they were scared. They didn't plead. Theirs was a world in which mercy was neither given nor expected; pain, even death, was their coinage and not for one moment did they doubt that the five masked men were of their own kind.

Philby flipped down the glove-compartment flap of the Cortina. He took out an automatic pistol; a tiny, but deadly .25 seven-shot Beretta Minx. He handed it to Blayde, and Blayde slipped it into a pocket of his boiler suit. The two collectors watched silently. Rath and Sykes kept the shotguns steady and level.

Preston brought a jack-handle from the van, and deliberately and systematically smashed the headlamps, windscreen, side-windows and rear-window of the Cortina.

Blayde said, "Strip." His voice was nasal and beyond recognition because of the stocking mask.

The collectors looked puzzled.

Rath poked one of the collectors in the guts with the business end of his shotgun, and growled, "Strip. Mother-naked."

With some reluctance, the collectors removed their clothes. When they hesitated, Rath growled, "All the way. Don't be shy."

Blayde fished in the discarded jackets until

he found a large manilla envelope. He slit it open and counted twenty used five-pound notes. He returned the money to the envelope, then stuffed the envelope into an inside pocket of his boiler suit.

Preston gathered the clothes together, opened the boot of the Cortina and threw them inside. He closed and locked the boot, then handed the keys to Blayde. Blayde leaned inside the car, flipped the gear-stick to neutral, inserted the key into the ignition, started the engine and left it to idle.

Despite the time of year, it was cool up there on the exposed moorland, and the flesh of the collectors showed goose-pimples. They looked a sorry pair, but still potentially dangerous.

Blayde faced them and said, "Any more trespassing, and you won't go back in the nude. You won't go back at all."

The Cortina passenger was bundled back into his seat. Philby had brought a roll of surgical tape from the van and the collector's left wrist was taped hard against the lower frame of the seat. His right hand was taped, equally firmly, to the stem of the gear lever. His companion was dumped onto the driver's seat, and both his hands were taped in "the correct driving position" to the rim of the steering wheel. Philby did the taping, and enjoyed doing it. Neither of them had a hope in hell of pulling a hand free until somebody cut through the tape.

As he slammed the driver's door, Blayde said, "Drive carefully."

Back in the van Preston, Philby, Sykes and Rath did nothing to control their mirth. It had been a giggle; something to talk about in years to come . . . when it was safe to talk. They shed their boiler suits and, as Blayde dropped them off near their respective homes, they emerged as decently dressed, off-duty policemen.

Blayde drove to his cottage. He garaged the van, pending its collection the next day by Joe Benton who, as a favour, had hired it from a van-hire firm. "And don't ask questions, Joe. You want a van for three days . . . *and that's all.*" He took the gear—the boiler suits, the stocking masks, what was left of the surgical tape and the two shotguns—and walked into the cottage. He didn't have to unload the shot guns, they'd never been loaded. He dropped the envelope containing the money and the

Beretta onto the kitchen table, then struggled out of his own boiler suit.

He walked into the hall, picked up the telephone and dialled a Lessford number. He draped a handkerchief over the mouthpiece as he waited for somebody to answer the call.

"Yeah?"

"Ric Blayde," said Blayde shortly.

"Who's calling?"

"If he wants you to know, he'll tell you."

There was a silence, then Richard's voice said, "Blayde, here. Who's the smart-arse?"

"You aren't," snapped Blayde. "You've moved out of your territory, Blayde. That Silver Stocking pick-up. Have some whisky and blankets ready for your goons when they arrive home. Next time, have a wreath waiting."

"Who the hell . . ."

"You want a war, you can have one."

"I don't want no damn war."

"So don't be greedy, little man. Keep well inside your own boundaries. I don't warn twice."

Blayde dropped the receiver. He used the handkerchief to wipe the sweat from his forehead . . . and he felt a complete nutter. Cheap gangland talk. Something from a pulp magazine. It had been necessary, but had it been worth it? Had any of it been worth it? Five careers hung out to dry, and for what? Something very personal. Something the others knew nothing about.

Over the weekend he destroyed the boiler suits and the stocking masks. The Police Widows and Orphans Fund received an anonymous donation of £100. On the Sunday, Houseman telephoned him at the cottage. "Mr. Blayde. You should know. That Lessford protection crowd. They're not alone. Somebody else. Here, inside your own area. Real hard men. I don't know names, yet, but I'll ask around." Blayde thanked him, and wondered how the collectors had reached sanctuary without the local newspaper sniffing something out. Maybe a holing-up place—somewhere Houseman didn't know—somewhere where they could drive in, be freed, get dressed and pick up an undamaged car. Palms had been greased, that for sure. Brother Richard ran a bigger organisation than he, Blayde, had realised. Two nude men, fastened to the steering-wheel and gear stick of a smashed-up car. They had to have been seen by somebody. And silence—that sort of silence—cost money. A lot of money, plus some very hard language. Brother Richard was doing very well for himself.

On the night of Saturday, September 6th, 1969, The Silver Stocking was gutted. Fire and forensic experts examined the burned out shell. They couldn't agree. They couldn't say it was arson. They couldn't say it wasn't arson. On the night of the fire Blayde watched the blaze, satisfied himself that nobody had been trapped and killed, then returned to his cottage. When the forensic report was made known, he also returned to his cottage, locked the door and, for the first time in his police career, drank neat whisky until he was in a state of stupor and beyond caring about anything.

16

THE bump up the promotion ladder, when it came, was something of a surprise. Despite the Silver Stocking fiasco, Blayde had Haggthorpe in the palm of his hand. He'd grown thinner than ever over the years; thinner, leaner and, if anything, more ruthless. The men and the women—by this time the percentage of policewomen in the force and in the division was growing fast—admired him and respected him. But he also tolerated fewer and fewer excuses. At its lowest level, he was a bastard . . . but a *just* bastard.

Perkins?

Who the hell was Perkins? It had almost come to that. Newcomers to the division—recruits or officers from other divisions—often asked that question in the chit-chat of bobby-talk. "Who the hell's Perkins?" A division carried a superintendent, therefore there had to be a superintendent, but in Haggthorpe Division the superintendent was nigh invisible and certainly carried no real weight. Blayde was Jack-the-Lad. Blayde was the boyo who scoffed slackers with his breakfast cornflakes. Perkins? You have to be kidding.

And the truth was that both Blayde and Perkins had come to terms with that situation. Perkins was on a very smooth-running roundabout; all his earlier spit-and-flash ideas had vanished; he trotted in front of the police medic once a year, was pronounced sound in wind and limb, and that was him happy for another twelve months. As for Blayde . . . a quarter of a century of hard policing had stamped its mark on him for life. "Once a copper, always a copper." Sure, but only if you were a certain kind a copper. Blayde's kind. The "us" and "them" kind . . . with very few of "us". Five more years, and he could retire on a two-thirds-chief-inspector's-pay pension. Which meant he wouldn't have to start hawking himself around looking for some hole-in-the-corner job to make ends meet. He had a home, he hadn't developed expensive tastes and with that sort of money coming in the rest of his life would be a length of old rope.

Then on March 15th, 1971 (it was a Monday) he was told to report to the chief's office at County Constabulary Headquarters.

It was a sort of "could-be-could-be" situation. He'd chanced his arm not a few times, and maybe some old rooster was coming home to peck him from his perch.

Having introduced himself to the cadet on entry hall duty, having climbed up to the third floor and introduced himself to the chief constable's secretary, he followed that stone-faced female across her carpeted outer-sanctum, entered the chief's office, chopped a fair-to-moderate salute at the man behind the king-sized desk and waited.

"Sit down, Blayde." The chief waved airily. "Just a few things to see to, then I'll be with you."

Blayde settled into a reasonably comfortable chair and eyed this High Priest of law enforcement with a slightly jaundiced eye.

Chief constables? Hell's bells, they weren't coppers . . . not *coppers.* With that acreage of fitted carpet, they'd be breathless before they reached the bloody door. Can-pushers. That's what they were, can-pushers. Three floors up, surrounded by a ten-foot-thick wall of practised sycophants . . . how the hell could they ever *bobby?* How the hell could they ever *know?* Some chinless goon from the Home

Office came up with a crackpot idea, and their job was to pass it down the line. One more can of worms for the real coppers to chew up and spit out. And from down under—coming in the opposite direction—pure flannel. "Yes, sir. No, sir. Three bags full, sir. What you don't know you won't regret, sir." That was the sum total. A bloody great salary, a bloody great desk and a bloody great vacuum where the know-how should be. And clowns like this . . .

"Now." The chief constable broke into Blayde's thoughts. He leaned back in his swivel-chair and said, "Haggthorpe. How long is it, now, Blayde?"

"On and off since 'forty-nine, sir."

"The 'off' period being when you were at Pinthead Pike?"

"And a spell at training college."

"Ah, yes, but you were still attached to Haggthorpe." Blayde reluctantly conceded that the chief must have done his homework. The chief constable smiled and added, "Almost on the inventory, in fact."

"I've seen a few people come and go, sir," agreed Blayde.

"Perkins." The chief watched Blayde's face. "Who runs the division? You or him?"

"He's the divisional officer," said Blayde carefully.

"That doesn't answer my question, chief inspector."

"It should," said Blayde bluntly. "You promoted him superintendent."

"Now . . . that *does* answer my question." The chief gave a quick, frosty smile. "Even chief constables make slight mistakes."

Blayde remained silent.

The chief said, "Bowland Division. Know it?"

"Not intimately, sir."

"Care to be its next superintendent?"

"Am I in the running, sir?" asked Blayde gently.

The chief nodded. "The divisional officer's retiring at the end of the month. That, by the way, isn't for public knowledge."

Blayde thought for a moment, then said, "I already have twenty-five in, sir. I've been thinking about retirement, too."

"A chief inspector's pension. A superintendent's pension. There's a difference, Blayde."

Blayde nodded.

"And," added the chief, "you ask me if you're in the running. The strict answer is, no. It's not a race. It's yours, if you want it."

"I—er—I have a house, sir. A cottage . . ."

"I know. I also know your reputation. You'll still want to live there."

"Yes, sir. If it's possible."

"If you make it possible, I've no objections."

"It shouldn't be too difficult," mused Blayde.

"So? You'll take over Bowland Division?"

Blayde hesitated, then said, "Yes, sir. As you say . . . a superintendent's pension."

"A wise choice. It's not a bad division, but I've no doubt you'll make it better. At least different."

"Thank you, sir."

"You'll receive official confirmation. Meanwhile make things as easy as possible for whoever takes your place at Haggthorpe."

"Yes, sir." Blayde stood up.

"Oh." The chief smiled. This time a slightly more friendly smile. "Don't forget you'll be the divisional officer. The crown you'll have on your shoulder. I'd hate you to think it was merely a symbol. The means of a free ride to a larger pension."

"It'll be more than that, sir," promised Blayde.

He saluted, left the office, walked past the

secretary without so much as an acknowledgement, left County Constabulary Headquarters building, then drove at a very moderate speed back to Haggthorpe.

This was, you see, "The Big 'Un". "The Big Apple" or "The Big Lemon". Chapman or Perkins or, come to that, Hale. Up there, from superintendent and above, the normally accepted laws of policing didn't apply. That thirty year stint. It didn't apply. An annual look-over by the police doctor and, while you were fit, you could stay in the force . . . that for starters. And on every damn form, there was a little box marked "Divisional Officer", and once you'd signed that you were alone and lonely. So many things; so many things he hadn't given much thought to in the past. But now he had to think about them. A team. That was one of the things—one of the very many things—he had to think about. As a chief inspector—even as a chief inspector under a berk like Perkins—he'd been able to play one-man-band antics. The Silver Stocking cock-up, for example. He'd had just enough freedom. But as a superintendent . . .

Christ! He'd be in the senior officer class. Up there with the elite. So, he'd have to have a team. Either make a team or collect a team.

He tried to remember what he knew about Bowland Division, and it wasn't much. Part industrial, part rural. But for the life of him he couldn't put a name to the retiring superintendent. Come to that, he couldn't put a name to a single officer from the damn division.

Some division!

Not a man there with enough sparkle to get his name known beyond the boundaries of his own neck of the woods. It wasn't promising.

Nevertheless, his division. Something to take and, if necessary, shake life into. By God, they'd soon know. These unknown slobs who, on the face of things, had led a gentle Toc-H existence. They'd bloody soon *know*.

On Monday, April 19th, 1971 Blayde strode into Bowland Divisional Headquarters, and started a week-long, dose-of-salts exercise. Within that week he'd seen the chief inspector, all four inspectors, all the sergeants, most of the working coppers and all the C.I.D. personnel. By the end of that week, the concensus of opinion was that Superintendent Robert Blayde was far too hot to handle other than with asbestos gloves.

"I see from the Sectional Diary that you lead a nine-to-five existence, inspector. It's three months since you needed a torch to see your way around. Visit the patrol constables at night in future. Often. *And* be around at six o'clock in the morning occasionally. For all you know there hasn't been a night cover . . .

"This is not a filing system, sergeant. These drawers are merely an extension of the waste-paper basket. Get it seen to, and I mean *you.* Not somebody who should be out on the beat. Then *keep* it tidy . . .

"Chief inspector, this may come as a shock to you, but you're not paid to be loved. You're paid to be respected, if you've enough about you to command respect. If not, you're paid to be hated. You're paid to be a bastard, when necessary. As from now, you'll be a bastard. Take my word for it, with practice it becomes easy . . .

"Officer, it says here you're a 'detective'. It lies. All you've done for weeks is record crime. A cadet can do that a damn sight cheaper, which makes you superfluous. You will, therefore, kindly get your arse away from that radiator, you'll get outside and you'll feel a few collars. You'll have a pinch—and a pinch worth calling a pinch—within the next fourteen days or you'll be back in uniform, pounding beats . . ."

And in six months Bowland Division began to be a division. While the pressure was on, they hated him. They hated his guts. Their main topic of conversation was the cold-blooded sod they'd inherited as a superintendent. But then, very gradually, it changed. Pride began to enter the scheme of things; pride in their job, pride in the division and (to their utter disbelief) pride in the man who'd taken the division by the scruff of the neck and shaken life into it.

The chief visited the division; an unannounced, personal look-see to check up on progress and the ability or otherwise of Blayde to cope with what Blayde had come to realise was just about the sloppiest run division in the force. The chief was pleased, and didn't hide the fact.

"I wondered," he admitted, over tea and biscuits in Blayde's office.

"They're good officers," said Blayde. "All they needed was riding a little."

"More than a little."

"To be told what the job's all about. To be reminded."

"Still looking forward to the thirty year pension?" asked the chief mischievously.

"They might be lost without 'father'," fenced Blayde.

The chief smiled knowingly.

"I see Hale's on the point of retiring," said Blayde by way of conversation.

"Uhu." The chief grunted, then frowned. Blayde's remark seemed to have touched a raw spot. He said, "The Police Authority. They come up with strange ideas sometimes. The latest . . . to combine Beechwood Brook and Pinthead Pike. Just the one division."

Blayde pursed his lips into a silent whistle, then said, "That will be one hell of a size."

"Bumper bundles," said the chief sourly. "People go in for them these days. From soap flakes to police divisions."

"Charlie Ripley'll cope," grinned Blayde.

"Ripley," said the chief grimly, "is very much like you. A law unto himself. I feel like an intruder whenever I visit his infernal division."

It was, and Blayde recognised it as such, a very high compliment. Some men do, indeed, achieve legendary status well within their own lifetime. In sport, in painting, in music—in any of the arts—and in policing. Capstick, Cherrill, Read, Mounsey, Wensley, Du Rose and, of course, Ripley. Ripley was a "copper's copper"; he'd crawl through hell backwards in support of any of his men receiving stick for doing something he, Ripley, would have done in similar circumstances. His division was a force within the force itself and, if (when) it was extended to include Pinthead Pike, Ripley would merely roll up his sleeves, spit on his hands and, in no time flat, leave the population of the old Pinthead Pike area in no doubt that their old king was dead and that their new king was ready and willing to knock some sense into the skulls of any wide boys who failed to realise that the joy-ride was over.

To be compared favourably with Ripley was, therefore a compliment, and Blayde felt a warm glow of pleasure.

Thereafter, he ran Bowland Division on oiled bearings.

The big break (and, for success, there always has to be a big break) came at close to midnight on Monday, November 15th, 1971. Blayde was at his cottage, relaxed in an armchair, sipping hot chocolate prior to going to bed. The telephone rang. Blayde answered it, and it was Nick Houseman from Haggthorpe.

"I got some hot stuff for you, Mr. Blayde."

Houseman sounded breathless. Almost afraid.

"I'm not at Haggthorpe now, Nick. But if . . ."

"No. Bowland. A heavy mob from Bordfield."

"I'm listening," said Blayde quietly.

"Remember The Silver Stocking?"

"I remember."

"Same mob. Bordfield branch, as you might say. There's a jewellers, next to Barclays in Bowland."

"I know the place."

Houseman seemed to hesitate, as if gathering courage, then said, "Thursday afternoon, Mr. Blayde."

"This coming Thursday?"

"Quarter to two. Copper's shift change, see? And the people who work in the shop. A couple won't be back from lunch till two." He increased the speed of his speech and said, "Three vans. One at each end to cut off any chase. The other to do the smash. It's well organised."

"You seem to know a lot, Nick," said Blayde gently.

"I'm—I'm supposed to be in it, Mr. Blayde."

"Nick, don't think . . ."

"I'm blowing, Mr. Blayde." Houseman sounded relieved at having passed on this priceless piece of information. "Me and the wife and kids. Somewhere down south. Maybe overseas, sometime."

"They might smell something."

"Naw." Houseman sounded certain. "Tomorrow, see. I've dropped a few hints. You people being after me, that sort of thing. They've a spare driver standing by in case." He paused, then added, "I'm straight, Mr. Blayde. Honest."

"I believe you," said Blayde solemnly.

"Just one thing," warned Houseman. "They're nasty. They'll have shooters. Sawn-offs."

"Thanks for mentioning it."

"That—that evens things I reckon," said Houseman awkwardly.

"I think it evens things very nicely," said Blayde. "Be good, Nick. And good luck in your new life."

"Thanks, Mr. Blayde. Thanks for everything."

Houseman rang off and Blayde returned to the armchair. He finished the drinking chocolate and smoked a cigarette as he mulled over the information he'd just received.

It could be relied on . . . *that* was the main thing. The time, the place, the plan. Nick Houseman had risked a great deal in passing the details, *ergo* it could be relied on. By the book, Blayde should have notified Headquarters; contacted the Head of C.I.D. and awaited orders. But screw the Head of C.I.D. This was strictly Bowland business. More than that—and bearing in mind the Silver Stocking cock-up—it was *Blayde's* business.

Guns; sawn-off shotguns; just about the most deadly, close-range weapon in any villain's armoury. Somebody meant business. Maybe that somebody was *the* somebody . . . but that was pure wishful thinking. Nevertheless, if Nick linked the forthcoming jewellery job with the protection caper of The Silver Stocking, somebody might cough up a few names. With luck, cough up a whole suite of furniture. If so, that would be a real bonus.

It was almost three o'clock in the morning before Blayde squashed out a last cigarette and went to bed. But by that time he'd worked out his plan of action.

The next day, Tuesday, November 16th, he talked to his chief inspector and his divisional detective inspector. The conversation was in the privacy of Blayde's office.

"And it stays between the three of us, pending the recruiting of the men needed. And it goes no farther than them until we have the bastards tucked away in a cell."

"Guns?" murmured the D.D.I. "Real Wild West stuff?"

Blayde glanced at the safe in the corner of his office. "Four Smith and Wesson .38 revolvers. Standard issue for each division. They'll be issued. You've both had range training?"

The two men nodded.

"Which leaves one question," said Blayde, sombrely. "Either of you likely to draw back when it comes to squeezing the trigger?"

"I won't like it," muttered the chief inspector.

"I'm not asking you to *like* it. Will you *do* it? Is there any likelihood that you'll hold off long enough for them to start blasting away with shotguns?"

"I'll do it," said the chief inspector.

"And you?" Blayde turned to the D.D.I.

"Me, too," grunted the D.D.I.

"Good." Blayde nodded his satisfaction. "Any shooting, we do it. And close enough not to miss. I want no civilians injured." He paused, then went on, "Two more men with range training. Pick 'em carefully. Don't tell 'em the details, but ask 'em the same questions. No hot-heads. *Our* way, not the TV cops-and-robbers way. And two unmarked cars. Mine . . ."

"And mine," cut in the chief inspector.

"Thanks. And two squad cars, tucked away out of sight. Just in case there's a slip-up and we have a chase on our hands."

"What about back-up?" asked the D.D.I.

"A Maria, within walkie-talkie distance. Again tucked away somewhere. Half a dozen uniformed men. Picked. A sergeant in charge. Tell him, don't tell the others."

They talked over the finer details, made suggestions and, when the Chief Inspector and the D.D.I. left the office, the plan was agreed upon. It was a good plan. It rested on split-second timing but, more than anything, it rested on Houseman's information being one hundred percent genuine.

Thursday, November 18th. It was a nice day; a cloudless sky, sunny but with a nip in the air as a reminder that the snows were on their way and that the frosts were already driving the night foot-patrol to flapping their arms to keep the circulation going.

Blayde was in civilian clothes (as, indeed, were the chief inspector, the D.D.I. and the two constables who were to spearhead the counter-attack on the thieves). Blayde had handed over his Jag to the D.D.I. "Don't bend it more than necessary, but if it comes to a choice between the car and the van's getaway, smash the car." Two streets away—one in a municipal car park, the other standing outside a supermarket—two squad cars were parked, their drivers and observers keyed up and waiting. The engines of the cars were ticking over, their normal radio sets were switched off and the observers were holding walkie-talkie radios at the ready.

A police van—a black Maria—was also parked in a cul-de-sac at the rear of the co-op stores; within easy distance of the jewellery shop. The uniformed sergeant, in charge of six uniformed constables inside the van, also had a walkie-talkie and had silenced the murmur of curiosity from the men, in order that he could the better hear any instructions.

The chief inspector and a range-trained D.C. waited in the chief inspector's VW. The VW was parked within sighting distance of the jewellers, but far enough away to quell any suspicion. Both men were armed with Smith and Wesson revolvers and they, too, were listening out to a walkie-talkie set nestling between the two front seats. Similarly, the D.D.I. pretended to be reading a newspaper in the driving seat of Blayde's Jag. He had his walkie-talkie on his lap, hidden by the opened newspaper. Alongside him was a police sergeant in plain clothes. Both men had revolvers, holstered and fastened to their waistbands.

In short, the target shop was neatly surrounded by coppers, four of them armed, but the positioning of the various vehicles formed an invisible noose, ready to be tightened when (if) the expected raid got under way.

It was a few seconds past 1.30 p.m.

Blayde strolled into the jewellers shop. He wore a loose-fitting mac over a sports jacket and twill trousers. In one pocket of the mac was the walkie-talkie, via which he could control the police at his disposal. In the other pocket nestled the seven-shot Beretta automatic, taken from the glove compartment of the Cortina during the Silver Stocking fiasco. The carrying of the automatic by Blayde was quite illegal, of course, but Bowland Division was limited to four revolvers for use in an emergency, and Blayde was damned if he was going to face sawn-off shotguns without something with which he could punch holes in the opposition's hide, should the occasion arise.

A neatly turned out young lady came to the counter, smiled a welcome and said, "Can I help you, sir?"

"Is the manager in?" asked Blayde pleasantly.

"He's at lunch, sir. He'll be back at two."

"Who's in charge?" asked Blayde.

"Well . . ." The assistant frowned, then said, "Mrs. Amber. I suppose you could call her the assistant manageress."

"Can I see her, please?"

"She's rather busy at the moment, sir. I'm sure I can do . . ."

"It's rather urgent, miss." Blayde fished his warrant card from an inside pocket, allowed the assistant to check the details, then said, "Now, don't be alarmed, miss. Just tell your Mrs. Amber that I must see her . . . now."

It transpired that Mrs. Amber was rather busy having a pee (which for the moment, lent the proceedings the air of a French farce) but, having emptied her bladder, she proved to be a very level-headed woman. She took Blayde into the privacy of the manager's office and, having checked his warrant card, answered his questions without hesitation.

"We carry good stock," she said. "Bowland isn't quite London, but on the other hand we pride ourselves on carrying better stock than most of the lesser London jewellers."

"We expect smash-and-grab," said Blayde. "But it may be something more."

"The window display is worth quite a few thousand."

"And inside?"

"The really expensive stuff is locked away in the safe, of course. But what we have on show is well worth stealing." She paused, then said, "I could telephone the manager. He's at lunch, but he'd . . ."

"No!" Blayde shook his head. "Nothing out of the ordinary. We want to catch them, not scare them off."

"It sounds sensible," she agreed quietly. "They might come again . . . when you're not expecting them."

"We expect them to be armed," said Blayde gently. "*We're* armed."

For the first time she looked startled.

"If there are customers in the . . ."

"Get them into here. Along with yourself and the assistant. And *stay* here. Away from the door. If possible behind solid furniture."

"And if Mr. Chisholme comes back?" she asked in a worried voice.

"Mr. Chisholme?"

"The manager. If he comes back from his lunch while all this is going on, he'll . . ."

"With luck, it'll be over before two."

"Oh!"

"And if he *does* arrive in the area before it's over, he won't be allowed through the police cordon."

"Are you . . ." She moistened her lips. "Are you staying in the shop?"

"Yes. I suggest you get your assistant in here. Don't tell her why, just get her in here and tell her to stay put."

"Of course. And—er—I'll stay in the shop?"

"If you don't mind. In case customers come in."

"Are *you* armed?" she asked a little breathlessly.

He nodded.

"Quite exciting, isn't it?" she murmured, and there was the hint of a shake in her voice.

"It could turn out to be," agreed Blayde.

It was 1.40 p.m.

The first van moved into position. It was a Vauxhall pick-up, carrying bricks and general building material. There was a tarpaulin sheet artistically draped so that this covered the rear number plate. It pulled in, alongside the kerb, less than three yards ahead of the chief inspector's VW.

"A wee bit stupid." The detective constable was from north of the border. His soft Highland burr gave no suggestion of panic. "We could cut them off, if we'd a mind."

"That's a well-tuned engine under that bonnet," said the chief inspector. He nodded to a nearby shop. "Go buy yourself a newspaper. Sort through the paperbacks till you see me leave the car."

The D.C. grunted agreement, climbed from the VW and strolled towards the newsagents.

The chief inspector bent forward, as if seeking something he'd dropped on the floor of the car, pressed the transmit toggle of the walkie-talkie, and murmured, "Number One Son to Father. Our target is at the bull."

The soft voice of Blayde answered, "Father to Number One Son. Handle target when necessary. Good luck."

Almost immediately, the voice of the D.D.I. came over the walkie-talkie, "Number Two Son to Father. Repeat as Number One Son."

"Thank you, Number Two Son. The same applies. Good luck."

The time was 1.43 p.m.

Blayde slipped his walkie-talkie back into the pocket of his mac, smiled at Mrs. Amber and said, "Make your way towards the office, ma'am. Pretend to be looking at the show cases. As if I'm here to buy something you can't quite put your hands on."

She nodded and moved quietly along the show-case covered wall behind the counter. Blayde moved slightly and positioned himself in order to watch the road from an angle, between the exhibits in the shop window. He saw the van arrive; a heavily built Commer, with the rear doors open and two lengths of six-by-four timber protruding about two yards beyond the open doors. The van swung left across the road and, inside the van, he saw two men drag balaclavas over their faces.

He snapped, "Into the office, ma'am." Then, pulling the walkie-talkie from his pocket, he gave the order. "Father to all the family. Get the show under way."

The time was 1.45 p.m.

The detective constable saw the chief inspector open the door of the VW. At a quick stroll he left the newsagents, crossed the pavement, drew the Smith and Wesson from its holster and thumbed back the hammer. The nearside window of the Vauxhall pick-up was conveniently wound down.

The D.C. placed the snout of the revolver against the ear of the man sitting watching the Commer, and in a quiet, conversational tone said, "Ye'll have a hell of an earache if ye do anything foolish, laddie."

The chief inspector dragged open the off-side door of the Vauxhall, levelled his revolver and said, "It's loaded, lad, and we're police officers. Be advised. Don't even look as if you're going to touch that shotgun."

The D.D.I. did it the fancy way; the "Dick Turpin" way. He flung open the door of the Jag, raced to the front of the Austin van then, less than two yards from the front of its bonnet, took up a classic bent-knees-two-handed-grip stance and aimed his revolver at the van's windscreen. He glimpsed the muzzle of a shortened shotgun come into view from below the windscreen, and squeezed the trigger twice. The two holes in the windscreen looked very business-like and the two villains ducked, the driver grabbing at his right shoulder. The sergeant arrived, dragged open the nearside door, pointed the Smith and

Wesson and warned, "Half a chance, and I'll blow both your bloody heads off."

By this time the citizenry had realised that something was amiss and there was a certain amount of scattering and shouting. Having verified that the sergeant had both men in the Austin under control, the D.D.I. turned to give what help he could to Blayde.

And Blayde needed help.

The two men wearing balaclavas had dropped from the rear of the Commer as the van began to reverse at speed. The ram of the two lengths of six-by-four shattered the window of the jewellers shop, then moved forward for a getaway. The helmeted villains each had a sawn-off shotgun and, as pedestrians screamed and Blayde raced from the shop, they swung the guns in opposing arcs. One blasted off in the general direction of Blayde, and Blayde took some shot in the left shoulder, was smashed against a wall and then went down. Before the villain could squeeze the second trigger, the D.D.I. let fly and, although he missed, he diverted attention long enough for Blayde to take aim with the Beretta. It was a very carefully aimed shot; from a prone position, with the crook of the left arm steadying the weapon and a deliberately slow squeezing of the trigger. The bullet blasted the villain's right knee-cap to hell; for the rest of his life he'd walk with a stiff leg, and for the moment his only interest in the world was the pain. He screamed—high-pitched and animal-like—as he buckled to the ground, and the shotgun went flying.

His companion whirled to meet all this unexpected opposition, and was caught between the cross-fire from Blayde and the D.D.I. He was no hero. He dropped his weapon, jerked his hands high into the air, and yelled, "No! Don't shoot! Don't shoot!"

Meanwhile, the Commer was accelerating for a last-chance getaway. It passed within a yard of the D.D.I., but the D.D.I. kept his cool, turned and, with the same stance he'd used against the Austin, emptied his revolver at the rear wheel. The offside rear blew, the Commer swerved, cushioned off a lamp-post and stopped as it nudged into the side of the squad car which had been parked in the municipal car park. The second squad car arrived to block off the other end of the road, then the van, complete with uniformed coppers and a sergeant.

In short, a beautifully-timed, immaculately executed ambush; less than three minutes of wild activity which the wide-eyed civilians who'd witnessed it would never forget. Three casualties. The villain with the shattered knee-cap who was writhing on the ground sobbing with pain. The driver of the Austin van who'd been clipped by a bullet from the gun of the D.D.I. And Blayde, who'd caught some of the spraying shot in his left shoulder. That, and a smashed shop window.

As Blayde hauled himself upright, with unnecessary assistance from the D.D.I., he muttered, "Not bad. Not bad at all."

The uniformed sergeant arrived alongside Blayde and said, "I've sent for an ambulance, sir."

"Good."

"And they're all unarmed and handcuffed. We'll have the uninjured in the van in no time."

"Any civilian casualties?" asked Blayde.

"Not so much as a scratch," grinned the D.D.I.

"They'll think twice in future." Blayde tried to return the grin, then winced as the pain in his shoulder built up from the original numbness. "Your case, inspector. 'From information received' . . . the usual crap. Put me down as witness. Oh, yes, there's a Mrs.

Amber and a girl assistant holed out in the manager's office. Nip in, and tell 'em the excitement's all over. Then statements. Statements from everybody who saw *anything*. And photographs. Bags of photographs. We want that bloody jury to be left in no doubt . . . no doubt at all."

"*My* case, sir," the D.D.I. reminded him gently.

"Your case," sighed Blayde. "It gets to be a habit. I'm sorry."

Nevertheless, Blayde did his share in interviewing, and he interviewed hard. The link-up . . . that was what he was after. The link-up with the burning down of The Silver Stocking. The link-up with Lessford. *The* link-up. Because of what he was—because of his rank and position in the force—he dare only go so far. He couldn't "suggest". He could only approach from various angles and hope that one of the villains might drop a word—give a hint—which, in turn, might send the D.D.I. in the right direction.

It did no good. They were hard nuts. Eight of the bastards and, to a man, they sat there and in effect spat in the faces of men who sought further information.

The man with the shattered knee looked up from the hospital bed, curled his lips, stared at Blayde's empty sleeve and the arm which was resting in a sling, and mocked, "It wasn't my day, copper. I should have wiped your face off."

There was hatred and counter-hatred. Far too much of it to make headway beyond what could be proved. Far too much for any give-and-take. It both worried and puzzled the D.D.I.

"Throw the book at them, inspector. Start at the top with attempted murder."

"For Christ's sake, sir. We haven't a hope . . ."

"We can *try.*"

"It's just that . . ."

"Attempted murder. All the way down to damage to the shop window. Dammit, inspector, if any of 'em haven't signed their driving licence, do 'em for *that.*"

"Yes, sir."

Blayde was called into the chief's office.

"That Beretta. You haven't a certificate for it, superintendent."

"No, sir. A war souvenir," lied Blayde.

"Do you carry it around often?"

"No, sir. We hadn't enough revolvers, that's all."

The chief tossed a buff-coloured piece of folded pasteboard across the desk surface and said, "Now you *have* a certificate. Back-dated, to save you extra trouble when you're cross-examined."

"Thank you, sir."

"But if it hadn't come off . . ." The chief left the sentence hanging in mid-air.

"The information was good."

"Obviously."

"Perfect, and very detailed."

"Quite." The chief nodded briefly. "But I don't like gun-play. Especially in busy streets."

"It was the only way."

"And I don't like being kept in the dark. When guns are issued, I want to know."

"Yes, sir. I'll bear that in mind in future."

"The hell you will," growled the chief. He sighed, then continued, "Men like you, Blayde. It's a damn good job you're on our side. As chief constable, I'm giving you another commendation. You and your divisional detective inspector . . ."

"Thank you, sir."

". . . but as a *man* I have grave doubts."

"Doubts?"

"It's too much of a crusade, Blayde." The chief's voice was soft and worried. "It's too much of a vendetta."

"I don't make excuses for 'em, sir," said Blayde flatly.

"No more do I. But I don't actively hate 'em."

"They hate us." The tone was still flat and expressionless.

"I suppose so." The chief frowned then, in a sorrowful voice, he capitulated to Blayde's unspoken argument. "I suppose we *need* men like you. This mad upsurge of violence."

"It isn't 'gentlemanly' any more, if it ever was."

"In a nutshell," agreed the chief sadly. "Therefore, my congratulations, superintendent. And I hope your shoulder heals quickly."

Bloody chief constables! Flash offices, worlds of their own, the luxury of feeling compassion. Whose blasted side were they on? The streets were becoming jungles, with animals prowling in the shadows. Dangerous animals. Animals prepared to kill, rather than be caged. And the damn chief constables still lived in the bull's-eye lantern and the come-along-a-me era. They refused to *see* these animals, or they mistook them for naughtily behaved kittens.

Blayde truly believed there was little hope. That unless open war was declared upon the criminal fraternity—all-out war with no holds barred—the villains and the tearaways would gradually get the upper hand. There wasn't a clever way. There wasn't a psychiatric way.

Not for the first time in his life, Blayde became a newspaper "hero". The abortive raid on the jewellers was headline stuff, in the nationals as well as in the locals. He refused, point-blank and with pithy language, to be interviewed. Not by columnists, not by radio talk-men, not by television smoothies. In army parlance, he put himself on "light duties". He'd refused to stay in hospital, once they'd dug the pellets from his arm and shoulder. By taking his arm from its sling, and driving carefully, he could use his car. But Bowland was his division and, without him around, Bowland was missing on one cylinder. He wasn't indispensable. He'd have been the first to agree—he'd have even *argued* that he wasn't indispensable—he merely acted as if he was.

On Saturday, November 27th, 1971, he strolled into Bowland D.H.Q. Charge Office.

it was about 10.30 a.m. and, as usual, the office was smooth-running and able to deal with any incident likely to crop up. He exchanged pleasantries with the sergeant in charge, chewed up a constable for having filthy finger-nails ("There's enough muck under there, lad, to sow a row of spuds") then picked up the Telephone Message Book to check incoming and outgoing calls. There was an Express Message recorded; underlined in red ink, as was the practice, originating from Bordfield and circulated to all police districts. Blayde read the text, initialled the message as proof that he'd seen it, then arranged for the telephone in his office to be connected with Bordfield D.H.Q.

Eventually, he was talking to Detective Superintendent Harris.

"Blayde, here."

"Who?"

"Blayde. Superintendent Blayde. Bowland Division, County Constabulary."

"Oh! Blayde?"

"That Express Message."

"What about it?"

"Anything else that isn't included in the circulation?"

"Not much. We fished him out of the canal

last night. An anonymous tip-off. Hands fastened behind his back with police handcuffs. Legs roped inside a sack, with bloody great boulders. According to documents on him, Nicholas Houseman." Harris paused, then added, "His tongue was cut out . . . that's not in the Express."

"God!" breathed Blayde.

"I'd like to have five minutes with the bastard responsible."

"So would I."

"Any ideas?" asked Harris.

"No," lied Blayde. Then, as an afterthought, added, "If Houseman was a snout. The tongue business, I mean."

"I've thought about it," said Harris grimly. "Some loud-mouthed copper not being able to keep his trap shut."

"Or Houseman."

"Possible." There was a reluctance in the admission. "They usually have more sense. My money's on some bloody copper."

"From your crowd?" asked Blayde gruffly.

"Possible," repeated Harris grudgingly. "I think not, though. I know my mob too well."

"I'll—er—I'll ask around. Quietly," said Blayde.

"You're uniform, aren't you?"

"Yes."

"Since when did uniformed men use informants?"

"We don't work the pigeon-hole system in the county," retorted Blayde. "Especially not in this division. We're *all* coppers."

"Oh, my word!" mocked Harris.

"It brings home sides of bacon," snapped Blayde. He added, "It's not easy to bag jewellers shops," and immediately wished he hadn't allowed Harris to get under his skin.

"I read about it," sneered Harris. "You damn near needed the Scots Greys."

"Maybe." Blayde grabbed his flying temper then, after a pause, asked, "How's Ruth?"

"Ruth?"

"Your wife . . . how is she?"

"She's okay. Why do you ask?"

"Politeness," said Blayde gently.

"She's okay," repeated Harris, then asked, "How's your wife?"

"It's something I've never had."

"What?"

"A wife."

"Oh, I haven't been interested enough to keep track of your emotional life."

"Well, now you're up to date."

In a slightly less aggressive tone, Harris said, "About Houseman."

"Yes?"

"If you hear anything, let me know."

"What makes you think I wouldn't?"

"We don't like each other, Blayde," said Harris bluntly. "But we're both coppers."

"Aye . . . we're both coppers."

Blayde replaced the receiver. He left the Bowland D.H.Q. building, called at a nearby off-licence shop and bought a bottle of whisky, then drove carefully back to his cottage. All that day he spent trying to get drunk, but when the whisky bottle was empty he was as sober as he'd been when he'd opened it. He didn't go to bed that night. Instead he sat in an armchair, chain-smoked and tried *not* to think about a man who'd paid for passing on priceless information by having his tongue cut out, then being drowned. He even toyed with the idea of handing in his resignation, but that would have been foolish; it would have deprived him of the one thing he needed most. Authority. The full weight and complexity of the Police Service. The "machine": the machine of justice—of vengeance as far as he was concerned—without which he couldn't hope to win. And that was the line along which his thoughts travelled. It had become a contest. A battle. Or, to be more precise, a personal duel within the general battle against law-breakers.

That was 1971. The tag-end of 1971. By Christmas, on the face of things, the policing of Bowland Division was back to its normal efficiency. Blayde's shoulder had healed and, if he was a shade more brusque than usual, it was accepted as a mere extension of his usual mannerism. In a surprisingly short time he'd polished a lack-lustre division into a single unit with pride and even with its own particular charisma.

Beyond the division Hale had retired and (as the chief constable had hinted) Pinthead Pike Division ceased to exist and was swallowed up within a vastly extended Beechwood Brook Division.

Thinking coppers had become worried. The age of the gun seemed to have dawned. Nor were mere flatfoots the only targets. In the immediate past authority—in particular uniformed authority—had acted like an invisible shield. Not too long before to shoot a policeman had been tantamount to committing slow-motion suicide. Every cop-killer had been traced, then topped. But, rightly or wrongly, the noose and the hanging-shed had been abolished and the life-for-a-life punishment no longer applied. It was, therefore, a short step to shoot any police officer and still live. Frederick Sewell underlined the new rules when he shot dead a Blackpool superintendent. The jewellery shop raiders would have, equally, killed Blayde in an attempt to carry out their purpose.

And in 1972 Chief Superintendent Charles Ripley stopped a bullet from a crazed killer and lived.[1] Nevertheless, Beechwood Brook Division lost its mentor. It was as if a grey and ice-cold mist had descended upon the whole force. A fear. A realisation. If it could happen to Ripley, it could happen to anybody. Nobody was safe. If it could happen to Ripley . . .

Even Blayde caught the feeling, but of more important personal concern was the fact that, earlier that same year, Harris earned himself a place on the short list and was then accepted by the County Constabulary as a chief superintendent and Head of C.I.D. Always, the bastard stayed one jump ahead. Always, he jockeyed himself into a position where he had

[1] A touch of Malice, Macmillan, 1973.

the edge over Blayde. Christ Almighty, why couldn't he have stayed in the Bordfield Force? Why—whichever way he turned—must Robert-bloody-Harris be grinning down at him from one rung higher? And now, in the same blasted force.

They met only once while Blayde was Bowland divisional officer. Harris was touring the divisions, checking the crime statistics and, wherever and whenever possible, finding fault.

In Blayde's office, after finding nothing whatever to form the basis of criticism, Harris unbent as far as his own pig-headed pride would allow.

"You run a tight division, superintendent."

"Coffee?" suggested Blayde. "Or would you prefer tea?"

"Tea, thanks." Harris cleared his throat. "Not like some of the Kate Karney set-ups."

Blayde lifted the receiver of his desk telephone and ordered tea and biscuits for two.

"I—er—I was lucky to get this job," grunted Harris. "Some of the opposition was red hot."

"I wouldn't know," said Blayde blandly.

"You still hate my guts," said Harris bluntly.

"I've just offered you tea and biscuits." Blayde smiled.

"And you can't even be honest about it."

"Sure . . . I hate your guts," said Blayde flatly. "But we're both in the same team . . . unfortunately."

"How does 'armed neutrality' grab you?"

"It could have its advantages," said Blayde warily.

"On the face of things, you seem to be able to handle your own crime."

"I *can* handle my own crime."

"So . . ." Harris sounded embarrassed. "So that's the deal?"

"Deal?" Blayde pretended puzzlement.

"Dammit, I'm new here," rasped Harris. "I'll find friends, eventually. But those who are coppers. I can do without *their* antagonism."

"Otherwise you'll need the Scots Greys."

Harris nodded slowly.

"Okay, a deal." Blayde leaned back in the desk chair and grinned wolfishly at the man he'd grown to dislike to a point which wasn't too far removed from hatred. "You keep off my back, I'll keep off yours. Y'see, I already *have* friends. Good friends. I could build a wall, figuratively speaking. It might hem me in. It *would* hem me in. I'd get no farther. I don't kid myself. That's the sacrifice, a full stop to any personal promotion prospects. But *you'd* be on top of that wall, doing a balancing act and, one day, I'd kick a brick away and you'd fall and break your neck. It's a trick I know. A trick I've perfected."

"I've heard," muttered Harris.

"So . . . that's the deal."

Harris nodded stone-faced agreement, then said, "For the present. Until I can build my own wall. And I won't have to tell you . . . you'll know when that is."

There was no need for formal agreement; no need for the mockery of a handshake. They both knew. They both knew they could walk into any force, dig around, and come up with similar "deals". The higher the rank, the greater the suspicion; the greater the suspicion, the more involved the wheeling and dealing. Up there at the top—among the real rank—friendship and trust were for suckers. The top dogs stayed top dogs because they could bite deeper than those snapping at their heels. Or, to be more accurate, they'd better bite deeper otherwise, sure as hell, they'd lose a leg.

Blayde knew he was on firm ground,

pending Harris vetting and collecting his own clique. The name of the game. Not cops-and-robbers . . . cops-and-cops.

For a few months Blayde kept a tight rein on Bowland. He'd pulled the whiskers of a tiger, and he knew it. Nevertheless, it had been a calculated risk and he prepared himself for whatever Harris might come up with. No real worries, though. He had a home, he had a neat little nest-egg tucked away in a building society, he'd no dependants and very few friends. As for policing . . . as far as that was concerned, there was nothing new under the sun. Harris? Harris was still in a strange land, surrounded by strange people, and would be for some time to come. He was a "comer-in". Somewhere on that short list the chances were that an ambitious county man's name had been included. Some copper from whom Harris had filched a plum job. It always happened, and *that* was the guy Harris had better watch, because *that* was the guy who'd be watching Harris. And Harris was no mug. That, at least in part, had been one reason for the proposed "deal"; because even Harris only had one pair of eyes, and even Harris had to sleep sometime. It didn't need a genius to work that one out. He wanted to be safe from

Blayde until such time as he'd secured his own position.

Meanwhile Bowland Division lived up to its own reputation. It had become a top drawer division, and Blayde made damn sure it stayed that way.

It was Christmas Eve, 1972 (a Sunday of all days) when the chief arrived, unannounced, at the D.H.Q. It was late morning—just after 11 a.m.—and Blayde was finishing off the paperwork chores he'd left from the previous evening. The chief constable tapped on the office door, then entered without invitation.

Blayde made as if to speak, then closed his mouth. There was a hard, worried expression on the chief's face and, as he flopped into a handy chair he sighed, as if he had the world's worries on his shoulders. Blayde waited. Some sixth sense told him that to wait, in silence, was what the chief required.

After a few moments, the chief raised his head, and said, "I'm glad you're here, superintendent. I called at your home. I hoped you'd be on duty. Here. Where I could contact you in person."

Blayde still waited.

"I called in to see Ripley." The chief's voice

was heavy. "Christmas . . . all the rest of it. To wish him . . ."

The chief's voice tailed off, and he moved his shoulders, helplessly.

"How is he?" asked Blayde.

"Finished." The single word was heavy with sorrow. "We thought he might recover. There seemed some slight chance, but . . . I doubt if he'll walk again."

"How's he taking it?" And, such was Ripley's reputation, that even Blayde's question held concern.

"How would you take it?" countered the chief bitterly. "How would any man take it?"

Blayde nodded.

The chief sighed, then said, "He has a good wife."

"Ah."

"In a way . . ." The chief paused, then said, "In a way she seems almost glad."

"But that's . . ."

"She doesn't have to share him any more. Beechwood Brook was more demanding than any mistress."

"Oh."

"You wouldn't know about that." The chief's smile was tight and humourless.

"No," agreed Blayde.

There was another pause, then the chief said, "It seemed only right—proper—to ask his advice."

"Advice?"

"About who should take over. It's been *his* division for so long. He's run it *his* way. He's never tolerated interference. He's never needed interference. For almost as long as I can remember, it's been 'Ripley's Patch'." The chief took a deep breath, then in a quiet voice, said, "He suggested you."

"Me?" Blayde frowned.

"It's a peg up. A chief-superintendentship."

"I don't give a damn about it being a . . ."

"That's what he'd have said," the chief smiled.

"He doesn't know me," protested Blayde. "We've hardly ever met. At senior officers conferences. Other than that . . ."

"He knows you, *of* you," interrupted the chief.

"And on his recommendation you're willing to . . ."

"My idea, too." The tone of the chief's voice stopped Blayde in mid-sentence. "Let's call Bowland a testing-ground. You've worked wonders."

"All it needed was . . ."

"What it needed was *you.* You're too self-opinionated to sell yourself short, Blayde. Modesty isn't your way. And now, you're the man for Beechwood Brook."

"Chief Superintendent Blayde," murmured Blayde quietly.

"It rolls very easily off the tongue."

"Thank you, sir. I'll take it."

"Of course you'll take it." The chief's voice was brusque. "I'll get confirmation off before the year's out." He paused, then continued, "Meanwhile, talk to Ripley. Visit him. He's asked to see you. He's worth a visit . . . he can even tell *you* things."

It was a little like the meeting of Mars and Vulcan. Not a clash, but an acknowledgement; two greats paying homage to each other on the last day of the year. It was early evening and Ripley, pale-faced and eyes burning with the inner fury of his own helplessness, sat propped up in bed and advised the man chosen to take over his beloved division. Blayde sat on a chair, alongside the bed, listened and occasionally asked questions. Not once were Ripley's injuries mentioned. It would have been in bad taste; unwanted sympathy; a tacit suggestion that a giant had hefted something he couldn't carry.

"Preston," said Ripley. "You know Preston?"

"I know Preston," agreed Blayde.

"Not many like him," said Ripley, with a wry grin. "Noisy, but in a tight corner he'll guard your back. No ambition. The only man I know who's genuinely surprised at his own rank. Trust him. He'll never let you down."

"Nice to know," murmured Blayde.

"And Sykes."

"I know Sykes, too."

"Salt of the earth. Loyal, and the men damn near worship him. Another man who'll slap the back-biters down. With Preston and Sykes on your side, you'll have the whole division behind you."

"Nice to know," repeated Blayde.

"And there's an inspector. McCoy. A young lad. Out to prove himself."

"He was winged at the shoot-out," contributed Blayde.

"That's the lad." Ripley grinned, and his bloodless lips seemed to almost crack. "He'll be hell on wheels, one day. Once he's learned not to waste too much time hating Harris."

"Harris?" It was a very carefully modulated

question; a simple, one-word question, but carrying with it the unspoken invitation to make known, as much as possible, the relationship between Harris and the whole of Beechwood Brook Division.

"Met Harris?" asked Ripley.

"A couple of times."

"Bouncy." Ripley moistened his lips and tried for another grin. "A real china-shop-bull type. Got a little peeved when he found Beechwood Brook crockery wasn't for smashing."

"Uhu." Blayde waited.

"Knotted McCoy up a little, until the penny dropped."

"The penny *did* drop?" coaxed Blayde.

"Blayde." Ripley's tone became almost paternal. "He's a chief superintendent. When you take over, *you'll* be a chief superintendent. Rank for rank, but with a difference. At Beechwood Brook you'll be *the* superintendent. The cock o' this particular midden. Harris is a visitor. I don't give a damn if he's from headquarters—I don't give a damn if he's from Outer Space—that's all he is, a *visitor*."

"He's been told that?"

"I gave him a present of the plan drawings."

"Worth knowing," observed Blayde.

"Don't let him screw the place up," said Ripley quietly.

"I won't."

"He'll try. I know the type."

"He'll get his toes trapped," promised Blayde.

Ripley nodded, as if satisfied. As if happy.

Blayde allowed the silence to grow until it formed a soft cushion of mutual respect and understanding then, very deliberately, he said, "Tallboy?"

"Detective sergeant," said Ripley, with equal deliberation.

"Your son-in-law."

"He has to be *somebody's* son-in-law."

"As uncomplicated as that?"

"Blayde," smiled Ripley, "this is a very uncomplicated division. The bloke in the top chair rules. Nobody tells him what to do. Nobody! Nobody gets all the favours. Nobody gets all the sewage. Nobody gets *anything* they don't deserve."

17

A police division. It is part of a force, and yet it can differ from that force. A fine force can have, within its limits, one or more very ropy divisions. Conversely, a ropy force can include the odd division which in itself is a law-enforcement gem. It is argued that a force is only as good as its chief constable, but this is a false truth; a truth which is far too simple, far too overall to stand up to serious examination. It is much nearer the basic truth to say that a chief constable is as good as the sum total of his superintendents and chief superintendents and to that extent—and by putting the cart before the horse—a force is, indeed, as good as its chief constable.

A division, sub-divided into sub-divisions, sections and beats, is a large area, but at the same time not an unwieldy area. It can be controlled or it can be let run to seed. The decision can be made and, once made, can be imposed. A force on the other hand—and especially a county constabulary—is unwieldy. What goes on in its out-of-the-way divisions is, in the final analysis, the concern of the chief constable. The chief's ultimate responsibility. But simple distance—sheer size—precludes him from having day-to-day or even a week-to-week control of the basic nuts and bolts of policing within that division. He must rely upon the capabilities and the conscience of his various divisional officers; his superintendents and his chief superintendents.

Thus, when Ripley was knocked out of the game and Blayde took his place, the county chief constable—figuratively speaking—held his breath and crossed his fingers. Beechwood Brook. "Ripley's Patch". One hell of an area, but an area which the chief had grown accustomed to take for granted; whatever happened elsewhere, Beechwood Brook would handle its own problems and handle them well.

This was all known to Blayde when he officially took over the post of divisional officer at Beechwood Brook D.H.Q. on Monday, January 8th. He was met by Chief Inspector Sanderson, Ripley's old second-in-command. They shook hands and, as they entered Ripley's old office, Sanderson said, "There's a chair . . ."

"It's arrived?" Blayde sounded pleased.

"Yes, sir." Sanderson pointed.

It was a new desk chair; so new, in fact that it still had its protective plastic covering in place.

Blayde said, "I ordered it from County Headquarters stores."

"But there's . . ."

"Ripley's chair." Blayde ended the sentence.

"Yes, sir. At least, the one he used. It's . . ."

"It's *Ripley's* chair," insisted Blayde.

"Yes, sir."

"And always will be."

"Sir, I don't see . . ."

"It stays in this office." Blayde looked around and saw a vacant place among the cabinets and filing drawers. "There, that's where it's going to stand. Kept clean, kept polished, but never used."

Sanderson looked puzzled.

"Chief inspector," Blayde spoke as to an equal, and as to a man who fully understood the psychology needed to run a good division. He offered an opened packet of cigarettes, Sanderson provided the lighter then, when they were both smoking, Blayde continued, "Ripley was very important. No, more than important. Vital. Irreplaceable. Therefore, I'm not going to attempt the impossible and try to 'replace' him. That chair," Blayde waved the hand holding the cigarette. "*His* chair. A sort of totem pole. Damn near an altar. Now, the men and the women of this division are going to look at me and say, 'That's not Ripley.' Some of 'em will go farther, and ask themselves 'What the hell's *he* doing, sitting in Ripley's chair?' So, I take the wind out of their sails by *not* sitting in his chair. I do more. I keep the chair in this office. I refuse to destroy their totem pole. I give it a place of honour. They can look at it. They can remember who once sat in it. But they can't make comparisons, because I'm *not* sitting in it."

Blayde inhaled cigarette smoke, then continued, "The others. Those who expect a complete new broom programme. Well, there's a new *chair*. They can read into it what the hell they like. A new regime, the relic of the old one sitting there in the corner reminding them of the good old times . . . maybe the bad old times. No, don't fanny me, chief inspector." Blayde waved Sanderson silent, as Sanderson was about to speak. "No divisional officer's universally popular in his division. The skivers. The smart-arse types who think they know a better way. The ones he's chewed up, when they didn't think they deserved chewing up. Not enemies. Not quite as bad as enemies. But those who have reservations. Those who don't 'quite like'. Even Ripley had 'em, and if you deny that you're a liar."

Again Blayde drew on the cigarette, then continued, "That chair. The new chair *and* the old chair. Together, they'll create one big question mark. Very enigmatic, see?" Blayde chuckled quietly and ended, "Even you. I've explained all the reasons. But even *you* don't know, can't make up your mind . . . yet."

"Not yet," agreed Sanderson gruffly.

"Right." Blayde's tone turned a little more brusque. "Arrange for the two chairs to be positioned, please. No explanations. No suggested explanations. Meanwhile, we'll look around the building. See if it's changed over the years. No criticism at this point. Just a look-see. And arrange for a conference at six o'clock this evening. All the inspectors—including yourself—and as many sergeants as possible, leaving skeleton cover. Plain clothes, as well as uniformed. I think I should perform a little unveiling ceremony . . . myself."

To some people it might have seemed foolhardy. Certainly unwise. To take over from a man like Ripley and, on the first evening of his command, to stand up amidst the men and women most likely to criticise him and in effect say, "This is me. I'm the guy you're all expected to despise. But have a damn good look, listen to some home-truths, then at least you can build a basis for your contempt."

Blayde's way. Never to duck the issue. Always to meet possible trouble, head-on.

The office wasn't small, but it was crowded. Sanderson was there, of course. So was Preston and Sykes. So was McCoy and Tallboy, although at that first meeting Blayde didn't recognise them. Seven other inspectors and as many sergeants—uniformed and C.I.D.—made up the audience and, as Blayde entered his office Sanderson brought the assembly to a slightly sloppy attitude of attention. He saluted Blayde, and Blayde had the sheer balls to keep the others at attention until he'd removed his peaked cap, peeled off his gloves and straightened what few files there were on the surface of his desk. It was a gesture. A deliberate and calculated gesture; a silent warning that this wasn't a vicarage garden party. There was a boss—*one* boss—and he was it and that important fact had better be digested.

Then he faced them—still standing—waved a hand and said, "Please relax. Sit down, if you can find a chair." He turned his head for a moment and added, "Nobody sits in *that* chair without my personal permission . . . and that isn't available."

There was a shuffling, a leaning against walls and radiators, a no-you-have-it rigmarole as far as the few chairs were concerned then, after a few moments, there was a waiting silence.

Blayde leaned his backside against the front of his desk, took out cigarettes and said, "Smoke, if you wish."

Again, it was a deliberate ploy. Keep 'em waiting. Keep 'em wondering. Then—just when they expect the firework display to start—put them at their ease. But a slightly worried ease. Good guy? Bad guy? Sucker? Slave-master? Spontaneous decisions were impossible . . . which was the object of the exercise.

Blayde spoke at a controlled speed. He

didn't waver. He spoke loudly enough for all to hear, but not loudly enough to risk being thought mouthy. And all the time his head moved slowly and he met every face eye-for-eye in turn. Again and again.

He said, "My name is Blayde. Something you all already know. Chief Superintendent Robert Blayde. I am *not* Chief Superintendent Ripley and, before I go into any more details, I give this solemn warning. Nobody—*nobody*—refers to my predecessor other than with full rank and name. Chief Superintendent Ripley. In this division—at least while I'm in charge—he'll hold that rank till the day he dies.

"I'm here from Bowland Division. I hold the convinced opinion that Bowland Division is far and away the best division in this force. In present company I may be in a minority of one, but that does not of necessity make me wrong. I'm open to correction, but it won't be easy. That's the message I want passing down the line to the newest recruit. That however good you all think you are, I'm the one you'll have to convince.

"There will be no great and immediate changes. Nobody need, therefore, get the breeze up. Everybody will continue to perform his or her duty in a way Chief Superintendent Ripley would have approved. The chances are, his way will satisfy me. If it doesn't I'll let you know, and from that moment you'll do it *my* way. A rule of thumb. There's a right way and a wrong way of doing everything. Right and wrong . . . not quite the same as official and unofficial. I credit you all with the full appreciation that no law enforcement is possible strictly according to the book. Arm-chancing is a daily occurrence, and I'm prepared to accept it as such. Which means I'll accept explanations, but not excuses. I expect loyalty. I expect trust. In return I'll back every man and woman in this division who, in the honest pursuit of duty, drops clangers. I want a minimum of Misconduct Forms. Any inspector—any sergeant—who has to use the threat of Misconduct Forms to keep his subordinates in line isn't worth the rank he carries. What is more, he'd better start packing his furniture because, when I spot him or her, Beechwood Brook Division will soon be losing a passenger.

"C.I.D. and uniformed branch. In this division, while this is my office, there's no difference. Anybody who thinks detecting the theft of milk bottles is more important than directing traffic has his priorities all to hell.

The same with snouts. A uniformed man cultivates an informant, I expect him to *use* that informant in the detection of crime. What I don't expect is some C.I.D. type to use the information obtained by the uniformed man for his own purpose. This is a single division . . . and it *stays* a single division. Not two halves.

"Generalities. Nobody salutes anybody unless the recipient of that salute is fully dressed and wearing the appropriate uniform. We may be servants of the public, we're not skivvies. I don't give a damn how much so-called pull a person has, unless he or she is a police officer, or an officer in Her Majesty's forces and, as such, is correctly dressed and deserving a salute . . . no saluting. It smacks too much of forelock touching. Our job is to enforce the law, and to enforce it without fear and without favour. If somebody has to be top dog on the street, it had better be us, however many noses are bloodied in the process. Drunkenness? Quite simple, you get pissed on your own time and, if it's in a pub, within licensing hours. Nobody puts himself in a position of either owning favours or being susceptible to moral blackmail. The same with women. I'm not looking for celibates. I'm not looking for saints. But fornication based upon what you are, as opposed to who you are, is out. That, too, is a form of moral blackmail."

Blayde paused long enough to take a deep drag on his cigarette, then in a slightly lower tone continued, "Those are the general guidelines. For myself . . . at some time or another in the future you'll all call me a bastard. It goes with the rank and has little or nothing to do with parentage. You have that freedom. You even have the freedom to call me it to my face, if you feel strongly enough about something. But having decided that I *am* a bastard, you'll also remember I'm Beechwood Brook divisional officer and, like it or lump it, you'll obey orders."

There was a silence. The assembled officers showed a variety of differing expressions. Sykes was almost grinning. Sanderson's eyes twinkled. One of the inspectors—a florid-faced man running to fat—looked a little like a turkey-cock and his nostrils fairly quivered with suppressed outrage. Some looked worried. Some looked relieved. Some looked satisfied almost to the point of smugness.

It had been quite a speech. Quite an opening broadside. A few minutes before every person in that room (Blayde himself excluded) had been convinced that, with the loss of Ripley, Beechwood Brook Division was on a downhill track. Now they weren't so sure. It was going to be different—as sure as God made green apples it was going to be different!—but not necessarily worse. Maybe as good as ever. Maybe even better.

The turkey-cock inspector cleared his throat and said, "Might I ask a question . . ."

"No." Blayde cut him short with the ruthless finality of a descending guillotine blade. "This isn't a conference. No votes. No suggestions. No questions. I've told you what I expect. I've told you what I'm prepared to accept. Later—when I'm in a position to answer questions—I'll answer 'em."

He moved from the desk and picked up his peaked cap. He still held the cigarette in his free hand. Sanderson stood up and made as if to bring the others to attention.

Blayde motioned and said, "The rules apply to me, too, chief inspector. I'm not properly dressed. Nobody need stand up. Nobody need salute. Talk what I've said out among yourselves, then get back on duty." Halfway to the door he paused and added, "And what I *don't* want is one of you to try currying favour by taking me into a corner and telling me what you do say. If anybody tries it, he's a marked man."

It was an explosive start. It had been meant to be. Blayde didn't believe in the easing-in technique. He was there and, having arrived, the sensible thing to do was make damn sure everybody knew he'd arrived. Launch the initial rocket and make sure everybody felt the blast and dodged the sparks. Then stand back and watch them all wait for the first splutter of the expected Roman candles; watch them all wince in expectation of a real Brock's Benefit Night.

But it didn't work that way and that, too, caught everybody on the hop. During those first few weeks—those first few months—he visited every nick and every police house. He saw and spoke to—indeed had fairly long conversations with—every man and woman in the division. They treated him with respect almost amounting to awe . . . because they'd all "heard". But by August 1973 each man, each woman, had reached a personal opinion. This guy Blayde had all his chairs at home. He was nobody's mug, but at the same time he was a damn good practical copper. Yes, by

God, as good as Ripley had been . . . well almost.

Blayde sensed the feeling and was satisfied. In Naval jargon, Ripley had run a "tight and happy ship". It had been no real problem stepping into the vacated shoes.

Harris had chanced his arm . . . once.

An unlawful wounding job; very messy, very nasty and the lunatic with the knife in his guts had been lucky to live. His buddy—his "best pal"—had been equally lucky not to have been facing a murder charge. As far as these two were concerned, the boozer had sold "fighting beer" and they'd each had a skinful. One thing had led to another and, before the publican had decided to enlist the services of the law a couple of women had fainted, the bar parlour floor was swimming in blood and, apart from a quartet of regulars who continued to play dominoes in one corner, the place was in an uproar.

Detection played no part in the fiasco. It was a simple, logical progression from a normal Saturday night punch-up, but with knobs on. God in all His glory knew why Harris saw fit to shove his nose into the routine and rather boring mopping-up operation, but he did. Perhaps he *was* chancing his arm; testing the new bath-water for temperature.

But for whatever reason, at about ten o'clock the following Sunday morning he bounded into Blayde's office, when Blayde was going over the more obvious bits and pieces of tidying-up, and let fly.

He ignored Blayde and snapped, "You handling last night's unlawful wounding, sergeant?"

The sergeant was Tallboy, Ripley's son-in-law, and—again, perhaps—that was *why* Harris ignored Blayde and showed what he thought were his superior muscles.

Tallboy said, "Yes, sir," in a very deadpan voice. He added, "There's not much to it. A handful of statements and . . ."

"You will take a statement from every person who saw or heard *anything*, sergeant. I don't want this clown walking away because of lack of evidence."

"But, sir . . ."

"Sergeant." Blayde's voice was very polite. Very gentle. Very pointed. "I must be getting absent-minded in my old age. I'm sure I left the keys of my car in the ignition. D'you mind strolling along and checking?"

Tallboy said, "Yes, sir," and without giving

Harris time to say anything left the office.

"If you're that bloody absent-minded . . ."

"Harris!" It wasn't loud, but figuratively speaking the broken ice rattled around the sides of the word and matched the gleam in Blayde's eyes. "This is my division. This is my office. Tallboy is one of my detective sergeants. In future, you'll await invitation before you stamp your size elevens on *my* petty crime. If you're asked, you'll knock on the door of *my* office, before you perform your elephant charge routine. And in my presence when talking to one of *my* officers you will reverse the order of those two words you saw fit to utter. Not 'You *will*'. But '*Will* you?'."

"What the bloody hell . . ."

"We have time." Blayde glanced at his watch. "I'll give him a ring. We'll sort it out, before he goes for lunch."

"Who?"

"The chief constable, who else? I'll drive you there in my car." He slipped the ignition key, on its ring, from his pocket and mocked. "Not quite as absent-minded as you thought, eh? Or would you prefer me to sand-blast you down to your true size in front of a detective sergeant?"

It wasn't so much a glare as a gawp. Harris

had never been met with such openly don't-give-a-damn opposition; had never *expected* to be so met. It was a little like a battle cruiser steaming, full-throttle, at Beachy Head. Something had to give . . . and Beachy Head wasn't likely to shift.

"You're—er . . ." Harris cleared his throat, then growled, "You're bloody touchy."

"Aren't I, though?" Blayde's eyes were still cold. He kept the key-ring ready.

"Just—y'know—I was passing."

"The hell you were passing," said Blayde softly.

"I thought . . ." Again Harris cleared his throat. "I thought you might be grateful for some help."

"When we need it, we'll ask."

"In that case . . ." Harris didn't end the sentence.

"Good morning."

Harris turned and left the office. He slammed the door unnecessarily hard.

Tallboy returned, looking puzzled.

"I'm sorry, sir. I can't . . ."

"No. They're here, after all." Blayde showed the key-ring and keys.

"Chief Superintendent Harris . . ."

"He's left."

"All those statements, sir."

"Use a yardstick you're used to," suggested Blayde gently. "What you think would have satisfied your father-in-law. It should suffice."

Word got round the division. Word always gets round. Blayde had backed Harris down a mouse-hole. How in hell's name he'd *done* it . . . Harris being Harris. Ripley could have done it, indeed Ripley had done it. But Blayde? Winks and knowing smiles were passed, and the division heaved a communal sigh of relief. It hardly seemed possible, but it had happened. Blayde really *was* a second Ripley. Beechwood Brook had been uncommonly fortunate.

1973. 1974. 1975. A damn good division, with a damn good boss and a team who appreciated their good fortune. Blayde and Harris? They didn't exactly kiss and make up. Not quite. Nevertheless, like dogs who each respect the other's fangs, there developed an unspoken armed neutrality between them. Protocol demanded that major crime be reported to the Head of C.I.D., and murder (whatever the circumstances) *was* a major crime. And within that time-span murders were committed within the boundaries of Beechwood Brook

Division. Some plain, some fancy, and each time Harris was allowed to barge in and say his piece. And each time Blayde answered. Some who heard the various exchanges thought it was the old "Bob Hope-Bing Crosby" routine, and both chief superintendents did nothing to dispel this belief. But it wasn't. Each smiled insult was barbed. Even civilised exchanges carried their own hidden meaning. Thus dislike fattened and grew to be a secret hatred.

Then in 1975 a bunch of gun-crazy lunatics, from Uncle Sam's country, figured that the British bobby was something of a patsy. They ran riot in a posh housing project called Robs Cully and for the first time Blayde and Harris put aside their personal enmity and worked in harness.[1] The Haggthorpe uniformed sergeant he'd met in 1949—Lennox—now a detective superintendent, took, and deserved, much of the kudos, but for once Harris and Blayde forgot their differences in what amounted to all-out war against armed and organised criminals.

But the dislike was too deep, too long-

[1] Landscape with Violence, Macmillan, 1975.

standing, to forget and it took little time for things to return to the old footing.

In May, 1976 Blayde completed thirty years in the force. He could have retired on a two-thirds-pay pension. Indeed, had he not held the rank he would have been required to retire. As it was, and as a chief superintendent, he could continue on a yearly basis consequent upon him being pronounced medically fit. As he saw things, fifty-four was no age to take up knitting; he was in his prime, he lived only for the job and there was no damn reason on earth why he shouldn't carry on doing it until his health ran out. That, of course, being Blayde's opinion, and an opinion favoured by many of his kind, but not always shared by the unknown constable, sergeant, inspector, chief inspector and superintendent whose respective promotions such an attitude holds in check.

1976 was quite a year. It saw Donald Neilson—the so-called "Black Panther"—caged for life after a trail of killings which included that of the young girl Lesley Whittle. That same year a man who became known as The Yorkshire Ripper had already terrified victims who would, eventually, top the teens in number.

And somewhere in Whitehall an inverted mastermind—convinced that big was a shortened way of writing beautiful—doodled lines on a map and created Lessford Metropolitan Police District. Nothing half-hearted. Nothing minor. If you're going to make a cock-up make one massive enough to take everybody's breath away. A million and a half acres . . . give or take a square inch here and there. Authorised strength of police personnel around the ten thousand mark . . . actual strength less than seven thousand. Population to be policed, teetering on the edge of three million. One hell of a law-enforcement area which overnight embraced the county constabulary, Lessford City Police Force and Bordfield City Police Force.

"Somebody," growled Blayde, "needs his bloody brain boiling."

The single pearl in this monumental pigswill of "amalgamation" was the choice of the man they sat in the hot seat. Gilliant. Until that moment the chief constable of Lessford City. Gilliant *made* it work. He divided the cake into two halves; Bordfield Region and Lessford Region. Beechwood Brook Division was in Bordfield Region. He upped Harris to the post of Assistant Chief Constable (Crime) for that region, and made the fat man, Lennox, detective chief superintendent and Bordfield Regional Head of C.I.D.

The rest didn't matter. Harris was one step removed from Blayde and between the two sat Lennox. Harris was happy; his ego had received one more shot in the arm. His area of responsibility was such that he hadn't time to give much thought to any single division and, anyway, Lennox was like a brick wall separating Harris from the various divisional officers.

It was a time of upheaval, but it passed, and through it all Blayde kept a firm hand on Beechwood Brook. His reputation grew. It equalled—and some thought outstripped—that of the legendary Ripley, but it differed from Ripley's. It lacked Ripley's basic humanity and this, perhaps, because Blayde himself lacked the humanising influence of a woman. Ripley had had a wife and a daughter. Blayde had nobody nor wanted anybody. His cottage was his retreat, his divisional headquarters was his castle and Beechwood Brook his personal realm. He'd seen it all. He'd done it all. Life no longer held either surprises or humour; it was an arrow-straight road along which he walked at a steady pace and always alone. Joe and Sarah Benton had been under the sod for years. Little Willie? God knew where Little Willie was; in some institution somewhere, surrounded by people who'd never understand him and whom he'd never accept. Blayde gave such things little thought. He had a life—the object of the exercise was to live it, and not waste time trying to live other people's lives.

Blayde didn't know it (such men never know these things) but he was the walking, living epitome of the police mind. He was a copper. In uniform, out of uniform, on duty, off duty, waking or sleeping . . . *always* a copper. His view of the world was blue-tinted. He never fully trusted anybody. Minor politenesses were looked upon with some suspicion, and with the unasked question, where's the catch? He spoke less and less, listened more and more and was progressively harder to convince.

He was like a rock and around him the swirls and splash of transfers, promotions, resignations and retirements went unheeded. He took cases other divisional officers might have marked as milestones in their career, handled them without panic, organised their successful conclusion and saw nothing wonderful in what he'd done. At times his complete objectivity was almost frightening.

By 1980 Tallboy had reached the rank of detective chief inspector and that same year, much to his own surprise, Blayde moved up a notch to take Lennox's old spot; detective chief superintendent and Head of Bordfield Regional C.I.D. and, again, one small step beneath Harris.

It made little difference, other than that his beloved Beechwood Brook Division came under the chief superintendentship of a weak and hopeless character called Blakey. What Ripley had done, and what Blayde had built upon, was allowed to crumble . . . but not for long.

The armed neutrality between Blayde and Harris had become a mutually accepted way of life; it was still there, but as ageing men they could now acknowledge the strengths of each other. Harris, too, saw that Blakey was the perfect square peg in the immaculate round hole and between them they had influence enough to put the real man in the real place. Tallboy, Ripley's son-in-law, deserved the division. He'd been the natural crown prince for too long. A double-shift up the ladder of promotion took him from C.I.D.

and placed him in his father-in-law's old chair, and both Blayde and Harris were happy.

And that was how things stood as 1981 brought a dismal start to a summer which followed a mild and miserable winter.

18

IT was Sunday, May 10th, 1981. The TV weatherman had said it was going to be nice—sunny periods with scattered showers—and, as usual, the TV weatherman had been talking out of the back of his neck. The bloody mist was almost thick enough to be called fog . . . and had been for two solid days. Blayde sat in an armchair in front of a good fire in his cottage, massaged his ankle and idly wondered whether these goons used seaweed. What the hell it was they used was on the blink, and had been for years. Some few weeks earlier nary a word had been said when, apparently out of nowhere, blizzards had raged the whole breadth of the country. It had been one of those all-hands-at-the-pump situations, and fifty-nine was the wrong age to be arsing around, up to the waist in snow, organising the rescue of lunatic motorists who should have had more gumption than to have been up there in that weather in the first place. That and this bloody mist. Those twinges of rheumatoid arthritis which he'd been able to dismiss at the last two medicals were giving him some stingo. One more medical though, eh? Just the one. A fortnight next Tuesday. Scrape past that one, then retire at sixty. A nice round number to retire at. A fat pension. This easy chair. Damn all to worry about.

"I'll be on a par with you, cat." He spoke to the moggy curled up on the hearth rug, well within reach of the warmth from the fire. A cat; a one-time, half-wild farm cat which had recognised its own kind and had ingratiated itself into his life. They knew each other well, this cat and Blayde. They could converse with each other and understand each other. It was no knee-cuddly ball of fur, nor would Blayde have insulted its pride by treating it as such. It was old, but still proud enough to keep itself scrupulously clean, and it wore the scars of past battles on its hide much as a soldier wears campaign medals. It opened an eye and stared as it heard his voice, and he continued to masage his ankle, and said, "Bore each other to death, eh?" He chuckled softly, and added, "Well, at least we won't bore other people, and there's always the cat-door when you've had enough."

Then, slightly muffled by the mist, he heard

the car door open and close. He heard the tiny squeak of the gate; a sound which to him was as familiar and as recognisable as an alarm signal. He even heard the slow, hesitant footsteps as the driver walked up the path and, before the ring of the doorbell, Blayde was out of his chair and on his way to the hall.

It was 8.30 p.m., still light, but because of the mist, approaching an early dusk.

He opened the door and for a moment the two brothers stared at each other.

Blayde spoke first.

He said, "Stranger," and his tone was flat and unemotional.

Richard Blayde didn't answer.

"There has to be a reason." Blayde's voice remained controlled and without emotion.

"Don't I get invited in?" The question was low-pitched, with the hint of a pleading quality.

"Brother? Twins? Of course . . . what else?"

Blayde stood aside and, as he passed, Richard Blayde muttered, "I need your help, Bob. I'm in the schnook. *Really* in it."

Blayde closed the door and followed his brother into the main room of the cottage. As the stranger entered the room the cat jumped to its feet, arched its back, spat, then turned and disappeared into the kitchen.

"Taste," murmured Blayde, and this time there was soft mockery in his voice.

"I can take it." Richard Blayde flopped into an empty armchair.

"Really?" Blayde took the companion armchair. "I thought you could only dish it out. Not you, personally, your trained apes."

"I need your help." The voice had a slight tremble in it, and he dropped his head and ran his hands through his hair.

"You keep telling me."

"The—the crowd from The Smoke." Richard Blayde's voice became something of a gabble. "You think you did it with the Richardsons. With the Krays. You think you cracked it. You think . . ."

"I don't think anything," interrupted Blayde calmly.

"Like—like a bloody vacuum. That's all you did. Create a vacuum. But it filled up again. That's all that happened."

"Two hundred miles south of here." Blayde smiled a quick, tight smile. "I've a big patch these days, but not that big."

"They're—they're coming."

"The Martians?"

"You know what I mean. Damn it, you know what I mean."

"Pretend I don't," suggested Blayde.

"They're taking . . . They're trying to take over."

"They've taken over," said Blayde softly.

"What?"

"Why the hell else would you be here?" Blayde's voice had that dangerous, rumbling quality of a volcano building up pressure, prior to eruption. "You've suddenly decided you're a rate-payer. You want protection."

"I've a right to it. I've a . . ."

"You've a right to sod-all," snarled Blayde. "The only right you have, little brother, is cell-space. The only right you've had for years. The only real right you can claim for the rest of your miserable life."

"They're—they're after me," choked Richard Blayde.

"I wouldn't doubt it."

"They—they won't be satisfied till they've stiffened me."

"You chose your own company . . .*Ric.*"

"You'd . . ." Richard Blayde stared unbelievingly. "You'd *let* them."

"I'd offer to dig the grave," said Blayde coldly.

"Oh, Christ! Oh, *Christ!*" Richard Blayde dropped his head again, and again ran fingers through his untidy hair. He raised his head and almost sobbed, "We're—we're *brothers*. You can stop it. You can nail the mad bastards. You can . . ."

"Let's talk about you." Blayde left his chair, walked to the sideboard, splashed whisky into two glasses, handed one glass to Richard Blayde, returned to his chair, and said, "I've heard things. Year after year, I've heard things. Specifics and non-specifics. I'd be very interested. From the horse's mouth, as it were."

Richard Blayde gulped at the whisky. It seemed to steady him a little. Liquid courage, perhaps, but courage of a sort. He leaned back in the chair, wiped his mouth with the back of a hand and, when he spoke, his voice was steadier.

"Don't gloat." The ghost of a smile held bitterness. "You've waited and it's come. But don't gloat."

"You still think you can claim police protection?" mocked Blayde.

"D'you think I *can't?*"

"A provincial gangster? A hoodlum? A

germ who's built his whole life on fear and violence? And you think . . ."

"Look who the hell's talking," said Richard Blayde.

"What?" Blayde frowned.

"All your damn life." Richard gulped more whisky. "The difference. 'Establishment violence' . . . that's all. The uniform. The authority. You've killed."

"Not many times," growled Blayde quietly. "And only in the course of duty."

"Neat, eh?" It was a death's-head grin of contempt. " 'The course of duty'. They're still dead. They're still . . ."

"I didn't drown the poor bastards. I didn't rip their tongues out."

"Let's say the course of *my* duty."

"You're not denying it?"

"Should I?"

"No," said Blayde bitterly. "We seem to be touching the truth, for a change."

"Like knee-capping." Richard Blayde finished off the whisky. "That was deliberate. Men saw it."

"Your men."

"A deliberate aiming. Knee-capping some poor bastard you didn't even know."

"Let's say," murmured Blayde, "I've done worse things."

He finished off his own whisky, left the chair, collected Richard Blayde's glass, poured re-fills, then returned to the chair.

"We're brothers . . . brother." Richard had almost recovered complete control of himself. He spoke in a steady, contemplative voice. "Twins. We're alike, brother. But I've had the guts to do it openly. You've needed official blessing. So, who's the biggest?"

"Fool?"

"Man."

"You'd run wild?" mocked Blayde gently. "That what you want? Freedom to rule by fear?"

"What do *you* rule by?"

"The law."

"Fear, wrapped up in some Act of Parliament."

"Punishment."

"A nice establishment word." Richard sipped at the whisky. He didn't gulp it any more. "It means fear, a polite way of putting it."

"You," mused Blayde, "once disclaimed belief in God. We were kids. Not old enough to know, one way or the other. But you said you didn't believe in God."

"And you?"

"I'm still not old enough to know . . . one way or the other."

"Still without the guts."

"Does it take guts?" asked Blayde gently. "Just to say words? Just to deny what nobody can prove?"

"I *am* God." Richard chuckled quietly.

"I've heard the argument," said Blayde softly.

"When I die, the world dies. It ceases to exist. It's only here while I'm here. When I go, it goes . . . as far as I'm concerned."

"And that makes you God?"

"The only God I'm interested in. The only God I know . . . the only one I can prove."

"And if you're wrong?"

"I'll take my chance." Again the quiet chuckle. "We'll both go to the same place, brother. Duty won't be an argument."

"Honour . . ." Blayde, too, sipped his whisky. In a soft, sing-song voice, he intoned, " 'Honour Thy Father and Thy Mother'. It's a nice let-out. For you, I mean. Being God excuses all things."

"Mug," murmured Richard.

Blayde raised an eyebrow.

Richard said, "Father. What do we know about him? What do we really know? A thief, who hadn't the nerve to face society when he'd been exposed for what he was. What the hell 'honour' does a craven bastard like that deserve?"

"What we know about him," agreed Blayde. "And ma?"

"The same." Richard's mouth twisted into a humourless smile. "Let me tell you something, brother. The truth, for a change. Not who she was. *What* she was. She couldn't make up her bloody mind. All three, all the same. While you were away, doing your king-and-country bit. I was on the make. Sure I was. Hundreds of us, we lacked nothing. Not a damn thing. Nor did they. I offered, and they took. Oh, sure, hands held high in horror. But they took. And later. Ma knew where the good life was coming from. She couldn't *not* know. She preached, but hell she preached in comfort. She preached on a full belly." He paused, then added. "The same with you. You could have . . ."

"I'd have told you where to ram it!"

"Maybe . . . just maybe." Richard's lip

curled. "You wouldn't have been the first cop on the take. Not by a few hundred."

"You daren't even *offer,*" sneered Blayde.

"Okay. A point for you. But that doesn't give you a halo."

"She ended up at Greenfields," said Blayde contemptuously.

"Ma?"

"I saw her . . . once."

"That must have been a treat for her. I visited her every month. I paid for her."

"Poetic justice," observed Blayde expressionlessly. "You put her there."

"No!" Richard Blayde seemed to suddenly lose his temper. "Damn and blast . . . what a bloody *family.* The greatest self-kidders in the world. She put herself there. She didn't want to accept, but she couldn't refuse. Shaw's middle-class morality. Those damn places are bulging with the type. Holier-than-thou, but give me the good things in life. It doesn't work that way. Three choices. You're born rich, you're a bastard or you stay poor."

"And you decided to be a bastard?" mocked Blayde.

"A *rich* bastard."

Blayde smiled.

"You aren't even rich," flashed Richard.

"But on the other hand I haven't London villains on my tail, eager to see my guts messing up the nearest pavement."

Richard tasted his whisky and, as if on cue, a car engine revved, then cut. They both knew a car was at the gate. The glass rattled gently against Richard's teeth before he lowered it.

"Them?" asked Blayde with mild interest.

Richard nodded. Some of his original terror returned. He threw the rest of the whisky down his throat and, again nodded.

"They knew you'd make for here?"

"They . . ." Richard rubbed his lips with the back of his hand. "They guessed."

"How?"

"They—they . . ."

"How in hell's name did they *know* about this place?"

"I knew. Some of the boys knew."

"Tell me." Blayde's tone had an almost academic quality. "Why not the nearest nick?"

"Eh?"

"The nearest police station? Why not run there?"

"You," said Richard shortly.

"I'm sorry."

"Dammit . . . *you!* You're you. Pick a phone up, that's all. They're nailed. You have the weight." Then, in little more than a mutter, he added, "Anyway, you're *you.*"

"Something extra?"

"Some coppers . . ." Richard waved his arms a little, and almost dropped the glass. "Okay, the law. But some coppers . . ."

"They go beyond the law?"

"I'm not complaining. I'm—I'm not . . ."

"Is that what you're saying?"

"They don't know when they're licked. They can't be licked."

"Ah."

They sat and listened. For all of two minutes they waited; Blayde waiting for the tell-tale squeak of the gate. They heard nothing.

"They're waiting," breathed Richard.

"They're parked," said Blayde with a lop-sided smile. "It's not illegal. We haven't double-yellow lines out here."

"They're waiting."

"That, too," agreed Blayde.

"You've a phone."

"Naturally."

"Then for God's sake . . ."

"Quieten down, little brother." The contempt for a man even fractionally weaker than himself was in Blayde's voice. "If they're as good as you say they are . . ."

"They're good. They're bad."

". . . they'll have thought of that, too. They won't be armed. A flick-knife, maybe. At a pinch, not even that."

"You can . . ."

"Nothing . . . *officially.*"

"You mean . . ."

"I mean, they're simply parked there. They're not even causing an obstruction."

"You're supposed to have pull," snarled Richard.

Blayde grinned. It was a grin of complete triumph; a grin which was in no way related to humour. Instead, it held the accumulation of years of loathing; a whole lifetime of growing contempt for this twin brother of his plus something else.

He pushed himself from the chair, walked to a bureau, unlocked then opened one of the drawers. He took out the Beretta Minx, slid the empty magazine from its housing then, from a box of cartridges, began to thumb rounds into place.

"I have a certificate," he said conversationally. "We haven't broken any law, yet."

"You're—you're going to . . ."

"I'm going to ask them in," said Blayde calmly. "Country hospitality . . . that sort of thing."

He pressed the last round home, re-housed the magazine, then cocked the automatic. As he made for the door he said, "If you need more whisky, help yourself."

They were neatly, but not flashily dressed. Two of them. Of an age, and slightly younger than Blayde had anticipated. Clean cut might have been the expression Blayde would have used, had he not known what they were. Polite, too. Charming, in fact, and without the smarm with which would-be smooth-guys try to emphasise the toughness of their ways. The impression was that these two didn't have to emphasise . . . any doubts and they'd happily *demonstrate.*

Richard almost shied away from them as they entered the room.

"This him?" Blayde waved a hand towards Richard.

"Richard Blayde. Your brother, I believe."

"My twin brother," agreed Blayde pleasantly.

"Really?"

The leader of the two—the spokesman—was

dressed in a mid-grey suit, with a white shirt and a carefully knotted tie. He was smoking a cigarette, and Blayde noticed the manicured fingernails and the odd, pear-shaped birth-mark on the back of the hand. Blayde estimated his age at mid- to late-twenties. *Very* young, for such a responsibility. But well-spoken. By the sound of things, well-educated.

Blayde waved them to be seated and, keeping his right hand in the pocket of his jacket, faced the two strangers and his brother from the hearth rug.

"He tells me you're—er—'after' him," he smiled.

The second man grunted.

The man with the birth-mark on his hand said, "We followed him here."

"Why?"

"We . . ." The young man smiled and showed well-kept teeth. "We represent rival interests."

"They're from London," said Richard breathlessly. "For Christ's sake, they're going to . . ."

"Are you?" asked Blayde.

"We represent a London firm." The man inhaled cigarette smoke, then continued,

"Personally, I'm from this part of the world. My friend's from Manchester."

"But you represent London?"

"Yes." The man nodded.

"Same busines as his?" Blayde glanced at Richard.

"More efficient, in our opinion."

"But the same business?"

"Less crude," smiled the man.

"In what way?"

"For Christ's sake!" exploded Richard. "It's my bloody *life* you're talking about. Business. Efficiency. They're evil buggers. Can't you understand that? You're supposed to be so bloody . . ."

"Are you?" asked Blayde, amiably.

"Evil buggers?" The man smiled. He moved a shoulder fractionally. "By some yardsticks, perhaps. We try not to be."

"But in your business?"

"Quite. Just occasionally, I'm afraid."

"Your car keys." Blayde changed the subject, without a change of tone.

"I beg your pardon?"

"The keys to your car. Where are they?"

"In the ignition."

"The door key? The key to the boot?"

"Same key," said the young man,

pleasantly. "It's a Ford Fiesta. You may have noticed. Same key for all locks, except the petrol tank."

"Fine." Blayde turned to his brother. "You. Outside. Get the key, get the wheel-brace and take every nut from all four wheels. Then sling 'em. Separately. Over the hedge, into the fields."

Richard blinked and said, "Why don't I just sling the key?"

"Because—little brother—these gentlemen don't really need a key to start a motor car. They may also have a spare key tucked away somewhere. What they won't have is spare wheel-nuts and they won't drive far when the wheels start dropping off. You'll find a torch in the hall. Go to it."

Blayde removed his hand from the jacket pocket and held the Beretta easily, but firmly. He spoke to the man with the birth-mark on his hand.

He said, "In case you're wondering. It's loaded. It's cocked. And if necessary I'm prepared to use it."

"You know your brother's a criminal," drawled the man.

"It's my job to know these things." Blayde lowered himself into the vacated chair. He rested the handgun on his knee, with the snout pointing in the general direction of the two young crooks. He added, "He's also very frightened."

"Do you intend riding nursemaid on him for the rest of his life?" asked the man pleasantly.

"What do you get out of it?" Blayde changed the subject smoothly.

"What have *you* got out of policing?" countered the man.

"It's a profession."

"More than that, surely?" A gentle smile touched the man's lips. "For some time—some years—you've been working at cut-price."

Blayde frowned.

The man said, "Two-thirds-pay pension. That, for doing nothing. That other third, that's been your real salary."

"Let's say I get satisfaction." It was almost an excuse; indeed, it had the hint of that ring which identifies an empty excuse. He said, "Why does an artist continue painting? A writer continue writing?"

"Creation," murmured the man.

"Fine." Blayde nodded. "I help to create a stable society."

"Have you succeeded?" asked the man mischievously.

Blayde didn't answer.

The man continued, "The crime rate rises every year. Shootings. Bombings. Arson. In America, entry into the White House is almost like putting yourself up as a target in a shooting-gallery. The Moors Murders. The Panther. A man claims to have received a message from God and kills women . . . and not just prostitutes. There is violence, chief superintendent. What you see—what the public knows about—that old tip-of-the iceberg argument underestimates the true situation."

"Probably," growled Blayde.

"Certainly."

"But without the police it would be . . ."

"The world is in need of another major war." The man chuckled, quietly. "What the pacifists never realise. Man—the average man—has an instinct for killing. It's there. Just below the surface."

"One bloody great bang," growled Blayde sarcastically.

"Oh, no." The man shook his head slowly. Solemnly. "That's the mistake. Nuclear weapons. They've done harm merely by being there. They've limited conventional warfare. You were in the last war."

"You've done your homework."

"The killing moments. The suicidal moments. The men who really won the medals . . . posthumously. A subject worthy of investigation in depth. A percentage were good men. Brave men. Patriotic men. Some of it an attempt at self-preservation, perhaps. But there was another reason. The killers . . . they were allowed to kill. They were encouraged to kill. They worked it out of their system. The rogue syndrome. You follow my argument?"

"I don't subscribe to it."

"Of course not. It would make you and your kind superfluous."

"It gives you and your kind a very empty excuse."

"I'm prepared to face the truth. You pay lip-service to civilisation. If you faced the truth you needn't have lived."

"So," mocked Blayde, "you're not crooks? You're merely playing at soldiers? What you're doing is a war-substitute?"

"You have the gun." The man smiled and glanced at the Beretta.

"They have other uses."

"Paper-weights?" The mockery matched

that of Blayde's. "I take it you'd use it?"

"Of course."

"To kill?"

"If necessary. It's not an ornament."

"And you'd enjoy killing. Just for that moment . . . you'd *enjoy* yourself?"

"I'd kill," said Blayde flatly.

The man chuckled quietly, as if at some private joke. As if at some great truth known only to himself.

Richard returned. His hands were grimy and he held them awkwardly, away from his clothes.

Blayde said, "Your friends believe in war."

Richard stared.

"As a natural stabiliser to civilisation," explained Blayde.

"I'll give 'em bloody war." Blayde had the gun, and Blayde was in control, therefore Richard was no longer afraid. "Let me get some lads together—a few I can count on—I'll give 'em more war than they can handle."

"Not quite the same thing." Blayde stood up from the chair and added, "Never mind your hands. Let's go. Pull the telephone cord from its socket as we pass." Then to the man, "There's a kiosk down the road. Turn left at the gate, about a mile."

As Blayde turned to leave the man said, "It is, you know."

"What?"

"The same thing. Exactly the same thing."

They found the Peugeot—Richard's Peugeot—out on The Tops the following day. Along a lane well away from the road. A group of ramblers found it: a group rather like the group who had found the body of his father more than half a century before.

They were both dead. *Very* dead. Richard was in the driving seat and the bullet had gone into the nape of his neck and killed him instantly. Blayde was in the rear of the car and half his head was missing; the pathologist verified that he'd placed the snout of the Beretta in his own mouth and, in all probability, squeezed the trigger with his thumb. The rear window and the upholstery was mapped with a mess of blood, brain tissue and shattered bone.

19

THE solicitor was a sun-bronzed, hawk-faced man, not yet old enough to carry noticeable grey in his dark, slicked-back hair. Around the forty mark and worn well. There was a certain smooth efficiency with which he went about his business; the unfolding of the card-table to be used as a makeshift desk; the placing of the chairs; the snapping open of his document-case. He faced his tiny audience, cleared his throat, smiled and began.

"First, my condolences. Other than in the making out of his will, I didn't know Chief Superintendent Blayde, but he struck me as a fine officer and a man who knew what he wanted and refused to be influenced by outside forces . . ."

Harris sniffed. Somebody else moved and the chair squeaked a little.

"It was his wish that those I asked to be here *be* here. It was also his expressed wish that any other person interested should be allowed to be present at this reading." The solicitor smiled a quick, tight smile. "Unfortunately, one of the men he wished to be here is now dead. His brother, Richard Blayde. The will, and my instructions, were completed some years ago."

The solicitor took a sealed envelope from the document-case, and slit it open as he continued, "Before the will proper, I am required to read this letter aloud. I do not know the contents. You will appreciate, therefore, although not part of the will, it may provide certain implied qualifications." The solicitor unfolded the letter, glanced at the heading, then continued, "It is addressed to Robert Harris—that will be you, Mr. Harris."

Harris straightened in his chair and concentrated his attention.

"It reads, On Saturday, November 27th, 1971 I telephoned you regarding the finding of the murdered body of a man called Houseman. Houseman was drowned, after having his tongue cut out. You were conducting enquiries into the matter. I have been unable to find enough proof to charge the man responsible but, for your information, Houseman was my informant and his death was as a direct result of his passing information to me personally. I have no doubt at all that the man responsible for Houseman's murder was my twin brother, Richard Blayde. If he is present, I suggest you arrest him immediately for serious questioning. If—the solicitor paused, cleared his throat, then continued. If you are as good at your job as you have always claimed to be, the shock of him hearing this open accusation, plus your own expertise, should result in one murderer being brought to justice." The solicitor looked up, met Harris's eyes, and said, "I'm sorry, Mr. Harris. My client seems to have taken the law into his own hands. However, the letter had to be read. You may get some satisfaction from its content."

"Not much," growled Harris. He seemed to be about to say something else, but changed his mind.

The solicitor reached into his document-case and unfolded the stiff-papered will. He glanced at the typed script, looked up, and said, "There is the usual preamble. It's a very simple will. I'll have it here for anybody to examine later, if they so wish. Two beneficiaries. The land, house and contents—including the motor car—and I quote from the will, *in belated recognition of the man mainly responsible for making Beechwood Brook Police*

Division what it now is . . . to his daughter, Susan Tallboy."

Tallboy reached out and squeezed his wife's hand. Susan paled, then dropped her head as the tears brimmed and ran down her cheeks.

The solicitor continued, "The second beneficiary. All else—meaning all monies, bonds, shares and so forth—amounting to approximately thirty thousand pounds, once tax and fees are deducted. Margaret Ogden, late of Sayworth. Unfortunately, she died some years ago. I instituted enquiries and found she left issue. A son. I—er—we examined the birth certificate. Robert Ogden. There is every reason to suppose that the deceased was his father, but was unaware of the fact." The solicitor glanced at the stranger dressed in a dark suit. "My reason for contacting you and asking you to be present, Mr. Ogden."

The stranger nodded and smiled solemnly.

Susan murmured something to Tallboy. Tallboy shifted his position—moved to the next chair—and whispered, "Congratulations, old son."

"Thank you."

As they shook hands Tallboy noticed the strange, pear-shaped birth-mark on the back of Robert Ogden's hand.

This book is published under the
auspices of the
ULVERSCROFT FOUNDATION,
a registered charity, whose primary object is to assist those who experience difficulty in reading print of normal size.

In response to approaches from the medical world, the Foundation is also helping to purchase the latest, most sophisticated medical equipment desperately needed by major eye hospitals for the diagnosis and treatment of eye diseases.

If you would like to know more about the
ULVERSCROFT FOUNDATION,
and how you can help to further its work,
please write for details to:

THE ULVERSCROFT FOUNDATION
The Green, Bradgate Road
Anstey
Leicestershire
England

GUIDE
TO THE COLOUR CODING
OF
ULVERSCROFT BOOKS

Many of our readers have written to us expressing their appreciation for the way in which our colour coding has assisted them in selecting the Ulverscroft books of their choice.

To remind everyone of our colour coding— this is as follows:

BLACK COVERS
Mysteries

★

BLUE COVERS
Romances

★

RED COVERS
Adventure Suspense and General Fiction

★

ORANGE COVERS
Westerns

★

GREEN COVERS
Non-Fiction

A Caribbean Mystery	*Agatha Christie*
Curtain	*Agatha Christie*
The Hound of Death	*Agatha Christie*
The Labours of Hercules	*Agatha Christie*
Murder on the Orient Express	*Agatha Christie*
The Mystery of the Blue Train	*Agatha Christie*
Parker Pyne Investigates	*Agatha Christie*
Peril at End House	*Agatha Christie*
Sleeping Murder	*Agatha Christie*
Sparkling Cyanide	*Agatha Christie*
They Came to Baghdad	*Agatha Christie*
Third Girl	*Agatha Christie*
The Thirteen Problems	*Agatha Christie*
The Black Spiders	*John Creasey*
Death in the Trees	*John Creasey*
The Mark of the Crescent	*John Creasey*
Quarrel with Murder	*John Creasey*
Two for Inspector West	*John Creasey*
His Last Bow	*Sir Arthur Conan Doyle*
The Valley of Fear	*Sir Arthur Conan Doyle*
Dead to the World	*Francis Durbridge*
My Wife Melissa	*Francis Durbridge*
Alive and Dead	*Elizabeth Ferrars*
Breath of Suspicion	*Elizabeth Ferrars*
Drowned Rat	*Elizabeth Ferrars*
Foot in the Grave	*Elizabeth Ferrars*

Murders Anonymous	*Elizabeth Ferrars*
Don't Whistle 'Macbeth'	*David Fletcher*
A Calculated Risk	*Rae Foley*
The Slippery Step	*Rae Foley*
This Woman Wanted	*Rae Foley*
Home to Roost	*Andrew Garve*
The Forgotten Story	*Winston Graham*
Take My Life	*Winston Graham*
At High Risk	*Palma Harcourt*
Dance for Diplomats	*Palma Harcourt*
Count-Down	*Hartley Howard*
The Appleby File	*Michael Innes*
A Connoisseur's Case	*Michael Innes*
Deadline for a Dream	*Bill Knox*
Death Department	*Bill Knox*
Hellspout	*Bill Knox*
The Taste of Proof	*Bill Knox*
The Affacombe Affair	*Elizabeth Lemarchand*
Let or Hindrance	*Elizabeth Lemarchand*
Unhappy Returns	*Elizabeth Lemarchand*
Waxwork	*Peter Lovesey*
Gideon's Drive	*J. J. Marric*
Gideon's Force	*J. J. Marric*
Gideon's Press	*J. J. Marric*
City of Gold and Shadows	*Ellis Peters*
Death to the Landlords!	*Ellis Peters*
Find a Crooked Sixpence	*Estelle Thompson*
A Mischief Past	*Estelle Thompson*

Three Women in the House	*Estelle Thompson*
Bushranger of the Skies	*Arthur Upfield*
Cake in the Hat Box	*Arthur Upfield*
Madman's Bend	*Arthur Upfield*
Tallant for Disaster	*Andrew York*
Tallant for Trouble	*Andrew York*
Cast for Death	*Margaret Yorke*